Arithmetic for Beginners, an Introduction to Cornwell and Fitch's Science of Arithmetic

SALZWASSER
VERLAG

James Cornwell

Arithmetic for Beginners, an Introduction to Cornwell and Fitch's Science of Arithmetic

Reprint of the original.

1st Edition 2023 | ISBN: 978-3-37514-360-2

Verlag (Publisher): Salzwasser Verlag GmbH, Zeilweg 44, 60439 Frankfurt, Deutschland
Vertretungsberechtigt (Authorized to represent): E. Roepke, Zeilweg 44, 60439 Frankfurt, Deutschland
Druck (Print): Books on Demand GmbH, In de Tarpen 42, 22848 Norderstedt, Deutschland

ARITHMETIC FOR BEGINNERS

BEING

AN INTRODUCTION

TO

CORNWELL AND FITCH'S

SCIENCE OF ARITHMETIC.

BY THE SAME AUTHORS.

LONDON:
SIMPKIN, MARSHALL, & CO., STATIONERS' COURT;
HAMILTON, ADAMS, AND CO., PATERNOSTER ROW;
EDINBURGH: OLIVER AND BOYD.

1858.

PREFACE.

THIS little work is intended to be the ordinary working school book of most classes in a school.

Its main peculiarities are these :—

I. It is eminently PRACTICAL, and, it is believed, contains a greater number of examples, wider in their range and more varied in their character, than are found in books of its size and price.

II. The method of treatment throughout is INDUCTIVE. It is not a book of practice only. In other words, each rule is shown to embody a general truth, resulting from the various processes of a simple example that has been pre-and introductory to them. The questions may, however, if viously worked in full.

III. It is copious in its EXPLANATORY EXAMPLES. After each rule has been discovered and enunciated, a second question is worked, as an illustration of the ordinary method, whether contracted or otherwise, in which the pupil is required to employ the rule. Thus, the working of the first example leads to the discovery of the Rule; the working of the second teaches its practical application.

IV. The first group of sums under each Rule consists of very simple questions, adapted for ORAL EXERCISE. Ample and systematic provision is thus made for mental calculation, not so much by a separate system of rules and questions, as in connection with the ordinary rules of school Arithmetic, desired, be worked in the usual way, and answers to them will be found with the rest at the end of the work.

V. In connection with each of the Compound Rules, allusion is made to the probable introduction of a DECIMAL SYSTEM of coinage. Rules are given for the reduction of our present money to the new denominations; and exercises for practice are appended. It is hoped that in this way learners may become prepared without difficulty to encounter a change which, though long delayed, is probably inevitable.

Reference is constantly made to the larger work of the authors, the "Science of Arithmetic," in which a fuller exposition of the theory of each Rule may be found. Such reference is often made in the contracted form (S. of A., 72 94, &c.)

TABLE OF CONTENTS.

PART I.

PART II.

ARITHMETIC FOR BEGINNERS.

1. **Arithmetic** is the art of reckoning or counting.

2. We reckon or count by the help of *words* and *figures*, which stand for certain numbers (*S. of A.*, 6).

3. **Numeration** teaches the meaning of the *words* which stand for numbers.

4. **Notation** teaches us the meaning of the *figures* or characters which stand for numbers.

NUMERATION.

5. The following are the words used in numbering:—

One	*Four*	*Seven*	*Ten*
Two	*Five*	*Eight*	*Eleven*
Three	*Six*	*Nine*	*Twelve.*

6. The number **Ten** is the most important of these; because all larger numbers are considered in counting as made up of tens. Hence the common numeration is called **Decimal**.* For example,

Teen at the end of a word means that ten is to be added; as,

Fourteen means four and ten; *sixteen*, six and ten.

Ty at the end of a word means that the number is to be taken *ten* times; as,

Forty means ten fours; *fifty*, ten fives; *eighty*, ten eights.

7. Other numbers used in decimal numeration are—

Hundred, which means ten tens; **Thousand**, or ten hundreds; **Million**, or ten hundred thousand.

8. All numbers whatever are expressed by the use of these words put together in different ways; thus,

Twenty-seven	means	two tens and seven.
One hundred and eighteen	,,	ten tens, eight, and ten.
Three thousand and thirty-five	,,	three tens of hundreds, three tens, and five.

* *Decimal*, from *decem*, a Latin word, meaning ten.

NOTATION.

9. Figures or characters are used in arithmetic, because it is not convenient to express all numbers in writing by words. The figures we use are—

1, one,	4, four,	7, seven,
2, two,	5, five,	8, eight,
3, three,	6, six,	9, nine.

10. All higher numbers can be expressed by these figures, if they are placed in different positions (*S. of A.*, 15); thus,

4 means four units or ones.
44 ,, four tens and four, the 4 to the left meaning 4 tens.
444 ,, four hundred, four tens, and four, the 4 to the left meaning 4 hundreds.
4444 ,, four thousand, four hundred, and forty-four, the 4 to the left meaning 4 thousands.
4444444 ,, four millions, four hundred and forty-four thousand, four hundred and forty-four, the 4 to the left meaning 4 millions.

Hence, in every line of figures each means ten times more than if it were one place further to the right. Thus,

hundreds of millions.	tens of millions.	millions.	hundreds of thousands.	tens of thousands.	thousands.	hundreds.	tens.	units.	
9	8	7	6	5	4	3	2	1	is to be read

Nine hundred and eighty-seven millions, six hundred and fifty-four thousands, three hundred and twenty one.

11. Sometimes we wish to express tens when there are no units, hundreds when there are no tens, or thousands when there are no hundreds or tens. We then use the character 0, or nought, which is called a *cipher,* and marks a vacant place; thus,

50 means five tens, *and no units.*
407 ,, four hundreds, *no tens,* and seven units.
2068 ,, two thousands, *no hundreds,* six tens, and eight.

12. In reading numbers it is usually convenient to break them up into periods of three, beginning at the right; thus,

1,384 One thousand, three hundred and eighty-four.
5,260,870 Five millions, two hundred and sixty thousand, *eight* hundred and seventy.

EXERCISE I.

(*a*)—*Oral.* Express in other words the meaning of the following numbers:—Twenty-four; three hundred and eighteen; seventy-nine; two hundred and forty-one; seven thousand three hundred and five; two millions and twelve; seven hundred and thirteen; twelve thousand three hundred and fourteen; sixty millions.

(*b*)—*Written.* Give the words for the following numbers:—

(1). 27, 15, 370. (2). 3185, 50, 617. (3). 4073, 219, 504.
(4). 1728, 312, 5172. (5). 10, 39, 821. (6). 71, 413, 586.
(7). 111, 3027, 515. (8). 320, 1100, 2171. (9). 1017, 2100, 11001.
(10). 6005, 1307, 16000. (11). 5028, 713901, 38705.
(12). 5000703, 20938415. (13). 63208753, 4098382075.
(14). 20740003, 500068370. (15). 7209865, 410320078.

EXERCISE II.

(*a*)—*Oral.* Give the figures representing the following numbers:—

(1). Eleven, seventeen, ten, twenty-three.
(2). Fourteen, one hundred and eight, thirty-six, fifty.
(3). Seven, nineteen, thirty-one, one hundred and eleven.
(4). Fifty-eight, three hundred, forty-one, two hundred and forty-four.
(5). Five thousand, two hundred and forty, six hundred and five.
(6). Seven hundred and fourteen, eighty-six, one hundred and one.

(*b*)—*Written.* Write in figures the following numbers:—

(1). Two hundred and thirteen; seven hundred and six; ninety-two.

(2). One hundred and eighty; seven hundred and one; eleven hundred and nineteen.

(3). Three thousand four hundred; nine hundred and six; five hundred and eight.

(4). Seven thousand and fourteen; nine hundred and ninety; fifty-eight hundreds.

(5). Six thousand three hundred and seventy-four; two thousand five hundred and eleven; seventy-eight thousand three hundred and twenty-four.

(6). Four millions seven hundred and eighty; five millions and seven; six hundred and forty-four thousand three hundred and fifty-eight; eighty millions and five.

(7). Eighty-four thousand three hundred and one; nine hundred and thirty-three thousand; forty-seven millions six thousand three hundred.

(8). Nine hundred and twenty millions six hundred and eight thousands; four hundred and thirty-eight thousand three hundred and forty-five; eleven thousand and eleven.

(9). Twenty-four millions three hundred and fourteen; seventy-nine thousand two hundred and one; sixty thousand and four.

(10). Eighty-seven millions three thousand and twenty; twenty-four millions seven hundred and nine; eighty thousand and six.

ADDITION.

13. Example I.—*There are nineteen sheep in one field, fifty-six in another, and seventy-four in a third; how many are there in all three fields?*

Explanation.—Because we want to find how many sheep there are in all the fields, we must add together the three numbers, and see how much they amount to (*S. of A.*, 18).

Now as the numbers are too large to be added together at once, we must break up the sum into pieces, and work it out part by part. We set the figures down in columns, thus:—

I. Tens.	Units.
1	9
5	6
7	4
13	19

II. Hund.	Tens.	Units.
	1	9
	5	6
	7	4
1	4	9

14. The 4, 6, and 9 are placed in the same column, because they all mean units, or single sheep. We add them together, and find they make 19.

Next we add together the 7, 5, and 1, because they mean tens of sheep. All together they make 13 tens.

The whole answer, as in I., therefore, is 13 tens of sheep. and 19 single sheep.

But 19 units are made up of 1 ten and 9 units, so we place the 9 only under the units' column, and remove the 1 ten to the column for tens, as in II.

15. This removal from one column to another is called carrying. The 1 ten thus *carried* from the units' place, and added to the thirteen tens, makes 14 tens; but as 14 tens are made up of 1 hundred and 4 tens, we *carry* the 1 hundred to its place in the next column to the left.

The whole answer, in its proper form, is 1 4 9 sheep.

16. This process is called Addition, because by it numbers are *added* together. The answer is called the Sum.

The sign of Addition is +, and is called *plus*.

Thus $4 + 9 = 13$, is read, Four *plus* nine *equals* thirteen.

17. Rule.—Arrange the numbers in columns, keeping all the units together, all the tens, all the hundreds, and so on. Begin on the right hand, add up the figures; if the sum be more than nine, carry the ten or tens to the next column, and set down the remaining units. Next add up all the tens, including the number carried. If there be more than 9 tens, *carry the hundreds* to the third place. Add up each column, *carrying the tens* in the same manner.

18. **Example of Working.—A man owes five sums of money; the first is 2,378 pounds, the second 476 pounds, the third 9,913 pounds, the fourth 1,671 pounds, and the fifth 835 pounds. How much does he owe altogether?**

In the right-hand column—5 and 1 and 3 and 6 and 8	2378
make 23 units.	476
Set down 3 *and carry* 2 *to the tens.*	9913
Then 2 and 3 and 7 and 1 and 7 and 7 make 27 tens.	1671
Set down 7 *and carry* 2 *to the hundreds.*	835
Then 2, 8, 6, 9, 4, and 3 make 32 hundreds.	———
Set down 2 *hundreds and carry* 3 *to the thousands.*	15273
Then 3 and 1 and 9 and 2 make 15 thousands.	———
Set down 15 *thousands.*	

The sum, therefore, of all five debts is fifteen thousand two hundred and seventy-three pounds, or in figures £15,273.

Or, $2378 + 476 + 9913 + 1671 + 835 = 15273$.

Exercise III.

(*a*)—*Oral.* (1). I have 5 marbles in one pocket and 16 in another; how many have I? There are 12 roses in 1 bed, 14 in another, and 8 in a third; how many are there in all?

(2). Add 5s., 8s., and 14s.; £12, £9, and £7; £14, £15, and £16.

(3). Add together 1, 2, 3, 4, 5, 6, 7, 8, 9; To 3 add 7 four times.

(4). Put 6 to 8 and 8 and 8 and 8; Add 3 to 9 and 9 and 9.

(5): To 5 add 4 seven times; To 3 add 8 six times; ten times.

(6). Add 14 to 15 and 16; Add together five thirteens.

(7). What is the united length of five roads, which are 7, 11, 14, 16, and 18 miles long respectively?

(8). Add 25, 32, and 14 together; Find the sum of 20, 30, 45, and 57.

(9). $18 + 9 + 7$; $16 + 12 + 3$; $25 + 19 + 10$.

(10). 21, 8, 3, 12 and 7; 14, 9, 6, 8 and 11; 29 and 35.

(11). When Monday is the 1st of March, on what days will the Sundays occur?

(*b*)—*Written.* (1). Work the following sums:—

(1)	(2)	(3)	(4)	(5)
15	167	47681	50981	52872
694	5280	2098	6253	109863
81	369	18	7109	729
1054	1283	12357	21862	84179
213	15392	6210	3971	6283

(6). There are fifteen children in one class, eighteen in another, twenty-one in a third, and only six in the fourth; how many are in the whole school?

(7). In a library there are eight compartments, containing respectively the following numbers of books—127, 430, 500, 91, 135, 102, 72, and 182; how many are there in all?

(8). John had thirty-two marbles, and won nineteen more; how many had he?

(9). There are forty counties in England, twelve in Wales, thirty-three in Scotland, and thirty-two in Ireland; how many counties are there in the United Kingdom?

(10). If a tradesman has fifty-six customers on Monday, twenty-nine on Tuesday, thirty-four on Wednesday, eighty on Thursday, ninety-four on Friday, and one hundred and fifty-six on Saturday, how many has he in the whole week?

(11)	(12)	(13)	(14)	(15)
20983	41096	217386	39876	61275
1273	82304	47258	1428	8236
607198	719	392164	39271	109
29384	6285	82716	4185	7832

(16)	(17)	(18)	(19)	(20)
73208	208654	329763	714638	314729
625	39728	85421	169372	72638
91718	176315	563092	54928	158472
4632	29182	72816	763050	93728
10729	736947	839628	159207	65417

(21). 17 + 12 + 30 + 18 + 301 + 19 + 7.
(22). 621 + 308 + 51 + 9 + 871 + 5346.
(23). 4083 + 2179 + 61728 + 317296 + 23.
(24). 5087 + 2163 + 8 + 19 + 374.
(25). 1072 + 39768 + 2047 + 54321.
(26). 7143 + 84 + 290 + 503 + 1306.
(27). 2186 + 3097 + 1200 + 8007 + 25.
(28.) 1931 + 6130 + 5070 + 3158 + 2132.
(29). 5041 + 6253 + 5836 + 2194 + 5271.
(30). 21379 + 8147 + 6325 + 4801 + 1963.

(31). There are two numbers; the less is 514, and the other exceeds it by 268; what is their sum?

(32). How many days are there in the three months of January, February, and March? (See Tables, p. 72.)

(33). What is the total number of members of the House of Commons, 467 being returned for England, 53 for Scotland, 105 for Ireland, and 29 for Wales?

(34). A fruitseller has 215 oranges, another has 37 more than this number, while another has 21 more than the first and second put together; how many have all three together?

(35). Find the sum of the following numbers:—twenty-seven, three hundred and five, four hundred and thirty-six, eighteen hundred and twenty-four, and forty-nine.

(36). Add together, three thousand four hundred and one, two thousand and nineteen, sixty-five millions two thousand and forty-three, and eighteen thousand three hundred and fifty.

(37). At an election there were two candidates, one had four hundred and seventeen votes, but was defeated by a majority of one hundred and twenty-four; how many people voted?

(38). State how many boys are in a large public school, in which there are fifty-six in the first class, sixty-four in the second, thirty in the third, forty-nine in the fourth, seventy-two in the fifth, and fifty-four in the sixth.

(39). Find the sum of three numbers, the first of which is made up of 124 and 69; the second of which exceeds the first by 35, and the third exceeds the sum of the other two by 60.

(40). From April 23 to October 19 inclusive, how many days?

(41). Julius Cæsar invaded Britain 55 B.C., how many years elapsed before the Norman Conquest in 1066 A.D.?

(42). An army consists of 27,563 infantry and 9,462 cavalry, it is reinforced by 13,261 infantry, 7,283 cavalry, and 4,106 engineers; what is the total number of men?

(43). What is that number from which, if I first take seven hundred and eighty-three, and then three hundred and fifty-six, there will remain ninety-eight?

(44). A farmer has in his poultry-yard thirty-eight ducks, forty-five fowls, nineteen turkeys, and fifty-three geese; how many has he in all?

(45). If a person was born in 1852, in what year will he be forty-nine years of age?

(46). In 1855, 27,883 emigrants sailed to the United States, 4,991 to the North American colonies, 29,868 to Australia, and 214 to other places; what was the total number?

(47). In the summer quarter of 1855, 87,646 deaths were registered in England, and in the same period of 1857 the number exceeded the former by 12,944; what was the number of deaths in the latter summer?

(48). In 1852 we imported 5,327,096 cwt. of raw cotton from the United States, 172,670 cwt. from Brazil, 131,392 cwt. from Egypt, 1,094,884 cwt. from British India, and 36,278 cwt. from other parts; what was the entire weight imported?

(49). In six months 32,682,415 persons were conveyed by railway in England and Wales, 3,905,724 in Scotland, and 2,661,466 in Ireland; find the entire number.

(50). Make a complete table, showing the dates of the accession of the Norman and Plantagenet kings: William I. began to reign in 1066, and reigned 21 years, William II. 13, Henry I. 35, Stephen 19, Henry II. 35, Richard I. 10, John 17, Henry III. 56, Edward I. 35, Edward II. 20, and Edward III. 50 years.

(51). In England and Wales there were in 1851 three millions two hundred and eighty thousand nine hundred and sixty-one inhabited houses, one hundred and fifty-two thousand eight hundred and ninety-eight uninhabited, and twenty-six thousand four hundred and thirty-four building. What was the total number?

SUBTRACTION.

19. *Example I.—A farmer had* 489 *sheep, he sold* 235; *how many had he left?*

Explanation.—We cannot at once tell how many are left if 235 are taken away from 489.

But the greater number, 489, is made up of the parts 4 hundreds, 8 tens, and 9. So, too, the smaller number is made up of 2 hundreds, 3 tens, and 5.

The smaller number can now be taken from the larger *in parts*, thus:—

5 sheep taken from 9 sheep leave 4 sheep.

3 tens, or thirty sheep, from 8 tens, or eighty sheep, leave 5 tens, or fifty.

2 hundreds from 4 hundreds leave 2 hundreds. Or,

From	4 hundreds	8 tens	9 sheep,
Take	2 ,,	3 ,,	5 ,,
There remain	2 ,,	5 ,,	4 ,,

The number left is therefore 254 sheep (*S. of A.*, 38).

20. *Example II.—A farmer has* 459 *sheep, he sells* 186; *how many has he left?*

We can here again separate these numbers into the parts of which they are made up, and say:—

From	4 hundreds	5 tens	9 sheep,
Take	1 ,,	8 ,,	6 ,,

But we cannot, as in Example I., take all the parts of the smaller number from the parts of the greater number, because one part of the less number, 8 tens, is greater than 5 tens, or fifty of the larger number.

21. We therefore adopt the plan of adding the same number to both the greater and the less. This does not alter their difference;* but it makes it easier to take one from the other.

We can take 6 sheep from 9, and the 3 sheep remain.

But we cannot take 8 tens from 5 tens, so we add ten tens to the 5, and also add ten tens, but in the form of 1 hundred, to the lower line. The new number will then be—

From 4 hundreds	15 tens (*i.e.* 5+10)	and 9 sheep
Take 2 hundreds (1+1)	8 tens	and 6 ,,
There remain 2 hundreds	7 tens	and 3 ,,

* We do not alter the difference between two unequal quantities if we add equal sums to both (*S. of A.*, Axiom VI.) For example: Take £2 and £5, their difference is £3. Now, add £7 to each, the £2 becomes £9, and the £5 becomes £12. The difference between these sums, £9 and £12, is £3, the same as between £2 and £5.

22. This process is called SUBTRACTION, because by it one number is subtracted or taken from another.

The character — is the sign of Subtraction, and is called *minus*.

Thus 459 — 186 = 273 is to be read,

Four hundred and fifty-nine *minus* one hundred and eighty-six *equals* two hundred and seventy-three.

23. RULE.—Place the less number under the greater, units under units, tens under tens, &c. Begin at the right, and take each number from the one above it, and set down the difference underneath. But when the lower number is greater than the upper, add ten to the upper, and in the next place on the left add 1 to the number in the lower line.

24. EXAMPLE OF WORKING.—If I have £7,968 in the bank, and draw out £3,287, how much remains?

7963	=	7 thousand	9 hundred	16 tens	13 units.
3287		3 „	3 „	9 „	7 „
4676		4 „	6 „	7 „	6 „

Seven from 3 cannot be taken; so add 10* to the 3.
Seven from 13, leave 6 units. *Set down 6 units.*
Add 1 to the 8 tens.*
Nine tens from six tens cannot be taken; so add 10 to the 6.
Nine tens from sixteen tens leave seven. *Set down 7 tens.*
Add 1 to the 2 hundreds.
Three hundreds from nine leave six. *Set down 6 hundreds.*
Three thousands from seven leave four. *Set down 4 thousands.*
The sum left in the bank, therefore, is 4,676 pounds.

EXERCISE IV.

(a)—*Oral.* (1). Take seven oranges from fifteen oranges, how many remain? Find the difference between sixteen and twenty-four.

(2). Take twelve from forty-three; eleven from twenty.

(3). Take four three times from twenty; eight twice from thirty.

(4). Take twenty-seven from forty; fifteen from thirty-three.

(5). What number must be added to thirty-one to make fifty?

(6). Take six and four and eleven from forty-eight.

(7). From eighty take six four times; from one hundred take nine five times.

(8). A boy who had a hundred and twenty marbles lost sixty-three; how many had he left?

(9). From the 7th of July to the 31st how many days?

(10). Add together the differences between sixteen and thirty; and between twelve and eighty.

* The *value* is the same which has been added to both numbers, though the addition has been made in parts of a different name. A person may pay for an article worth £2, either 2 sovereigns or 40 shillings.

(11). A is 25 years old, B is 34, and C is 59; what is the difference between A's age and B's, between A's and C's, and between B's and C's?

(12). 28 − 5; 40 − 16; 90 − 18.

(13). 100 − 51; 84 − 19; 23 − 17.

(14). (27 + 13) − 19; (18 + 16 + 10) − (7 + 3 + 4).

(15). 70 − 9 − 9 − 9; 100 − 6 − 6 − 6; 23 − (12 − 8)

(16). 18 − 15; 29 − 13; 56 − 49; 21 − 19.

(17). 95 − 76; 82 − 17; 56 − 28; 104 − 18.

(*b*)—*Written.* (1). A train contains 241 passengers, of whom one hundred and fifty are in the first and second classes; how many third class passengers are there?

(2). Of 283 trees in a park 94 were cut down; how many remained?

(3). Find the difference between three thousand four hundred and fifty-six, and two thousand seven hundred and ninety.

(4). Take eleven hundred and twenty-eight from four thousand and five hundred and seventy-two from two thousand six hundred.

(5). What is the difference between thirty-seven thousand six hundred and eleven, and one million?

(6)	(7)	(8)	(9)	(10)
283112	21685	170462	200000	5062
190476	9127	39287	78310	1397

(11)	(12)	(13)	(14)	(15)
21703	470126	567209	10271	2000
16928	139278	287360	5693	1796

(16). 7283 − 1296; 302709 − 5682; 500 − 72.

(17). 308700 − 54729; 526387 − 149613; 20000 − 18621

(18). 3972413 − 1369871; 1000000 − 729836.

(19). (274 + 381) − (109 + 62); 81 + 39 + 41 − 128.

(20). 5968 − 2473 − 1068 − 35; 4078 − (692 + 3257).

(21). (1408 + 5623 + 308) − (6792 − 5431 + 409).

(22). In 1811, there were altogether 640,500 men in the army, navy, and merchant service; of these the two branches of the military force amounted to 501,488; how many were there in the merchant service?

(23). If the expenses of a commercial house are £23,659, and the receipts £37,867, what are the profits?

(24). What was the interval of time between the signing of Magna Charta in 1215 and the Revolution of 1688?

(25). The first Punic war commenced in 263 B.C., and the third terminated 146 B.C.; what was the length of the interval?

(26). What number, subtracted from a million, would leave seven hundred and fifty-three thousand six hundred and eighteen?

(27). The Duke of Wellington was born in 1769, and died in 1852; how old was he?

(28). In 1851 there were in England and Wales 8,762,588 males, and 9,160,180 females; find the difference.

(29). The total population of Great Britain, in 1801, was 10,267,893; in 1821, 15,180,351; and in 1851, 20,936,468; what was the difference between the increase in the former 20 years and the latter 30?

(30). In 1852, the value of our exports to India was £7,382,907, and to Australia £4,222,205; what was the excess?

(31). How much must be added to the sum of 8,263 and 4,059 to make the sum of 10,562 and 5,837?

(32). In the year 1855, 635,043 births and 425,703 deaths were recorded; what was the increase of population?

(33). The distance of Mercury from the sun is 36,791,000 miles, that of Venus 68,748,000, and that of the Earth 95,044,000 miles; find the distance from the orbit of Mercury to that of Venus, and from Venus to that of the Earth.

(34). Milton was born in 1608, and died in 1674; how long did he live?

(35). At an election the successful candidate polled 5,384 votes, and his opponent 4,796; what was the majority?

(36). At an election the whole number of votes was 7,936, of which the unsuccessful candidate received 3,428; what was the majority?

(37). The Great Fire of London, in 1666, occurred fifty-three years after the accession of James I., and thirty-one years after that of Charles I.; when did each of them begin to reign?

(38). A town traveller collected £1,200 from four customers; from the first £352, from the second £67 more, and from the third £94 less; how much did he receive from the fourth?

(39). A tradesman has in his shop goods worth five hundred and sixty-four pounds, and twenty-five pounds in his cash-box: he owes three hundred and thirty-four pounds, and debts to the amount of four hundred and fifty-nine pounds are due to him; what is he worth?

(40). Find the sum and difference of 783 and 297.

(41). There are two numbers, of which the less is 682, and the sum is 1,500; what is their difference?

(42). Charles I. was beheaded in 1649, and his son succeeded in 1660; what was the length of the interregnum?

(43). The battle of Bannockburn was fought in 1314, and that of Waterloo in 1815; how many years elapsed between them?

(44). From the sum of 8,760,432,964 and 5,769,087,579 subtract their difference.

(45). It is 18 miles from London to Watford, and Wolverton is 34 miles beyond it; how much further is Birmingham, which is 113 miles from London?

(46). Chimborazo, the highest mountain in America, is 21,427 feet high, and Mont Blanc, the highest in Europe, is 15,732 feet. By how much does the height of the one exceed that of the other?

(47). Take the sum of 12,936, 17,832, and 5094, from the sum of 20,968, 35,798, 21,531, and 6,190.

MULTIPLICATION.

25. *EXAMPLE I.—In a kitchen garden there are five rows of cabbages, and in each row are* 135 *plants; how many cabbages does the garden contain?*

EXPLANATION.—In each row there are 135 plants, and there are 5 rows. Therefore the whole number of plants is 5 times as many as there are in one row, or 5 times 135 plants.

This number might be found by adding together 135 five times, according to the Rule of Addition (17).

But a number five times as great as 135 may be found by a shorter way than that of addition.

Since the number 135 is too large for us to increase it five times at once by the help of the tables, we take the number to pieces and make each separate part five times greater.

I.	Hundreds.	Tens.	Units.
	1	3	5
			5
	5	15	25

II.	
	135
	5
	675

Here 5 times 5 units make 25 units, 5 times 3 tens make 15 tens, and 5 times 1 hundred make 5 hundreds; the whole number is therefore 5 hundreds, 15 tens, and 25 units, as in I.

But by the method of transferring, or carrying (15), as the 25 units are made up of 2 tens and 5 units, we set down the 5 units and carry 2 to the tens. Then, as 2 and 15 tens make 17 tens, or 1 hundred and 7 tens, we set down 7 under the tens, and carry 1 to the hundreds. This added to the 5 makes 6 hundreds. See II.

There are therefore six hundred and seventy-five cabbages in the garden.

26. This process is called MULTIPLICATION, because the number 135 has been *multiplied* or repeated five times.

27. The character × is the sign of Multiplication. Therefore the answer might be thus expressed:—

135 × 5 = 675; which is to be read,
135 *into* 5 *equals* 675.

The number multiplied is called the *multiplicand;* the number by which it is multiplied is the *multiplier*, and the answer, or result, is called the *product* (*S. of A.*, 56).

Hence Multiplicand × Multiplier = Product.

28. Rule.—Set down the multiplier under the unit figure of the multiplicand. Multiply the unit by it, and if the answer be more than 9 set down the units and carry the tens; then multiply the tens; add the tens which were carried, and if they make more than 9 set down the tens and carry the hundreds; proceed in this way until the sum is worked.

29. Example of Working.—There are 7 regiments of soldiers, and in each regiment 856 men; how many are there in the whole?

	7 times 6 are 42.
856	*Set down* 2 *units and carry* 4 *tens.*
7	7 times 5 are 35, and 4 carried from the units make 39.
——	*Set down* 9 *tens and carry* 3 *hundreds.*
5992	7 times 8 are 56, and 3 carried from the tens are 59 hundreds.
	Set down 9 *hundreds and* 5 *thousands.*

The answer is, five thousand nine hundred and ninety-two soldiers; or, in figures, 5992 soldiers; or,

$$856 \text{ soldiers} \times 7 = 5992 \text{ soldiers.}$$

Exercise V.

(a)—*Oral.* (1). How many pence are in six boxes, containing 13 pence apiece? Fifteen children sit on each form in a school, and there are eight forms; how many children are there?

(2). When apples are four for a penny, how many can I buy for 24 pence? There are sixteen ounces in a pound, how many ounces in 9 pounds?

(3). Multiply 5 by 4 and by 3; multiply 6 by 8 and 5.

(4). Seven times 18; 8 times 14; 9 times 17.

(5). Three times four times six; Twice eight times nine.

(6). Multiply together 2, 3, 4, and 5; Also 4, 7, and 8.

(7). 6 times 28. 4 times 43. 8 times 65.

(8). There are 5 drawers in a cabinet of coins, each drawer contains 8 compartments, and each compartment 12 coins; how many coins are there altogether?

(9). There are 12 houses in a row, and each house has 27 windows; how many windows are there in all?

(10). In each window there are nine panes of glass; how many panes in 824 windows?

(11). On every page of a book there are 36 lines, there are 12 pages in every sheet, and the book contains 9 sheets; how many lines are there?

(12). Multiply 5 by 3 four times in succession; 2 by 8 three times.

(13). Multiply all the nine digits together.

(14). If seven boys have 26 marbles each, how many have they all together?

(15). In a house of 4 stories, having 3 rooms on each story, each room contains 2 windows of 16 panes each; how many panes of glass are in the house?

(16). 23 × 5; 17 × 9; 21 × 11.
(17). (2 + 4) × (5 + 12); (17 + 16) × 8.
(18). 29 × 6; 123 × 3; 542 × 8.
(19). 35 × 12; 41 × 7; 126 × 5.
(20). 262 × 8; 154 × 9; 317 × 11.

(*b*)—*Written.* (1). What is the total weight of forty-three parcels weighing seven pounds each, and eighty-seven weighing ten pounds each?

(2). In a train consisting of fifteen third-class carriages, each in four compartments, which hold six persons on each of the two seats, how many persons can travel?

Work the following sums :—

(3) 729846	(4) 5729608	(5) 1730298	(6) 397241
3	4	5	6
(7) 208465	(8) 320987	(9) 162145	(10) 2746209
6	7	8	9
(11) 50768	(12) 309628	(13) 723698	(14) 506832
8	7	6	9

(15). 23684 × 10. (16). 329708 × 12. (17). 32897 × 6.
(18). 4236 × 5 × 8. (19). 27368 × 5 × 3. (20). 274 × 10 × 9.
(21). 123 × 11 × 12. (22). 508 × 6 × 9. (23). 172 × 6 × 3.
(24). (508 + 62) × 5 × 6. (25). (723 + 64) × 4 × 8.
(26). (128 + 146) × 5 × 9. (274 − 38) × (82 − 75).

(27). How many shots will be fired in seven rounds by three frigates of forty-two guns each?

(28). How many words in 8 columns of a dictionary, containing fifty-three words each?

(29). Find the product of seventy-six and eight.

(30). Find the difference between the sum and the product of nine and fifty-six.

(31). Suppose twelve trains of nine carriages each run daily on a railway, and each carriage contains, on an average, 47 people; how many people are conveyed in a week?

(32). How many pages in 7 half-yearly volumes of a monthly publication, each number of which contains 48 pages?

(33). A wholesale dealer employs twelve clerks, three at salaries of £250, five at £160, and the rest at £90. He has also eight servants, five of whom receive £21 per annum, and the rest £18. The rent and taxes of the premises amount to £1,250; the household expenses to £2,855. His sales amounted in the year to £126,785, and the money he laid out to £111,297. What was his profit?

(34). How many persons can be seated in a church in which there *are 98 pews,* 45 holding five persons, and the rest six each?

LONG MULTIPLICATION.

30. *Example.—There are* 27 *regiments of soldiers in an army, and in each regiment* 856 *men; how many men are in the whole army?*

Explanation.—As each regiment consists of 856 men, the whole army will contain 27 times as many. We must therefore multiply 856 by 27.

But 27 is a larger multiplier than can be found in the tables, so we first multiply by 7, and then by 20.

$$\begin{array}{r} 856 \\ 27 \\ \hline 5992 = 856 \times 7 \\ 17120 = 856 \times 20 \\ \hline 23112 = 856 \times 27 \\ \hline \end{array}$$

We first multiply by 7; and the product, according to Rule (28), is 5,992. But 7 times 856 is only part of the required answer; and we have also to multiply by 20. Now 20 is ten times two. If, therefore, we multiply 856 by 2, and place the unit figure of the answer in the tens' place, we shall be multiplying at one step by 20 (*S. of A.*, 69). In this way we find that 1,712 tens, or 17,120, equal twenty times 856. On adding the two partial answers together, we get the whole product. Hence

$$856 \times 27 = 23112$$

There are therefore 23,112 soldiers in the army.

31. Rule.—Place the multiplier under the multiplicand. Multiply first by the unit, and set down the answer as in the simple rule. Next multiply by the tens, and place the unit of this product under the tens of the former answer. Place in like manner the first figure of the hundreds' product under the hundreds, the first figure of the thousands under thousands, and so on. Add all the answers together to find the total product.

32. Worked Example.—Multiply 5063 by 768.

$$\begin{array}{r} 5063 \times 768 \\ 768 \\ \hline 40504 = 5063 \times 8 \\ 30378 = 5063 \times 60 \\ 35441 = 5063 \times 700 \\ \hline 3888384 = 5063 \times 768 \end{array}$$

EXERCISE VI.

(*a*)—*Oral.** (1). At thirteen for a shilling, how many buns can I buy for eleven shillings?

(2). There are twenty-four sheets in a quire; how many are there in fourteen quires? How many in eighteen quires?

(3). How many oranges in fifteen bags, containing 80 in each?

(4). Thirteen times twenty-five? Eighteen times fifty-six?

(5). Three times five times seventeen? Four times seven times twenty-three?

(6). There are twenty quires in a ream. How many quires are there in forty-seven reams? In sixty-one? In eighty-nine?

(7). Thirty times twenty-eight? Forty times eighty-six?

(8). How many calendar months are there in forty-nine years?

(9). How many minutes are there in 150 hours?

(10). Five times five times seventy? Eight times three times seventeen?

(11). $3 \times 2 \times 5$; $7 \times 18 \times 2$; $14 \times 12 \times 4$.

(12). $17 \times 16 \times 3$; $20 \times 30 \times 40$; $15 \times 9 \times 6$.

(*b*)—*Written.* Work the following sums:—

(1) 2963 18	(2) 50962 27	(3) 40786 58	(4) 219376 347
(5) 223954 137	(6) 70983 216	(7) 41832 307	(8) 693215 1098
(9) 141326 182	(10) 216831 594	(11) 150839 76	(12) 728603 95

(13). A town contains 4,253 houses, and, on an average, four grown persons and five children in each. What is the population of the town?

(14). Add seventeen dozen to eighteen score.

(15). Multiply three thousand four hundred and seventy-six by two hundred and forty-five; also by seven hundred and nine.

(16). If I buy eighteen horses at twenty-five pounds each, and sell eleven of them at thirty-three pounds each and the rest at thirty-seven pounds, how much do I gain?

(17). Multiply one hundred and seventeen by itself twice.

(18). What is the value of a row of 27 houses, valued at seven hundred and sixty-five pounds each?

(19). If I travel by railway 14 hours at thirty-four miles an hour, and next day walk seven hours at four miles an hour, how far do I travel?

(20). In a Government department there are fifty-three clerks, whose incomes average one hundred and forty-three pounds a year; what is the whole sum paid to them per annum?

* These may be worked mentally by the use of the extended table which is *given in the Appendix*.

(21). 28645 × 34. (22). 345068 × 135. (23). 406832 × 359.
(24). 108692 × 312 × 5. (25). 14196 × 15 × 8.
(26). 108 × 19 × 25. (27). 32850 × 46. (28). 5076 × 132.
(29). 30172 × 164. (30). (5082 + 176) × (32 + 51).
(31). (1362 − 71) × (81 − 19). (32). 47268 × 3047.
(33). 41960 × 3287. (34). 21968 × 5012.
(35). Multiply the sum of 3005 and 1862 by their difference.
(36). Find the product of 50832, 146, and 94.
(37). Add the product of 197 and 506 to their difference.
(38). What is the difference between sixty-five dozen and thirty-nine score?

(39). How many men are there in 16 regiments of soldiers, each containing 6 companies of 85 men each?

(40). If a railway company pays, on an average, fourteen hundred and twenty-five pounds per mile for the land, and sixteen hundred and twenty-eight pounds per mile as the expense of construction, what will be the total cost of one hundred and twenty-seven miles of the road?

(41). In a spelling-book there are fifty-nine pages, containing lists of words; these are arranged in triple columns, each column containing forty-eight words; how many words are there?

(42). In a large public room there are eighteen chandeliers, each of which has four branches, and each branch holds seven candles; how many candles are there?

(43). A grazier who owned fifteen hundred sheep lost, during the prevalence of an infection, at the rate of thirteen a day for three weeks; how many had he left?

(44). In a book of 352 pages, each page contains twenty-four lines, and each line, on an average, eleven words; how many words are in the book?

(45). If one mile of telegraph wire weighs 139 lbs., what is the total weight supported by the posts of a telegraph 17 miles long, and consisting of 16 wires?

(46). A man bought seventy-nine shares of the Great Western Railway when they were worth a hundred and fifty pounds each, and sold them when they were at a hundred and sixteen; how much did he lose?

(47). Take the numbers 47 and 65; find the difference between their product and their sum.

(48). What is the total weight of seventeen packages, containing three hundred and seventy-five pounds each?

(49). If, in a certain district, thirty-eight persons die per day on an average, how many deaths take place in the year?

(50). Multiply the number five hundred and seventy-six by itself, and subtract the result from a million.

(51). The equator is divided into 360 degrees, each of about 69 miles; what is the total circumference of the earth?

(52). Find the product of the sum and difference of five hundred and *eighty-four* and seven hundred and fifty-six.

DIVISION.

33. *Example.—A father left the sum of £2,352 to be divided equally among his six children. What should be the share of each?*

Explanation.—The whole sum has to be parted into six equal shares; we have therefore to find a sixth part of it.

But the sixth part of so large a sum as £2,352 cannot be found all at once, and must therefore be found in portions.

Let us set down the whole sum, and place the six on the left side of it, thus:—

	Thousand.	Hundred.	Tens.	Units.
6)	2	3	5	2
		3	9	2

The first part is 2 thousands, but we cannot find the sixth part of this in thousands, so we call it 20 hundreds, and join it to the 3 hundreds.

We next try to take the sixth part of 23 hundreds. But the nearest answer to this is 3 hundreds, which is the sixth part of 18 hundreds, so we set down the 3 *hundreds*, and carry on the 5 hundreds which have not been divided.

These 5 hundreds added to the 5 tens make 55 tens. But the nearest sixth part of 55 tens mentioned in the tables is 9 *tens*, which we therefore set down, carrying on the remaining 1 ten which is not yet divided.

This 1 ten and the 2 units make 12 units or single pounds. But the sixth part of 12 units is 2 *units*, which we set down under the units. Thus:—

Because	3 hundred	is the sixth part of	1800
And	9 tens	is the sixth part of	540
And	2 units	is the sixth part of	12
Therefore	392	is the sixth part of	2352

The answer therefore is, Three hundred and ninety-two pounds, which is the share of each (*S. of A.*, 93).

34. This process is called Division, because the number is divided, or separated into parts. The number so divided (2352) is called the Dividend, the dividing number (6) is called the Divisor, and the answer (392) is the Quotient.

The character ÷ is the sign of Division; or sometimes the Dividend is put over the Divisor: thus—

$56 \div 8 = 7$; or, $\frac{56}{8} = 7$, may be read,

Fifty-six *divided by* eight *equals* seven; or, fifty-six *upon eight equals seven.*

35. Rule.—Place the divisor on the left of the dividend, divide the first figure of the dividend, and place the answer underneath. If anything remains, carry it to the next figure, and divide the new number by the divisor. Set each figure of the quotient beneath that of the same value in the dividend.

36. Example of Working.—*If I have* 43,268 *apples, how many baskets can I fill, holding nine apiece?*

I.

$$\begin{array}{r} 9)43268 \\ \hline 4807\frac{5}{9} \end{array}$$

II.

$$\begin{array}{rcl} 9)43268 & & \\ \hline 4000 & = & 36000 \div 9 \\ 800 & = & 7200 \div 9 \\ 7 & = & 63 \div 9 \\ \frac{5}{9} & = & 5 \div 9 \\ \hline 4807\frac{5}{9} & = & 43268 \div 9 \end{array}$$

Nine into four cannot be found. Carry 4. Nine into forty-three thousands gives 4 thousands and 7 over.

Set down 4 *thousands and carry* 7.

Nine into 72 hundreds gives 8 hundreds.

Set down 8 *hundreds.*

Nine into 6 tens cannot be found.

Set down 0 *under tens and carry* 6.

Nine into 68 units gives 7 units and 5 over.

Set down 7 *units and carry* 5.

Nine into 5 cannot be found.

Set down the ninth part of five as not found; $\frac{5}{9}$.

The answer is $4807\frac{5}{9}$; or,

$\frac{43268}{9}$ = Four thousand eight hundred and seven and the ninth part of five.

Exercise VII.

(*a*)—*Oral.* (1). Thirty soldiers are ranged in rows of five each; how many are there in each row?

(2). In twenty-four pages of this book how many leaves are there?

(3). How many piles of twelve pence each can be made from 100 penny pieces?

(4). Add the half of fourteen to the third of thirty.

(5). Find the seventh of fifty-three and the twelfth of eighty.

(6). What is the difference between the seventh and the eighth of fifty-six?

(7). What number multiplied by 14 will make 112?

(8). Divide 120 by 6; by 5; by 4; and by 12.

(9). How many threes, fives, and sevens are there in 105?

(10). Add the tenth of 200 to the sixth of 240.

(11). Find the half, the third, and the fourth of 162.

(12). $\frac{45}{9}$; $\frac{63}{7}$; $\frac{108}{12}$. (13). $\frac{273}{3}$; $\frac{106}{2}$; $\frac{288}{3}$. (14). $\frac{412}{4}$; $\frac{128}{4}$; $\frac{175}{5}$

(15). $270 \div 9$; $144 \div 6$; $200 \div 8$. (16). $(7 + 12 + 5) \div (8$

(*b*)—*Written*. (1). A thousand nuts have to be divided among 7 children; how many will each have?

(2). If a cow be worth as much as 5 sheep, and eight cows cost £120, what is the value of a sheep?

(3). 6)47928 (4). 7)32047 (5). 8)210869 (6). 9)20047

(7). $\frac{32784}{6}$ (8). $\frac{20000}{3}$ (9). $\frac{96541}{4}$ (10). $\frac{1270506}{8}$ (11). $\frac{32741}{7}$

(12). $\frac{2198654}{7}$ (13). $53825 \div 9$ (14). $\frac{36096}{5}$ (15). $\frac{216850}{8}$

(16). There are 144 children in a school; how many more rows do they form as they walk two and two than if they were to walk in threes?

(17). There are 21,392 persons in a town, and on an average seven live in each house; how many houses are there in the town?

(18). I counted nine hundred and four windows in a street in which each house had eight windows; how many houses were there?

(19). Divide the sum of three hundred and fifty-four and four hundred and eighty-six by five.

(20). In a multiplication sum 11 is the multiplier and 34,848 is the product. What is the multiplicand?

(21). What is that number which, multiplied by nine, will give two thousand nine hundred and forty-three?

(22). Divide the product of fifty-six and two hundred and eighty-six by seven.

(23). The circumference of the earth is 24,900 miles; how many hours would it take to go round it at the rate of nine miles an hour?

(24). A gentleman left at his decease £4,800. From this three legacies of £500 each had to be paid, one of £450, one of £528, and the rest was to be divided equally among six persons. What did each of the six receive?

(25). Find the difference between the fifth of seven hundred and ninety-three and the twelfth of nine hundred and sixty-two.

(26). Divide the sum of eighty-nine and ninety-seven by their difference.

(27). If I distribute five thousand eight hundred and eight pence amongst a number of children, giving to each boy 5d., to each girl 3d., and to each an equal number, how many children receive the gift?

(28). Divide the sum of five thousand and sixteen and three hundred and fifty-nine into twelve equal parts.

(29). Add the sixth of 1,278 to the eighth of one thousand.

(30). What is the ninth part of the difference between twelve times ninety-seven and eight times three hundred and six?

(31). Find the difference between the seventh and the eleventh of ten millions.

LONG DIVISION.

37. *Example.—Thirty-six thousand seven hundred and eighty-four articles have to be made up into parcels of twenty-seven each; how many parcels can be made?*

Explanation.—The whole number has to be divided into parcels of twenty-seven; and the number twenty-seven is therefore the divisor.

But since *twenty-seven* is a larger number than any multiplier in the tables, we cannot do this sum by the short method of Division.

```
27)36784(1000     = the twenty-seventh of 27000
   27000  300     =    „         „        8100
   -----   60     =    „         „        1620
    9784    2     =    „         „          54
    8100   10/27  =    „         „          10
    ----                                 -----
    1684  1362 10/27 = „         „       36784
    1620
    ----
      64
      54
      --
      10 Remainder.
```

We first inquire how many times 27 is contained in 36 thousand. The answer is 1 thousand times only, for 2 thousand would be too much. We therefore set down 1 thousand as the first part of the answer, and subtract 1,000 times 27 from the dividend.

There now remain 9,784 to be divided by 27.

We next try to find the twenty-seventh part of 97 hundreds, and the nearest answer in hundreds is 3 hundreds. We set down the 3 hundreds, multiply 27 by 3, and take 8,100 from the undivided part.

There now remain 1,684 not yet divided by 27.

We take the 168 tens, and find how many times 27 is contained in this number. The nearest answer is 6 tens. We therefore set down 6 tens, and take 6 times 27 tens away from the former remainder. 64 now remain.

But 64 divided by 27 gives 2 as the nearest quotient, and twice 27 makes 54. We therefore subtract 54 from 64, and leave 10 remaining undivided (*S. of A.*, 99).

The answer is therefore, One thousand three hundred and sixty-two parcels, and 10 articles remaining, or $1362\frac{10}{27}$.

38. Rule for Long Division.—Write the divisor to the left of the dividend, and separate them by a line. Take as many figures from the left of the dividend as there are in the divisor, find how many times the divisor is contained in it, and set this number on the right as the first part of the quotient. Multiply the divisor by it, and subtract this product from the dividend, setting down the remainder. To this remainder bring down the next figure of the dividend, and try how many times the divisor is contained in it, and set down this number as the next part of the quotient. Multiply as before, and subtract each new product from the part of the dividend remaining, until the whole is divided.

39. Example of Working.—Divide 732,506 by 153.

```
153)732506(4787
    612
    ----
    1205
    1071
    ----
     1340
     1224
     ----
      1166
      1071
      ----
        95
```

732 thousands divided by 153 give 4 thousands. 4 times 153 makes 612. *Set down 4 thousands.*

612 from 732 leaves 120 thousands.

Bring down 5 hundreds.

1205 hundreds divided by 153 gives 7 hundreds. 7 times 153 makes 1071. *Set down 7 hundreds.*

1071 from 1205 leaves 134 hundreds.

Bring down 0.

1340 tens divided by 153 gives 8 tens.

8 times 153 makes 1224. *Set down 8 tens.*

1224 from 1340 leaves 116 tens.

Bring down 6 units.

1166 units divided by 153 gives 7 units.

7 times 153 makes 1071. *Set down 7 units.*

95 remain undivided.

Answer.—Four thousand seven hundred and eighty-seven and the hundred and fifty-third part of ninety-five.

Exercise VIII.

(*a*)—*Oral.* (1). Find the eighteenth part of thirty-six. The twenty-fourth part of 144.

(2). How many times is thirteen contained in fifty-two?

(3). Five hundred marbles have to be divided among twenty boys. How many will each receive?

(4). A hundred and fifty bushels of corn were eaten by 25 horses. What was the share of each?

(5). Divide 240 by 16, by 20, by 15, and by 8, and add the quotients together.

(6). Add the twenty-third of ninety-two to the fourteenth of 112.

(7). In a row of twenty-eight houses there are five hundred and sixty windows; how many are there in each house?

(8). What is the difference between the hundredth part of a million and the fiftieth part of ten thousand?

(9). What is the average of 15, 16, 18, and 19?
(10). Out of £250 how many persons can be paid £8 each?
(11). $\frac{280}{14}$; $\frac{720}{18}$. (12). $\frac{1000}{20}$; $\frac{960}{24}$. (13). $\frac{1080}{8}$; $\frac{2480}{4}$.
(14). $(120 + 24) \div (30 - 6)$. (15). $810 \div (7 + 2)$.
(16). One man can do a certain work in 72 days; in how many days would 3 men do it? In how many would 4? would 8? would 12?
(17). What is the fifteenth part of three millions?

(*b*)—*Written.* (1). How many vessels capable of holding 780 men can transport an army of 30,000?
(2). How many times can three hundred and twenty-seven be subtracted from five thousand five hundred and seventeen?
(3). If in the year 1855, 635,043 children were born in England, how many were born, on an average, per day, and how many per week, throughout the year?
(4). In a town, 9,836 deaths were registered in 74 days, how many is that per day?
(5). In a coalpit where 519 miners are employed, the number of tons of coal produced annually is 206,652; what, on an average, does each man obtain?
(6). If 19,460 is the dividend, and 695 is the quotient, what is the divisor?
(7). Out of an estate of five thousand pounds an executor has to pay one legacy of six hundred and fifty-two pounds, four others of five hundred and fifty pounds each, and to divide the remainder equally among six persons. How much will each receive?
(8). Divide the sum of 1,856 and 2,037 by their difference.
(9). What number multiplied by 387 will give 48,762?
(10). $287632 \div 19$. (11). $5068415 \div 23$.
(12). $9862013 \div 41$. (13). $5086291 \div 53$.
(14). $217968 \div 102$; $1086234 \div 521$; $4098763 \div 143$.
(15). $\frac{32986}{27}$; $\frac{408629}{503}$. (16). $\frac{7290831}{615}$; $\frac{1000000}{219}$.
(17). $\frac{5086762}{315}$; $\frac{7103826}{429}$. (18). $\frac{2050308}{732}$; $\frac{6219834}{136}$.
(19). $\frac{273 + 584}{56}$; $\frac{5086 + 519}{312-119}$. (20). $\frac{10000-713}{94-71}$; $\frac{21783+5046}{27+18}$.
(21). A legacy of six thousand one hundred and forty-four pounds was left to the poor of a large town; nine pounds were to be given to each man, and seven pounds to each of an equal number of women. How many persons received the benefit of the bequest?
(22). The answer to a multiplication sum is 1,404,336, and the multiplicand is 5,163; what is the multiplier?
(23). How many times can I subtract fifty-nine from 10,000.
(24). If 19,113 be the dividend, 516 the quotient, and 21 the remainder of a Division sum, what is the divisor?

MULTIPLICATION, DIVISION, &c., COMBINED.

40. *EXAMPLE I.—There are five and a half yards in a pole; how many yards in 8,692 poles?*

EXPLANATION.—We have here to take five times 8,692, and also the half of 8,692. One part of the sum will, therefore, be done by Multiplication, another by Division, and another by Addition, thus:—

```
2)8692
     5
------
 43460 = five times 8692
  4346 = the half of 8692
------
 47806 = the number of yards in 8692 poles.
```

41. *EXAMPLE II.—Find four-sevenths of 2,772.*

EXPLANATION.—One-seventh of this number must be found by Division, and four times one-seventh must be found by Multiplication. We have therefore to divide by seven, and to multiply by four. But this may be done either by multiplying first and dividing afterwards, as in II., or by dividing first and multiplying afterwards, as in I.

```
I. 7)2772                         II.  2772
     ----                                 4
      396 = 1-seventh of 2772         ------
        4                           7)11088 = 4 times 2772
     ----                             ------
     1584 = 4-sevenths of 2772         1584 = the 7th of 4 times 2772
```

EXERCISE IX.

(*a*)—*Oral.* (1). Find half as much again as 18.

(2). Twice the third of nine; Three-sevenths of seven.

(3). Multiply 12 by 1½, by 2½, and by 3½.

(4). One boy has 30 marbles, another has half as many again, another has a third as many, another a fifth as many, and another a sixth as many. How many has each?

(5). Multiply 10 by 2¼, by 4½, by 7⅕.

(6). Find three-fifths of twenty; five-ninths of sixty-three.

(7). Four-sevenths of twenty-one; six-ninths of eighty-one.

(8). Four-elevenths of ninety-nine; three-fifths of forty-five.

(9). What is the difference between three-fourths of twenty-four and six-sevenths of fourteen?

(10). What number is a sixth as much again as twenty-four? an eighth as much again as thirty-two?

(*b*)—*Written.* (1). What is the eleventh part of six score?

(2). 4193 × 5⅛; 2047 × 10½. (3). 4082 × 7¼; 2193 × 18⅓.

(4). 1068 × 18⅓; 219 × 5⅐. (5). 72816 × 13⅕; 32789 × 11⅛.

(6). Three-eighths of two hundred and seventy-two; five-ninths of ten thousand and eight; seven-ninths of a million and seventeen?

(7). A mile, or 1760 yards, of road, had to be mended by three labourers; of whom the first could do twenty yards a day, the second half as many again, and the third a fifth as many again as the other two together. When they had been at work two weeks of six days each, how much remained to be done?

(8). In a glasshouse 30 men are employed making bottles; what will be the total number made per week, if 3 men can make 500 in a day?

(9). A brickmaker can make 2,000 bricks in a day; how long will it take four men to make 120,000?

(10). $(196347 + 2035914) \times (918635 - 817209)$.

(11). $(235 + 627) \div (4172 - 4096)$.

(12). $\dfrac{796 + 487 - 98}{523 - 397}$; $\dfrac{406 \times (382 - 194)}{(26 + 18) \times 7}$.

(13). $\dfrac{(2067 + 818 + 519) \times (327 + 41 - 68)}{411 + 71 + 56 - 108}$.

(14). In a school there are 108 boys aged twelve years; 46 aged eleven; 29, ten; 56, eight; 23, seven; 14, six; and 10, five. How many boys are in the school, and what is their average age?

(15). By the Great Northern Railway it is 32 miles from London to Hitchin, 44 from Hitchin to Peterborough, 44 from Peterborough to Newark, 36 from Newark to Doncaster, and 35 from Doncaster to York. How far is it from London to Newark, and from London to York; and what is the average distance between the stations?

(16). From London to Exeter is 193 miles; how long would a man be walking the distance, if he walked 4 miles an hour for 8 hours per day?

(17). Divide £1,000 between A, B, and C, giving A £160 more than C, and C £105 more than B.

(18). How many pence will be taken in a day by an omnibus conductor who has 73 passengers paying threepence each, forty-nine paying fourpence each, and fifty-eight paying sixpence each?

(19). Four hundred and eighty marbles are divided among three boys according to their ages. The first, who is twelve years old, takes twelve parts; the second takes seven; and the third, five parts. How many does each receive?

(20). How many times greater is the population of Lancashire, which was 2,063,913 in 1851, than that of Rutland, which was 24,272?

(21). In Middlesex, Kent, Surrey, and Stafford, the populations were at the last census, 1,895,710; 619,225; 684,805; and 630,506 respectively; what was the average for each county?

(22). What is that number whose fifteenth part is made up of two gross, nine score, and eight dozen?

(23). In how many days will a traveller, who drives at the rate of seven miles an hour for eight hours a day, accomplish a journey of five hundred miles?

REDUCTION BY MULTIPLICATION.

42. *Example.—How many inches are there in 30 yards?*

Explanation.—If we know how many inches there are in one yard, we can find the answer at once by multiplying that number by 30.

But it is more usual to work the answer, step by step, in this way:—

```
  30 yards
   3
  ──
  90 feet in 30 yards, because 3 feet make 1 yard
  12
────
1080 inches in 90 feet, because 12 inches make 1 foot.
```

There are therefore 1,080 inches in 30 yards.

43. This is called Descending Reduction, because by it we reduce any quantity from a higher to a lower name.

All Descending Reduction is worked by multiplication, and the multipliers are always those given in the tables.

44. Rule.—Begin with the number of the highest name, and multiply by the number which will reduce it to the next lower name. Add in the figures of the lower quantity from the top line. Multiply the result by as many of the next lower name as make one of the greater. Add in as before, and continue this process until the required denomination is reached. (See Tables, p. 69.)

45. Example of Working.—*Reduce* £4 17s. 9¾d. *to farthings.*

```
   £  s. d.
   4 17 9¾
  20
  ──
  97 shillings in £4 17s.
  12
────
1173 pence in £4 17s. 9d.
   4
────
4695 farthings in £4 17s. 9¾d.
```

Twenty times four are 80. Add 17 shillings. *Set down 97 shillings.*

Twelve times 97 are 1164, and 9 pence are 1173. *Set down* 1173 *pence.*

Four times 1173 are 4692, and 3 are 4695. *Set down* 4695.

46. If our Money were Decimal, so that Ten Mils made One Cent, Ten Cents One Florin, and Ten Florins One Pound, Reduction would be worked without trouble, and without the use of multipliers, because we can multiply by ten at sight (*S. of A.*, 296). Thus the same sum of £4 17s. 9¾d. would be equal to £4 8 fl. 9 c. 1 m.

Now Reduce £4 8 florins 9 cents 1 mil to mils:—

```
£ fl. c. m.
4  8  9  1 = 48 florins 9 cents 1 mil, because 10 florins are £1.
           = 489 cents 1 mil, because 10 cents are 1 florin.
           = 4891 mils, because 10 mils are 1 cent.
```

EXERCISE X.

(*a*)—*Oral*. (1). How many farthings in 4¾d.; in 6¼d.; in 10½d.?

(2). Reduce to pence 1s. 9d.; 4s. 3d.; 5s. 8d.; 12s. 4d.; 7s. 6d.

(3). To how many persons can I give twopence out of 6s. 8d.?

(4). How many inches are there in 3 ft. 8 in.; in 4 ft. 9 in.?

(7). How many sixpences are there in £1; in 18s.; in £2 5s.?

(8). Reduce to pence three half-crowns; twelve shillings.

(9). How many times does the clock tick in 3 hours? In 1¼ hour?

(10). Reduce £1 to farthings; to halfpence; to threepenny pieces; to fourpenny picees.

(11). How many sixpences may I obtain in change for a £5 note?

(12). Reduce to farthings. 2¾d.; 1s. 8½d.; 2s. 6d.

(13). To halfpence. 5s. 7½d.; 10s. 6d.; 8s. 4½d.; 12s. 10d.

(14). To pence. 13s. 8d.; 5s. 6d.; 14s. 9d.; 17s. 2d.

(15). To shillings. £6 10s; £8 13s.; £1 17s.; £7 11s.

(16). To half-pints. 3 qts. 1 pint; 2 gal. 3 qts.; 5 gal. 2 qts.

(17). To ounces. 1½ lb.; 3 lbs. 4 oz.; 12 lbs.; 4 lbs. 6 oz.

(18). To minutes. 2 hours; 5½ hours; 1 day; 15 hours 47 min.

(*b*)—*Written*. (1). Reduce the following sums to farthings:—
£17 8s. 9¾d.; £45 6s. 8½d.; £29 13s. 7¾d.; £106 14s. 7d.

(2). How many halfpence in £25; in £16 13s. 4d.; in £59 8s. 8d.?

(3). Reduce to pence £29 17s.; £213 12s. 8d.; £49 5s. 6d.

(4). In £56 how many shillings; fourpenny pieces; and pence?

(5). Reduce £58 to pence; 872 shillings to halfpence.

(6). How many sixpences in £84 15s.? Farthings in 27 crowns?

(7). In £18 10s. how many half-farthings? In 125 florins how many pence? In 19 half-crowns how many farthings?

(8). Bring £16 15s. 4½d. to halfpence; £294 6s. 2d. to pence.

———————*

(9). How many inches in 17 m. 3 fur. 18 p.? In 10 yds. 2 ft.?

(10). Reduce 38 miles to feet; 1 league 1 m. 1 fur. to yards.

(11). 2 m. 6 fur. 3 p. to yds.; 176 yds. to in.; 8 m. 3 fur. to feet.

(12). 5 tons to pounds; 9 cwt. 3 qrs. to ounces; 15 cwt. 18 lbs. to pounds.

(13). To ounces, 72 cwt.; 13 st. 12 lbs. 5 oz.; 3 tons 2 qrs.

(14). To grains, 19 lbs. troy; 5 oz. 8 dwts.; 17 oz. 5 dwts. 6 grs.

(15). 8 lbs. 7 oz. 2 dwts. to dwts.; 27 oz. to grains; 5 lbs. 7 oz. 3 dwts. 9 grs. to grains.

(16). 17 ells 4 qr. 2 nl. 1 in. to half inches.

(17). 5 a. 2 r. 16 p. to sqare yards; 3 a. 1 r. 9 p. to perches.

(18). 17 sq. yds. 8 sq. ft. 71 sq. in. to square inches.

(19). 25 acres to poles; 13½ a. to square yards; 5 a. 2 r. to roods.

(20). 28 gals. to pints; 17 bush. to quarts; 35 gals. to half-pints.

(21). 17 pks. 3 qr. 1 pt. to pints; 5 qr. 2 c. 2 bush. 1 pk. to quarts.

(22). 17 wks. 1 d. to hours; 15 yrs. to days; 19 hrs. 3 m. to seconds.

(23). 21 wks. 5 days to hours; 3 yrs, 17 wks. 5 days to days.

* The pupil is recommended to pass over the sums beneath this line for the present, and to return to them as soon as he shall have worked all the sums in addition, subtraction, multiplication, and division of money.

REDUCTION BY DIVISION.

47. *Example.—In 3,286 farthings how many pounds?*

Explanation.—If we knew how many farthings are in one pound, we might obtain the answer at once by dividing 3,286 by that number; but it is more usual to divide step by step in such cases; thus:—

4)3286	farthings.
12)821-2	pence and farthings
20) 68-5	shillings and pence
£3 8s. 5½d.	pounds, shillings, pence, and farthings.

Because there are four farthings in one penny, we may find how many pence are in 3,286 farthings by dividing by 4.

In 3,286 farthings, therefore, there are 821 pence and 2 farthings. But as there are 12 pence in a shilling, we find how many shillings are in 821 pence by dividing by 12.

In 821 pence, therefore, there are 68 shillings and 5 pence. And because there are 20 shillings in one pound, we may find how many pounds are in 68 shillings, by dividing by 20.

In 68 shillings there are £3 8s.

There are therefore £3 8s. 5½d. in 3,286 farthings.

48. This process is called Ascending Reduction, because by it we reduce any quantity from a lower to a higher name. All ascending reduction is worked by division, and the series of divisors is always that given in the tables (*S. of A.*, 116).

49. On a Decimal method, instead of 960 farthings, 1,000 mils would make a pound, and the reduction would then be worked at sight; for,—

3,286 mils = 328 c. 6 m., or 32 fl. 8 c. 6 m., or £3 2 fl. 8. c. 6 m.

50. Rule.—Divide the number by as many of the less as make one of the greater; leave the remainder, and divide the first quotient by as many of that name as make one of the next higher. Continue to divide by the numbers given in the tables until the required denomination is reached.

51. Example of Working.—*Reduce* 10,007 *ounces avoirdupois to hundredweights.*

16)10007	By Long Division the sixteenth of 10,007 is 625, and 7 over.
28)625-7	*Set down* 625 *pounds, and a remainder*, 7 *ounces.* The twenty-eighth part of 625 is 22 and 9 over.
4)22-9	*Set down* 22 *quarters, and a remainder*, 9 *lbs.* The fourth part of 22 is 5 and 2 over.
5-2	*Set down* 5 *cwt. and* 2 *qrs.*

Answer—10,007 *ounces are* 5 *cwt.* 2 *qrs.* 9 *lbs.* 7 *oz.*

Exercise XI.

(*a*)—*Oral.* (1).—What are nine farthings worth? thirteen farthings? twenty-two farthings?

(2). Twenty-seven farthings? thirty-five? sixty-three farthings?

(3). Add seven farthings to twelve; nine farthings to eighteen.

(4). Seven articles at nine farthings each? eight at eleven farthings? thirty at forty farthings.

(5). Forty pence? fifty-three pence? seventy-six pence?

(6). Add fifteen pence to eleven pence; twenty-two to eighteen pence; ninety-four pence?

(7). Three articles at seventeen pence each? five at nine pence?

(8). Thirty-nine shillings? fifty-eight shillings? 209 shillings?

(9). Add seventeen, eighteen, and nineteen shillings together.

(10). Four articles at sixteen shillings? eight at twenty-one shillings? nine at eighteen shillings?

(11). What sum could be changed into 230 halfpence? into 117 farthings? 28 half-crowns?

(12). Find the worth of 17 fourpenny pieces; 35 sixpences.

(13). In 100 threepenny pieces, how many shillings? In 69 half-crowns how many pounds?

(14). Change the form of the expressions, 100 oz.; 132 lbs.

(15). 125 minutes; 23 days; 53 hours; 47 months.

(16). 39 inches; 84 feet; 17 furlongs; 40 inches; 29 feet.

(*b*)—*Written.* (1). Reduce to pounds 1,176 shillings; 20,978 pence.

(2). 500 farthings; 3248 pence; 107,962 farthings.

(3). 186,234 pence; 5,096 shillings; 82,634 farthings.

(4). 72,108 halfpence; 6,096 farthings; 819,436 half-farthings.

(5). 21,679 pence; 8,274 shillings; 10,832 crowns.

(6). 72,436 fourpenny pieces; 82,456 threepenny pieces.

(7). 1,200 halfpence; 75,000 farthings; 62,189 pence.

(8). How many £5 notes are there in 7,286 pence? in 31,965 pence? in 20,836 farthings?

(9). Reduce to pounds 187,563 mils; 12,796 cents; 175 florins.

(10). How many florins in 7,286 mils? In 2,178 cents?

---

(11). Reduce to miles 96,834 ft.; 17,200,786 inches.

(12). To furlongs 1,760 poles; 23,478 yards; 185,634 feet.

(13). To acres 125,000 poles; 72,984 roods; 326,584 sq. yds.

(14). To roods 2,500,000 sq. inches; 185,634 sq. ft.

(15). Reduce to cwts. 1,000,000 oz.; 3,972 lbs.; 200,000 drs.

(16). To tons 18,563,947 oz.; 21,847 lbs.; 500,000 qrs.

(17). Reduce to stones 276 lbs.; 319,768 oz.; 25,068 lbs.

(18). Reduce to troy pounds 11,263 gr.; 518 dwts.; 207 oz.

(19). Reduce 2,967 cub. ft. to cub. yds.; 72,863 cub. in. to cub. ft.

(20). How many weeks are there in 1,000,000 minutes? How many days in 314,728 hours?

(21). The "Times" of June 10th, 1858, bore the number 23,108, on what day did it first appear?

COMPOUND ADDITION.

52. *Example.—A gentleman pays the following sums to tradesmen,—to the butcher,* £9 3s. 6½d.; *to the baker,* £1 17s. 6d.; *to the grocer,* £12 18s. 4¾d.; *and to the upholsterer,* £39 15s.; *how much does he pay in all?*

Explanation.—As these sums of money have to be added together, they should be arranged in columns, so that only those numbers stand together which have the same meaning.

£	s.	d.	
9	3	6½	Butcher's bill.
1	17	6	Baker's "
12	18	4¾	Grocer's "
39	15	0	Upholsterer's "
£63	14	5¼	Total.

We first add the farthings together, and find that there are five in all; but because four farthings make a penny, we set down 1 farthing in the form ¼, and carry the 1 penny to the column of pence.

Then 1 penny and 4 and 6 and 6 make 17 pence; but because 12 pence make 1 shilling, 17 pence make 1 shilling and 5 pence; we therefore set down 5 under the pence and carry 1 to the column of shillings.

We next add 1, 15, 18, 17, and 3 together, because they all mean shillings; these we find to make 54 shillings: but because 20 shillings make 1 pound, 54 shillings are equal to 2 pounds and 14 shillings; we therefore put the 14 down under the shillings, and carry 2 to the pounds.

On adding the 2 to the other pounds, we find that they amount to 63.

The whole sum paid to all the tradesmen is £63 14s. 5¼d.

53. This is called Compound Addition, because the quantities are of different kinds—pounds, shillings; yards, feet; tons, cwts., &c., and are related to each other according to the special rules given in the tables.

54. If our money were decimal, the carrying from each column would be the same as in Simple Addition.

The same amounts would be then thus expressed:—

	£	fl.	c.	m.	
	9	1	7	7	Butcher's bill.
	1	8	7	5	Baker's "
	12	9	1	9	Grocer's "
	39	7	5	0	Upholsterer's "
The total would be	£63	7	2	1	and this is the same amount as

the former (£63 14s. 5¼d.), only decimally expressed.

55. Rule.—Place the numbers which refer to the same quantities in separate columns, according to the tables. Add the numbers in each column by themselves, beginning with those of the lowest value; carry to the column on the left as many of the less as make one or more of the greater, placing the remainder only under the column on the right. Proceed in this way until all are added.

56. Example of Working. — *Five parcels of goods weighed respectively* 3 *qrs.* 18 *lbs.* 5 *oz.*; 1 *cwt.* 1 *qr.* 7 *lbs.*; 2 *qrs.* 11 *lbs.* 12 *oz.* 8 *drs.*; 27 *lbs.* 6 *oz.* 11 *drs.*; *and* 2 *cwt.* 1 *qr.* 17 *lbs.* 8 *oz.*; *what was their entire weight?*

cwt.	qrs.	lbs.	oz.	drs.
	3	18	5	0
1	1	7	0	0
	2	11	12	8
		27	6	11
2	1	17	8	0
5	1	26	0	3

11 and 8 make 19 drams. But 19 drams are 1 oz. 3 drs.
Set down 3 *drs. and carry* 1.
1 and 8 and 6 and 12 and 5 are 32 oz. But 32 oz. are 2 lbs.
Set down 0 *oz. and carry* 2.
2 and 17 and 27 and 11 and 7 and 18 make 82 lbs. But 82 lbs. make 2 qrs. 26 lbs.
Set down 26 *lbs. and carry* 2.
2 and 1 and 2 and 1 and 3 make 9 qrs. But 9 qrs. make 2 cwt. 1 qr.
Set down 1 *qr. and carry* 2.
2 and 2 and 1 make 5 cwt.
Set down 5 *cwt.*

Exercise XII.

(*a*)—*Oral.* (1). I bought three articles, costing 7½d., 4¾d., and 1s. 6d.; what did I spend altogether?

(2). A man earns 11s. a week, his wife 3s., and his son 2s. 9d.; what are their total earnings?

(3). I have a half crown, a florin, a shilling, and two penny pieces in my pocket; how much is there altogether?

(4). How many weeks and days are there from the first of August to the end of October?

(5). Add 1s. 7d. to 5s. 3d. Find the sum of 3¼d., 7¾d., and 6½d.

(6). Two forms are placed together, measuring 5 ft. 8 in. and 4 ft. 9 in.; express the whole length in yards.

(7). Add 3 sixpences, four fourpenny pieces, 7 pence, and 5 halfpence together.

(8). I bought a hat for thirteen and sixpence, an umbrella for seventeen and ninepence, and a pair of gloves for three shillings and sixpence; how much did I spend?

(9). Three books cost 9d., 1s. 4d., 4s. 6d.; what is the total cost?

(10). 3¼d. + 4¼d. + 7½d.; 10s. 6d. + 4s. 8d. + 3s. 9d.

(11). £1 10s. + 15s. 6d. + 4½d.; 3¼d. + 4½d. + 1s. 9½d.; 11s. 2d. + 7½d. + 8s.

(12). £3 2s. 8d. + £1 2s. 6d. + 15s.; £2 9s. 8d. + [illegible]; £3 19s. 6d. + 11s. 3d.

(*b*)—***Written.*** (1). What sum will pay four bills, of which the first amounts to four pounds seven shillings and sixpence halfpenny, the second to eight pounds thirteen and fourpence, the third to seventeen shillings and ninepence three farthings, and the last to twenty-three pounds fifteen shillings?

(2). Add together £4 3s. $7\frac{1}{2}$d., £17 8s. 9d., £29 11s. $6\frac{1}{4}$d., and £124 13s. $6\frac{3}{4}$d.

	£	s.	d.		£	s.	d.		£	s.	d.		£	s.	d.
(3)	28	19	$4\frac{1}{2}$	(4)	128	6	9	(5)	18	6	4	(6)	29	1	$3\frac{1}{4}$
	11	13	2		45	13	$2\frac{1}{4}$		2	3	9		18	0	$5\frac{1}{4}$
	123	9	$6\frac{1}{4}$		1	10	11		5	12	$7\frac{3}{4}$		7	9	$2\frac{1}{2}$
		17	$4\frac{3}{4}$		17	3	$2\frac{1}{2}$		41	2	$9\frac{1}{4}$		2	1	8

	£	s.	d.		£	s.	d.		£	s.	d.		£	s.	d.
(7)	0	14	$7\frac{1}{4}$	(8)	2	1	$7\frac{1}{2}$	(9)	21	8	$10\frac{1}{4}$	(10)	1	4	$7\frac{1}{2}$
	0	3	9		1	5	$6\frac{1}{4}$		18	6	$4\frac{1}{2}$		0	19	6
	1	2	$8\frac{1}{2}$		2	17	$3\frac{3}{4}$		2	1	$9\frac{1}{4}$		2	18	$3\frac{3}{4}$
	0	17	$2\frac{1}{4}$		0	11	$9\frac{1}{2}$		0	19	$8\frac{1}{2}$		3	2	6

(11). £2 8s. 3d. + 5s. $6\frac{1}{2}$d. + 14s. $3\frac{3}{4}$d. + £5 2s. $8\frac{1}{2}$d.
(12). £17 2s. 6d. + £1 10s. + 3s. $7\frac{1}{2}$d. + £14 + £53 5s. $7\frac{1}{4}$d.
(13). £21 9s. 8d. + £7 2s. $3\frac{3}{4}$d. + £52 14s. $3\frac{1}{2}$d. + £103 2s. $8\frac{1}{4}$d.
(14). £2,168 13s. 2d$\frac{1}{2}$. + £407 3s. 6d. + £812 10s. $5\frac{1}{4}$d. + £410 18s.
(15). £728 1s. 2d. + £619 3s. 4d. + £5 12s. 6d. + £10 10s. 10d. + £7 9s.
(16). £13 2s. 6d. + £40 13s. $2\frac{1}{2}$d. + £1 9s. $7\frac{3}{4}$d. + 16s. $2\frac{1}{2}$d. + 1s. $7\frac{3}{4}$d. + £100.
(17). £81 3s. $6\frac{1}{4}$d. + £7 12s. $6\frac{1}{2}$d. + £3 12s. $4\frac{1}{2}$d. + £76 6s. 8d.
(18). £3,047 18s. 6d. + £2,098 17s. 4d. + £312 6s. 8d. + £4,127 13s. 8d.
(19). Add £10 2 fl. 8 c. to £6 2 fl. 5 m., and to £3 2 fl. 6 c. 8 m.
(20). £27 5 fl. 6 c. 3 m. + £7 2 fl. 1 c. 8 m. + 17 fl. 2 m. + 635 mils.
(21). Add together 47 fl. 85 c. and 153 m., 29 c., 16 fl. 43 m.
(22). Add £6 3 fl. 5 c. 4 m. to £1 3 fl. 7 c. 2 m. and to £12 8 fl. 9 c. 6 m.
(23). £5 4 fl. 8 m. + 6 fl. 7 c. 4 m. + 1 fl. 9 m. + 12 fl. 6 c. + £9 8c.
(24). A taxgatherer collected five pounds four shillings and sixpence halfpenny from one house, three pounds fifteen shillings from the next, eight pounds and ninepence three farthings from another, and twelve pounds five shillings and ninepence from another; how much had he altogether?

---

(25) 3 tons 19 cwt. 2 qrs. + 5 tons 17 cwt. 1 qr. + 16 cwt. 5 qrs. 27 lbs. + 2 qrs. 21 lbs.
(26). 4 tons 7 cwt. 3 qrs. 19 lbs. + 1 ton 5 cwt. 16 lbs. 8 oz. + *1 cwt. 21 lbs.* 9 oz. + 3 lbs. 7 oz.

(27). 5 cwt. 3 qrs. 17 lbs. 4 oz. + 2 cwt. 1 qr. 18 lbs. + 2 qrs. 19 lbs. 7 oz. + 21 lbs. 14 oz.

(28). 3 oz. 4 dwts. 19 grs. + 2 lbs. 8 oz. 18 dwts. 9 grs. + 4. oz. 17 dwts. 9 gr. + 8 dwts. 17 grs.

(29). 2 oz. 13 dwts. 17 grs. + 1 oz. 9 dwts. 16 grs. + 6 oz. 17 dwts. 23 grs. + 5 oz. 17 dwts. 17 grs.

(30). 5 miles 2 fur. 13 p. + 3 m. 1 fur. 17 p. + 7 fur. 18 yds. + 19 p. 3 yds. 2 ft.

(31). 7 leagues 4 m. 2 fur. + 17 miles 3 fur. 7 p. + 2 m. 5 fur. 27 p. + 185 yards.

(32). 73 yds. 2 ft. 7 in. + 16 yds. 1 ft. 11 in. + 5 ft. 10 in. + 7 ft. 4 in. 2 bc.

(33). 19 a. 2 r. 4 p. + 3 a. 1 r. 16 p. + 4 r. 21 p. + 11 a. 3 r. 18 p.

(34). 22 a. 1 r. 19 p. + 17 a. 4 r. 17 p. + 3 a. 3 r. 33 p. + 2 a. 1 r. 15 p.

(35). What is the cost of flooring two surfaces, one the size of 196 sq. yds., and the other 120 sq. yds. 8 sq. ft., at 7d. per sq. ft.

(36). There are six flagstaffs arranged along a road at the following distances, 28 yds. 2 ft., 30 yds. 1 ft., 56 yds. 2 ft. 8 in., 19¼ yds., and 25¼ yds.; how far were the first and sixth apart?

(37). If a man works 5 days 8 hrs. one week, 4 days 8 hrs. the next, 3 days 9 hrs. the next, and 5 days 2 hrs. the next, what will be his wages for the month, if 10 hours is considered a working day, and if he is paid at the rate of 5d. per hour?

(38). Three oxen, weighing 54 st., 61 st. 5 lb., and 58 st. 7 lbs. respectively, were sold together at the rate of 3½d. per lb.; what was paid for them?

(39). The floor of a room contains 17 sq. yds., 3 sq. ft. 18 sq. in., of another 21 sq. yds. 1 sq. ft. 126 sq. in., of a third 32 sq. yds. 2 sq. ft., and a fourth is half as large again as the sum of the other three; what is their united area?

(40). If a coat takes 2 yds. 1 qr. 3 nls. of broadcloth, a waistcoat 3 qrs. 1 nl., and a pair of trowsers 1 yd. 1 qr. 2 nls.; how much cloth is wanted for a suit?

(41.) What is the united length in yards of three roads, measuring respectively 3 m. 2 fur. 7 p., 2¼ m., and 7 m. 3 fur. 18 p.; and what will it cost to lay down a curbstone along all three at 3d. per yard?

(42). A man receives at his banker's, in change for a cheque, four twenty pound notes, seven notes of ten, and thirteen of five pounds, 59 sovereigns, 14 half-sovereigns, 38 crowns, 87 shillings, and 31 sixpences; what was the amount of the cheque?

(43). An estate consists of 79 a. 3 r. 21 p. pasture, 125 a. 1 r. 18 p. arable, 2¼ a. orchard, and a fir plantation of 7 a. 2 r. 8 p.; what is its whole extent?

(44). What time elapses from 5.30 p. m. on the 27th of September to 11.25 a.m. on the 3rd of February?

(45). In four vessels, containing respectively 2½ hogsheads of beer, 3¼ barrels, 5 firkins, and 9 gallons, how many pints?

COMPOUND SUBTRACTION.

57. *Example.—Out of a sum of* £7 9s. 6d. *I have to pay the sum of* £3 12s. 8d.; *how much will be left?*

Explanation.—There is enough money in my hands to pay the debt, yet if I have the money in the form of 7 sovereigns, 9 shillings, and six penny-pieces, it will not be possible to pay the 12 shillings and 8 pence. In practice we should get change for one of the sovereigns and one of the shillings (*S. of A.*, 50); but in working the sum we will suppose a sovereign and a shilling to be added to both lines (*S. of A.*, 44 & 51).

£	s.	d.
7	9	6
3	12	8
3	16	10

£	s.	d.
7	9 + 20	6 + 12
3 + 1	12 + 1	8
3	16	10

We first try to take 8 pence from 6 pence; but this is impossible, *so we add* 12 *pence to the upper line*, and say, 8 from 18 pence. The answer is 10 pence, which we set down.

But because 12 pence were added to the upper line, something equal to it must be added to the lower; *so we add* 1 *shilling to the* 12 *shillings*, and say, 13 from 9.

But, because 13 cannot be taken from 9, *we add* 20 *shillings to the* 9, and say, 13 shillings from 29. The answer is 16 shillings, which we set down.

As 20 shillings were added to the upper line, something equal to it must be added to the lower, *so we add* 1 *pound to the* £3, and say, £4 from £7. This leaves £3, which we set down.

We have now found that—

The difference, therefore, between £7 9s. 6d. and £3 12s. 8d. is £3 16s. 10d.;

Or, £7 9s. 6d. — £3 12s. 8d. = £3 16s. 10d.

58. With Decimal Money, it would only have been necessary to add 10 instead of 12 or 20. Thus,

£	fl.	c.	m.
7	4	7	5
3	6	3	3
3	8	4	2

£	fl.	c.	m.
7	4 + 10	7	5
3 + 1	6	3	3
3	8	4	2

This answer, £3 8 fl. 4 c. 2 m., is nearly equal to £3 16s. 10d.

59. **Rule.**—Place the less number under the greater, arranged as in Compound Addition. Begin at the right hand, and take away each number from that above it, setting down the difference underneath. Whenever the number in the lower line is greater than the number above it, add to the upper line as many of that quantity as make one of the next greater, according to the tables: then add one of the greater to the next figure of the lower line.

60. **Example of Working.**—There is a road measuring 18 miles 3 furlongs 27 poles 2 yards 1 foot: it is proposed to extend it to the length of 24 miles 2 furlongs 4 poles 3 yards; how much must be added?

m.	fur.	p.	yds.	ft.
24	2	4	3	1
18	3	27	2	2
5	6	17	0	2
24	10	44	3	4
19	4	27	3	2
5	6	17	0	2

2 feet from 1 cannot be taken, add 3 ft. to the upper line.
2 from 4 leaves 2 feet. *Set down* 2 *ft.*
Add 1 to the 2 yds.
3 from 3 yds. leaves nothing. *Set down* 0.
27 poles from 4 cannot be taken.
Add 40 to the 4 poles.
27 from 44 leaves 17. *Set down* 17 *poles.*
Add 1 furlong to the 3.
4 furlongs from 2 cannot be taken.
Add 8 furlongs to the 2.
4 from 10 leaves 6. *Set down* 6 *furlongs.*
Add 1 mile to the 18.
19 from 24 leaves 5. *Set down* 5 *miles.*

Exercise XIII.

(*a*)—*Oral.* (1.) I had 5s. in my pocket, and lost 3s. 6d.; how much was left?

(2). If two articles cost me 3½d. and 7½d. what change shall I have out of a shilling?

(3). I have to pay 17s. 7d. out of £1 2s. 8d., how much will be left?

(4). Take each of the following sums severally from one shilling; 3¾d., 7½d., 2¼d., 10¾d., 8½d., 9½d., 6½d.

(5). Take each of the following sums severally from a florin; 10½d., 1s. 4½d., 7¾d., 1s. 8¼d., 1s. 10d., 1s. 6¾d.

(6). Take each of the following sums severally from half a crown; 7¾d., 1s. 8¾d., 2s. 1½d., 1s. 11¼d., 1s. 9½d., 1¼d., 7½d., 1s. 3½d.

(7). Take each of the following sums severally from a crown; 4s. 8½d., 1s. 3¼d., 2s. 6½d., 11¼d., 8½d., 3s. 7½d., 4s. 2¼d.

(8). Take each of the following sums severally from half a sovereign; 7s. 3¼d., 8s. 6½d., 2s. 1¼d., 11½d., 3s. 7¼d., 1s. 7½d., 4s. 5¾d.

(9). Take each of the following sums severally from a sovereign; 14s. 9d., 7s. 6d., 3s. 8d., 2s. 7¼d., 18s. 9½d., 3s. 7¾d.

(10). From a sovereign take 4s. 3½d., 2s. 7¾d., 18s. 6¾d., 16s. 8d., 11s. 7d., 2s. 4½d.

(11). Cut off a foot and a half from a two-yard rod, how many inches remain?

(12). Out of a five weeks' holiday I have 17 days left, how much has past?

(13). (7½d. + 5¾d.) − 6d.; 2s. 9½d. − 1s. 3¾d.

(14.) 3s. 9½d. − (1s. 7d. + 8¾d.); 7s. 6d. − 5s. 7¾d.

(*b*)—***Written.*** (1). Take £2 9s. 6d. and 17s. 4d. from £5.

(2). What change out of a five pound note will remain after paying the following sums; 18s. 6d., £1 9s. 4¼d., and 13s. 8½d.?

(3). How much is a man worth who has £500 in his possession, and who owes £189 14s. 7½d.

(4). Take the sum of 17s. 3½d., 18s. 9½d., £2 4s. 7¼d., and £5 6s. 8d., from £523 14s. 7d.

	£	s.	d.		£	s.	d.		£	s.	d.		£	s.	d.
(5)	7284	16	5	(6)	6050	11	4½	(7)	1287	14	5	(8)	3250	17	9
	1093	9	8½		1972	5	8¾		645	9	6		187	6	11

(9). £2,057 16s. 3d. − £1,874 1s. 6d.; £1,057 18s. 4d. − £822 10s. 6d.

(10). £150 − £81 9s. 3d.; £2,384 5s. + £569 2s. 7d. − £147 10s. 3d.

(11). £2,178 + £4,163 10s. − £817 13s. 5d.; £3,168 5s. − £1,094 17s. 3½.

(12). £1,078 + £214 15s. + £519 16s. 7d. − (£238 17s. 4d. + £156 11s. 7d.)

(13). What is the difference between 37 florins and 48 half-crowns?

(14). At a collection at a church-door two plates are held. The one has in it a sovereign, three half-sovereigns, seventeen half-crowns, eleven florins, fifty-eight shillings, thirty-four sixpences, and eight fourpenny pieces; the other has three sovereigns, one half-sovereign, three crown pieces, eight half-crowns, thirty-seven shillings, nineteen sixpences, and a cheque for three guineas and a half. By how much did the sum of the one exceed the other?

(15). A man buys 1,000 yards of ribbon at 2¾d. a yard; he sells half of it at 3½d. per yard, and the rest at 4½d.; how much does he gain?

(16). Take £3 8 fl. 5 c. 6 m. from £10; £7 8 c. 6 m. from £15 3 fl. 4 c.

(17). £19 7 fl. 8 c. 3 m. − £8 6 fl. 3 c. 8 m.; £21 2 fl. 6 m. − £8 1 fl. 3 c. 7 m.

(18). What is the difference between 10 florins and 417 mils?

(19). By how many farthings does £18 10s. exceed £7 9s. 4¼d.?

(20). From 1,000 guineas take 10,000 pence.

---

(21). From a tea-service, weighing in all 120 oz. 17 dwts., several articles are stolen, whose total weight is 4 lbs. 9 oz. 18 grs.; how much remains?

(22). 22 lbs. troy 6 oz. 3 dwt. — 19 lbs. 7 oz. 5 dwts. 18 grs.

(23). 17 dwts. 18 grs. — 192 grs.; 3 oz. 5 dwts. 15 grs. — 1 oz. 6 dwts. 3 grs.

(24). 5 tons 7 cwt. 3 qrs. — 2 tons 6 cwt. 18 lbs.; 4 cwt. — 1 cwt. 3 qrs. 27 lbs.

(25). 4 cwt. 3 qrs. — 1 qr. 17 lbs.; 15½ cwt. — 7 cwt. 1 qr. 20 lbs.

(26). 18 lbs. 15 oz. 12 drs. — 9 lbs. 6 oz. 12 drs.; 32 lbs. — 17½ oz.

(27). 7 m. 2 fur. 8 p. — 2 m. 6 fur. 25 p.; 3½ m. — 1 m. 5 fur. 28 poles; 100 m. 2 fur. — 78 m. 3 fur. 6 p.

(28). 100 m. — 17 m. 283 yds.; 27 m. 6 fur. — 19 m. 28 yds.; 10 fur. 3 poles — 196 yds.

(29). A cart, weighing 12 cwt. 2 qrs. 17 lbs., loaded with sand, weighs on the machine of a toll-bar 1 ton 7 cwt. 1 qr.; how much does the sand weigh?

(30). The total or gross weights of 2 hogsheads of sugar are 12 cwt. 1 qr. 7 lbs. and 14 cwt. respectively; and the tare or allowance on the first is 1 cwt. 2 qrs., and on the second 2 cwt. 27 lbs.; what is the nett weight of both?

(31). If a railway truck weighs 2 tons and a half, and when loaded with goods weighs 9 tons 3 cwt. 18 lbs., what is the weight of the goods?

(32). A man sets out to walk 154 miles; he walks 21 miles the first day, 18¾ the next, 30 m. 3 fur. the next; how far further has he to go?

(33). A farm of 134 acres is thus apportioned, 17 a. 3 r. 14 p. are sown with wheat, 26 a. 2 r. 29 p. with barley, 50½ a. with oats, 4 a. 2 r. 19 p. are occupied by the house, outbuildings, and farm-yard, 3¼ roods as a kitchen-garden, and the rest as pasture land; how much pasture is there?

(34). By how much does the size of a field of 36 a. 2 r. 14 p. exceed that of two others, which are 17 a. 1 r. 9 p. and 12 a. 3 r. 27 p. respectively?

(35). Mont Blanc is 15,780 feet above the level of the sea, and Dhawalagiri is about 5 m. 8 p.; express the difference in inches.

(36). Subtract the sum of 7 qrs. 3 bush. 1 peck, and 8 qrs. 1 bush. 1 gallon, from 50 qrs.

(37). 10 gals. — 7 gals. 3 qts. 1 pt.; 8 gals. 2 qts. — 19 qts. 7 pints.

(38). 7 qrs. 5 gals. — 18 gals. 1 peck; 24 qrs. 7 gals. — 9 qrs. 3 gals. 7 qts.; 6 combs — 3 bush. 7 gal.

(39). From a cask of beer, containing 4¼ gals., which is worth 1¾d. per pint, 13 qts. 2 pints are lost by leakage; for what sum will the remainder be sold?

(40). From 216 days 17 hrs. 8 min. take 178 days 9 hrs. 43 min.

(41). From 1,000 troy pounds take 1,000 ounces; from 1,000 avoirdupois pounds take 1,000 ounces.

(42). If I walk for 2¾ hours at the rate of 100 yards in a minute, how much further shall I have to go to finish a journey of 15 miles?

(43). How much shall I gain, if, after purchasing 3 cwt. 2 qrs. of sugar at 3¼d. per pound, and losing 29 lbs. of it, I sell the rest at 4½d. per pound?

COMPOUND MULTIPLICATION.

61. *Example I.—What is the price of five copies of a book published at £1 17s. 6d.?*

Explanation.—The price of the 5 books must be five times the price of one. We have therefore to find five times £1 17s. 6d. by multiplication. This must be done by multiplying the parts one by one:—

	£	s.	d.			£	s.	d.
I.	1	17	6		II.	1	17	6
			5					5
	5	85	30			9	7	6

We first find five times 6 pence; this is 30 pence.

But as thirty pence make 2 shillings and 6 pence, we set down the 6 pence and carry the 2 shillings, as in II.

We next find five times 17 shillings; this makes 85 shillings, which added to the 2 carried makes 87 shillings.

But as 87 shillings make 4 pounds 7 shillings we set down the 7 and carry the 4.

As 5 times 1 are 5, and the 4 carried make 9, we set down 9 under the pounds.

We have thus found five times 6 pence, five times 17 shillings, and 5 times £1, and the three answers taken together make £9 7s. 6d.

The cost of the five books is therefore £9 7s. 6d.

62. *Example II.—What is the price of 37 pieces of silk, worth £4 12s. 8½d. each?*

Explanation.—Here the multiplier, 37, is larger than any contained in the tables. But we cannot work this sum by the Rule of Long Multiplication (30), because a compound number, such as £4 12s. 8½d., cannot be multiplied by 10 by moving the figures to the left.

We therefore find what numbers multiplied together will make 37, in order that we may multiply by these in succession (*S. of A.*, 66).

Now no two numbers multiplied together will make 37, but 9 times 4 make 36, and 1 more will make 37. We therefore work the sum thus:—

£	s.	d.	
4	12	8½	× 37, or (9 × 4) + 1
		9	
41	14	4½	= £4 12s. 8½d. × 9
		4	
166	17	6	= £4 12s. 8½d. × 36
4	12	8½	= £4 12s. 8½d. × 1
171	10	2½	= £4 12s. 8½d. × 37

Because the £4 12s. $8\frac{1}{2}$d. has been multiplied by 4 and afterwards by 9, it has been multiplied altogether by 4 times 9, or by 36. And because the £4 12s. $8\frac{1}{2}$d. has been added once to this result, that sum of money has been multiplied altogether by 36 and 1, or by 37.

63. On a system of Decimal Money the two sums would be worked thus :—

	£	fl.	c.	m.
I.	1	8	7	5
				5
	9	3	7	5

	£	fl.	c.	m.
II.	4	6	3	5
				37
	32	4	4	5
	139	0	5	
	171	4	9	5

64. In Example II. the sum of money may be multiplied by 37 in two lines as in (30), because florins, cents, and mils are in a tenfold relation to each other, like the thousands, hundreds, and tens of simple numbers.

65. Rule.—When the multiplier is not greater than 12, begin with the numbers of the lowest name, multiply each in turn, and carry as in Addition: but when the multiplier is greater than 12, find its factors (*S. of A.*, 56), and multiply by each of them in succession. If factors cannot be found exactly, take those which make the number nearest to the multiplier, multiply by each of them, and then multiply the top line by the difference between this number and the multiplier, and add this product to the rest.

66. Example of Working.—Multiply 5 cwt. 3 qrs. 21 lbs. 3 oz. by 17. 17 equals twelve and five.

tons	cwt.	qr.	lb.	oz.
	5	3	21	3
				12
3	11	1	2	4
1	9	2	21	15
5	0	3	24	3

12 times 3 are 36 oz., or 2 lbs. 4 oz. *Set down* 4 *and carry* 2.

12 times 21 are 252, and 2 are 254 lbs.

254 lbs. are 9 qrs. 2 lbs. *Set down* 2 *and carry* 9.

12 times 3 are 36, and 9 are 45.

45 qrs. are 11 cwt. 1 qr. *Set down* 1 *and carry* 11.

12 times 5 are 60, and 11 are 71.

71 cwt. are 3 tons 11 cwt. *Set down* 3 *tons* 11 *cwt.*

In like manner five times 5 cwt. 3 qrs. 21 lbs. 3 oz. are 1 ton 9 cwt. 2 qrs. 21 lbs. 15 oz.

These added together make the answ—

Exercise XIV.

(*a*)—*Oral.* (1). Three articles at 4½d. each; five at 6¼d.?

(2). How much must I give for six books at 1s. 6d. each; for seven at 2s. 9d.; for ten at 11d.; for nine at half-a-crown?

(3). A gentleman gave to each of five poor men 1s., to each of seven poor women ninepence, and to each of eleven children fourpence; how much did he give away?

(4). A boy takes in a monthly publication which costs him sevenpence, and has it bound in half-yearly volumes for 10d. each; what does it cost him per annum?

(5). 3 lbs. of sugar at 5½d.; 7 lbs. at 4¾d.; 9 lbs. at 7½d.; 6 lbs. at 8d.?

(6). 12 lbs. of tea at 3s. 6d.; 10 lbs. at 2s. 9d.; 7 lbs. at 4s. 2d.; 8 lbs. at 5s. 6d.?

(7). 3 yards of ribbon at 6¼d.; five at 8½d.; seven at 10¾d.?

(8). 13 yards at 6d.; 17 yards at 9d.; 20 yards at 10d.?

(9). What does a weekly paper published at 4d. cost in a year?

(10). The price of a dozen articles at 2d.; at 4½d.; at 7¼d.; at 6¾d.?

(11). Twelve times 8d.; 1s. 4d.; 3s. 2d.; 7s. 3d.; 6s. 6d.; and 3¾d.?

(12). A score of articles at 1s 6d.; at 3s. 4d.; at 7s.; at half a crown; at five shillings?

(13). Five half-crowns; seven fourpenny pieces; fifteen sixpences?

(14). 7½d. × 5; 2s. 8½d. × 2.   (15). 4d. × 16; 9½d. × 12.

(16). 2s. 4½d. × 10; 5s. 6d. × 12.   (17). 1s. 2½d. × 11; 1s. 6¼d. × 9.

(*b*)—***Written.*** (1). At three pounds seventeen shillings and sixpence each, what is the price of twelve silver watches?

(2). At 5s. 6d. per pound, what is the price of 27 lbs. of tea?

	£	s.	d.		£	s.	d.		£	s.	d.
(3)	27	19	4	(4)	18	16	10	(5)	123	13	6¼
			5				7				11

(6)	£36	18	10¼	(7)	£4	16	10¾	(8)	£29	0	7½
			17				20				35
(9)	£12834	16	7	(10)	£328794	14	3½	(11)	£563	18	7¾
			29				12				15

(12). £2,798 10s. × 40; £868 13s. 2d. × 21; £4,197 10s. 6d. × 56.

(13). £3,297 15s. 8¾d. × 28; £1,097 15s. 2d. × 55.

(14). £8,312 15s. 6d. × 49; £12,741 15s. 4¼d. × 63.

(15). £2,917 10s. × 98; £10,471 16s. 3d. × 58; £2,169 12s. 4d. × 79.

(16). £8,641 13s. 2d. × 131; £1,072 11s. 5½d. × 69; £4 5s. 6d. × 39.

(17). £2,097 15s. 4½d. × 76; £103 12s. 10d. × 135; £67 7s. 8d. × 196.

(18). Multiply £9 7 fl. 6 c. 3 m. by 17; £18 6 fl. 3 c. 4 m. by 73.

(19). £28 7 c. 4 m. × 117; £57 3 m. × 29; £1 6 fl. 8 c. × 19.

(20). £7 5 fl. 8 c. 9 m. × 36; £12 7 fl. 3 c. 1 m. × 48.

(21). £8 2 fl. 6 c. 3 m. × 100; £128 6 c. × 1000.

(22). Of 1,700 people who went by an excursion train, six hundred and forty paid sixpence each, five hundred and eighty paid ninepence, and the rest 1s. 3d. each; what were the railway receipts?

(23). Forty-seven pounds of tea at 5s.; sixty-three at 4s. 6d.?

(24). Fifty-four pounds at 3s. 9d; twenty-nine at 5s. 4d.?

(25). Sixty-four oranges at 1¼d.; 92 at ¾d.; 111 at 1¾d.?

(26). A person owes me £27, and pays only 7s. 4½d. in the pound; what do I lose?

(27). If a glover buys seventeen dozen pairs of gloves at 2s. 6¾d. each, and sells them at 3s. 4d., what does he gain?

(28). A grocer's bill contains the following items:—4 lbs. of tea at 4s. 3d., 6 lbs. of sugar at 4¾d. and 7 lbs. at 6½d., 11 lbs. of candles at 10d. and 6 lbs. at 8½d., 2 gallons of oil at 4s. 9d., and 7 lbs. of soap at 7½d.; what is the amount?

---

(29). 7 lbs. 8 oz. 19 dwts. 5 grs. × 6; 11 ozs. 19 dwts. × 17.

(30). 7 oz. 15 dwts. 11 grs. × 27; 5 lbs. 3 dwts. 16 grs. × 115.

(31). The weight of 7 spoons at 15 dwts. 16 grs. each; of thirteen forks at 1 oz. 17 grs. each?

(32). Find the weight of 5 casks of sugar weighing 4 cwt. 27 lbs. each, and also of 13 casks weighing 3 cwt. 1 qr. 19 lbs. each.

(33). 5 cwt. 1 qr. 21 lbs. × 18; 7 tons 3 cwt. 19 lbs. × 26.

(34). 7 lbs. 6 oz. × 47; 2 lbs. 9 oz. 1 dr. × 18.

(35). Gold may be beaten out so that 282,000 leaves make the thickness of one inch; how many such leaves would form a pile a mile high?

(36). There are five roads measuring 3 miles 4 furlongs each, four measuring 7 miles 6 fur. 20 p. each, and seven measuring 6½ miles each; what is the total length?

(37). How much ditching will a man do in nine weeks of 6 days each, if he can do 3 poles 2 yards 1 foot daily?

(38). How far does a railway engine travel in 17 days if it works 9 hours per day, and goes at the rate of 27 m. 5 fur. 27 p. 3 yds. per hour?

(39). 7 m. 3 fur. 3 p. × 18; 18 m. 1 fur. 4 yds. × 29.

(40). What is the price of 16 cwt. at 1s. 7½d. per lb.?

(41). The average daily sale of a baker, excluding Suudays, is 15 cwt. 3 qrs. 17 lbs. of the best, and 24 cwt. 2 qrs. 17 lbs. 13 oz. of seconds bread; what weight does he sell in the year?

(42). How much cloth will be required to make 5 coats at 2 yds. 1 qr. each, 7 waistcoats at 3 qrs., and 15 pairs of trousers requiring 1 yd. 3 qrs. 1 nl. each?

(43). A cubic foot of water weighs 62 lbs. 7 oz. 4 drs.; what is the weight of 176 cubic feet?

(44). 8 qrs. 3 bush. 5 pk. × 17; 5 qrs. 1 bush. 3 pk. × 351; 6 bush. 1 pk. × 85.

(45). Sound travels at the rate of 1 fur. 27 p. 4 yd. 2 ft. 6 in. per second; how far will it travel in an hour and 3 quarters?

COMPOUND DIVISION.

67. *Example I.—A company of seven persons staid at a hotel for a week, and the bill amounted to £23 10s. 2d., what was each person's share?*

Explanation.—The whole sum has to be divided into seven equal parts. In order to do this we first divide the pounds, then the shillings, and afterwards the pence.

	£	s.	d.
7)	23	10	2
	3	7	2

We first try to find the seventh part of £23. But the nearest answer is £3, which is the seventh part of £21. We therefore set down the £3 as the first part of the answer, and carry on the £2 which remains undivided.

The two remaining pounds, with the 10s. of the dividend, must now be reduced to shillings by Descending Reduction (44). They make fifty shillings.

Now the nearest seventh part of fifty shillings is seven shillings, which is the seventh of forty-nine. We therefore set down the seven shillings as part of the answer, and carry one shilling, which is yet undivided.

On adding this 1 shilling to the 2 pence, we find by Reduction that they make 14 pence.

But the seventh part of 14 pence is 2 pence. We therefore set down 2 pence as the third part of the answer.

The share of each person is therefore £3 7s. 2d.

68. Decimal Money could be divided without the use of Reduction; just as if the pounds, florins, cents, and mils, were thousands, hundreds, tens, units. Thus the same sum of money, decimally expressed, is £23 5 fl. 0 c. 8 m.—

	£	fl.	c.	m.	
7)	23	5	0	8	
	3	3	5	8	= £3 7s. 2d.

69. *Example II.—How many times will a wheel, 2 ft. 3 in. in circumference, turn in going five miles and a quarter?*

Explanation.—By the rule of Descending Reduction (42) we find that there are 332,640 inches in 5¼ miles and that there are 27 inches in 2 ft. 3 in.

The question therefore is, How many times are 27 inches contained in 332,640 inches?

This may now be found by Division (38), for 332,640 ÷ 27 = 12,320, the number of revolutions made by the wheel.

70. Rule.—Divide the number of the highest name as in Simple Division. Reduce the remainder and the next figure of the dividend into the next lower name. Divide this number and reduce the remainder as before. Each figure of the quotient is of the same name as the number from which it is obtained.

When the divisor is a compound number, reduce divisor and dividend to the same name, and divide the greater by the less (*S. of A.*, 108).

71. Example of Working.—Divide a piece of land measuring 20 a. 3 r. 14 p. into fifteen equal allotments.

```
15)20  3  14(1 a.
   15
   --
    5
    4
   --
15)23(1 r.
   15
   --
    8
   40
   ---
15)334(22 p.
   330
   ---
     4
   30¼
   ---
15)121(8 sq. yds.
   120
   ---
     1
```

Fifteen into 20 gives 1 and 5 over.
Set down 1 *a., and reduce* 5 *a.* 3 *r. to roods.*
Fifteen into 23 gives 1 and 8 over.
Set down 1 *r., and reduce* 8 *r.* 14 *p. to poles.*
Fifteen into 334 gives 22 and four over.
Set down 22 *p., and reduce* 4 *p. to sq. yards.*
Fifteen into 121 give 8 and 1 over.
Set down 8 *sq. yds.*
1 square yard remains undivided.

The answer is 1 acre 1 rood 22 poles 8 sq. yds. and the fifteenth part of 1 sq. yd.

Exercise XV.

(*a*)—*Oral.* (1). Divide nine pence among six persons; a shilling among eight; ten pence among twenty.

(2). The fourth of 5d.; the eighth of eighteen pence; the twelfth of ninepence?

(3). Divide half a crown among three persons; among 5, 6, 4, 12, 8.

(4). Part a florin into 4 parts; into 6, 3, 12, 8, 16.

(5). What is the tenth of a crown? the fourth? the sixth? the twentieth? the twelfth?

(6). The half of ten shillings; the third; the twelfth; the sixth; the fourth?

(7). Of a pound take the third; the fourth; the fifth; the sixth.

(8). The eighth of a sovereign; its tenth; its twelfth; its fifteenth; its sixteenth?

(9). Divide a sovereign by 20; by 24; by 30; by 32; by 48.

(10). Part 5s. 4d. among 8 persons; 7s. 6d. among 3.

(11). Take the fourth of a crown from the tenth of a sovereign.

(12). Add the eighth of 3s. 4d. to the sixth of 10s. 6d.

(13). How many bottles containing a pint and a half can be filled from six quarts?

(14). How many coins, worth 2½d. each, are equal in value to nine shillings?

(15). 2s. 8d. ÷ 4; £1 1s. ÷ 6. (16). 15s. ÷ 10; 10½d. ÷ 7.

(17). 2s. 4d. ÷ 7; 13s. 6d. ÷ 6; 18s. 6d. ÷ 4.

(18). £1 1s. 7d. ÷ 14; £3 5s. ÷ 6; £20 ÷ 12.

(19). 4s. 9d. ÷ 7; 13s. 2d. ÷ 8; £1 11s. 6d. ÷ 7.

(20). 17s. 6d. ÷ 9; 21s. 6d. ÷ 5; 36s. ÷ 18.

(*b*)—*Written*. (1). One hundred and fifty pounds are to be divided equally among six persons, what will be the share of each?

(2). A master paid among 21 workmen, in equal sums, the sum of £24 13s. 6d.; what did each receive?

(3) 6)2 7 6 7)5 8 4 (4) 5)276 13 2½ 4)56 3 6

(5). £728 13s. 9d. ÷ 12; £1,000 ÷ 17; £459 13s. 6d. ÷ 10.

(6). £847 13s. 6d. ÷ 35; £234 12s. 8d. ÷ 54; £1,500 10s. ÷ 83.

(7). £2,198 5s. 4d. ÷ 59; £1,268 10s. ÷ 184; £30,743 14s. ÷ 219.

(8). £3,256 0s. 7d. ÷ 71; £2,386 1s. 2d. ÷ 354; £2,500 ÷ 294.

(9). £632 12s. 3½d. ÷ 49; £2,456 14s. 3d. ÷ 7; £68 12s. 5d. ÷ 11.

(10). £729 11s. 4d. ÷ 46; £1,063 ÷ 15; £2,986 3s. 1d. ÷ 21.

(11). £3,562 8s. 5d. ÷ 724; £10,000 ÷ 582.

(12). £23,827 5s. 6d. ÷ 176; £12,683 14s. 6d. ÷ 275.

(13). £106,895 10s. ÷ 425; £327 16s. 9d. ÷ 111; £985 10s. 4d. ÷ 273; £5,289 12s. 4d. ÷ 63.

(14). Divide £78 6 fl. 5 c. 4 m. among 17 persons; among 23.

(15). £34 5 fl. 6 c. 8 m. ÷ 27; £2 3 fl. 4 c. 2 m. ÷ 7.

(16). £25 1 fl. 4 c. ÷ 18; £19 3c. 8 m. ÷ 14; £63 4 fl. 7 m. ÷ 45.

(17). £129 6 fl. 4 m. ÷ 111; £354 7 fl. 6 c. ÷ 215.

(18). 68 mils ÷ 11; 197 fl. ÷ 35; 428 c. ÷ 17; 5,328 m. ÷ 17.

(19). What is the nineteenth part of twenty guineas?

(20). A master paid on Saturday night £20 3s. 8d. in wages; four servants received 7s. 6d. each; five received a crown each; and the rest was paid in equal portions to 8 journeymen: what did each of them receive?

(21). How many fifty pound shares are there in the capital of a railway company which amounts to £13,375,850?

(22). How long will a person be in saving £360, at the rate of £2 10s. per month?

(23). How many guineas are there in £589 10s.?

(24). If there were a new coin worth 3½d., how many of them might be had in change for seven guineas and a half?

---

(25). 4 yds. 2 ft. 1 in. ÷ 7; 16 yds. 1 ft. 11 in. ÷ 5.

(26). 3 fur. 6 p. 2 yds. ÷ 8; 14 m. 3 fur. 100 yds. ÷ 9.

(27). 2 leagues 2 m. 2 fur. ÷ 11; 12 m. 1 fur. 50 yds. ÷ 17.

(28). 5¼ m. ÷ 16; 4½ furlongs ÷ 21; 500 yards ÷ 23.

(29). How many times will a coach wheel, $3\frac{1}{2}$ yds. in circumference, turn in traversing $47\frac{1}{2}$ miles?

(30). How many steps will a man take in walking $6\frac{3}{4}$ miles, who walks at the rate of 5 ft. 6 in. in two steps?

(31). How far apart must cabbages be planted if a row of fifty is 19 yds. 1 ft. 4 in. long?

(32). 5 a. 2 r. 7 p. ÷ 6; 14 a. 1 r. ÷ 7; 7 a. 5 r. 3 p. ÷ 8.

(33). 17 a. 5 r. 7 p. ÷ 16; 40 a. 19 p. ÷ 11; 21 a. 2 r. ÷ 15.

(34). A land society, consisting of 36 members, buys a plot of 15 a. 2 r.; what will be each man's share?

(35). A farm of 104 a. 2 r. 16 p. has one-fourth covered with wheat, one-sixth with barley, and one-half with grass; how much is left for the house and farmyard?

(36). A meadow, 73 acres in extent, is divided by four long trenches into 5 equal parts; each trench occupies a surface of 1 r. 17 p.: what is the area of each part?

(37). 12 oz. 5 dwts. 6 grs. ÷ 7; 3 oz. 17 grs. ÷ 8; 19 dwts. ÷ 3.

(38). 100 oz. (troy) ÷ 13; 60 oz. 11 dwts. ÷ 9; 7 oz. 3 dwts. 3 grs. ÷ 5.

(39). How many coins, containing $5\frac{1}{2}$ grains of silver each, can be made out of a bar of silver, weighing 14 lbs. 11 oz.?

(40). A silversmith makes 2 dozen tablespoons out of 52 oz. of silver, what is the weight of each?

(41). 3 tons 5 cwt. ÷ 6; 14 cwt. 1 qr. ÷ 8; 1 cwt. 1 qr. 1 lb. ÷ 10.

(42). 17 lbs. 5 oz. 6 dr. ÷ 13; 56 lbs. 7 oz. ÷ 16; 13 tons 7 cwt. 1 qr. ÷ 234.

(43). How many parcels of sugar, weighing respectively $\frac{1}{4}$ lb., $\frac{1}{2}$ lb., 1 lb., 2 lbs., and 4 lbs., can be made up out of a cask weighing 3 cwt. 1 qr., there being an equal number of each?

(44). 9 cwt. 1 qr. 26 lbs. of bread, and 36 gals. 3 qts. 1 pint of ale, were distributed among 236 poor people, what was the share of each?

(45). 17 bush. 2 pecks ÷ 5; 19 qrs. 7 gals. ÷ 12; 21 qrs. 6 bush. ÷ 7.

(46). 115 gals. $4\frac{1}{2}$ pints ÷ 9; 67 gals. 3 qts. ÷ 16; 25 gals. 1 qt. 1 pt. ÷ 18.

(47). The weight of a cubic foot of water is 1,000 oz. avoirdupois; find the weight of a cubic inch.

(48). An estate of 305 a. 2 r. is divided into 80 equal allotments; what is the area of each?

(49). Light travels 192,000 miles in a second; in what time does a ray come from the sun to the earth, a distance of 95,000,000 miles?

(50). Sound travels 1,142 feet in a second; in what time will the report of a gun which is $4\frac{1}{2}$ miles off be heard?

(51). A kilderkin of ale is drawn off into bottles containing $1\frac{1}{4}$ pint each; suppose three pints and a half are lost in the process, how many bottles will be filled?

(52). A tax levied at the rate of £3 17s. 5d. per house produces £919 6s. 5d.; how many houses are subject to the rate?

BILLS AND RECEIPTS.

72. When a tradesman sells several articles to the same person, it is usual to make out an account of their prices in the following form:—

Example I.—Mrs. Smith,

To W. Jones, Draper.

March 10.—	£	s.	d.
1 piece of flannel, $28\frac{1}{2}$ yds., at 3s. 4d. per yd.	4	15	0
35 yds. of calico at $5\frac{1}{2}$d. per yd. . . .	0	16	$0\frac{1}{2}$
$3\frac{1}{2}$ doz. pairs of stockings at 18s. 6d. per doz.	3	4	9
7 pairs of gloves at 3s. 3d. per pair . .	1	2	9
$12\frac{1}{4}$ yds. of Irish linen at 5s. 6d. per yd. .	3	7	$4\frac{1}{2}$
4 pairs muslin curtains at 12s. 8d. per pair.	2	10	8
	15	16	7

73. In the case of a retail account such as this, a Receipt for the money is generally written on the bill itself, thus:—

Received the above, William Jones.

74. *Example II.—Mr. James Williams,*

To Samuel Carter, Wholesale Grocer.

Aug. 14.—				£	s.	d.
To 14 hhds. of sugar, at £5 11s. 6d. per hhd.				78	1	0
„ 17 cwt. of coffee at 1s. 4d. per lb. .				126	18	8
„ 3 chests of tea—viz.						
A B 256 lbs. at 4s. 6d. .	£57	12	0			
C D 174 lbs. at 4s. . .	34	16	0			
E F 187 lbs. at 3s. 9d. .	35	1	3			
				127	19	3
„ 4 cwt. rice at $3\frac{1}{2}$d. per lb. . . .				6	10	8
„ 6 boxes of raisins, 15 lbs. each, at $9\frac{1}{2}$d. .				3	11	3
				343	0	10

75. A separate receipt for a large sum like this is made out in the following form:—

Received this seventeenth day of December, 1858, of Mr. James Williams, the sum of three hundred and forty-three pounds and tenpence, for goods delivered.

£343 0s. 10d. Samuel Carter.

Exercise XVI.

Write the following accounts as bills, and find their amounts:—

(1). Seven lbs. of sugar at $4\frac{3}{4}$d.; three and a half pounds of tea at 4s. 6d.; seven pounds of coffee at 1s. 4d., and a drum of figs, containing $7\frac{1}{2}$ lbs., at $10\frac{1}{2}$d. per lb.

(2). 12 yds. superfine black cloth at 9s. 6d. per yd.; 17 yds. doeskin at 7s. 9d.; 13 yds. black alpaca at 3s. 4d.; 25 yds. of red padding at 1s. 5d.; 9 yds. black beaver at 11s. 6d.; 7 yds. black cloth at 8s.; 34 yds. canvas at 9d.; 4 doz. pairs black kid gloves at 4s. per pair; 6 doz. pairs India rubber straps at 9d. per pair.

(3). 650 ft. of bar iron at 8d. per foot; 2 cwt. of cut nails at 50s. per cwt.; 2 16-gallon coppers at 48s. 9d. each; 3 parlour stoves at £1 10s. each; 5 brass locks at 2s. 6d.; 8 scythes at 7s. 8d. each.; 4 guns at £2 7s.

(4). 6 tons of tin ore at 50s. per ton; an iron chain of 90 links at 2d. per link; 90 yds. of iron piping at 8s. per yd.; 70 feet of American deal at 3s. per foot.

(5). 26 ft. of lead pipe at 1s. 8d. per foot; 1 pump, £18; 1 tank, £4; 4 joints at 3s. 6d. each; 1 tap, 5s. 6d.; labour in fixing, £5 6s. 8d.

(6). 3 pieces of black cloth, 25 yards each, at 11s. 6d. per yd.; 124 yds. of calico at 4d. per yd.; 18 yds. of canvas at 8d. per yd.; 56 vest pieces at 9s. 4d. each.

(7). Making a silk dress, 8s.; 25 yds. of ribbon trimming, at 6½d.; 3½ yds. of Irish linen at 2s. 8d.; making a jacket, 3s. 6d.; making 3 children's pelisses, at 4s. 6d. each; 6 doz. trimming buttons, at 1s. 2d. per doz.

(8). An upholsterer sends the following account:—26½ yds. blue Kidderminster carpet at 3s. 3d.; making, 3s.: 12½ yds. chintz carpet at 3s. 6d.; making, 3s.: 46 yds. Brussels at 4s. 6d.; 2 hearth-rugs at 15s. each; 1 piece of floorcloth, 16½ yds., at 3s.; 1 piece, 16 yds., at 3s. 6d.; 9¾ yds. of stair carpet at 3s. 8d. per yd.; 8¾ yds. for landing at 4s. 6d.: what is the amount?

(9). Dining-room curtains, 33½ yds. crimson damask, at 2s. 6d.; 44 yds. of trimming at 4½d.; 32 hooks, 1s. 6d.; 2 pairs loops and tassels, 6s.; cutting out and making two sets for dining-room, 16s. 6d.

(10). Ploughing fallow field, a man and pair of horses, 4 days, at 7s. per day; 1 man and pair of horses, harrowing 2 days, at 7s.; 20 bush. wheat-seed at 9s.; drilling and harrowing, 15s.; two men digging and cleaving, 3½ days each, at 2s. 6d. per day.

(11). 16 yds. super broadcloth at 27s. 6d.; 18 second ditto, at 14s. 9d.; 13 brown ditto, at 11s. 10d.; 14½ scarlet at 24s. 4d.; 62¾ black kerseymere at 9s. 8d.

(12). Two reams of foolscap paper at 10d. per quire; 1½ reams note paper at 5d. per quire; 2,000 envelopes at 1s. 2d. per 100; 3 bundles quill pens at 1s. 6d. per bundle.

(13). 23 Reading Books at 1s. 4d.; 35 Arithmetics at 1s. 6d.; 12 Higher Arithmetic at 4s. 6d.; 6 Atlases at 7s. 9d. each.

(14). 53 qrs. of wheat at 48s.; 47 qrs. barley at 23s; 38 of rye at 27s. 6d.; and 15 of oats at 39s.

(15). Silk dress, 18½ yds., at 5s. 6d. per yd.; 64 yds. of sheeting at 1s. 4½d.; 4 pairs of blankets at 18s. 4d. per pair; 3 ditto at 12s. 8d.; 26 yds. of huckaback at 10½d.; 9 damask tablecloths, 4 at 19s. 6d., 5 at £1 6s. 6d.

PRACTICE.

76. *Example.—Find the value of* 7,263 *articles at* £2 12*s.* 4½*d.*

Explanation.—This is a question in Compound Multiplication, for the sum of £2 12s. 4½d. has to be multiplied by 7,263.

But 7,263 is a large and inconvenient number to be used as a multiplier. We therefore take this number, consider it as £7,263, and by multiplication and division find what would be the value of 7,263 articles, at £2, at 10s., at 2s., at 3d., and at 1½d. each. By adding all these results together, we find the value of the articles at the whole sum each.

				£	s.	d.	
				7263	0	0	=7263 articles at £1 each.
						2	
Twice	£7263	0	0=	14526	0	0	=7263 articles at £2 each.
Half of	7263	0	0=	3631	10	0	= „ „ 10s. „
Fifth of	3631	10	0=	726	6	0	= „ „ 2s. „
Eighth of	726	6	0=	90	15	9	= „ „ 3d. „
Half of	90	15	9=	45	7	10½	= „ „ 1½d. „
The sum of all the lines			=	19019	19	7½	= „ „ £2 12s. 4½d.

77. The same sum might have been worked by considering the 7,263 as shillings, and by taking parts for the pence, thus:—

	7263		= 7263 articles at 1s. each.
	52		
	14526		
	36315		
	377676		= 7263 articles at 52s. each.
Third of 7263s. =	2421		= „ „ 4d. „
Eighth of 2421s. =	302	7½	= „ „ ½d. „
	2,0)38039,9	7½	= „ „ £2 12s. 4½d.
	£19019 19	7½	

78. This process is usually called Practice. Before using it we must know how to divide a pound into any number of equal parts. When these parts can be expressed exactly without a remainder, they are called Aliquot Parts. It is also necessary to break up the whole price of one article into portions, so that each of them, taken in order, may be an *aliquot part of* the last, or of some one preceding it.

79. RULE.—Multiply the number of articles by the number of pounds or shillings of the price, and take aliquot parts for the rest.

EXERCISE XVII.

(*a*)—*Oral.** (1). Fourteen articles at twopence farthing each?
(2). Multiply three halfpence by 76; five farthings by 48.
(3). A hundred articles at 2d. each; at 3¼d.; at 7½d.?
(4). 50 articles at 6¼d.; at 4½d.; at 8¾d.?
(5). 45 times 1s. 6d.; 38 times 2s. 4d.; 75 times 1s. 2½d.
(6). The cost of a cwt. at 4d. per lb.; at 6d.; at 7½d.; at 5¼d.?
(7.) Multiply 3½d. by 108; 6¼d. by 270; 9¾d. by 360.
(8). Find 365 times 2d.; 365 times 4½d.; 365 times 7d.
(9). Multiply 1s. 3d. by 48; 4s. 6d. by 53; 2s. 2d. by 54.
(10). 7 lbs. of tea at 3¼d. per oz.; 4 lbs. at 2½d.; 11 lbs. at 4¾d.?
(11). 2 tons at 7d. per lb.; 1 ton at 9d.; 5 tons at 1s. 2d. per lb.?
(12). A gross of articles at 4d.; at 6½d.; at 9¾d.; at 2¼d.?

(*b*)—*Written.* (1). Find the price of 1,926 articles at 7½d. each.
(2). 14,372 at 4¾d.; 90,685 at 10½d.; 43,928 at 6½d.
(3). 7,963 articles at 7½d.; 2,154 at 9¾d.; 4,182 at 10¼d.
(4). 2,068 at 13s. 6d.; 41,923 at 11¾d.; 20,578 at 1s. 2½d.
(5). 50,196 at 14s. 2¼d.; 21,608 at 7s. 6¾d.; 10,962 at 8s. 4d.
(6). 21,623 at 7s. 3½d.; 18,096 at 12s. 4½d.; 3,102 at 9s. 6½d.
(7). 4,083 at 2s. 7¼d.; 86,924 at 3s. 3½d.; 21,687 at 3s. 4d.
(8). 5,198 at 14s. 7d.; 2,013 at 6s. 4½d.; 30,985 at 7s. 6d.
(9). 20,687 at 3s. 5¾d.; 51,861 at 4s. 9d.; 72,168 at 13s. 1d.
(10). 3,569 at £1 3s. 7d.; 4,087 at £1 1s. 6d.; 2,178 at £1 5s.
(11). 1,023 at £2 5s. 3d.; 2,347 at £3 7s. 8d.; 8,694 at £7 6s.
(12). 72,185 at £7 2s. 9d.; 54,186 at £1 7s. 4d.
(13). 10,587 at £1 5s. 6d; 2,198 at £4 12s.; 5,184 at £3 9s. 6d.
(14). 72,163 at £43 12s. 6d.; 10,386 at £5 9s. 6d.
(15). 5,165 at £1 6 fl. 5 c.; 72,389 at 5 c. 6 m.; 1,274 at £5 6 c. 8 m.
(16). How much will 52,384 yards cost at 17 fl. 5 c. per yd.?
(17). Find the price of 2,784 articles at 48 mils each.
(18). Find the cost of 1,285 yards of silk at 4s. 3½d. per yard.
(19). During a year 255,255 qrs. of oats, 133,167 qrs. of wheat, nd 12,553 qrs. of barley were imported into Liverpool from Ireland. uppose oats to be worth 2s. 8½d. per bushel, wheat 7s. 2½d., and arley 4s. 1½d., what is the total value?
(20). In 1852, 1,377,671 half-sovereigns were issued from the Mint. Suppose that in the course of ten years' use each loses a veight of gold worth 3¼d., what will be the value of the coins?
(21). During 1846 the mines of Austria produced 5,549 lbs. of pure gold, and 85,653 lbs. of silver. Suppose the gold to be worth £3 17s. 10½d., and the silver 5s. 6d. an ounce, what was the total value of the yield?

* In these Exercises it is better at once to consider the articles as so many pence, shillings, or farthings, and to perform the multiplication. Thus, fourteen pence are 1s. 2d.; multiply 1s. 2d. by two and a quarter.

COMPOUND PRACTICE.

80. *Example.—What will be the cost of 3 cwt. 3 qrs. 16 lbs. at £18 9s. 5d. per cwt.?*

Explanation.—Here the number of times the price has to be taken is not expressed by a simple number, but by the compound number, 3 cwt. 3 qrs. 16 lbs.

We must therefore multiply the price of 1 cwt. by the number of cwts., and take aliquot parts for the remaining portions of the weight. Thus—

	£18	9	5	= value of 1 cwt.
			3	
	55	8	3	= value of 3 cwt.
Half the price of 1 cwt.	9	4	8½	= value of 2 qrs.
Half the price of 2 qrs.	4	12	4¼	= value of 1 qr.
Half the price of 1 qr.	2	6	2	= value of 14 lbs.
⅐th of the price of 14 lbs.	0	6	7	= value of 2 lbs.
	£71	18	0¾+	= value of 3 cwt. 3 qrs. 16 lbs.

Here it was necessary to resolve the whole weight (3 cwt. 3 qrs. 16 lbs.) into such parts that each might be obtained from the former, or from 1 cwt., either by multiplication or division. These parts are—

3 cwt., or 3 times 1 hundred weight.
2 qrs., or half a hundred weight.
1 qr., or half of 2 quarters.
14 lbs., or half of 1 quarter.
2 lbs., or one-seventh of 14 lbs.

Since all these parts together make the whole weight, the prices of these parts added together make up the price of the whole weight. This is called Compound Practice.

81. Rule.—Multiply or divide the price of one part so as to find, in succession, the price of each part of the whole quantity. Add these results together.

82. Example of Working.—What will a colonist pay for 35 a. 3 r. 34 poles at £9 17s. 6d. per acre?

	£	s.	d.		£	fl.	c.	m.
	9	17	6	= price of 1 acre =	9	8	7	5
			7					7
	69	2	6	= price of 7 acres =	69	1	2	5
			5					5
	345	12	6	= price of 35 acres =	345	6	2	5
Half the price of 1 a.	4	18	9	= „ 2 roods =	4	9	3	7+
Half „ 2 r.	2	9	4½	= „ 1 „ =	2	4	6	8+
Half „ 1 r.	1	4	8¼	= „ 20 poles =	1	2	3	4
Half „ 20 p.	0	12	4	= „ 10 „ =	0	6	1	7+
⅕th „ 20 p.	0	4	11	= „ 4 „ =	0	2	4	6+
	355	2	6¾		355	1	2	7

EXERCISE XVIII.

(*a*)—*Oral.* (1). Two pounds and a half at fourpence per oz.?

(2). At two shillings per lb., what is the price of 3½ oz.?

(3). Multiply 2s. 6d. by 4½; 4s. 8d. by 5¼; 7s. by 3⅓.

(4). 17¾ yards at 4d. per yard; 5¼ yards at 6d.

(5). What are the wages of a man for 5 days 6 hours at 4s. 6d. a day, reckoning 9 hours a working day?

(6). On the same supposition, find the wages—for 7 days 3 hours at 3s. 6d. per day; for 4 days 4 hours at 18d. a day.

(7). 3 weeks 4 days' wages at 10s. per week; 7 weeks 5 days at 15s.?

(8). 4 weeks 3 days at £1 1s. per week; 5 weeks 2 days at a guinea and a half?

(9). 6 weeks 4 days at 1s. 6d. per day; 7 weeks 3 days at 2s. 8d.?

(10). At £120 per annum, what is the salary for 2 years 5 months?

(11). At £60 per annum, what is the salary for 3 years 7 months; for 1 year 11 months?

(12). At £100 per annum, what is the salary for 2 months; for 4 years 3 months; for 16 months?

(*b*)—*Written.* (1). Find the worth of 3 cwt. 2 qrs. at £17 6s. per cwt.

(2). 3 lbs. 7 oz. 6 dwts. of gold at £3 17s. 10½d. per oz.; 7 lbs. 10 dwts. at £3 15s. per oz.

(3). 27 qrs. 7 bush. at 68s. per qr.; 5 qrs. at 5s. 3d. per bushel.

(4). The wages for 7 weeks 2 days at £2 15s. per week; for ¾ of a year at 17s. 6d. per week?

(5). What is the value of 27 a. 3 r. 29 p. at £23; and 14 a. 1 r. 11 p. at £37 per acre?

(6). What is the cost of paving 5 miles 3 fur. 200 yds. of road at £35 10s. 6d. per mile?

(7). Estimate the cost of constructing a railway 17 m. 2 fur. 3 p. long, at the rate of £12,372 12s. per mile.

(8). Find the rent paid by the owners of two fields, one of 16 a. 3 r., and the other of 27 a. 1 r. 20 p., at £2 1s. 8d. per acre.

(9). A person engaged at a salary of £150 per annum, leaves his post at the end of 29 weeks 4 days: what ought he to receive?

(10). What is the worth of 6 hides of leather, 4 of which weigh 28¼ lbs. each, and the others 29 lbs. 6 oz. and 33 lbs. 4 oz. respectively, the value of the leather being 1s. 6¾d. per lb.?

(11). Nine men find a lump of gold weighing 15 lbs. 7½ oz.; what will be each man's share if the gold be worth £3 17s. 10½d. per oz.?

(12). Find the price of 166 cwt. 7 lbs. of lead at £5 7s. per cwt.

(13). Find the value of 5 cwt. 2 qrs. 8 lbs. at £3 4s. 2d.; and of 711 at £1 17s. 4½d. per cwt.

(14). Find the rent of a house for 3 years 7 months (of 4 weeks each) 4 days, at 17s. 6d. per week.

(15). Make out a bill for the following articles:—156 yds. 1 qr. 3 n. at 6s. 8d. per yd.; 48 yds. 1 qr. 1 n. at 1s. 5½d. per yd.; and 117 yds. 1 qr. 1 n. at 5s. 1½d. per yd.

REDUCTION TO DECIMAL MONEY.

83. The English Sovereign is now divided into 960 parts, called Farthings. If it were divided into 1,000 parts, called Mils, some of our present coins could easily be represented by the new names, while others would not (*S. of A.*, 296). Thus—

A Sovereign would be £1, or	10 fl., or	100 c., or	1,000 m.
A Half-Sovereign would be	5 fl., or	50 c., or	500 m.
A Crown piece „	$2\frac{1}{2}$ fl., or	25 c., or	250 m.
A Half-Crown „	$1\frac{1}{4}$ fl., or	$12\frac{1}{2}$ c., or	125 m.
A Florin „	1 fl., or	10 c., or	100 m.
A Shilling „	$\frac{1}{2}$-fl., or	5 c., or	50 m.
Sixpence „	$\frac{1}{4}$-fl., or	$2\frac{1}{2}$ c., or	25 m.

A Penny is now 4 farthings, but would become 4 mils.
A Halfpenny 2 „ „ 2 mils.
*A Farthing would become 1 mil.

84. Our present money can therefore be accurately reduced to a decimal form, when the sum is not lower than sixpence. When smaller sums occur, if we reduce them to farthings, and call the farthings mils, the error is very slight, and will not affect the answer unless in multiplication sums, when the error itself is of course increased.

85. Rule.—For every two shillings take 1 florin, or 100 mils; for every shilling, 5 cents, or 50 mils; for sixpence, 25 mils; and for every additional farthing, 1 mil.

Examples.—I. Reduce to decimal money the sums of 10s. $6\frac{3}{4}$d. and £3 5s. $7\frac{1}{2}$d.

	fl.	c.	m.
10 shillings =	5	0	0
6 pence =	0	2	5
3 farthings =	0	0	3
10s. $6\frac{3}{4}$d. =	5	2	8

	£	fl.	c.	m.
3 pounds =	3	0	0	0
4 shillings =	0	2	0	0
1 shilling =	0	0	5	0
$7\frac{1}{2}$d. = 30 far. =	0	0	3	1
	£3	2	8	1

II. Reduce to present money £7 2 fl. 6 c. 4 m. and £1 1 fl. 3 c. 2 m.

£	fl.	c.	m.		£	s.	d.
7	0	0	0	=	7	0	0
0	2	0	0	=	0	4	0
0	0	5	0	=	0	1	0
0	0	1	4	=	0	0	$3\frac{1}{2}$
7	2	6	4	=	7	5	$3\frac{1}{2}$

£	fl.	c.	m.		£	s.	d.
1	0	0	0	=	1	0	0
0	1	0	0	=	0	2	0
0	0	3	2	= 31 far. =	0	0	$7\frac{3}{4}$
					1	2	$7\frac{3}{4}$

* It is evident that all the money below sixpence would become slightly lowered in value, and that new coins of one mil, two mils, five mils, and one cent would be *required to supersede* the farthing, halfpenny, penny, and threepenny pieces.

EXERCISE XIX.

(a)—*Oral.* Reduce to Decimal Money—

(1). 10s. 4d.; £1 6s. 10d.; £2 0s. 7d.

(2). £7 15s. 6d.; £1 18s. 5d.; £1 3s. 3¾d.

(3). £6 2s. 1d.; £2 9s. 8d.; £1 17s. 3d.

(4). £4 13s. 9d.; £1 6s. 3d.; £2 5s. 8½d.

(5). £3 2s. 2d.; £5 0s. 7¼d.; £9 6s. 6d.

(6). £1 7s. 6d.; £3 18s. 4¼d.; £2 7s. 2d.

(7). £1 0s. 10d.; £7 1s. 9d.; £8 2s. 5d.

(8). £2 3s. 4¼d.; £1 19s. 6¾d.; £2 7s. 4¼d.

(9). 17 farthings; 18 pence; half-a-crown; half-a-guinea.

Reduce to present money—

(10). £1 3 fl. 4 c. 6 m.; £8 1 fl. 3 c. 7 m.; £9 2 fl. 8 m.

(11). 6 fl. 5 c.; £1 2 fl. 4 c. 2 m.; £8 2 fl. 1 c. 1 m.

(12). £10 9 fl. 3 c. 4 m.; £6 4 fl. 5 c. 3 m.; £5 3 fl. 4 c. 6 m.

(13). £1 8 fl. 9 c. 3 m.; £2 4 fl. 3 c. 5 m.; £7 2 fl. 4 c.

(14). £61 2 fl. 8 m.; £9 1 fl. 3 c. 8 m.; £12 3 fl. 4 c. 5 m.

(15). £17 3 fl. 4 c. 8 m.; £2 4 fl. 1 c. 8 m.; £1 3 fl. 4 c. 7 m.

(16). £2 9 fl. 9 c. 9 m.; £1 1 fl. 1 c. 1 m.; £5 3 fl. 4 c. 2 m.

(17). 18 florins; 72 cents; 64 mils; 23 mils.

(b)—*Written.* Work the following sums by the Decimal method:—

(1). Questions 12, 13, 14, 15, and 16 in Exercise XII.

(2). Questions 5, 6, 7, 8, 9, 10, 11, and 12 in Exercise XIII.

(3). Questions 2, 12, 23, in Exercise XIV.

(4). Questions 3 to 12, in Exercise XV.

(5). Add together 8s. 6d., 13s. 4d., £5, £7 5s., and 9½d.

(6). What sum must be added to £75 6s. 4d. to make £155 10s.?

(7). What will be the cost of 11 cwt. 2 qrs. at £51 7s. 6d. per cwt.?

(8). Divide £1,023 18s. 4½d. by 76, and also by 43.

(9). Make out the bills 4, 7, 10, and 14, in Exercise XVI., decimally.

(10). Find the difference between £13 5s. 6d. and £50, in farthings and in mils.

(11). Find in mils the difference between the fourteenth and the fifteenth of £50.

(12). If the price of a four-pound loaf were raised from 4½d. to 20 mils, what would be the weekly gain to a baker who sells, on an average, 519 quartern and 843 half-quartern loaves on each working day?

(13). If at Waterloo Bridge 4,000 persons pass in a day, paying a halfpenny, 261 cabs paying 2d., and 153 carriages and waggons paying 3d., what would be the daily difference in the bridge receipts if the tolls were altered to 2 mils, 1 cent, and 12 mils respectively?

(14). In 1851, 360,500,000 letters were delivered in the United Kingdom. Suppose the postage of each letter had been 4 mils instead of 1 penny, what would have been the loss to the Post Office revenue? If the postage had been 5 mils what would have been gained?

MEASUREMENT OF SURFACES.

86. *Example.—A surface is* 3 *feet* 4 *inches long and* 2 *feet* 5 *inches broad; what is its area?*

Explanation.—The size of the whole surface is to be found by multiplying the number of feet and inches in the length by the number of feet and inches in the breadth.

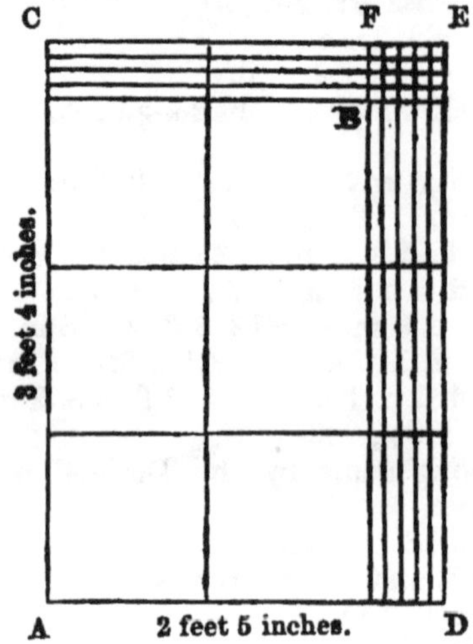

In the figure, let the line CE represent 2 ft. 5 in., and the line ED 3 ft. 4 inches.

The whole area, CD, is made up of pieces of three different sizes.

The largest pieces measure 1 foot each way, and are called *square feet.*

There are *six* of these; they form the figure AB.

Other pieces measure 1 foot one way, and 1 inch the other. Each of these contains one *twelfth of a square foot*, and is called a *prime.* There are eight of these in the figure CB, and fifteen of these in the figure BD.

The smallest pieces measure 1 inch each way, and are called square inches.

There are 20 of these pieces; they form the figure BE.

The whole area is therefore 6 feet 23 primes 20 inches, as in I.

But since 12 of the smallest pieces, or square inches, make 1 of the larger or primes; and 12 primes make 1 of the largest pieces, or square feet; each part of the answer must be reduced by 12, as in II.; and thus the whole answer is—

		ft.	in.	
I.		3	4	
		2	5	
			20	=5 in. × 4 in. = BE
		15		=3 ft. × 5 in. = BD
		8		=2 ft. × 4 in. = CB
	6			=3 ft. × 2 ft. = AB
	6	23	20	=CEDA

		ft.	in.	
II.		3	4	
		2	5	
		16	8	= FD
	6	8		= AF
	8	0′	8″	= ACED

square feet no primes and 8 *square inches.*

87. This kind of computation is called DUODECIMAL* because both the linear foot and inch, and the superficial foot or inch, are divided into 12 parts.

But it is necessary to observe that though there are 12 inches in a foot of length, there are 12 times 12 inches in a foot of surface. Therefore, the twelfth part of a square foot is not a square inch, but a piece measuring 1 foot by 1 inch.

1 foot of length = 12 inches = 144 seconds = 1728 thirds.
1 foot of surface = 12 primes = 144 inches = 1728 thirds.

88. It is usual to express these subdivisions by accents, thus—

7 ft. 8′ 5″ 4‴ = 7 ft. 8 inches 5 seconds 4 thirds.
8 sq. ft. 9′ 4″ 7‴ = 8 sq. ft. 9 primes 4 inches 7 thirds.

89. The same principle must be kept in view in all square measurement. Three feet make one yard; but 3 times 3 sq. feet make one square yard. 320 poles make one mile; but 320 × 320 square poles make a square mile.

90. RULE.†—Multiply the feet, inches, and seconds in the length by the feet, inches, and seconds in the breadth, according to the following table:—

Feet × feet = square feet.
Feet × inches = square primes.
Inches × inches = square inches.
Feet × seconds = square inches.
Inches × seconds = square thirds.
Seconds × seconds = square fourths.
Links × links = square links.
Yards × yards = square yards.—(*S. of A.*, 483.)

91. EXAMPLE OF WORKING.—I. Find the area of a floor 17 feet 2 inches 6 seconds by 11 feet 8 inches 9 seconds.

ft.	in.	sec.					
17	2	6					
11	8	9					
1	0′	10″	10‴	6⁗	= 17	2′	6″ × 9″
11	5′	8″			= 17	2′	6″ × 8′
189	3′	6″			= 17	2′	6″ × 11 ft.
201	10′	0″	10‴	6⁗	= 17	2′	6″ × 11 ft. 8′ 9″

* From *duodecim*, a Latin word meaning twelve.

† In all former multiplications, quantities, lengths, values, or numbers have been taken or repeated a *certain number of times*, and the product has always been a number *of the same kind as the multiplicand*. In strictness, this is the only true multiplication. But in this rule we multiply figures together which mean *length*, and the product is a number which means *surface*. This is an artificial and peculiar kind of compound multiplication, which therefore requires distinct explanation.

92. Land is measured by Gunter's chain, which is 4 poles or 22 yards long, and is divided into 100 parts, each of which is called a link.

An acre is equal to a parallelogram 40 poles long and 4 poles broad; that is, 10 chains or 1,000 links long, and 1 chain or 100 links broad. There are therefore 1,000 × 100, or 100,000 square links in an acre.

It is usual, in measuring fields, to reduce both length and breadth to links, and then to find the number of acres by cutting off five figures from the right of the product. This is the convenient way of dividing by 100,000, which is the number of square links in an acre. The remaining figures must be reduced to roods and poles by ascending reduction.

93. EXAMPLE OF WORKING.—II. A field in the form of a rectangle measures 17 chains 25 links by 21 chains 50 links; find its area in acres.

```
21 chains 50 links = 2150 links.
17   „    25   „   = 1725   „
                     -----
                     10750
                     4300
                    15050
                    2150
                    --------
                    37,08750 square links = 37 a. 8750 lks.
```

But 8,750 sq. links are by reduction 14 poles.
The area of the field is therefore 37 acres 14 poles.

EXERCISE XX.

(1). A rectangular parallelogram measures 4 ft. 3 in. by 6 ft. 7 in.; what is its area?

(2). Multiply 14 ft. 5 in. by 2 ft. 6 in.; and 21 ft. 5′ 4″ by 18 ft. 2′.

(3). Multiply 9 ft. 2′ by 4 ft. 3′ 7″; and 16 ft. 8′ 3″ by 12 ft. 4′ 8″.

(4). Find the area of a floor 9 ft. 3′ 7″ by 11 ft. 9′ 11″.

(5). Find the area of a floor 14 ft. 3′ by 16 ft. 7′ 10″.

(6). How many sq. yards are there in a surface 16 ft. 4 in. by 23 ft. 5 in.?

(7). How many rods of brickwork are there in a wall 14 ft. high, and 73 ft. 6 in. long?

(8). Divide a floor 23 yds. 4 in. long, and 17 yds. 5 in. broad, into squares of 100 feet.

(9). Find the number of sq. feet of paper required in a room 12 ft. 6 in. long, 10 ft. 5 in. broad, and 11 feet high.

(10). Two rooms open into one another; the one is 17 ft. 3 in. long and 12 ft. 5 in. broad, and the other is 19 ft. 7 in. long and 13 ft. 4 in. broad; how much carpet will cover both?

(11). I have a piece of drugget 5 yds. 1 ft. 7 in. long and 3 ft. 4 in. broad, to lay down in a room containing 100 sq. ft.; how much will be left uncovered?

(12). What is the area of a square field whose side measures 15 chains 40 links?

(13). How many stones, 9 in. broad and 12 in. long, will be required to pave a courtyard 15 ft. 8 in. long, and 12 ft. 6 in. broad?

(14). A schoolroom was 54 ft. long and 36 ft. wide; how many children would it accommodate, supposing 6 sq. ft. sufficed for each? On the same supposition, how many more children will be accommodated in a room 32 ft. by 24 ft. than in one 36 ft. by 20 ft.?

(15). How many desks, 14 ft. long and 20 in. broad, can be made out of a piece of timber 120 ft. long and 5 ft. broad?

(16). How many yards of paper, 42 in. wide, will be required to cover a wall 18 ft. long and 13 ft. high?

(17). The base of a triangular field is 26 chains 3 poles, and its perpendicular 7 chains 1 pole; what is its area? *

(18). A rectangular field, whose breadth is 4 chains, has to be divided into plots, some of which are to contain an acre and others half an acre; what is the width of each allotment?

(19). How many sq. ft. of paper will be required to cover a room, if the height be 15 ft., the breadth 18 ft. 6 in., and the length 27 ft. 4 in., and if there be in it a door 7½ ft. by 3 ft. 6 in., two fireplaces, each 4 ft. 6 in. long and 4 ft. high, and three windows, each 10 ft. by 4 ft. 6 in.?

(20). What will a piece of marble, 7 ft. 4 in. long and 5 ft. 6 in. broad, cost at 6s. per sq. ft.?

(21). What is the difference between the number of acres in a parallelogram, one of whose sides is 738 yds. and the other 514 yds., and those in a square whose side measures 1,720 feet?

(22). 4 sq. ft. 4 sq. in. being the area of a map which is laid down on the scale of an inch to a mile, required the number of acres represented?

(23). Find the difference between 25 sq. ft. and 25 ft. square.

(24). The area of a floor contains 771 sq. ft. 10′ 6 in., and its length is 32 ft. 6 in.; what is its breadth?

(25). If a space is 2 ft. 9 in. broad, and contains in all 34 ft. 4′ 6″, what is its length?

(26). A sheepfold, in the form of a square, is enclosed by 80 hurdles, each 5 ft. 6 in. long; what is its area?

(27). A room is 36 ft. sq.; suppose it were a third as long again, how wide should it be in order that it may contain the same area?

(28). How many yards of carpet, two feet wide, will cover a floor 17 feet long by 12 ft. 6 in. wide?

(29). A room, measuring 11 ft. in length, 8 ft. 6 in. in breadth, and 10 ft. 6 in. in height, has to be covered with a paper, measuring 2 ft. 6 in. in width; how many yards will be required?

(30). A table contains in its surface 44 sq. ft., and it is 8 ft. long; what is its breadth?

* A triangle is always half the area of a parallelogram of the same base and altitude (*S. of A.*, 460).

MISCELLANEOUS QUESTIONS.

(*a*)—*Oral.* (1). Add seven times thirteen to the third of forty-two.

(2). Add together the third, the fourth, and the fifth of sixty.

(3). How many times is the seventh of sixty-three contained in ninety?

(4). What is the difference between the fourth and the seventh of fifty-six?

(5). By how much does the product of six and five exceed their sum?

(6). Add the half of ninety-four to the third of sixty-three.

(7). Take the eleventh of ninety-nine from its ninth.

(8). Find the product of the three numbers—four, seven, and nine.

(9). Divide the sum of nineteen and fifteen by their difference.

(10). What change shall I have out of a sovereign, after paying for five articles at 2s. 7½d. each, and three at 1s. 9d.?

(11). A quarter of a pound of tea at 4s. 4d., a pound and a half of coffee at 1s. 6d., and 3 pounds of sugar at 5½d., have to be paid for with a crown piece; what is the change?

(12). What is the amount of the following bill:—2 yds. at 1s. 7d., 1½ yds. at 2s., 5 yds. at 3¾d., and 6 reels of cotton at ¾d. each?

(13). 7¼ lbs. of meat at 6d.; 5½ lbs. at 7d.; 12½ lbs. at 11d.

(14). What are the wages of two men for 5½ days at 1s. 6d. per day each?

(15). Find the number of threepenny pieces in a sovereign.

(16). How many 3-mil pieces are there in 4 florins?

(17). Multiply the number of farthings in 7¾d. by 4.

(18). Find the number of halfpence in three sixpences, two fourpenny pieces, and a half-crown.

(19). Multiply the third of a crown by seven.

(20). What are the dimensions of a square plot measuring 15 feet each side?

(21). At 3d. a foot what will it cost to pave a courtyard measuring 20 feet by 12?

(22). At sixpence a yard what will it cost to paint a fence, half a mile in length?

(23). Multiply three-fourths of forty by two-thirds of twelve.

(24). A boy is employed in a field at eightpence a day, what will he earn in five weeks?

(25). How long will a labourer, who earns 8s. 6d. a week, be in earning £5?

(26). Walking 12½ miles a day, how long shall I be on a journey of 100 miles?

(27). A hoop is a yard and a half in circumference, how many times will it turn in 600 yards?

(28). Add together 7, 9, 11, 16, 8, 5, 7, and 10.

(29). Add together 6s. 4d., 7s. 6d., 3s. 4d., 4s. 7d., and 11½d.

(30). Add five hundred and eleven to two hundred and seventeen, and take the result from a thousand.

(31). Multiply 34 by 15, and take the result from 1,000.

(32). Nine dozen pence; Seven score farthings; One hundred and fifty threepenny pieces?

(33). Take the third of a half-crown, the fourth of a crown, and the fifth of half a sovereign, from the half of a five-pound note.

(*b*)—*Written.* (1). A farmer expends £371 10s. 3d. in buying horses and oxen; 12 of the former cost £21 9s. each, and he buys 9 of the latter, what is the price of each ox?

(2). What will be the expense of restoring a public monument, if it is paid for by 280 persons, who contribute a guinea each; by a penny subscription from 8,400 contributors; and by the proceeds of a sale, amounting to £56 5s.?

(3). If the first of February in leap-year fall on Monday, on what day of the week will the 2nd of December fall?

(4.) A butcher has five oxen, whose average weight is 399 lbs.; out of these pieces have to be cut, weighing 7, 8½, 9, 11¾, 17, 20¼, and 21½ lbs., and of each an equal number. How many pieces can be cut?

(5). Find the difference in acres between a field of 12 chains square, and one of 12 square chains.

(6). A grocer mixes 24 lbs. of tea, worth 5s. per lb., 42 lbs. at 4s. 6d., and 19 lbs. at 4s. together; he sells the mixture at 5s. 4d. per lb.: what is his whole profit?

(7). An officer's pay is 12s. 3d. per day; if out of this he spend £3 12s. per week, how much will he be able to save in half a year?

(8). The stones of a windmill are so connected with the perpendicular shaft that they go round 3½ times for every revolution of the shaft; the shaft revolves 3 times as often as the sails, and the sails revolve 9 times per minute; how many revolutions will the stone make in a day of 12 hours?

(9). A manufacturer of woven silk employs 200 hands, each of whom makes on an average 4 yds. per day, and receives wages at the rate of 6½d. per yd.; what sum will he pay in wages every year?

(10). How many days elapsed from January 19th, 1856, to June 24th, 1857?

(11). Seven men found a nugget of gold, weighing 45¼ lbs.; on selling it each man received as his share £276 18s. 4d.; what was the worth of the gold per oz.?

(12). 22 cwt. of tea were bought in China for £28 14s. 6d. The freight was £3 1s. 4d. per cwt.; the duty 1s. 3d. per lb.; the wharfage and other expenses, £23 7s. 6d.; the whole was sold at 3s. 4d. per lb.: what was gained or lost?

(13). A man has to go a journey of 400 miles. He walks 11 hours a day, at the rate of a mile in 20 minutes. When will he reach the end of his journey, supposing him to go 78 miles out of his way, to walk 6 days in the week, and to be detained 5 hours by illness?

(14). If sailcloth be bought for 10d. per yard, and sold for 1s. 4½d., what would be the total gain on 100 pieces, measuring 3 yds. 3 qrs. each, and 54 of 2 yds. 3 qrs. each?

(15). If 2 cwt. 3 qrs. of sugar be bought at the rate of 4d. per pound, and sold for £5 15s. 6d., how much is gained?

(16). In a wire-mill there are 50 wire-drawers and 20 labourers. If each drawer receives 30s. per week, what must be paid to each of the labourers, so that the sum paid in wages per week shall be £90?

(17). How long will a man be walking 15 miles, supposing he takes 80 steps a minute, and walks at the rate of 2 ft. 6 in. each step? By how many feet does the equatorial diameter of the earth, which is 7,924 miles, exceed the polar, which is 7,898 miles?

(18). The distance of Jupiter from the sun is 496,494,000 miles. In what time does the light of the sun, which travels at the rate of 192,000 miles in a second, reach that planet?

(19). By how much does a field of 7 a. 3 r. 2 p. exceed one which measures 7 chains 57 links in length and breadth?

(20). The average prices of wheat, barley, and oats during the seven years preceding 1851 were 7s. 1½d., 4s. 1½d., and 2s. 9½d. per bushel respectively. What, at that rate, would have been the difference in the value of two farms, the one producing 53 bushels of wheat, 27 of barley, and 40 of oats, and the other 29 of wheat, 60 of barley, and 34 of oats?

(21). In Middlesex the property rated for the relief of the poor is of the annual value of £7,584,668. Suppose on an average the poor rate amounts to 5¼d. in the pound throughout the county, what will be the total sum raised?

(22). The Blackwall Railway is 5¼ miles long, and cost at the rate of £256,050 per mile; what was its total cost?

(23). A butcher gave 28 lbs. of mutton to a grocer for 18 lbs. of sugar at 8½d. per lb.; what was the price of the mutton?

(24). There are 1,175 casks in a cellar, each containing 3 gals. 3 qts. 3 pts. and 3 half-pints; how much do they all hold?

(25). Divide £357 12s. 2d. amongst 3 men 4 women and 6 children, so that each man shall have twice as much as a woman and four times as much as a child.

(26). What quantity of shalloon that is ¾ yd. wide will line 7½ yds. of cloth 1⅓ yds. wide?

(27). If a spoon weigh 15 dwts. 11 grs. how many such spoons can be formed out of 122 oz. 9 dwts. 1 gr.?

(28). How many acres are there in a field 387 yds. long and 275 wide?

(29). Suppose each person consumes 5 bushels of corn per annum, what is the yearly consumption of England, the population being 20,936,468?

(30). At £2 16s. 10d. per cwt., what is the cost of 176 cwt. 1 qr. 14 lbs.?

(31). It is calculated that an acre of ground sown with wheat yields sufficient for the annual consumption of two persons; how many square miles ought to be under cultivation to supply the people of Kent, who amount to 619,225?

(32). If a fence cost 2s. 8d. per yard, how much will it cost to enclose a field 427 yds. long and 128 wide?

(33). If I purchase 16 yards of silk at 6s. 8d. per yd., 27 yds. of calico at 2½d., and 35 yds. of ribbon at 1s. 1d., what is the amount of my bill?

(34). There are two boxes of raisins, the one weighing 1 cwt. 1 qr., and the other 127½ lbs.; what is the difference in their value, supposing the raisins are worth 5¼d. per lb.?

(35). How many tenpenny pieces in £17 10s. 6d., and how many American dollars, value 4s. 6d. each, in the same sum?

(36). If one-twelfth of a gold coinage be alloy, how much pure gold is there in 753 pieces, weighing 61 grains each?

(37). Find the difference between the weekly income of two persons, one of whom receives £350, and the other £480 per annum.

(38). If, out of an income of £500 per annum, a gentleman spends a guinea a day, what does he save?

(39). Three persons embark in business, the first contributing five shares of the capital, the second three, and the third two: the whole sum required is £5,350; what are their several shares?

(40). What number subtracted from the product of 26 and 14 will leave the product of seventeen and nineteen?

(41). A line 35 yards long is used to measure a road 14 miles long; how many times will the line be used?

(42). A house is rated at £85, its actual rent is £95, the poor rate is at 1s. 2d. in the pound, the lighting and paving 2½d., the church rate at 6½d., and the house tax at 5d.; what sum does the owner pay for rent and taxes every quarter?

(43). What is the entire length of 65 pieces of cloth, each measuring 45 yds. 1 qr. 1 nl.?

(44). When the income tax was reduced from 1s. 2d. to 5d. in the pound, a professional man estimated that he should save £22 10s. per annum by the change; what was his income?

(45). The annual value of rateable property in the county of Kent is £2,340,836; what sum would be produced by a uniform rate of 1½d. in the pound throughout the county?

(46). If the weight of 255,255 qrs. of oats is 36,465 tons, what is the average weight per quarter?

(47). If the value of 133,167 qrs. of wheat is £339,022, what is its value per quarter?

(48). Find the value of 240 sacks of potatoes at 8s. 6d. per sack; 120 sheep, 80 lbs. each, at 6d. per lb.; 60 stone of wool at 17s. 6d. per stone; and 30 pigs at 30s. each.

(49). What will be the rent of a house for 3 months, 2 weeks, and 4 days, at £4 14s. 6d. per month?

(50). If tea which cost 2s. 3d. per lb. is sold at 3s. 6d., how much will be gained on 1 cwt. 3 qrs.?

(51). If I pay £28 per cwt. for tea, and sell it for £32 10s., how much must I sell to gain £169 17s. 6d?

(52). How many times is £24 11s. 6¼d. contained in £8,060 8s. 10d.?

(53). How many times will a wheel 16½ feet in circumference turn round in a distance of 24 m. 3 fur. 25 p.?

(54). If 48 dozen of wine, each bottle containing 1 pint and a half, cost £76 16s., what is the worth of the wine per pint?

(55). How many parcels of 3 oz. each are there in 16 cwt. 1 qr. 18 lbs.?

(56). Make out a bill, and find the amount of the following articles:—274 yds. of linen at 3s. 5¼d.; 239 yds. at 2s. 11d.; 179 yds. of Irish at 2s. 3½d.; 175 at 1s. 9¾d.

(57). The number of receipt stamps used in 1852 was 5,290,661: of these, 14,256 were ten shilling; 15,878 were seven shillings and sixpence; 28,112 were five shilling; 44,109 were four shilling; 165,947 were half-a-crown; 360,628 were eighteenpenny; 1,051,828 were one shilling; 1,568,136 were sixpenny; and the rest were threepenny stamps. What was the total amount of duty?

(58). The expense of distributing the stamps mentioned in the last sum was £3,881, and £13,586 was allowed in the form of discount to purchasers; what did the Government actually receive?

(59). How many yards of cloth worth 18s. 1½d. per yd. must be given in exchange for 720 yards at 3s. 7½d.?

(60). At the rate of £2 15s. per yd., what will be the expense of constructing a railway 78 miles in length?

(61). A man has three debts owing to him by persons who become bankrupts: the first owes £427, and pays 5s. in the pound; the second owes £128, and pays 4s. 6d. in the pound; and the third owes £57, and pays 11s. 9d. in the pound; how much does he lose in all?

(62). A person with £10 5s. 2d. in his pocket goes on a journey. His railway fare is 6 fl. 4 cents.; his cab-hire, 1 fl. 2 c. 5 m.; he spends at a hotel 7 fl. 3 c. per day for 4 days; and returns in a first-class carriage, the fare being half as much again as he paid before: how much will he bring back?

(63). The sum of £9 3 fl. 4 c. 5 m., and £21 5 fl. 5 m. has to be divided among 18 persons; how much will each receive?

(64). A pipe of wine is bottled off, so that three-fourths is in quart bottles, and the rest in pints; how many dozen bottles will be filled?

(65). Suppose 1,524 yds. of cloth are bought at 6s. 9½d. and sold at 8s. 6d. per yd., how much is gained?

(66). A house and furniture are together worth £3,745 10s., but the house is worth four times as much as the furniture; what is the worth of the house?

(67). A man receives £3 3s. per week, and spends £35 per quarter; how much will he be able to save in 6 years?

(68). From a piece of ground of 24 acres, 1 a. 2 r. are given for a church and churchyard, and 2 r. 15 p. for a school and play-ground; how many perches remain?

(69). How long will a person be in walking from London to Sydenham, a distance of 6½ miles, if he takes 16 steps per minute of 2 ft. 3 in. each?

(70). If I buy 6 bales of cloth, each bale containing 5 pieces, and each piece 25 yards, at 7s. 4d. per yard, what does it cost?

(71). Divide 58 gallons of oil into an equal number of gallons, quart, pint, and half-pint measures.

(72). How many grains of alloy are there in 3 lbs. of jewellers' gold, 18 carats fine (24 carats being the standard)?

(73). How many more grains are there in the avoirdupois pound than in the troy pound?

(74). A horse runs round a field in 15 seconds; how many times will he go round it in 6 minutes 45 seconds?

(75). Rome was founded 753 B.C., which is called the year 1 A.U.C.; in what year of Rome was Jerusalem destroyed by Titus, 70 years A.D.?

(76). Find the rent of 500 a. 3 r. 25 p. of land, at £2 7s. 4d. per acre.

(77). How many square feet of deal are wanted to make a box, the length of which is 3 ft. 6 in., the depth 2 ft. 3 in., and the width 1 ft. 6 in.?

(78). What is the area in square feet of a rectangular garden, the length of which is 125 yds., and the breadth 68 yds.?

(79). $\frac{72 + 56 + 374}{419 - 56}$; $\frac{274 - 84 + 419}{18 + 6 + 5}$.

(80). $51 \times 4 \times 6 \times 18$; $(215 + 35 + 8) \times (41 + 6 + 8)$.

(81). $(175 + 48 + 62) \times (327 + 153 - 219)$.

(82). (£27 4s. 10d. + £16 3s. 8d.) × (193 + 15).

(83). £29 11s. 4½d. ÷ 1s. 7½d; £3 8s. 2½d. ÷ 4½d.

(84). How many acres are there in a triangular field, the base of which is 1,520 yds., and the altitude 854 yds.?

(85). Find the difference between the area of a square table, the side of which is 5 ft. 8 in., and that of another, measuring 6 ft. 4 in. by 4 ft. 6 in.

(86). Make out the following bill, and find the amount:—Material for laying water pipes. 54 ft. 6. in. of piping, at 7½d. per foot. Labour, 2 men, 1 day, at 4s. 6d. per day; 2 men, 1 day, at 2s. 9d. per day. Re-roofing outhouses, 2 (25 ft. 6 in. × 30 ft.) stables, at 7s. per square; 15 ft. × 9 ft, lodge; and 12 ft. 9 in. × 12 ft. hen-roost, at 4s. 6d. per square. Building kitchen, £29. Bricklayer and labourer, 3 days, at 7s. 3d. per day; 15 drain tiles, at 13s. per score.

(87). How many hurdles, 2½ yds. long, will surround a square field, measuring exactly an acre?

(88). What will it cost to paint a room, measuring 21 ft. 6 in. long, 18 ft. 3 in. broad, and 12 ft. high, at 2½d. per sq. foot, allowing for two fireplaces, each 7 ft. 4 in. by 4 ft. 5 in., and for three windows, each 9 ft. 6 in. by 3 ft.?

TABLES.

MULTIPLICATION TABLE.—I.

1	2	3	4	5	6	7	8	9	10	11	12
2	4	6	8	10	12	14	16	18	20	22	24
3	6	9	12	15	18	21	24	27	30	33	36
4	8	12	16	20	24	28	32	36	40	44	48
5	10	15	20	25	30	35	40	45	50	55	60
6	12	18	24	30	36	42	48	54	60	66	72
7	14	21	28	35	42	49	56	63	70	77	84
8	16	24	32	40	48	56	64	72	80	88	96
9	18	27	36	45	54	63	72	81	90	99	108
10	20	30	40	50	60	70	80	90	100	110	120
11	22	33	44	55	66	77	88	99	110	121	132
12	24	36	48	60	72	84	96	108	120	132	144

MULTIPLICATION TABLE.—II.

	13	14	15	16	17	18	19	20
13	169	182	195	208	221	234	247	260
14	182	196	210	224	238	252	266	280
15	195	210	225	240	255	270	285	300
16	208	224	240	256	272	288	304	320
17	221	238	255	272	289	306	323	340
18	234	252	270	288	306	324	342	360
19	247	266	285	304	323	342	361	380
20	260	280	300	320	340	360	380	400

MEASURES OF VALUE.—MONEY.

I. Present English Money.

A Farthing (¼)
1 Penny (1d.) =4 farthings
1 Shilling (1s.) =12 pence =48 farthings
1 Sovereign or Pound (£1)=20 shillings=240 pence=960 farthings.

II. Pence Table.

	£	s.	d.
12 pence		1	0
20 "		1	8
24 "		2	0
30 "		2	6
36 "		3	0
40 "		3	4
48 "		4	0
50 "		4	2
60 "		5	0
70 "		5	10
72 "		6	0
80 "		6	8
84 "		7	0
90 "		7	6
100 "		8	4
120 "		10	0
200 "		16	8
240 "	1	0	0
300 "	1	5	0
400 "	1	13	4
480 pence	2	0	0
500 "	2	1	8
600 "	2	10	0
700 "	2	18	4
720 "	3	0	0
800 "	3	6	8
900 "	3	15	0
1000 "	4	3	4

III. Shillings Table.

	£	s.	d.
20 shillings	1	0	0
30 "	1	10	0
40 "	2	0	0
50 "	2	10	0
60 "	3	0	0
70 "	3	10	0
80 "	4	0	0
90 "	4	10	0
100 "	5	0	0

IV. Proposed English Money on a Decimal System.

A Mil = one-thousandth of a pound.
A Cent = 10 mils, or one-hundredth of a pound.
A Florin = 10 cents = 100 mils, or one-tenth of a pound.
A Pound = 10 florins = 100 cents = 1000 mils.

V. Miscellaneous and Obsolete English Coins.

A Moidore = 27s.	A Guinea = 21s. 0d.	A Noble = 6s. 8d.
A Jacobus = 25s.	A Mark = 13s. 4d.	A Crown = 5s. 0d.
A Carolus = 23s.	An Angel = 10s. 0d.	A Groat = 4d.

MEASURES OF LENGTH.

I. Long Measure.

1 Inch.
1 Foot =12 inches.
1 Yard =3 feet = 36 inches.
1 Pole =5½ yards=16½ feet =198 in.
1 Furlong=40 poles =220 yards=660 feet =7920 in.
1 Mile =8 fur. =320 poles=1760 yds.=5280 ft.=6336[illegible]

II. Surveyor's Measure.

1 Link (lk.) = $7\frac{23}{25}$ inches.
1 Chain = 100 links = 22 yards.
1 Furlong = 10 chains = 1000 links = 220 yards.
1 Mile = 8 furlongs = 80 chains = 8000 links = 1760

III. Cloth Measure.

1 Nail = $2\frac{1}{4}$ inches.
1 Quarter = 4 nails = 9 inches.
1 Yard = 4 quarters = 16 nails = 36 inches.
1 English Ell = 5 quarters.
1 French Ell = 6 quarters.
1 Flemish Ell = 3 quarters.

IV. Miscellaneous or Obsolete Measures of Lengti

A Line = $\frac{1}{12}$ of an inch.
A Palm = 3 inches.
A Hand (for measuring horses) = 4 inches.
A Span = 9 inches.
A Cubit = 18 inches.
A Fathom = 6 feet.
A Degree = 69·1 miles.
A Geographical Mile = $\frac{1}{60}$ of a degree.
A Greek Stadium = ·1149 English mile.
A Parasang = 30 stadia, or $5\frac{1}{2}$ English miles.
A Log Line, used by sailors = 48 feet.
A Piece of Calico = 28 yards.
A Piece of Irish Linen = 25 yards.
A Piece of Muslin = 10 yards.

MEASURES OF AREA OR SURFACE.

I. Land or Square Measure.

1 Square Inch.
1 Square Foot = 144 sq. inches.
1 Square Yard = 9 sq. feet = 1296 sq. in.
1 Square Pole or Perch = $30\frac{1}{4}$ sq. yds.
1 Square Rood = 40 sq. poles or perches = 1210 sq.
1 Acre = 4 sq. roods = 4840 sq.
1 Square Mile = 640 acres.

II. Surveyor's Measure.

1 Square Link.
1 Square Chain = 10000 square links.
1 Rood = 25000 square links.
1 Acre = 100000 square links.

III. Miscellaneous or Obsolete Measures of Surfac

A Hide of land = 100 acres. A Square of Flooring = 100
A Yard of land = 30 acres. 1 Rod of Brickwork = $272\frac{1}{4}$

1 Quire of paper = 24 sheets.
1 Ream = 20 quires.
1 Printer's Ream = $21\frac{1}{2}$ quires.

MEASURES OF SOLIDITY.—I.

1 Cubic Inch		
1 Cubic Foot	=	1798 cubic inches.
1 Cubic Yard	=	27 cubic feet.

II.—Miscellaneous Measures of Solidity.

1 Load, or Ton of Hewn Timber	=	50 cubic feet
1 Load, or Ton of Rough Timber	=	40 „
1 Ton, in Shipping	=	42 „
1 Ton of Marble	=	12 „
1 Ton of Portland Stone	=	16 „
1 Ton of Bath Stone	=	20 „

MEASURES OF CAPACITY.

I. Imperial Measure.

1 Gill				
1 Pint	=	4 gills		
1 Quart	=	2 pints	=	One-fourth of a gallon
1 Gallon	=	4 quarts		
1 Peck	=	2 gallons	=	8 quarts
1 Bushel	=	4 pecks	=	8 gallons
1 Coomb	=	4 bushels	=	32 gallons
1 Quarter	=	2 coombs	=	8 bushels = 64 gallons
1 Load	=	5 quarters	=	320 gallons.

II. Wine Measure.

1 Anker	=	10 gallons
1 Tierce	=	42 „
1 Puncheon	=	84 „
1 Hogshead	=	63 „
1 Pipe	=	126 „
1 Tun	=	252 „

III. Ale and Beer Measure.

1 Firkin	=	9 gallons
1 Kilderkin	=	18 „
1 Barrel	=	36 „
1 Hogshead	=	54 „
1 Butt	=	208 „
1 Tun	=	216 „

IV. Miscellaneous Measures of Capacity.

1 Sack	=	3 bushels
1 Chaldron	=	36 „

MEASURES OF WEIGHT.

I. Troy Weight.—(For Weighing the Precious Metals.)

1 Grain						
I Pennyweight	=	24 grains				
1 Ounce	=	20 dwts.	=	480 grains		
1 Pound	=	12 oz.	=	240 dwts.	=	5760 grs.

II. Apothecaries' Weight.

(For Drugs and Medical Prescriptions.)

1 Scruple (℈)	= 20 grains			
1 Drachm (ʒ)	= 3 scruples	= 60 grains		
1 Ounce (℥)	= 8 drachms	= 24 scruples	= 480 grains	
1 Pound	= 12 ounces	= 96 drachms	= 288 scr.	= 5760 grs.

III. Avoirdupois Weight.—(For Ordinary Purposes.)

1 Dram				
1 Ounce	= 16 drams			
1 Pound	= 16 ounces	= 256 drams	= 7000 grains	
1 Quarter	= 28 lbs.	= 448 ounces	= 7168 drams	
1 Cwt.	= 4 qrs.	= 112 lbs.	= 1792 oz.	= 28762 drs.
1 Ton	= 20 cwt.	= 80 qrs.	= 2240 lbs.	= 35840 oz.

IV. Wool Weight.

1 Clove	=	7 lbs. (avoirdupois)
1 Stone	=	2 cloves
1 Tod	=	2 stones
1 Wey	=	6½ tods
1 Sack	=	2 weys
1 Last	=	12 sacks

V. Miscellaneous and Obsolete Measures of Weight.

1 Stone	= 14 lbs.	1 Pocket of Hops	= 112 lbs.
1 Stone of Meat	= 8 lbs.	1 Firkin of Soap	= 64 lbs.
1 Sack of Coals	= 2 cwt.	1 Gallon of Salt	= 7 lbs.
1 Truss of Straw	= 36 lbs.	1 Bag of Rice	= 168 lbs.
1 Truss of Hay	= 60 lbs.	1 Chest of Tea	= 84 lbs.
1 Load	= 36 trusses	1 Quintal of Fish	= 112 lbs.
1 Pack of Wool	= 240 lbs.	1 Barrel of Anchovies	= 30 lbs.
1 Firkin of Butter	= 56 lbs.	1 Barrel of Flour	= 196 lbs.
1 Fother of Lead	= 19½ cwt.	1 Gallon of Oil	= 9 lbs.
1 Stone of Glass	= 5 lbs.		

MEASURES OF TIME.

I. Time Table.

1 Second		
1 Minute	= 60 seconds	
1 Hour	= 60 minutes	
1 Day	= 24 hours	
1 Week	= 7 days	
1 Lunar Month	= 4 weeks	= 28 days
1 Year	= 365 days	= 52 weeks 1 day

The year is divided also into 12 calendar months; of which February has 28 days in ordinary years, but 29 in leap-year, or evèry 4 years.

The others have 31 days, except those mentioned in the following couplet—

"Thirty days hath September,
April, June, and November."

II. Miscellaneous Measures of Time.

1 Lustrum	= 5 years	1 Lunar Cycle	= 19 years
1 Century	= 100 years	1 Solar Cycle	= 28 years

PART II.

PRIME AND COMPOSITE NUMBERS.

94. The number *fifteen* is made up of *three* times *five*.

95. Three and five are called its FACTORS or MEASURES.

96. When a number has factors or measures it is called a COMPOSITE NUMBER, or a MULTIPLE of its factors.

Thus Twenty-two has the factors eleven and two, and
Sixty-three . . . . . . nine and seven;
Therefore, twenty-two and sixty-three are Composite Numbers. The one is a Multiple of eleven and two, and the other of nine and seven.

97. The number *seventeen* is not made up of factors. No two numbers multiplied together make seventeen. When any number has no measure, it is called a PRIME NUMBER.

Thus three, eleven, and nineteen are prime numbers.

98. Suppose we wish to find whether the number 345 is a prime number or not, we must try whether any number will divide it; thus,—

$$\begin{array}{r} 3\underline{)345} \\ 5\underline{)115} \\ 23 \end{array}$$

As the number is an odd one, it cannot be divided by two; so we try three as a divisor, and afterwards five, which is the next prime number. The quotient 23 is a prime number, for it is divisible by no other number.

We have now found that $345 = 3 \times 5 \times 23$; and because 3, 5, and 23 are prime numbers, we have resolved the number into PRIME FACTORS.

99. RULE.—To resolve a number into prime factors, divide by the smallest prime number which will measure it; then by the smallest prime number which will measure the quotient, and so on, until the quotient is a prime number.

EXERCISE XXII.

(*a*)—*Oral.* Distinguish the prime numbers, and find the prime factors of the composite numbers, in the following list:—

(1). 8, 15, 22, 29. (2). 7, 35, 63, 100.
(3). 27, 19, 37, 39. (4). 11, 36, 120, 68.
(5). 64, 34, 49, 78. (6). 23, 54, 132, 141.

(*b*)—*Written.* (1). 340, 587, 624. (2). 74, 518, 193.
(3). 412, 1000, 218, 615. (4). 723, 514, 862, 500.
(5). 167, 219, 347, 281. (6). 2174, 3052, 4096.
(7). 3261, 5782, 149, 320. (8). 2172, 3638, 1236.
(9). Make a list of the prime numbers between 1 and 200.

GREATEST COMMON MEASURE.

100. *Example.—What is the greatest number which will divide* 105 *and* 266 *without a remainder?*

Explanation.—If these numbers were in the tables, we could compare them at once; but as they are so great, we must use another method.

```
105)266(2
    210
     56)105(1
         56
         49)56(1
            49
             7)49(7
               49
               ..
```

Whatever number measures the divisor and dividend of a division sum measures the remainder also (*S. of A.*, 151). We therefore make the greater number, 266, the dividend, and the less, 105, the divisor. Thus we find that the required number must also be the measure of 105 and 56. These numbers are smaller than the first pair; but as they are too large, we make the greater the dividend, and the less the divisor, of a new sum. In this manner we find that the number required is also a measure of 49 and 56. But we know from the tables that *seven* is the greatest number which will divide both 49 and 56.

Seven is therefore the greatest number which will divide both 105 and 266.

101. This number is called the Greatest Common Measure of the two numbers, because it is the largest number which will divide both of them without a remainder.

102. Rule.—Divide the greater number by the less; if there be no remainder, the less measures the greater; but if there be a remainder, bring down the first divisor, and divide it by the remainder; afterwards bring down each former divisor in the same way, until there is no remainder. The last divisor is the greatest common measure.

Exercise XXIII.

(a)—*Oral.* Find the G. C. M. of the following numbers:—

(1). 35 and 25, 15 and 12. (2). 16 and 10, 14 and 63.
(3). 55 and 100, 64 and 28. (4). 20 and 30, 108 and 90.
(5). 27 and 60, 80 and 120. (6). 75 and 33, 96 and 110.
(7). 1s. 3d. & 4½d., 3s. & 9s. 4d. (8). 10s. & 6s. 8d., 2s. 6d. & 9d.

(b)—*Written.* Find the G. C. M. of the following numbers:—

(1). 570 and 720, 618 and 314. (2). 162 and 2763, 323 and 1700.
(3). 85 and 204, 473 and 1100. (4). 285 and 3819, 946 and 4300.
(5). 602 and 1032, 12987 and 1494, 1147 and 961.
(6). 6006 and 3318, 57690 and 82719, 43902 and 49593.
(7). 8246 and 6727, 13195 and 5655.
(8). 4s. 11½d. and 7s. 7d. (9). £5 and £1 17s. 6d.
(10). 8s. 3d. and 15s. 1½d. (11). 13s. 11d. and 16s. 6d.

LEAST COMMON MULTIPLE.

103. *Example.—What is the smallest number which contains both* 12 *and* 18 *as factors?*

Explanation.—The product of these numbers is 216; and this number is of course a multiple of both 12 and 18, for it contains 12 eighteen times, and 18 twelve times.

But the two numbers 12 and 18 have the common measure six (102). Therefore the sixth part of the product will contain both factors (*S. of A.*, 163). For, because 12 is made up of twice six, and 18 of three times six,

$$12 \times 18 = 2 \times 6 \times 3 \times 6 = 216,$$

and $2 \times 6 \times 3$, or 36, contains 12 three times and 18 twice.

Thirty-six is therefore a Common Multiple of eighteen and twelve, though it is less than their product.

104. The Least Common Multiple of two or more numbers is often required in Arithmetic, and must always be found by throwing out the Common Factors of the numbers.

105. Rule.—To find the Least Common Multiple of any numbers, divide as many of them as possible by any prime number which is a common measure; bring down the undivided numbers, and divide those in the second line by any prime number which measures two or more of them. Proceed in this way, until no common divisor can be found. The product of all the divisors, and of the numbers remaining in the lowest line, will be the least common multiple.

106. Example of Working.—Find the least common multiple of 15, 18, and 20.

5) 15 18 20	Five measures 15 and 20. *Set down* 3, 18, *and* 4.
3) 3 18 4	But 3 will measure two of these numbers, 3 and 18. *Set down* 1, 6, *and* 4.
2) 1 6 4	Two measures 6 and 4. *Set down* 1, 3, *and* 2.
1 3 2	

$$5 \times 3 \times 2 \times 3 \times 2 = 180 = \text{L. C. M. of } 15, 18, 20.$$

Exercise XXIV.

(*a*)—*Oral.* (1). Find the L. C. M. of 6 and 8; of 10 and 12.
(2). 15 and 10, 24 and 30, 18 and 15. (3). 20 and 30, 48 and 27.
(4). 50 and 60, 35 and 55. (5). 63 and 18, 56 and 40.
(6). 25 and 75, 120 and 80, 132 and 77, 99 and 12.
(7). 3, 4, and 6; 10, 12, and 15. (8). 20, 30, and 40; 14, 21, and 70.

(*b*)—*Written.* (1). Find the L. C. M. of 24, 32, 10, and 15.
(2). 54, 81, 63, and 90; 21, 11, 17, and 3; 16, 17, 18, and 19.
(3). 30, 75, and 1515; 56, 54, 88, 21, and 33; 108, 11, and 99.
(4). The nine digits; 581, 923, and 249; 52, 81, 13, 90, and 33.
(5). 620, 540, 75, and 27; 451, 55, and 289; 5, 11, 9, 21, and 30.
(6). 14, 19, 20, 24, and 38; 206, 100, and 309; 12, 35, 28, and 40.
(7). 8, 12, 20, and 100; 72, 54, 108, and 500; 560, 760, and 960.

VULGAR OR COMMON FRACTIONS.

107. ***Example.—What is the fifth part of two inches?***

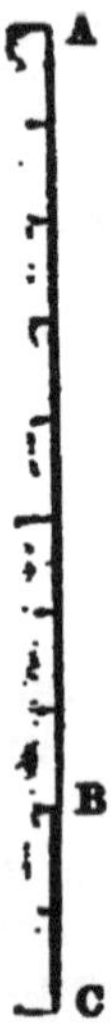

Explanation.—The fifth part of two inches must be less than a whole inch; and we have to find what part of an inch it is. Let A C represent a line two inches long; and let each inch be divided into five parts. There are in all ten such parts, and the fifth of ten is two; therefore the part C B is the fifth of two inches.

But C B is made up of two parts, each of which is the fifth of one inch; therefore C B is two-fifths of one inch.

The fifth part of two inches is therefore the same as two-fifths of one inch.

108. The expression $\frac{2}{5}$ is used to mean the fifth part of two, and is called a Fraction. The lower number (5) shows how many parts the inch has to be divided into, and is called the Denominator. The upper number (2) shows how many of these parts have to be taken, and is called the Numerator.

109. The Numerator is in fact the Dividend in a Division sum, of which the Divisor is the Denominator, while the Quotient is the whole Fraction itself. In ordinary division the quotient is generally a whole number; in Fractions it consists of a part or parts of a whole number.

110. In the diagram the part enclosed within the dark line is three-fourths of the whole, because the whole is divided into four equal parts, of which three are separated from the rest. The enclosed part may therefore be called $\frac{3}{4}$ of the figure.

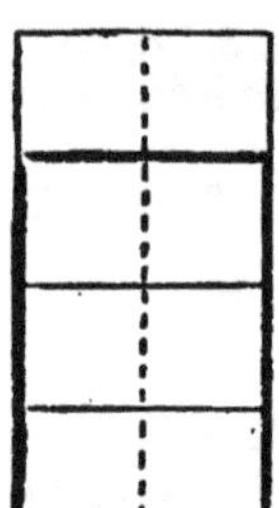

But the same diagram is divided into eight parts, of which six are separated from the rest. The enclosed part may therefore be called $\frac{6}{8}$ of the figure.

So if the whole were divided into 24 equal parts, the dark line would include 18 of them, or $\frac{18}{24}$ of the whole.

$\frac{3}{4}$, $\frac{6}{8}$, and $\frac{18}{24}$, are therefore different names for the same part or Fraction of the whole.

For if we multiply or divide the number of parts into which the whole is divided (or the Denominator), and also multiply or divide the number of parts taken (or the Numerator) by the same number, we do not alter the value of the Fraction (*S. of A.*, 194). In this way we may change *the form of* any fraction in a great many ways.

111. **Rule.**—To express a fraction in its lowest terms, divide both numerator and denominator by their greatest common measure.

112. **Example of Working.**—Reduce $\frac{100}{125}$ to its lowest name.

$$\frac{100 \div 25}{125 \div 25} = \frac{4}{5}$$

By (102) 25 is the greatest common measure of the numbers.

100 divided by 25 gives 4 as quotient.

125 divided by 25 gives 5 as quotient.

$\frac{4}{5}$ is therefore the lowest expression for the fraction $\frac{100}{125}$.

Exercise XXV.

(*a*)—*Oral.* (1). Four-sevenths of thirty-five; five-ninths of 108.
(2). $\frac{7}{12}$ of 84, $\frac{3}{7}$ of 28, $\frac{4}{5}$ of 60. (3). $\frac{11}{12}$ of 72, $\frac{3}{8}$ of 160, $\frac{2}{9}$ of 99.
(4). $\frac{9}{10}$ of 40, $\frac{3}{8}$ of 72, $\frac{3}{7}$ of 49. (5). $\frac{5}{6}$ of 18, $\frac{8}{11}$ of 77, $\frac{4}{7}$ of 63.
(6). $\frac{5}{6}$ of 1s., $\frac{3}{8}$ of 1d., $\frac{5}{12}$ of 2s. (7). $\frac{4}{5}$ of 2s. 6d., $\frac{3}{5}$ of 5s., $\frac{7}{10}$ of 2s. 6d.
(8). $\frac{4}{15}$ of £1 10s., $\frac{7}{12}$ of 9s., $\frac{3}{8}$ of £1.
(9). $\frac{5}{12}$ of a week, $\frac{1}{8}$ of 2 lbs., $\frac{11}{12}$ of 16 feet.
(10). What fraction is 20 of 25; 17 of 19; 33 of 100; 15 of 75?
(11). What fractions of a shilling are $4\frac{1}{2}$d., 7d., $9\frac{3}{4}$d., $10\frac{1}{2}$d.?
(12). What fractions of £1 are 9s. 6d., 10s. 8d., 14s. 3d., 17s. 6d.?
(13). Of what number is 20 $\frac{4}{7}$? of what is 15 $\frac{3}{5}$? of what is 25 $\frac{5}{9}$?
(14). Of what is 96 $\frac{12}{13}$? of what is 17 $\frac{17}{18}$? of what is 100 $\frac{25}{36}$?
(15). Of what sum is 2s. 6d. $\frac{5}{6}$? of what is 3s. $\frac{3}{7}$?
(16). Of what sum is 5s. the fifth? of what is 2s. $\frac{4}{5}$? of what is 9d. $\frac{3}{4}$? of what is 1s. 7d. $\frac{19}{20}$?
(17). What fraction is 1s. of 2s. 6d.? 7d. of 2s. 8d.? $5\frac{1}{2}$d. of 6d.?
(18). Express in lower terms the fractions $\frac{15}{18}$, $\frac{6}{9}$, $\frac{10}{15}$, $\frac{8}{10}$, $\frac{14}{35}$.
(19). Reduce to the lowest name $\frac{45}{144}$, $\frac{50}{110}$, $\frac{44}{132}$, $\frac{27}{108}$, $\frac{132}{240}$.
(20). Express in higher terms the fractions $\frac{3}{7}$, $\frac{4}{11}$, $\frac{3}{10}$, $\frac{5}{9}$.

(*b*)—*Written.* (1). Find $\frac{15}{16}$ of £5; $\frac{8}{100}$ of £35; $\frac{15}{960}$ of £2.
(2). $\frac{7}{56}$ of 2 cwt.; $\frac{8}{60}$ of a week. (3). $\frac{155}{1760}$ of 4 miles; $\frac{17}{28}$ of $1\frac{1}{2}$ cwt.
(4). What fraction is $7\frac{3}{4}$d. of 15s.? 19s. $7\frac{1}{2}$d. of £2 10s.?
(5). What part is 177 sq. yds. of $2\frac{1}{4}$ sq. m.? 17 lbs. 6 oz. of 3 qrs.?
(6). Express $\frac{475}{1000}$, $\frac{392}{1764}$, and $\frac{128}{4096}$ in lower terms.
(7). Reduce to the lowest name, $\frac{4991}{2573}$, $\frac{555}{930}$, and $\frac{1888}{3008}$.
(8). Find £$\frac{5}{16}$; $2\frac{7}{12}$ cwt. (9). $3\frac{5}{9}$ weeks; $4\frac{5}{11}$ tons.
(10). What fractions of a ton are 2 cwt. 3 qrs., 1 qr. 19 lbs., and 17 lbs. 5 oz.?
(11). What fractions of a mile are 15 yds., 3 fur. 27 p., 5 p. 4 yds.?
(12). Reduce to the lowest name $\frac{4}{7}$, $\frac{63}{135}$, $\frac{35}{315}$.
(13). $\frac{240}{384}$, $\frac{1242}{4646}$, $\frac{275}{2000}$. (14). $\frac{440}{1054}$, $\frac{81}{4872}$.
(15). $\frac{1060}{1484}$, $\frac{2422}{3941}$, $\frac{510}{630}$. (16). $\frac{2343}{7865}$, $\frac{555}{950}$. (17). $\frac{333}{1037}$, $\frac{2513}{18797}$.
(18). Of what sum is £1 17s. 6d. five-nineteenths? what length of road is that of which 175 yds. 2 ft. are $\frac{3}{17}$?
(19). Of how much is 18 lbs. 6 oz. twelve twenty-fifths.
(20). In how many ways can the fraction $\frac{24}{36}$ be expressed by lower figures?

IMPROPER FRACTIONS AND MIXED NUMBERS.

113. *Example.—Find another expression equal to $\frac{8}{5}$ of an inch.*

Explanation.—In this case the numerator is greater than the denominator. The number of parts, therefore, into which the whole is divided, is less than the number of parts required. To find eight-fifths of an inch, we must divide more than a whole inch. Thus, in the figure, five-fifths, or A B, are one inch; while eight-fifths, or C B, are one inch and three-fifths of an inch.

114. The expression $\frac{8}{5}$ is called an Improper Fraction, because it does not mean a part, but more than the whole, of a number. When an Improper Fraction is changed into the form of a whole number and a part, it is called a Mixed Number.

Thus, $1\frac{3}{5}$ is a mixed number (*S. of A.*, 185).

115. Rule.—To reduce an Improper Fraction to a Mixed Number, divide the numerator by the denominator, set down the quotient as the whole number, and the remainder is the numerator of the remaining fraction.

To convert a Mixed Number to an Improper Fraction, multiply the whole number by the denominator of the fraction; add the numerator, and place the denominator under the sum.

Examples of Working.—Reduce $\frac{175}{16}$ to a mixed number, and $21\frac{3}{11}$ to an improper fraction.

I. $175 \div 16 = 10\frac{15}{16}$. II. $11 \times 21 = 231$; therefore $21 = \frac{231}{11}$.

$$\frac{231}{11} + \frac{3}{11} = \frac{234}{11}.$$

Exercise XXVI.

(*a*)—*Oral.* (1). Ten-thirds of a shilling; $\frac{9}{4}$ of £1; $\frac{28}{16}$ of an oz.?
(2). Twenty-seven elevenths; $\frac{15}{6}$ of 6d.; $\frac{25}{12}$ of 1s.; $\frac{23}{4}$ of 1d.?
(3). $\frac{16}{10}$ of 2s. 6d.; $\frac{27}{20}$ of 5s.; $\frac{16}{5}$ of £1?
(4). $\frac{29}{10}$ of 20, $\frac{15}{4}$ of 12, $\frac{29}{3}$ of 3? (5). $\frac{16}{15}$ of 30, $\frac{35}{6}$ of 24, $\frac{45}{7}$ of 42?
(6). $\frac{26}{5}$, $\frac{25}{14}$, $\frac{46}{9}$. (7). $\frac{23}{11}$, $\frac{47}{3}$, $\frac{68}{9}$. (8). $\frac{110}{9}$, $\frac{130}{12}$, $\frac{49}{2}$.
(9). Reduce to improper fractions $4\frac{1}{9}$, $5\frac{3}{8}$, $7\frac{4}{5}$. (10). $1\frac{1}{12}$, $5\frac{6}{13}$, $4\frac{1}{9}$.
(11). Express 7, 8, and 9 as fractions, with the denominator 4.

(*b*)—*Written.* (1). Reduce to mixed numbers $\frac{1014}{20}$, $\frac{565}{11}$.

(2). $\frac{1327}{6}$, $\frac{4274}{15}$, $\frac{796}{18}$. (3). $\frac{2341}{21}$, $\frac{1685}{18}$, $\frac{2174}{23}$.

(4). Express 17 as a fraction with the denominator 24; 12 with the denominator 11; 14 with the denominator 15.

(5). Reduce to improper fractions $17\frac{3}{11}$, $26\frac{5}{18}$, $4\frac{7}{25}$, $5\frac{6}{31}$.

(6). $21\frac{3}{14}$, $5\frac{8}{15}$, $6\frac{7}{34}$. (7). $1\frac{101}{125}$, $15\frac{7}{19}$, $26\frac{196}{275}$.

(8). $5\frac{17}{35}$, $2\frac{713}{960}$, $4\frac{35}{98}$. (9). $7\frac{1}{108}$, $3\frac{516}{928}$, $10\frac{921}{1007}$.

COMMON DENOMINATORS.

116. *EXAMPLE.—Compare the fractions $\frac{3}{5}$ and $\frac{4}{9}$.*

EXPLANATION.—Fifths and ninths are fractions of different values, and cannot be easily compared. But by (110) we may express the value of a fraction by higher numbers whenever it is convenient to do so, provided that both numerator and denominator are multiplied by the same number.

If we multiply the numerator and denominator of $\frac{3}{5}$ by 9 the fraction $\frac{3}{5}$ becomes $\frac{27}{45}$.

And if we multiply the numerator and denominator of $\frac{4}{9}$ by 5 the fraction $\frac{4}{9}$ becomes $\frac{20}{45}$.

We can now compare the two fractions $\frac{27}{45}$ and $\frac{20}{45}$ because they both have the same denominator (*S. of A.*, 199).

117. Finding one denominator to two or more fractions is called reducing them to a COMMON DENOMINATOR. This denominator must always be a Common Multiple of all the denominators (*S. of A.*, 201).

118. RULE.—To reduce Fractions to a Common Denominator, multiply the numerator and denominator of each fraction by all the denominators of the other fractions.

Note.—When a less common multiple than the product of all the denominators can be found, make the least common multiple the new denominator of each of the fractions; divide this multiple by each denominator in succession; and multiply the numerator by the quotient thus found.

119. EXAMPLE OF WORKING.—Reduce to a common denominator $\frac{5}{8}$, $\frac{4}{7}$, and $\frac{3}{5}$.

$\frac{5}{8} = \frac{5 \times 7 \times 5}{8 \times 7 \times 5} = \frac{175}{280}$ Because both numerator and denominator are multiplied by 7×5.

$\frac{4}{7} = \frac{4 \times 8 \times 5}{7 \times 8 \times 5} = \frac{160}{280}$ Because both numerator and denominator are multiplied by 8×5.

$\frac{3}{5} = \frac{3 \times 8 \times 7}{5 \times 8 \times 7} = \frac{168}{280}$ Because both numerator and denominator are multiplied by 8×7.

EXERCISE XXVII.

(*a*)—*Oral.* (1). Reduce $\frac{1}{3}$ and $\frac{1}{4}$ to a common denominator.

(2). Which is the greater fraction, $\frac{2}{3}$ or $\frac{3}{4}$, $\frac{5}{6}$ or $\frac{6}{7}$?

(3). Compare together $\frac{1}{4}$ and $\frac{1}{7}$, $\frac{1}{10}$ and $\frac{3}{5}$, $\frac{4}{20}$ and $\frac{9}{10}$.

(4). Reduce to common denominators $\frac{1}{3}$ and $\frac{5}{7}$, $\frac{2}{5}$ and $\frac{5}{6}$, $\frac{3}{8}$ and $\frac{1}{4}$.

(*b*)—*Written.* Reduce the following to common denominators :—

(1). $\frac{4}{5}$, $\frac{7}{9}$, and $\frac{3}{10}$; $\frac{7}{12}$ and $\frac{5}{10}$; $\frac{5}{9}$, $\frac{4}{11}$, and $\frac{6}{15}$.

(2). $\frac{5}{6}$, $\frac{7}{15}$, $\frac{11}{12}$, and $\frac{14}{20}$; $\frac{15}{18}$, $\frac{16}{32}$, and $\frac{9}{56}$; $\frac{7}{11}$, $\frac{21}{15}$, $\frac{19}{25}$, and $\frac{9}{10}$.

3. $\frac{15}{16}$, $\frac{18}{27}$, and $\frac{6}{18}$; $\frac{21}{15}$, $\frac{6}{11}$, $\frac{3}{24}$, and $\frac{1}{12}$; $\frac{2}{7}$, $\frac{3}{16}$, $\frac{4}{18}$, and $\frac{13}{24}$.

4. $\frac{6}{100}$, $\frac{5}{125}$, $\frac{17}{20}$, and $\frac{5}{60}$; $\frac{9}{12}$, $\frac{14}{24}$, $\frac{7}{15}$, and $\frac{3}{20}$; $\frac{6}{20}$, $\frac{3}{15}$, and $\frac{14}{14}$.

ADDITION AND SUBTRACTION OF FRACTIONS.

120. *Example.—Add three-sevenths to five-twelfths.*

Explanation.—It is never possible to add numbers together unless they have the same meaning. For instance, £2 and 7s. do not make either £9 or 9s.; but if the £2 are reduced to 40s., the two sums may be added together, and found to make 47s. In the same manner, fractions cannot be added together until they are reduced to a common name or denominator (116). When reduced, the fractions $\frac{3}{7}$ and $\frac{5}{12}$ take the form $\frac{36}{84}$ and $\frac{35}{84}$.

But the sum of 36 and 35 is 71; therefore the sum of $\frac{36}{84}$ and $\frac{35}{84}$ is $\frac{71}{84}$.

121. In the same manner the difference between $\frac{36}{84}$ and $\frac{35}{84}$ is equal to $\frac{1}{84}$, because $36 - 35 = 1$.

We cannot therefore add or subtract fractions until they are reduced to a common denominator; when this is done, we may add or subtract their numerators.

122. Rule.—To add or subtract fractions, reduce them to a common denominator, and add or subtract their numerators.

123. Example of Working.—I. Add together $\frac{5}{9}$, $\frac{4}{7}$, and $\frac{3}{5}$.

By (118) $\frac{5}{9}$, $\frac{4}{7}$, and $\frac{3}{5}$ are reduced to the form—

$\frac{175}{315}$, $\frac{180}{315}$, $\frac{189}{315}$, and the sum of these is—

$$\frac{175 + 180 + 189}{315} = \frac{544}{315} = 1\frac{229}{315}.$$

Note.—When mixed numbers have to be added, the whole numbers should be added separately, thus:—

$$4\tfrac{1}{3} + 2\tfrac{2}{7} = 4 + 2 + \tfrac{7}{21} + \tfrac{6}{21} = 6\tfrac{13}{21}.$$

124. Example of Working.—II. Find the difference between $\frac{12}{15}$ and $\frac{7}{11}$.

By (118) $\frac{12}{15}$ and $\frac{7}{11}$ are reduced to $\frac{132}{165}$ and $\frac{105}{165}$.

Therefore $\frac{12}{15} - \frac{7}{11} = \frac{132 - 105}{165} = \frac{27}{165}$.

Exercise XXVIII.

(*a*)—*Oral.* (1). Add together a half and a third.

(2). $\frac{3}{12}$ and $\frac{7}{12}$, $\frac{5}{6}$ and $\frac{2}{15}$. (3). $\frac{7}{10}$ and $\frac{3}{20}$; $\frac{1}{3}$, $\frac{1}{4}$, and $\frac{1}{6}$.

(4). What is the difference between $\frac{1}{6}$ and $\frac{1}{7}$; between $\frac{2}{3}$ and $\frac{3}{4}$?

(5). A boy gives away a third of his cake to one schoolfellow, a fifth to another, and a sixth to another; how much has he left?

(6). $2\frac{1}{3}$ and $5\frac{1}{3}$, $7\frac{1}{5}$ and $3\frac{1}{4}$. (7). $\frac{21}{4} + \frac{5}{8}$; $4\frac{3}{5}$ and $\frac{13}{5}$.

(8). Take $\frac{3}{7}$ from 4; $\frac{5}{8}$ from $\frac{5}{6}$. (9). $9 - \frac{13}{7}$, $10 - 2\frac{1}{4}$.

(10). Add $\frac{3}{8}$ of a shilling to $\frac{2}{3}$ of £1; $\frac{5}{12}$ of 1s. + $6\frac{3}{4}$ of 1s. + $\frac{9}{8}$ of 1d.

(11). Take a third from a half; two-fifths from seven-eighths.

(12). What fraction added to $\frac{4}{7}$ will make $\frac{9}{10}$?

(13). Take $4\frac{3}{7}$ from 5; take $12\frac{1}{6}$ from 20.

(14). Add together $5\frac{1}{3}$ and $2\frac{1}{4}$; add $7\frac{1}{3}$ to $12\frac{1}{6}$ and $5\frac{1}{8}$.

(*b*)—*Written.* (1). Add $\frac{2}{3}$, $\frac{5}{8}$, and $\frac{3}{7}$ together; also $\frac{3}{17}$ and $\frac{2}{19}$.

(2). $\frac{5}{6} + \frac{7}{11} + \frac{3}{13}$; $\frac{14}{15} + 2\frac{1}{6}$. (3). $16\frac{3}{5} + \frac{81}{4}$; $7\frac{3}{9} + \frac{100}{19}$.

(4). $2\frac{3}{4} + \frac{5}{7} + 6\frac{1}{12} + 18\frac{1}{6}$. (5). $8\frac{3}{5} - 4\frac{1}{7}$; $\frac{17}{5} - \frac{5}{9}$.

(6). $2\frac{1}{3} + 6\frac{2}{7} - (3\frac{1}{9} + \frac{41}{11})$. (7). $(\frac{4}{5} + \frac{5}{6} + \frac{6}{7} + \frac{7}{8}) - (\frac{1}{3} + \frac{1}{4})$.

(8). $4\frac{11}{15} + \frac{93}{100}$; $16\frac{3}{41} - 3\frac{9}{17}$. (9). $\frac{1547}{12} + \frac{319}{60}$; $4\frac{21}{95} + 3\frac{11}{18}$.

(10). To what number can I add $11\frac{3}{7}$, so as to make $15\frac{5}{9}$?

(11). Subtract from 20 its third, fourth, and fifth, and find what fraction the remainder is of 50.

(12). Add $\frac{5}{9}$ of £1 to $\frac{3}{5}$ of 1s., and $\frac{3}{7}$ of 1d.

(13). By how much does the sum of $53\frac{1}{7}$ and $12\frac{5}{8}$ exceed the sum of $9\frac{4}{5}$ and $\frac{521}{16}$?

(14). What is the difference between $(\frac{4}{5} + \frac{5}{6})$ and $(\frac{61}{4} - \frac{3}{7})$?

(15). When stock, bought at $92\frac{3}{8}$, is sold at $95\frac{3}{4}$, what is gained?

(16). A and B can build a boat in 18 days, and, with the assistance of C, they can build it in 11 days; in what time can C build it by himself?

(17). What is that number of which $\frac{1}{3} + \frac{1}{4} + \frac{1}{12}$ is equal to 36?

(18). If a cistern can be filled by one pipe in three hours, by another in five hours, and by another in six, in what time will it be filled by all running together?

(19). Add £$\frac{1}{3}$, £$\frac{3}{4}$, and £$\frac{11}{12}$ together.

(20). What is that number whose third exceeds its fourth by 20?

(21). Three persons undertake to do a piece of work; the first could finish it alone in $\frac{3}{4}$ of a day, the second in $\frac{2}{3}$ of a day, and the third in $\frac{4}{5}$ of a day; in what time will they finish it, working together?

(22). After paying away $\frac{3}{8}$ of the money in my purse, I find I have £$4\frac{1}{6}$ remaining; how much had I at first?

(23). If $\frac{8}{15}$ of a post are in the water, $\frac{2}{9}$ above the water, and 12 feet under the water, what is its entire length?

(24). If I have to travel 72 miles, and go $\frac{1}{3}$ of the way by train, $\frac{3}{8}$ by coach, and walk the remainder, how many miles do I walk?

(25). If a tank would be filled in 6 hours by one pipe, and emptied in 10 hours by another, how soon would it be filled if both pipes were opened at the same time?

(26). A jar, when filled, weighs $81\frac{1}{3}$ lbs., and when empty, $4\frac{3}{8}$ lbs., what is the weight of its contents?

(27). Add together $17\frac{3}{7}$ yds., $3\frac{1}{9}$ yds., and $12\frac{1}{4}$ yds., and take the result from 50 yds.

(28). After losing a third, a fourth, and a fifth of a sum of money, what portion of the whole remains?

(29). If $4\frac{1}{4}$ yds. be required for a coat, $2\frac{1}{4}$ yds. for a pair of trowsers, and $1\frac{1}{8}$ yds. for a waistcoat, how much will remain, after cutting sufficient for a suit, from a piece of $12\frac{1}{2}$ yds.?

(30). Add together the sum and difference of forty-seven nineteenths, and thirty-five elevenths.

MULTIPLICATION AND DIVISION OF FRACTIONS BY WHOLE NUMBERS.

125. *Example.—Multiply five-twelfths of a shilling by six.*

Explanation.—Five-twelfths of a shilling have to be taken or multiplied six times. There are two ways of doing this: If we multiply the numerator by six, the fraction becomes $\frac{30}{12}$, and this is six times as much as $\frac{5}{12}$.

But if we divide the denominator by six, and convert $\frac{5}{12}$ into $\frac{5}{2}$, we also multiply the fraction by six, for $\frac{1}{2}$ is six times as much as $\frac{1}{12}$. The fraction $\frac{5}{2}$ is the same as $\frac{30}{12}$.

For $\frac{5}{12}$ of a shilling is 5d.; and this sum multiplied by 6 gives 30 pence, or $\frac{30}{12}$ of a shilling; but the same sum may also be expressed as $\frac{5}{2}$ of a shilling, or $2\frac{1}{2}$ shillings.

126. We may therefore multiply a fraction by a whole number, either by multiplying the numerator or by dividing the denominator by that number (*S. of A.*, 191).

127. Rule.—To multiply a fraction by a whole number, multiply the numerator by the number; or if the multiplier is a measure of the denominator, divide the denominator by it.

Example of Working.—$\frac{7}{15} \times 5 = \frac{7 \times 5}{15} = \frac{35}{15}$,

$$\text{or } \frac{7}{15} \times 5 = \frac{7}{15 \div 5} = \frac{7}{3}.$$

128. *Example II.—Divide six-eighths of a shilling by three.*

129. Explanation.—To divide $\frac{6}{8}$ by three is to find its third part. But this may be done in two ways. If we divide the numerator by three, the fraction becomes $\frac{2}{8}$, and this is the third of six-eighths.

But if we multiply the denominator by three, we also divide the fraction; for $\frac{1}{24}$ is a third of $\frac{1}{8}$. The answer, $\frac{6}{24}$, is the same as $\frac{2}{8}$ (110).

For $\frac{6}{8}$ of a shilling is ninepence, and the third of this is threepence, which equals $\frac{2}{8}$ of a shilling, and also $\frac{6}{24}$ of a shilling.

130. We may therefore divide a fraction by a whole number, either by dividing the numerator, or by multiplying the denominator by that number (*S. of A.*, 192).

131. Rule.—To divide a fraction by a whole number, multiply the denominator; or if the divisor be a measure of the numerator, divide the numerator by it.

Example of Working.—$\frac{14}{11} \div 7 = \frac{14 \div 7}{11} = \frac{2}{11}$,

$$\text{and } \frac{14}{11} \div 7 = \frac{14}{11 \times 7} = \frac{14}{77}.$$

EXERCISE XXIX.

(*a*)—*Oral.* (1). Multiply $\frac{3}{7}$ by 6; $\frac{1}{9}$ by 3; $\frac{5}{12}$ by 4.

(2). $\frac{5}{7} \times 8$; $\frac{4}{15} \times 5$.
(3). $\frac{27}{50} \times 2$; $\frac{9}{48} \times 12$.

(4). $\frac{7}{16} \times 4$; $\frac{3}{70} \times 7$.
(5). $\frac{7}{30} \times 10$; $\frac{5}{33} \times 11$.

(6). $\frac{15}{108} \times 12$; $\frac{14}{17} \times 12$.
(7). $\frac{8}{54} \times 9$; $\frac{7}{85} \times 5$.

(8). $4\frac{1}{3} \times 3$; $5\frac{3}{7} \times 6$.
(9). $1\frac{7}{8} \times 4$; $3\frac{5}{12} \times 3$.

(10). $7\frac{1}{9} \times 9$; $\frac{18}{7} \times 7$.
(11). $6\frac{7}{11} \times 5$; $4\frac{3}{5} \times 10$.

(12). Divide $\frac{8}{14}$ by 4, $\frac{1}{5}$ by 3, $\frac{9}{15}$ by 2.

(13). $\frac{25}{29} \div 5$; $\frac{4}{11} \div 7$.
(14). $\frac{3}{5} \div 21$; $\frac{8}{9} \div 9$.

(15). $\frac{49}{50} \div 7$; $\frac{48}{49} \div 8$.
(16). $\frac{6}{19} \div 6$; $\frac{33}{41} \div 3$.

(17). $2\frac{1}{7} \div 5$; $6\frac{3}{5} \div 11$.
(18). $3\frac{3}{5} \div 3$; $1\frac{1}{17} \div 9$.

(19). Three-fifteenths of £1 are given to each of six persons, how much do they receive altogether?

(20). Five-eighths of a ship are held in equal portions by seven persons, what does each person possess?

(*b*)—*Written.* (1). Multiply $\frac{15}{38}$ by 2; $\frac{35}{44}$ by 4.

(2). $14\frac{2}{3} \times 6$; $18\frac{5}{9} \times 9$.
(3). $\frac{27}{4} \times 4$; $3\frac{1}{8} \times 8$.

(4). £1 16s. $7\frac{1}{12}$d. $\times$ 7; £2 0s. $9\frac{1}{16}$d. $\times$ 11; £35 17s. $2\frac{5}{8}$d. $\times$ 7.

(5). 7 yds. 2 ft. $3\frac{1}{3}$ in. $\times$ 9; £$2\frac{5}{8} \times 15$; 7 cwt. 3 qrs. $19\frac{1}{12}$ lbs. $\times$ 11.

(6). $\frac{23}{5} \times 10$; $\frac{109}{115} \times 12$.
(7). $\frac{27}{14} \times 7$; $(\frac{1}{3} \times \frac{1}{4}) \times 6$.

(8). £$64\frac{3}{5} \times 5$; £$102\frac{5}{16} \times 9$.
(9). £$12\frac{4}{5} \times 10$; £$59\frac{3}{10} \times 16$.

(10). What is the price of 7 shares at $97\frac{3}{8}$, and four at $77\frac{3}{5}$?

(11). Divide $\frac{10}{17}$ by 5, $\frac{12}{21}$ by 3, $3\frac{1}{9}$ by 14.

(12). $\frac{57}{218} \div 8$; $\frac{14}{151} \div 21$.
(13). $\frac{34}{87} \div 17$; $\frac{310}{98} \div 30$.

(14). £$5\frac{3}{4} \div 9$; £$12\frac{11}{16} \div 8$.
(15). £$97\frac{5}{8} \div 11$; £$99\frac{3}{10} \div 20$.

(16). £1 2s. $8\frac{1}{4}$d. $\div$ 6; £7 2s. $9\frac{1}{3}$d. $\div$ 7.

(17). 15s. $6\frac{3}{8}$d. $\div$ 7; £1 0s. $7\frac{1}{12}$d. $\div$ 5.

(18). $(\frac{7}{12} + \frac{5}{10}) \div 11$; $(\frac{1}{4} - \frac{1}{9}) \div 18$; $(6\frac{1}{4} + 2\frac{2}{7}) \div 17$.

(19). When £100 stock is worth $88\frac{1}{8}$, what is the value of £7,500 stock?

(20). If a vessel contains $\frac{1}{8}$ of a pint, what will 23 such vessels contain?

(21). If mercury is $13\frac{3}{5}$ heavier than water, what is the weight of a quantity of mercury equal in bulk to 17 lbs. of water?

(22). Multiply the sum of $\frac{1}{15}$ and $\frac{1}{16}$ by the product of 15 and 16.

(23). If a piece of cloth is $17\frac{3}{16}$ yds. in length, what is the length of one-fourteenth part of it?

(24). What is the difference in value between 24 shares in a railway company at £$47\frac{2}{3}$, and 52 shares at $29\frac{3}{4}$?

(25). If a coin be $1\frac{1}{8}$ inches in diameter, how far would 1,200 of them reach if laid side by side in a line?

(26). Add together seven times $95\frac{3}{11}$ and the seventh of $210\frac{31}{12}$.

MULTIPLICATION BY FRACTIONS.

132. *Example.—Multiply five-ninths by four-sevenths.*

Explanation.—Here the fraction $\frac{5}{9}$ has to be multiplied, not by a whole number, but by the fraction four-sevenths. It has therefore to be taken the *seventh part of four* times. If we multiply by 4 it becomes, by (127), $\frac{5 \times 4}{9}$, or $\frac{20}{9}$. But it was required to multiply it only by the seventh part of four. Therefore the true answer is the seventh part of $\frac{20}{9}$. But, by (131), the seventh of $\frac{20}{9}$ is $\frac{20}{9 \times 7}$, or $\frac{20}{63}$ (*S. of A.*, 212).

133. The same question in Multiplication may take this form—Find $\frac{4}{7}$ of $\frac{5}{9}$. This expression ($\frac{4}{7}$ of $\frac{5}{9}$) is called a Compound Fraction; but it is really a problem in Multiplication, for to multiply $\frac{5}{9}$ by $\frac{4}{7}$ is to take $\frac{4}{7}$ of $\frac{5}{9}$. We first take $\frac{1}{7}$ of $\frac{5}{9}$, which is $\frac{5}{63}$, and then multiply the result by 4, and the answer, $\frac{20}{63}$, is the same as before.

134. Rule.—Multiply the numerators together for the numerator of the product, and the denominators for the denominator of the product.

Example of Working.—$\frac{8}{13} \times \frac{7}{11} = \frac{8 \times 7}{13 \times 11} = \frac{56}{143}$.

Note.—When mixed numbers occur in multiplication, it is generally more convenient to reduce them to improper fractions.

Exercise XXX.

(*a*)—*Oral.* (1). Half of a third; $\frac{2}{3}$ of $\frac{4}{5}$; $\frac{1}{2}$ of $\frac{1}{5}$?

(2). A man owns half a ship, and sells two-thirds of his share; what portion of the whole has he left?

(3). What is a third of a fourth of half a sovereign?

(4). What fraction is equal to $\frac{3}{4}$ of $\frac{2}{9}$?

(5). What is one-third of $2\frac{1}{2}$? one-seventh of $5\frac{1}{4}$?

(6). Multiply $2\frac{1}{5}$ by $4\frac{1}{2}$; $1\frac{3}{7}$ by $2\frac{4}{5}$; $7\frac{2}{9}$ by $3\frac{1}{11}$.

(*b*)—*Written.* (1). $\frac{7}{9} \times \frac{3}{4}$; $\frac{6}{7} \times \frac{2}{5}$; $3\frac{1}{2} \times 4\frac{1}{7}$.

(2). $41\frac{2}{7} \times \frac{1}{9}$; $\frac{51}{8} \times \frac{7}{8}$. (3). $\frac{21}{10}$ of $\frac{3}{5} \times \frac{6}{8}$; $2\frac{1}{7} \times 1\frac{9}{11}$.

(4). $2\frac{1}{2} \times 4\frac{1}{3}$; $\frac{7}{19} \times \frac{12}{14}$. (5). $\frac{63}{4} \times 3\frac{1}{9}$; $\frac{21}{25} \times \frac{3}{17} \times \frac{1}{10}$.

(6). $\frac{1}{3}$ of $\frac{2}{7}$ of $\frac{5}{16}$; $\frac{5}{7}$ of $2\frac{1}{2}$ of $8\frac{1}{13}$; $\frac{12}{13}$ of $\frac{5}{14}$ of $\frac{28}{39}$.

(7). $(\frac{7}{8} + \frac{2}{9}) \times \frac{6}{11}$; $(\frac{3}{8} - \frac{1}{12}) \times 5\frac{1}{3}$; $(4\frac{1}{9}$ of $15) - 2\frac{4}{11}$.

(8). Find the product of the sum and difference of $\frac{2}{9}$ and $\frac{1}{5}$.

(9). £7 2s. $10\frac{1}{2}$d. $\times 5\frac{1}{6}$; £1 3s. $8\frac{1}{12}$d. $\times 2\frac{1}{4}$; £7 2s. $3\frac{1}{16}$d. $\times \frac{5}{8}$.

(10). If $60\frac{5}{8}$ yds. of brickwork can be built in a day, how much can be finished in $15\frac{3}{5}$ days?

(11). If $\frac{1}{4}$ of a piece of work be done in 1 day, and $\frac{3}{5}$ of the remainder in the next, how much remains to be done?

(12). What is the united area of two floors, the one measuring $15\frac{3}{7}$ by $12\frac{1}{6}$ yds., and the other $20\frac{3}{4}$ by $17\frac{1}{8}$?

(13). Take $\frac{5}{7}$ of $3\frac{1}{8}$ from $\frac{4}{5}$ of $5\frac{1}{9}$; and $5\frac{1}{2}$ of $27\frac{1}{4}$ from $150\frac{1}{3}$.

DIVISION BY FRACTIONS.

135. *EXAMPLE.—Divide six-sevenths by eight-ninths.*

EXPLANATION.—We have here to divide six-sevenths by the ninth part of eight. If we first divide the fraction by 8, the answer, by (131), becomes $\frac{6}{7\times 8}$, or $\frac{6}{56}$. But it was required to divide only by the ninth part of eight. Hence nine times $\frac{6}{56}$ must be the true answer; but by (127) nine times $\frac{6}{56}$ is $\frac{6\times 9}{56}$, or $\frac{54}{56}$.

136. This answer is the same as would be obtained if we had multiplied by $\frac{9}{8}$, which is called the reciprocal of $\frac{8}{9}$. Hence dividing by a fraction is the same thing as multiplying by its reciprocal (*S. of A.*, 225).

137. Sometimes a question in Division takes this form, $\frac{\frac{6}{7}}{\frac{8}{9}}$. It is then generally called a COMPLEX FRACTION; the lower fraction being the divisor, and the upper the dividend.

138. RULE.—To divide by a fraction, invert the terms of the divisor, and multiply by it.

EXAMPLE OF WORKING.—$\frac{11}{13} \div \frac{10}{13}$, or $\frac{\frac{11}{13}}{\frac{10}{13}} = \frac{11}{13} \times \frac{13}{10} = \frac{143}{130}$.

Note.—When a divisor is a mixed number, convert it into an improper fraction.

EXERCISE XXXI.

(*a*)—*Oral.* (1). Divide $\frac{2}{3}$ by $\frac{3}{4}$; $\frac{5}{6}$ by $\frac{4}{7}$; $\frac{30}{5}$ by $\frac{10}{3}$.

(2). How many times is $\frac{1}{7}$ contained in 2? $\frac{3}{5}$ in 8?

(3). Divide 6 by $\frac{2}{5}$; 10 by $\frac{3}{7}$; 20 by $\frac{10}{11}$.

(4). What number, multiplied by $\frac{3}{10}$, would make 18?

(5). How many times is $2\frac{1}{3}$ contained in 20? $5\frac{1}{4}$ in 210?

(6). A person who has $\frac{2}{5}$ of a mine sells $\frac{3}{4}$ of his share for £1,500, what is the worth of the whole mine?

(*b*)—*Written.* (1). Divide $\frac{3}{7}$ by $\frac{11}{12}$; $\frac{4}{9}$ by $\frac{6}{7}$; $\frac{11}{13}$ by $\frac{3}{4}$ of $\frac{1}{5}$.

(2). $6\frac{1}{3} \div 2\frac{1}{7}$; $\frac{15}{8} \div \frac{3}{8}$.

(3). $\frac{2110}{2330} \div 1\frac{3}{4}$; $50\frac{1}{3} \div 6\frac{3}{8}$.

(4). $\frac{27}{2\frac{1}{5}}$; $\frac{11\frac{2}{3}}{6\frac{5}{8}}$; $\frac{2\frac{1}{5}}{9\frac{1}{7}}$.

(5). $\frac{12}{3\frac{3}{37}}$; $\frac{4\frac{3}{5}}{2\frac{3}{8}}$; $\frac{8\frac{1}{7}}{3\frac{1}{5}}$.

(6). $\frac{\frac{7}{9}}{\frac{3}{4}}$; $\frac{3\frac{1}{7} \text{ of } 2}{5\frac{1}{3} \text{ of } 6}$; $\frac{\frac{1}{4} \text{ of } 23}{\frac{1}{5} \text{ of } 19\frac{1}{4}}$.

(7). $\frac{21\frac{1}{4}}{5\frac{3}{19}}$; $\frac{\frac{3}{5} \text{ of } \frac{7}{11} \text{ of } 19}{\frac{1}{4} \text{ of } \frac{3}{7} \text{ of } 20}$.

(8). £2 9s. 6d. $\div \frac{3}{7}$; £1 2s. $4\frac{1}{2}$d. $\div \frac{4}{5}$; £32 5s. $8\frac{1}{12}$d. $\div 1\frac{7}{8}$.

(9). How many times can a vessel containing $1\frac{3}{8}$ pints be filled from one containing $27\frac{3}{8}$ pints?

(10). How many times are £$12\frac{3}{10}$ contained in £$236\frac{3}{13}$?

(11). $\frac{(\frac{4}{5} + \frac{2}{7}) \quad \frac{1}{6} \text{ of } \frac{3}{8}}{\frac{2}{3} + \frac{7}{12} - \frac{1}{3}}$; $\frac{\frac{5}{9} \text{ of } \frac{7}{8} \text{ of } \frac{6}{15}}{\frac{3}{4} + 1\frac{5}{7} - \frac{18}{10}}$; $\frac{4\frac{3}{10} \text{ of } 2\frac{1}{5}}{7\frac{3}{5} - 3\frac{1}{5}}$.

REDUCTION OF FRACTIONS TO OTHER NAMES.

139. *EXAMPLE I.—What fraction of a shilling is $\frac{4}{5}$ of a pound?*

EXPLANATION.—Because there are twenty shillings in one pound, there must be twenty times $\frac{4}{5}$ of a shilling in $\frac{4}{5}$ of a pound. Hence we must multiply $\frac{4}{5}$ by 20. But by (127) $\frac{4}{5} \times 20 = \frac{80}{5}$.

Therefore, $\frac{4}{5}$ of £1 $= \frac{80}{5}$ of a shilling.

140. *EXAMPLE II.—What fraction of a pound avoirdupois is equal to $\frac{2}{5}$ of an ounce?*

EXPLANATION.—Because there are 16 oz. in a pound, there must be a sixteenth part of $\frac{2}{5}$ of a pound in $\frac{2}{5}$ of an ounce. Hence we must multiply the denominator of the fraction by 16. But by (131) $\frac{2}{5} \div 16 = \frac{2}{80}$.

Therefore, $\frac{2}{5}$ of an ounce $= \frac{2}{80}$ of a pound avoirdupois.

141. *EXAMPLE III.—What fraction of 12s. is 7¾d.?*

EXPLANATION.—Sevenpence three farthings is not an aliquot part of twelve shillings, therefore both sums must be reduced to some common name. But 7¾d. = 31 farthings, and 12s. = 576 farthings.

Hence 7¾d. $= \frac{31}{576}$ of 12s.

142. RULE.—When the fraction has to be altered to one of a lower name, multiply the numerator by as many of the less as make one of the greater.

But when the fraction has to be altered to one of a higher name, multiply the denominator by as many of the less as make one of the greater.

If the less is not an aliquot part of the greater, reduce both to a common name.

143. EXAMPLES OF WORKING.—I. Reduce $\frac{5}{7}$ of a yard to the fraction of a mile.

$$\frac{5}{7} \text{ of a yard} = \frac{5}{7} \text{ of } \frac{1}{1760} = \frac{5}{12320} \text{ of a mile.}$$

II. Reduce $\frac{13}{14}$ of a ton to the fraction of a pound.

$$\frac{13}{14} \text{ of a ton} = \frac{13}{14} \text{ of 20 cwt.} = \frac{260}{14} \text{ of 1 cwt.}$$

$$\frac{260}{14} \text{ of 1 cwt.} = \frac{260}{14} \text{ of 112 lbs.} = \frac{260 \times 112}{14} = \frac{29120}{14} \text{ of 1 lb.}$$

III. Reduce 7 lbs. 3 oz. to the fraction of 3½ cwt.

By descending reduction, 7 lbs. 3 oz. = 115 oz.

And 3 cwt. 2 qrs. = 6272 oz.

Therefore 7 lbs. 3 oz. $= \frac{115}{6272}$ of 3 cwt. 2 qrs.

EXERCISE XXXII.

(*a*)—*Oral.* (1). What part of sixpence is $\frac{3}{5}$ of a shilling?

(2). How much of a crown is $\frac{1}{5}$ of a shilling?

(3). Reduce $\frac{3}{5}$s. to the fraction of a pound; £$\frac{1}{5}$ to the fraction of 1s.

(4). What part of a week is $\frac{3}{4}$ of a day? $\frac{4}{7}$ of a day?

(5). How much of 1 lb. is $\frac{3}{5}$ of an oz.? $\frac{5}{16}$ of a dram?

(6). Reduce to fractions of £1, $\frac{4}{7}$s., $1\frac{1}{4}$d., $\frac{3}{7}$ of sixpence.

(7). What part of a yard is $2\frac{3}{4}$ inches? $2\frac{5}{12}$ feet?

(8). What part of a farthing is $\frac{4}{7}$ of a penny? $\frac{1}{9}$ of a shilling?

(9). How much of 2s. 9d. is $4\frac{3}{8}$d.? how much of 5s. is 3s. $6\frac{1}{4}$d.?

(*b*)—*Written.* (1). Reduce $\frac{3}{7}$s. to the fraction of £1.

(2). $\frac{5}{8}$ of 2s. 6d. to the fraction of 1s.; $\frac{3}{17}$ of 6d. to the fraction of 1d.

(3). £$\frac{5}{8}$ to the fraction of a guinea; $\frac{1}{12}$d. to the fraction of a florin.

(4). $5\frac{1}{2}$ of £2 10s. to the fraction of 5s.; $3\frac{3}{7}$ of 1s. 6d. to the fraction of 10s.

(5). $3\frac{1}{4}$ of 2s. 6d. to the fraction of 4s. 2d.; $\frac{2}{5}$d. to the fraction of 16s.

(6). $\frac{7}{11}$ of a day to the fraction of a week; $\frac{5}{8}$ of a week to the fraction of an hour.

(7). $3\frac{1}{4}$ lbs. to the fraction of a ton; $2\frac{1}{12}$ tons to the fraction of a quarter.

(8). $17\frac{1}{2}$ dwts. to the fraction of a grain; $\frac{5}{8}$ of a grain to the fraction of a troy pound?

(9). Express $\frac{5}{17}$ of a day in terms of a minute, an hour, and a week.

(10). Reduce $\frac{13}{15}$ of an avoirdupois ounce to the fractions of a cwt., a pound, a dram, and a grain.

(11). Express 3 roods 7 perches as the fractions of an acre and a square mile.

(12). What part of 11 miles is $\frac{1}{4}$ of $2\frac{1}{5}$ of $\frac{9}{11}$ of 1,200 yards?

(13). Reduce $\frac{3}{16}$ of a shilling to the fractions respectively of a penny, a florin, a sovereign, and a five-pound note.

(14). Express $3\frac{3}{7}$ weeks as the fraction of $2\frac{1}{5}$ days; and $\frac{10}{11}$ of $\frac{3}{4}$ of a day as fractions respectively of $4\frac{1}{5}$ hours and of $1\frac{5}{8}$ weeks.

(15). How much is 5 a. 3 r. of 100 acres?

(16). Reduce 2 weeks 5 days 4 hours 3 minutes to the fraction of a lunar month.

(17). What fraction of a mile is $17\frac{3}{8}$ fathoms?

(18). Reduce 12 links to the fraction of a yard.

(19). What fraction of a barrel is $19\frac{1}{7}$ quarts?

(20). Reduce $5\frac{7}{12}$ yds. to the fractions of an inch and of a mile.

(21). How many square feet are there in $5\frac{7}{12}$ acres?

(22). What fraction of $7\frac{1}{2}$ tons is $192\frac{1}{7}$ lbs.?

(23). Express $\frac{2036}{5}$ yards in the usual form.

(24). How many cwts. are there in $\frac{53284}{3}$ lbs.?

MISCELLANEOUS QUESTIONS.—XXXIII.

(*a*)—*Oral.* (1). What number is that of which three times nine is three-ninths?

(2). How often is the fraction $2\frac{1}{4}$ contained in 35?

(3). What number, added to the third of ninety, will make three-fifths of 100?

(4). Multiply $\frac{4}{5}$ of 75 by $\frac{3}{4}$ of 60.

(5). Add $\frac{5}{6}$ of a shilling to $\frac{1}{5}$ of half-a-crown, and state the result as a fraction of £1.

(6). If a man does $\frac{2}{9}$ of a piece of work in a day, in how many days will he do the whole?

(7). From a piece of cloth worth £10 I sell to one person a third, and to another a fourth; what is the worth of what remains?

(8). How many times is $\frac{3}{5}$ of a shilling contained in $\frac{1}{5}$ of £1?

(9). What are the lowest expressions for the fractions $\frac{2410}{3600}$ and $\frac{2520}{3600}$?

(10). Add $3\frac{1}{6}$, $2\frac{1}{4}$, and $5\frac{2}{12}$ together.

(11). Find $\frac{1}{3}$ of $\frac{6}{7}$ of $\frac{7}{12}$; also $\frac{2}{3}$ of $\frac{10}{12}$ of 2s. 6d.

(12). What number is that of which $\frac{3}{4}$ of $\frac{2}{3}$ equals 12?

(13). What is the difference between the sixth of seven and the seventh of six?

(14). How long will two men be in completing a work, if one of them could finish it in 12 days alone, and the other in ten?

(15). What part is $2\frac{1}{4}$ days of a week? How much is 12s. 7d. of 15s. 6d.?

(16). If a boy can earn $\frac{3}{7}$ of a shilling in an hour, in how many hours will he earn three shillings?

(17). If I walk at the rate of 3 yards in five steps, what is the length of each step in feet?

(18). What sum of money is that which, being divided equally among twelve persons, gives to three of them the sum of 2s. 9d.?

(*b*)—*Written.* (1). From the difference between $\frac{1}{5}$ and $\frac{1}{4}$ take the difference between $\frac{1}{6}$ and $\frac{1}{7}$.

(2). Find the product of $(\frac{3}{7} + \frac{1}{3})$ and $(\frac{4}{5} - \frac{1}{6})$.

(3). If a person inherits $\frac{3}{7}$ of 1,000 acres, and sells $\frac{7}{10}$ of his estate, how many poles remain?

(4). Find the sum, difference, and product of $\frac{1}{3}$ and $\frac{1}{5}$.

(5). Multiply the sum of $5\frac{1}{5}$ and $4\frac{1}{6}$ by their difference.

(6). Express the answers to the following questions as fractions of £1:—

£4 3s. 5d. ÷ 7; £2 11s. $9\frac{1}{4}$d. ÷ 9; £128 4s. $3\frac{1}{12}$d. ÷ 5.

(7). 7s. $6\frac{1}{3}$d. — 1s. $9\frac{1}{5}$d.; £2 3s. $6\frac{7}{12}$d. — £1 4s. 9d.

(8). £1 2s. $6\frac{5}{10}$d. × 9; £4 12s. $7\frac{1}{3}$d. × $2\frac{1}{4}$; 2s. $9\frac{3}{8}$d. × $5\frac{1}{6}$.

(9). 2 cwt. 3 qrs. $17\frac{3}{5}$ lbs. × $4\frac{2}{7}$; $109\frac{1}{3}$ lbs. ÷ $\frac{2}{5}$; 47 weeks $5\frac{7}{12}$ days × $11\frac{1}{3}$.

(10). What number, multiplied by $\frac{2}{5}$ of $\frac{5}{9}$, will give $\frac{1}{10}$ of 12?

(11). What must be paid for 63 shares in the Eastern Counties Railway at £$59\frac{1}{2}$; 123 shares in the London and North-Western at *$88\frac{3}{4}$; and 26* shares in the Great Northern at $99\frac{1}{8}$?

(12). If I buy 120 shares in the Brighton Railway when they are at $106\frac{3}{8}$, and sell half of them at $107\frac{1}{4}$, and the other half at $108\frac{1}{4}$, what do I gain?

(13). Thirteen persons have equal allotments of a piece of ground; the portion of seven of them amounts to 3 a. 2 r. 21 perches; what is the extent of the whole piece of ground?

(14). Express the height of a mountain, which is 7,263 feet high, as a fraction of the earth's diameter, which is 7,926 miles.

(15). Take from 50 its fourth, fifth, and sixth; and express the remainder as a fraction of $24\frac{1}{2}$.

(16). If two men working together can build a wall in 20 days, and one of them working alone could build it in 30 days, in what time would the other do it alone?

(17). Divide the product of $\frac{2}{13}$ and $\frac{8}{13}$ by their sum?

(18). Find the difference between $\frac{1}{5}$ of $\frac{1}{7}$ of $\frac{1}{3}$ and $\frac{3}{11}$ of $\frac{4}{5}$.

(19). Gunpowder is composed of $\frac{1}{10}$ sulphur, $\frac{3}{20}$ charcoal, and $\frac{3}{4}$ nitre; how much of each material will be required to make $2\frac{1}{2}$ cwt. of gunpowder?

(20). What number, when divided by $\frac{1}{5}$, will give $\frac{3}{5}$ as quotient?

(21). What number, multiplied by $3\frac{1}{15}$, will give 1 as product?

(22). If the greatest common measure of 2,500 and 2,142 be the divisor, and the least common multiple of 12, 10, and 5 be the dividend, what is the quotient?

(23). Express $\frac{2}{5}$ of $\frac{10}{11}$ of 1 shilling as a fraction of a £5 note.

(24). A person owns $\frac{3}{5}$ of a ship, and sells $\frac{3}{4}$ of his share for £342; what is the whole ship worth?

(25). Add together $2\frac{3}{4}$, $5\frac{3}{7}$, and $8\frac{9}{10}$, and divide the sum by the product of $\frac{12}{25}$ and $25\frac{4}{5}$.

(26). What is the sum of $\frac{3}{5}$ of 17s., and $\frac{2}{5}$ of 21s. 8d.?

(27). Multiply $\frac{3}{5}$ by $\frac{5}{8}$, and divide the product by $\frac{4}{9}$.

(28). Of what distance is $4\frac{1}{2}$ miles seven-tenths?

(29). If A can reap $\frac{1}{5}$ of a field in $2\frac{2}{3}$ days, and B can reap $\frac{3}{5}$ of it in $4\frac{1}{2}$ days, in what time can A and B reap the whole field together?

(30). Reduce to their simplest terms the expressions—

$$\frac{\frac{3}{5}+\frac{3}{7}}{4\frac{5}{7}-3\frac{2}{9}}; \quad \frac{78\frac{4}{7}}{157\frac{4}{5}} \div \frac{29\frac{7}{17}}{71\frac{8}{11}}; \quad \frac{(\frac{1}{3} \text{ of } \frac{3}{7}) + (\frac{5}{8} - \frac{5}{9})}{(\frac{1}{2} \times 6\frac{1}{5}) - \frac{3}{8} \text{ of } \frac{3}{7}}.$$

(31). $(\frac{3}{7} + \frac{3}{8} - \frac{5}{9}) \times 2\frac{1}{5} + 7\frac{2}{3}$; $(\frac{1}{2} + \frac{1}{3} + \frac{1}{4} + \frac{1}{6}) \times (4\frac{1}{2} + \frac{15}{4} - 3)$.

(32). Add together $\frac{2}{5}$ of $\frac{6}{7}$ of $\frac{5}{8}$, and $\frac{3}{4}$ of $\frac{6}{7}$; and divide the sum by $\dfrac{\frac{1}{7} \text{ of } \frac{6}{9}}{3\frac{4}{9}}$.

(33). If $\frac{5}{11}$ of an article be worth £3 5s., what is the price of $\frac{1}{4}$ of $\frac{3}{5}$ of it?

(34). A daughter receives as a bequest from her father £533 6s. 8d., which is $\frac{4}{5}$ of $\frac{3}{8}$ of the legacy left to her brother: but the brother's share was $\frac{5}{23}$ of the whole property; what was the father worth?

(35). What number is that of which the difference between one-fifth and one-nineteenth is equal to $10\frac{11}{19}$?

DECIMAL FRACTIONS.

144. *Example.—Express the fraction $\frac{7}{10}$ in a decimal form.*

Explanation.—Since all our Simple Arithmetic is Decimal (6), and we deal more easily with all numbers when they are expressed as multiples of ten, it would be more convenient if all fractions could be expressed in the form of tenths, hundredths, thousandths, &c., in order that they may be easily compared.

Now, in the number 777

we have three figures, of which that on the left means seven hundreds, the next seventy, or one-tenth of seven hundreds, and the third seven units, or the tenth of 7 tens. So we can carry the same arrangement further—

777·77.

Here the third figure from the left means 7 units as before, but the figure to the right of the point means one-tenth of seven, or $\frac{7}{10}$; and the figure farthest to the right means one-hundredth of seven, or $\frac{7}{100}$.

Hence, $\frac{7}{10}$ may be conveniently expressed as ·7. Such an expression is called a Decimal Fraction.

145. By the use of the point (·), which is called the Decimal Point, we can extend the Decimal Notation below units, and express tenths, hundredths, and thousandths, without *writing* the denominator.

Thus, 7·6 is read, Seven *point* six, or Seven *decimal* six, and means 7 whole numbers and 6 tenths, or $\frac{76}{10}$.

In like manner 2·38 means 2 and 3 tenths and 8 hundredths, or $\frac{238}{100}$.

" 1·0398 " 1 and 3 hundredths 9 thousandths and 8 tens of thousandths, or $\frac{10398}{10000}$.

146. Because the numbers in Decimal Fractions all stand in a tenfold relation to one another, it is easy to multiply or divide by ten, a hundred, or a thousand, merely by shifting the decimal point one, two, or three places. Thus:—

35·067 divided by 10 gives 3·5067; for in the second expression every figure is diminished ten times.

147. Rule.—To form decimal fractions, place tenths in the first place to the right of the decimal point, hundredths in the second place, and thousandths, tens of thousandths, &c., in order.

To convert decimal into ordinary fractions, take for the denominator the figure 1, with as many ciphers as there are places to the right of the decimal point, and for the numerator the whole line of figures, omitting the point.

148. Examples of Working.—I. Express fifteen hundredths in a decimal form.

$$\frac{15}{100} = \frac{1}{10} + \frac{5}{100} = \cdot 15.$$

II. Analyze the expression 69·385 :—

$$\begin{aligned} 69\cdot385 &= 60 + 9 + \frac{3}{10} + \frac{8}{100} + \frac{5}{1000}. \\ &= 69 + \frac{3}{10} + \frac{8}{100} + \frac{5}{1000}. \\ &= \frac{693}{10} + \frac{8}{100} + \frac{5}{1000}. \\ &= \frac{6938}{100} + \frac{5}{1000}. \\ &= \frac{69385}{1000}. \end{aligned}$$

III. Multiply 73·684 by 10, and divide 619·098 by 100.

$$73\cdot684 \times 10 = 736\cdot84; \quad 619\cdot098 \div 100 = 6\cdot19098.$$

IV. Divide 1·698 by one thousand.

Here we cannot remove the point three places to the left without prefixing two ciphers. Hence—

$$1\cdot698 \div 1000 = \cdot001698.$$

Exercise XXXIV.

Write the following fractions in the decimal notation:—

(1). Three tenths, fifty-one hundredths, eighty-five thousandths.

(2). Eleven tenths, seven thousandths, one hundred and ninety three millionths.

(3). $\frac{7}{10}$; $\frac{14}{100}$; $\frac{85}{1000}$. (4). $\frac{108}{100}$; $3\frac{6}{10}$; $12\frac{3}{100}$. (5). $7\frac{6}{10000}$; $\frac{238}{100}$

(6). $\frac{3}{1000}$; $\frac{101}{10000}$; $5\frac{7}{10000}$. (7). $9\frac{108}{1000}$; $12\frac{7}{10}$; $\frac{204}{10}$.

(8). $\frac{3024}{100}$; $\frac{509}{10}$; $\frac{215}{100}$. (9). $\frac{6}{10}$; $3\frac{14}{100}$; $2\frac{5}{10}$.

Write the following as vulgar fractions, and state the separate value of each figure:—

(10). 4·1; 7·086; 13·47. (11). 12·938; ·017; 7·103.

(12). 1·0007; 13·4705. (13). 6·18753; 1·0029; 2·9706.

(14). 25·36; 1·0007805. (15). 79·680352; 4·1073285.

(16). 21·096; ·03507. (17). 210·973; ·5638271.

(18). 7·235 × 100; 41·069 × 10; 2·7 × 100.

(19). ·07 × 10; 7·38 ÷ 10; 4·096 × 1000.

(20). 328·7 ÷ 1000; 5·069 ÷ 100; 1·3728 ÷ 10000.

(21). 3·079 × 10000; 71·684 ÷ 1000; ·7963 × 1000.

(22). 1·8 ÷ 10; 17·538 × 1000; 70·638 ÷ 100.

(23). Multiply the following by ten :—
70·386; 159·085; ·7263; ·0862; 5763·894.

(24). Divide the following by ten :—
·069; 5·8321; 1796; 3·057; 27·86; ·9072.

(25). Multiply the following by 100 :—
1·23; ·0796; 58·3; 150·7; 32·786; 5·0978.

(26). Divide the following by 1,000 :—
17·96; 2·083; ·0590; 723; 215; 17·29; 346·25.

REDUCTION OF VULGAR TO DECIMAL FRACTIONS.

149. *EXAMPLE.—Express seven-eighths as a decimal fraction.*

EXPLANATION.—We require here to find another fraction equal to $\frac{7}{8}$, but so expressed that its denominator shall be ten, a hundred, or a thousand, &c. Now, since $\frac{7}{8}$ is the eighth part of seven, we may work this question by reduction, thus:—Let us reduce the seven to tenths. The eighth part of 70 tenths is 8 tenths, and 6 tenths over. Reduce the 6 tenths to hundredths. The eighth part of 60 hundredths is 7 hundredths, and four over. Reduce the four hundredths to thousandths. The eighth part of 40 thousandths is 5 thousands. $\frac{7}{8}$ is therefore equal to $\frac{8}{10} + \frac{7}{100} + \frac{5}{1000}$, and this fraction, by (145), may be expressed as ·875.

```
8) 7(0
   10
8)70(8 tenths.
  64
   6
  10
8)60(7 hundredths.
  56
   4
  10
8)40(5 thousandths.
  40
  ..
```

The usual way of working this would be as follows:—

```
8)7·000
   ·875
```

150. It is not possible to express all fractions exactly with decimal denominators. For instance, the number six cannot be multiplied by any number so as to make 10, 100, or any number of this series (*S. of A.*, 269). Therefore, no fraction with 6 as its denominator can be exactly expressed in a decimal form.

In the same manner, any other fraction whose denominator, when resolved into factors, contains any other prime numbers than 2 and 5, which are the prime factors of 10, 100, 1000, &c., cannot be so reduced as to take a decimal form. Thus, $\frac{5}{14}$ cannot take a decimal form, because the factors of 14 are 2 and 7; but $\frac{7}{50}$ can be reduced to a decimal, because the factors of 50 are $2 \times 5 \times 5$ (*S. of A.*, 270).

The fraction $\frac{5}{6}$ can only be approximately expressed:—

```
6)5·000
  ·833 . . .
```

The same quotient, 3, will occur again and again, as long as the division is continued. Thus, ·83 is very near to $\frac{5}{6}$; ·833 is still nearer, and does not differ so much as one thousandth from the truth; while ·833333 does not differ from $\frac{5}{6}$ by one-millionth of a unit. Such a fraction is called a *RECURRING* DECIMAL, and is written thus, 8·$\dot{3}$.

151. **Rule.**—To reduce a vulgar to a decimal fraction, divide the numerator by the denominator. If there be a quotient, it is a whole number; if not, or if there be a remainder, add a cipher, and place a point before the first figure of the quotient which occurs after doing so. Continue adding ciphers and dividing as far as is required.

152. **Examples of Working.**—Reduce to decimals the vulgar fractions $\frac{7}{12}$ and $\frac{18}{7}$ true to the fifth place.

I. 12)7·0 ——— ·58333|3 II. 7)18·0 ——— 2·57142|8

Ans. $\frac{7}{12}$ = ·58333. *Ans.* $\frac{18}{7}$ = 2·57143.

Note.—Because in I. the first of the omitted figures (3) is less than 5, it should be neglected in the answer; but because in II. the first of the omitted figures (8) is more than 5, it is nearer the truth to add one to the previous figure than to neglect it altogether. Hence the answer in the first case is ·58333, or $\cdot 58\dot{3}$; and in the second, 2·57143.

Exercise XXXV.

(*a*)—*Oral.* (1). What decimal of a pound is a florin?
(2). Express as decimals of £1, 5s., 10s., and 15s.
(3). What decimal of a shilling is sixpence?
(4). Reduce to the decimal of £1, 4s., 18s., and 11s.
(5). State what sums of money are expressed as follows:—
£·1, £·2, £·7, £6·5.
(6). £·25; £·342; £1·6; £183·4; £20·47.
(7). £2·9; £4·15; £1·07; £627·8; £1224·32.
(8). How many tenths are in one-half? one-fifth?
(9). How many hundredths are there in one-fourth? one-tenth?
(10). Reduce to decimals three fifths, five eighths.
(11). Find a decimal expression for three fourths; for four twentieths; for three eighths.
(12). Reduce to decimals $\frac{1}{25}$, $\frac{5}{100}$, and $\frac{4}{8}$.

(*b*)—*Written.* Reduce to decimals true to five places the fractions—

(1). $\frac{5}{7}$; $\frac{2}{9}$; $\frac{3}{10}$. (2). $\frac{4}{13}$; $\frac{5}{8}$; $\frac{15}{17}$. (3). $\frac{13}{16}$; $\frac{8}{15}$.
(4). $\frac{37}{75}$; $\frac{88}{300}$; $\frac{14}{90}$. (5). $\frac{23}{54}$; $\frac{7}{16}$; $\frac{213}{547}$. (6). $8\frac{1}{2}$; $5\frac{1}{4}$.
(7). $2\frac{7}{8}$; $21\frac{4}{19}$. (8). $\frac{1}{6}$ of $\frac{5}{9}$; $\frac{2}{3}$ of $\frac{6}{7}$. (9). $12\frac{1}{9}$; $\frac{1}{6}$ of $\frac{4}{15}$.
(10). $2\frac{1}{4} + 1\frac{4}{11}$; $5 - 3\frac{3}{7}$. (11). $\frac{2}{3} + \frac{5}{6} - \frac{1}{8}$; $\frac{\frac{4}{7}}{1\frac{5}{6}}$.
(12). $\frac{\frac{3}{7}\frac{1}{4}}{\frac{5}{9}\frac{4}{6}}$; $\frac{\frac{5}{6}}{\frac{1}{7}\frac{3}{4}}$.
(13). $\frac{\frac{3}{4} \text{ of } 6\frac{1}{3}}{\frac{1}{2} \text{ of } 18\frac{1}{5}}$; $\frac{\frac{5}{9} \times 1\frac{1}{4}}{6\frac{1}{8} - 5\frac{1}{9}}$.
(14). $\frac{\frac{2}{3} + \frac{5}{6}}{\frac{1}{3} \text{ of } \frac{5}{6}}$; $\frac{8\frac{1}{4} - 3\frac{1}{7}}{2\frac{1}{3} \text{ of } 1\frac{1}{3}}$. (15). $\frac{\frac{1}{11} + 7\frac{3}{4}}{12\frac{5}{6} - 11\frac{7}{8}}$; $\frac{\frac{5}{7} \text{ of } \frac{10}{17}}{\frac{2}{3} \text{ of } \frac{3}{7}}$.
(16). Express decimally the product of the sum and difference of three sevenths and four elevenths.

ADDITION OF DECIMALS.

153. *Example.—Add* ·6, 1·8, ·703, *and* ·2196 *together.*

Explanation.—It was shown in (120) that fractions can be easily added when they have the same denominator. The principal advantage of decimal fractions is, that all the figures are the numerators of fractions which are easily reduced to a common denominator by a simple arrangement. Thus the numbers 6, 8, 7, and 2, all mean tenths, and should therefore be placed in one column; 1 and 0 both refer to hundredths, the 3 and 9 to thousandths, and the 6 to ten-thousandths. Since they are so arranged that ten units in any one column are equal in value to one in the next, the addition may be worked exactly as in the simple rule (17), and the answer is 3·3226.

```
  ·6
 1·8
  ·703
  ·2196
 ------
 3·3226
```

When decimal fractions are added it is always necessary that the figures should be so placed that the points are all in one column. If this is done, all the figures in any one column are numerators of fractions which have the same denominator, and therefore by (122) they may be added together (*S. of A.*, 273).

154. Rule.—Arrange the figures so that the decimal points in all the lines shall fall in the same column. Add up as in Simple Addition, placing a point in the answer exactly underneath the other points.

Exercise XXXVI.

(1). 4·5 + 70·63 + 1·079 + 25. (2). ·508 + 11·23 + 4·197.
(3). ·126 + 3·05 + ·07 + ·528 + 7·093.
(4). 111·306 + ·0317 + 2·793 + ·007.
(5). 470·05 + 72·701 + 3·0315 + 413·2658.
(6). 12·3987 + 4·1462 + ·02063 + 13 + 10·962.
(7). 210·7 + 14563·21 + ·0173 + 382·74156.
(8). 9·127 + 17·62 + ·0041 + 2·31 + 170·96.
(9). ·101285 + 17·061 + 3·2001 + 5·38706.
(10). 2·325 + ·0012 + 5·086 + 219·6832 + ·407.

(11). Add together three tenths, five hundredths, and seven thousandths.

(12). Find the sum of eleven thousandths, seventeen hundredths, and 12 tenths.

(13). Add together fifteen millionths, 173 thousandths, and 23 hundredths.

(14). Find the sum of 4 ten-millionths, 311 ten-thousandths, and 58 tenths.

(15). Add together the weights of a sovereign, a shilling, and a *penny*—which weigh 123·274 grs., 87·272 grs., and 291·6$\dot{6}$ *respectively.*

SUBTRACTION OF DECIMAL FRACTIONS.

155. *Example.—Take* 8·143 *from* 27·02.

Explanation.—The difference between any two fractions can always be found, when they have a common denominator, by subtracting the numerator of the less from that of the greater (121). It is necessary, therefore, to arrange the numbers so that each figure shall be subtracted from another which has the same value. Thus,—

I.	
	27·02
	8·143
	18·877

II.	Tens.	Units.	Tenths.	Hundredths.	Thousandths.
	2	7 + 10	10	2 + 10	10
	1	8 + 1	1 + 1	4 + 1	3
	1	8·	8	7	7

The first figure, 3, of the subtrahend means 3 thousandths, and as there are no thousandths in the upper line we add 10, as in Simple Subtraction (21). We must therefore add $\frac{10}{1000}$, but in the form of $\frac{1}{100}$, to the lower line. In the same manner we add $\frac{10}{100}$ to the 2, and $\frac{1}{10}$ to the 1; also $\frac{10}{10}$ to the upper line and 1 to the lower; ten to the upper and one to the lower. The actual work is shown in II., and the ordinary form in I.

The first fraction is $\frac{2702}{100}$ or $\frac{27020}{1000}$, and the second is $\frac{8143}{1000}$, and by (122) the answer is $\frac{27020-8143}{1000}$, or $\frac{18877}{1000}$.

156. Rule.—Arrange the figures so that the decimal point of the subtrahend shall fall immediately below that of the minuend. Place another point in the same place of the answer.

Exercise XXXVII.

(1). Take 7·39 from 18·035; and 1·9704 from 16·238.
(2). 118·92 — 75·38; 4·065 — ·9382; 4·147 — 2·096.
(3). 45·7208 — 18·096; 12·3972 — ·56; ·058 — ·0058.
(4). 1·072 — ·7368; ·5421 — ·0728; 123·96 — 76·854.
(5). 2·067 + 3·274 + 4·06 — 8·1975; 43·76 + 62·85 — 101·527.
(6). (6·197 + ·0015) — (1·238 + ·709); 17·28 + 25·6 — 9·38.
(7). (128·416 + 73·29 — 41·802) — (7·162 + 51·386 — ·09863).
(8). 673·5 — 29·086; 1·08 — ·963; 54 — ·0054.
(9). Take $\frac{3}{8}$ of $\frac{2}{5}$ from 1, and express the answer in decimals.
(10). The length of a seconds pendulum is 39·1392 inches, and that of a French metre 39·371 inches. Find the difference between them.
(11). A sovereign weighs 123·274 grs., and a shilling 87·272 grs.; find the difference.
(12). Take eleven thousandths from eleven hundredths.
(13). Add together the sum and difference of seventy-three thousandths and one hundred and fifteen millionths.
(14). What is the difference between $3\frac{2}{7}$ and $1\frac{5}{8}$ in decimals?
(15). Take ·754 from the sum of $\frac{3}{4}$ and $\frac{4}{5}$.

MULTIPLICATION OF DECIMAL FRACTIONS.

157. *Example.—Multiply* 7·09 *by* ·673.

Explanation.—We learn from (132) that fractions are to be multiplied together by multiplying the numerators together for a new numerator, and the denominators for a new denominator. Now 7·09 is a fraction of which 709 is the numerator, and 100 the denominator, and ·673 is a fraction whose numerator is 673, and whose denominator is 1000. Therefore, if we multiply 709 by 673 we obtain the numerator of the product; and the denominator of the product will be 100 × 1000, or 100000. Thus:—

I.
```
   ·673
   7·09
   ----
   6057
  4711
 -------
 4·77157
```

II. 7·09 × ·673 =

$$\frac{709}{100} \times \frac{673}{1000} = \frac{709 \times 673}{100 \times 1000} = \frac{477157}{100000} = 4{\cdot}77157.$$

The number of decimal places in the product will always be as many as in the multiplier and multiplicand together. For in the example above, the number ·673 has 1000 for its denominator because it has three decimal places, and 7·09 has 100 for its denominator because it has two decimal places; therefore the product must have 100 × 1000 for its denominator, or five decimal places.

If the multiplier be a whole number, there will, of course, be the same number of decimal places in the product as in the multiplicand.

158. Rule.—Multiply as in whole numbers, and cut off as many decimal places from the product as there are in all the factors together.

159. Examples of Working.—I. Multiply together ·7, 3·9, and ·12.

```
  3·9
    7
 ----
 2·73
   12
 ----
·3276
```

Take the largest number as the multiplicand, multiply by 7, and cut off two figures from 273, multiply by 12, and cut off two more figures from the product.

II. Multiply ·002 and 1·0005 and ·0032 together.

```
      1·0005
           2
      ------
       20010
          32
      ------
       40020
      60030
------------
·00000640320
```

Here, in the multiplication, the ciphers which stand before the significant figures may be neglected, and the factors multiplied together as whole numbers. Since 11 figures need to be cut off from the answer, we must add ciphers to make up the number.

EXERCISE XXXVIII.

(1). 807·29 × 5; 62·317 × 12; 20·683 × 7.
(2). 54·3812 × 17·1; 156·072 × 273.
(3). 107·96 × 3 × 7; 801·056 × 7·2.
(4). 506·847 × 20·368; 213·796 × 5·017.
(5). 327·08 × 50·6; 213·87 × 5·192.
(6). Multiply 17 hundredths by thirty-five thousandths.
(7). Find the product of 127 ten-thousandths and 153 tenths.
(8). Multiply 1·07, 2·038, and 41·25 together.
(9). Find the continued product of twenty-seven tenths, thirty-seven hundredths, forty-five thousandths, and twelve millionths.
(10). (1·23 + ·586) × (50·3 + 61·28); (17·56 + 4·093) × $18\frac{1}{2}$.
(11). 2·07 × 5·1 × 3·092; 15·99 × 1·03 × ·11.
(12). (5·1 + 3·27 + 4·069) × (12·7 + 3·14 — 2·106.)
(13). (3·71 × 4·613 × 8) — (2·5 × 7·18 × ·13.)
(14). Find in decimals the product of $\frac{1}{3}$, $\frac{3}{5}$, and $\frac{4}{7}$.
(15). 2·7 of $5\frac{1}{8}$; $6\frac{1}{2}$ of ·2439; 12·5 of $18\frac{3}{4}$.
(16). Express in decimals of £1 the rent of 67·34 acres, at £5·65 per acre.

(17). A square link contains 62·726 square inches; what is the area in inches of 5,327 square links?

(18). A gallon contains 277·274 cubic inches; what are the cubic contents of 5 qrs. of corn?

(19). A pint of water weighs 1·25 lbs. avoirdupois; what is the weight of 7·9 pints?

(20). Gold is 19·26 times heavier than water; what weight of gold is of the same bulk as 17·342 lbs. of water?

(21). The circumference of a circle measures 3·14159 times its diameter; what will be the length of the circumference of a circle whose diameter measures 37·258 miles?

(22). Find the product of the sum and difference of ·27 and 27.

(23). If the side of a square piece of land be 37·25 perches, what is its area?

(24). What is the weight of five cubic yards of water, if a cubic foot weighs 62·455 lbs. avoirdupois?

(25). Carbonic acid gas weight is 1·524 heavier than air; what is the weight of a volume of the gas equal in bulk to 72·53 lbs. of air?

(26). A French metre is 3 ft. 3·371 inches long; what is the length in inches of 54·61 metres?

(27). Multiply together the sum and difference of $\frac{4}{7}$ and $\frac{3}{8}$, and give the answer in decimals.

(28). If I possess ·76 of a ship, and sell $\frac{3}{4}$ of my share, what fraction of the whole is left?

(29). How much silver is there in 273·5 francs, containing 69·453 grains of pure silver each?

(30.) What is the rent of 47·38 acres of land at £12·563 per acre?

DIVISION OF DECIMAL FRACTIONS.

160. *Example I.—Divide* 7132·506 *by* 9.

$$9)\underline{7132{\cdot}506}\qquad 792{\cdot}5006\dot{6}$$

Explanation.—The ninth part of this number may be found by ordinary division. For 71 is the first part of the dividend taken, and means 71 hundreds. Therefore the first part of the quotient, or 7, is also a number of hundreds. Ciphers may be added, and the division carried as far as we please, but each part of the quotient is of the same value as that of the part of the dividend from which it is derived.

161. *Example II.—Divide* ·703 *by* ·0012.

Here both divisor and dividend are fractions. But by (116) whenever fractions have the same denominator, we may compare them by comparing their numerators. Now, by adding a cipher to ·703, and making it ·7030, we do not alter its value, but we reduce it to the same denominator as ·0012; for—

$$\cdot703 = \tfrac{703}{1000}, \text{ or } \tfrac{7030}{10000}, \text{ and } \cdot0012 = \tfrac{12}{10000}.$$

$$\cdot0012)\underline{\cdot7030}\qquad 585{\cdot}83\ldots$$

The question is, therefore, "How many times are $\frac{12}{10000}$ contained in $\frac{7030}{10000}$?" But this question is the same as "How many times are 12 contained in 7030? (*S. of A.* 228). Whenever, therefore, the dividend and divisor have the same number of decimal places, they may be treated in division as whole numbers, and the quotient is a whole number, although, by adding ciphers, the answer may be carried as far below unity as we please.

162. *Example III.—Divide* 1·0563 *by* ·8.

$$\cdot8)\underline{10{\cdot}563}\qquad 13{\cdot}203$$

Explanation.—Here it would be possible, as in the last example, to equalize the decimal places in dividend and divisor, and so to convert the question into one in Simple Division; for 10·563 $\div$ ·8 = $\frac{10563}{1000} \div \frac{800}{1000}$, or 10563 $\div$ 800: but 800 is an inconvenient divisor, and it is therefore better simply to divide by 8. The question is, "What number, multiplied by ·8, will make 10·563?" But by (157) the product of any two decimal expressions has as many places to the right of the point as there are in both the factors. Therefore, the number of decimal places in the quotient must be the *difference* between the number in the dividend and the number in the divisor. And as there are here three decimal places in the dividend, and only one in the divisor, there must be two in the quotient, and the answer, before ciphers are *added, is* 13·20.

163. **Rule.**—When the divisor is a whole number, divide as in Simple Division, setting down the first figure of the quotient as of the same value as that of the dividend.

When the divisor has a greater number of decimal places than the dividend, add ciphers to the dividend, so as to make them equal, and proceed as in Simple Division.

When the dividend has more decimal places than the divisor, divide as in Simple Division, and cut off from the quotient as many decimal places as the difference between the number in the dividend and that in the divisor.

Exercise XXXIX.

(1). Divide 7·9302 by three, by five, and by seven.

(2). 1·086 ÷ 13; 15·72 ÷ 19; 3·072 ÷ 211.

(3). 471·82 ÷ 25; 2036·931 ÷ 8; ·5032 ÷ 17.

(4). 1·02 ÷ 7·13; 5 ÷ ·05; 18·9 ÷ ·007.

(5). 3·2 ÷ ·16; 23 ÷ ·14; 528·6 ÷ ·912.

(6). 54·3 ÷ ·009; 2·798 ÷ ·011; 7·163 ÷ ·25.

(7). 318·7 ÷ 2·1; 416·79 ÷ 2·35; 412·8 ÷ 1·7.

(8). 176·582 ÷ 2·7; ·4087 ÷ 13·2; 51·347 ÷ 2·05.

(9). (21·63 + 4·139) ÷ (8·72 + ·107); 4·4 ÷ ·706.

(10). A gallon contains 277·274 cubic inches; what are the cubic contents of a gill?

(11). A yard measures 4·545 links; what fraction of a link is an inch?

(12). The weight of a sovereign is 123·274 grs.; what should be the weight of a gold crown piece?

(13). One-twelfth of the weight of a sovereign is alloy; find the quantity of pure gold in 25 sovereigns.

(14). Divide seven tenths by seventeen hundredths.

(15). Divide forty-five thousandths by nine millionths.

(16). What decimal, multiplied by 14 ten-thousandths, will give 235 hundredths?

(17). Divide the sum of ·763 and 1·2854 by their difference.

(18). Multiply 237·6 by 2·5, and divide the result by 7.

(19). ($\frac{4}{5}$ of $21\frac{3}{8}$) ÷ ·16; (21·3 of $35\frac{1}{4}$) ÷ 7·2.

(20). Divide the product of $28\frac{1}{2}$ and 10·5 by that of 7·2 and $2\frac{1}{4}$.

(21). What is the difference between the twelfth and the thirteenth of 25·413.

(22). Divide 3·14159 by $19\dot{7}$, by 2·3, and by 1·067.

(23). Divide $3\frac{1}{8}$ of $21\frac{5}{12}$ by 1·5 of 29·38.

(24). How many times is 123·274 grs. contained in 23 troy lbs.?

(25). If the breadth of a board be 1·32 feet, what length will be required to give an area of 1 square foot?

(26). What must be the length of a field 7·25 perches in breadth, if its area is 2 acres?

(27). If the circumference of a circle be 88·75, what is its diameter? (See Exercise xxxviii. 21.)

(28). If the circumference be one foot, what is the diameter?

REDUCTION OF DECIMAL FRACTIONS TO THOSE OF OTHER NAMES.

164. *Example I.—Reduce* ·17 *cwt. to the decimal of* 1 *lb.*

```
·17 cwt.
  4
 ——
·68 qr.
 28
 ——
544
136
 ——
18·04 lb.
```

Explanation.—We have here to reduce a certain quantity, which is a fraction, ·17 of 1 cwt., to the fraction of a lb. But by (139) it will be a greater fraction of a pound, and we must therefore multiply.

The fraction ·17 of a cwt. must be four times ·17, or ·68 of a quarter. So also the weight, which is ·68 of a quarter, is 28 times ·68, or 18·04 of a pound. We multiply, as in ordinary Descending Reduction (42), by whole numbers, and therefore the number of decimal places in each line is always the same as in the first (157). The answer is 18·04 pounds.

165. *Example II.—Reduce* 3 052 *inches to the fraction of a yard.*

```
12)3·052
   ————
 3)·25433̇
   ————
  ·08477̇
```

Explanation.—The length, which is equal to 3·052 inches, must be a less fraction of a yard (140), and therefore we must divide, as in Ascending Reduction (45). On dividing by 12 we find that 3·052 inches is equal to ·2543 feet, and on dividing by 3 we find that the same length is equal to ·08477 yards.

166. Money may be reduced to the decimal of a pound by Rule (85), when accuracy is only required to the third place; for florins, cents, and mils being respectively tenths, hundredths, and thousandths of £1, may always stand in the first, second, and third decimal places.

Thus, £13 4 fl. 5 c. 9 mils = £13·459.

167. Rule.—To reduce a fraction to a decimal of a lower name, multiply by as many of the less as make one of the greater, pointing off as many decimal places as are in the multiplicand.

But to reduce decimals to fractions of a higher name, divide by as many of the less as make one of the greater, placing the point according to the value of the dividend (172).

168. Examples of Working.—Reduce £7·638 to decimals of a shilling and a penny; and 3 lb. 2 oz. 15 dwts. 7·2 grs. to decimals of a troy pound.

```
I.  £7·638                II.  24)7·2 grs.
        20                     20)15·3̄  dwts.= 15 dwts. 7·2 grs.
    ———————                    12)2·765̄ oz.  = 2 oz. 15 dwts. 7·2 grs.
   152·760 shillings             3·2304 lb.  = 3 lb. 2 oz. 15 dwts. 7·2 grs.
        12
    ———————
      ·120 pence
```

EXERCISE XL.

(*a*)—*Oral.* (1). Express as pounds, shillings, and pence—
£2·938; £5·06; £1·792.

(2). £1·856; £·23; £1·478. (3). 3·26 fl.; 7·2 fl.; £1·008.

(4). £·811; £1·302; 5·8 fl; 1,728 florins.

(5). 17·2 cents; £186; £·627; 732,654 cents.

(6). Express in decimals of £1 true to the third place—
£1 9s. 8d.; £12 1s. 7d.; £185 6s. 4½d.

(7). 2s. 8d.; 5s. 3½d.; 10s. 6d.; £124 13s. 9d.

(8). £22 11s. 3d.; £4 1s. 10½d.; £1 7s.

(9). 16s. 4d.; 8s. 3½d.; 19s. 11d.; £208 6s. 6d.

(10). 4½d.; 1s. 7¾d.; 1¼d.; 2s. 6¾d.

(11). 6¾d.; 11s. 2½d.; 9¾d.; 14s. 9½d.

(*b*)—*Written.* (1). Reduce to the decimal of £1 true to the fifth place—£1 17s. 8½d.; £28 16s. 10¾d.; £12 7s. 9¼d.; £47 13s. 2¼d.

(2). Reduce to decimals of 1s.—£1 7s. 4½d.; £2 9s. 3¾d.; 11½d.; 4¾d.

(3). Reduce to decimals of 1d.—3·7 far.; 23·6 shillings; £12 3s.

(4). 1s. 7d. to the dec. of 10s.; 5s. 8½d. to the dec. of 14s. 6d.

(5). Reduce 3 days 17 hrs. to the dec. of a week; 14·7 minutes to the dec. of a day.

(6). 2 bush. 3·1 pecks to the dec. of a quarter; 5 qts. 1 pt. to the dec. of a gallon.

(7). 7 fur. 35·27 poles to the dec. of a mile; 17·63 yds. to the dec. of an inch.

(8). 118·37 feet to the decimal of a mile, a furlong, and a yard.

(9). 27·6 bushels to the decimals of a quarter, a quart, and a pint.

(10). 3 hours 14 minutes to the dec. of a week, a day, and a minute.

(11). 11 lbs. 6 oz. avoirdupois to the dec. of a cwt. and a ton.

(12). What is the length in feet of 1·32 miles, and of 17·1 yards?

(13). Find ·5 of £3 15s.; ·68 of 17s. 6d.; ·1 of 1s. 8d.

(14). What is ·29 of a mile? ·117 of a cwt.? ·39 of a ton?

(15). 17·36 gals.? 218·7 troy pounds? 11·35 avoir. lbs.?

(16). 21·392 acres? 31·85 acres? 412·27 sq. roods?

(17). Find the difference, in decimals of a minute, between the length of the true year, which is 365·242264 days, and that of the Julian year, which is 365¼ days.

(18). Express the height of Chimilari, which is 29,000 feet, as the decimal of a mile.

(19). The French metre is 39·371 English inches in length. Express the length of 25 such metres as fractions of an English mile.

(20). The kilometre is 1,000 French metres long; what is the length of 7 kilometres in English miles?

(21). Reduce a kilometre to the decimal of an English foot.

(22). The French gramme weighs 15·444 grains; how many troy pounds are there in a kilogramme, which contains 1,000 grammes?

(23). In ·155 of an estate, consisting of 205·65 acres, how many acres, roods, and poles?

MISCELLANEOUS EXERCISES.—XLI.

(1). Multiply $\frac{7}{8}$ by $\frac{5}{16}$, and take the result from 1·32.

(2). Find the sum and difference of $\frac{3}{20}$ and ·47.

(3). What is the number which, multiplied by $\frac{1}{108}$, will produce ·2?

(4). A rectangular field is 79·386 chains long, and 48·357 broad, what is its area?

(5). Find the difference between the product of ·72 and 1·12 and that of $\frac{1}{5}$ and $\frac{1}{6}$.

(6). If an oz. of gold, $\frac{1}{12}$ of which is alloy, is worth £3 17s. 10½d., express in decimals of £1 the value of an ounce of perfectly pure gold.

(7). What sum of money would be required to give 72 persons ·35 of a florin each?

(8). The circumference of every circle is 3·14159 times its diameter, what is the circumference of a circle whose diameter is 1¾ miles?

(9). The diameter of an imperial bushel measure is 18·789 inches, what is its circumference?

(10). How many postage stamps, each $\frac{13}{25}$ of a square inch, would cover a surface of 518⅜ square inches?

(11). By what decimal fraction does $\frac{3}{4}$ exceed $\frac{5}{8}$?

(12). What is the worth of 722·5 pounds at £1·345 per pound?

(13). If a cubit was equal to 1 ft. 9·888 inches, and a span equal to half a cubit, express the height of "six cubits and a span" in inches.

(14). What fraction of an English yard was a "hand-breadth," which was one-sixth of a cubit?

(15). The French metre is equal to 3·9371 English feet, and is a ten-millionth part of a quarter of the earth's circumference; express the length of the earth's circumference in miles.

(16). The specific gravity of brass is 8·396 times that of water; the specific gravity of air is $\frac{1}{770}$ of that of water; how many times does the weight of a piece of brass exceed that of an equal volume of air?

(17). A cubic foot of air contains about 2·03 grains of vapour; what bulk of air will contain 1·25 avoirdupois pounds of vapour?

(18). If ·1875 of a ship cost £273, what is her value?

(19). Find the decimal of £1, which is equivalent to ·54 of a guinea, and reduce £3 2s. 6d. to the decimal of £5.

(20). Multiply ·0082 by 7·05, and divide the product by ·0000705.

(21). Find the sum of £·775, ·824s., and ·305 of a crown, and express the result in decimals of a guinea.

(22). Find the value of $(3·0005 \times ·006) \div ·0009$.

(23). Add together £258 and ·365 of a guinea.

(24). What is that number, of which 15 is ·75?

(25). The sun's diameter is 111·454 times the equatorial diameter of the earth, which is 7925·648 miles; what is the diameter of the sun?

(26). Divide ·001 by ·02, and prove the result by Vulgar Fractions.

(27). The bulk of the planet Mars is ·1386 that of the Earth; *how many times* is the Earth greater than Mars?

(28). A possesses ·25 of a ship, whose value is £6,800, and B possesses ·5 of the remainder; what is the united value of their shares?

(29). Find the value of $603\frac{3}{8}$ yards of cloth at 9s. $7\frac{5}{8}$d. per yard, and give the result in decimals of £1.

(30). If ·375 of a ship is worth £9,900, what is its value?

(31). After spending $\frac{1}{3}$ of the money in my purse, I find that $\frac{5}{12}$ of the remainder amounts to 4s. $10\frac{1}{3}$d.; how much had I at first?

(32). Express decimally $\frac{1}{7}$ lb. troy and $\frac{1}{8}$ lb. avoirdupois.

(33). Find a fourth of that sum of money of which $\frac{3}{17}$ is £28·6.

(34). What number, added to the sum of $\frac{3}{8}$, $\frac{1}{8}$, ·72, and 1·071, will make up the number 4?

(35). Add together £·27318, ·5423s., and 11·053d.

(36). Multiply ·00728 by 3·14, divide ·628 by ·005, and add the results together.

(37). What fraction of 2·5 days is 3·47 minutes?

(38). Take 3·728 yards from 28·316 feet, and give the result in inches.

(39). Find half a year's rent of 12·48 acres of land at £11·35 per acre.

(40). Add together $\frac{1}{4}$, $\frac{1}{5}$, $\frac{1}{6}$, and $\frac{1}{7}$, both as vulgar fractions and as decimals.

(41). If the price of an oz. of tea is 3·75d., what is the price of 17·28 lbs.?

(42). What is the difference in lbs. between ·0583 of 1 cwt. and ·0056 of a ton.

(43). Add together 2·796 yds. and ·1 of half a mile.

(44). What is the average of 32·58, 33·47, and 35·61?

(45). If 27·38 be quotient, and $45\frac{3}{19}$ the divisor, what is the dividend?

(46). Find the value of $23\frac{5}{8}$ yds. of cloth at $1\frac{1}{8}$s. per yd.; 23·$\dot{7}$ yds. of linen at 3·4s. per yd.; and 12·7 yds. of calico at £·007 per yd.

(47). If a business produce an annual return of £1,500, and of three partners one has ·475 and another ·35 share of the profit, how much money falls to the share of the third partner?

(48). To find the area of a circle, multiply the diameter by itself, and that product by $\frac{1}{4}$ of 3·14159: what is the area of a circle whose diameter is 17·2 feet in length?

(49). Find the united areas of 2 circles, whose diameters are 69·5 inches, and 3 ft. 4 inches.

(50). From what weight can I subtract 1·72 lb. so as to leave 0·5 cwt.?

(51). If a person buys $603\frac{3}{8}$ yards of cloth for 9s. 7·625d. per yd., at what price should he sell it per yard, so as to gain $£37\frac{5}{8}$ on the whole?

(52). In an assembly of 1,500 persons, ·22 of the whole are men, ·34 are women, and the rest are children; how many children are there?

PROPORTION.

169. *Example.—What number bears the same relation to 10s. which £24 does to £8?*

Explanation.—We have here to find a number which is as many times greater or less than 10s. as £24 is greater or less than £8. But we know that as 24 is three times 8, the number of shillings required must be three times ten. 30s. therefore bears the same relation to 10s. which £24 does to £8.

170. This fact is generally stated in the following form:—

£8 : £24 : : 10s. : 30s.

The relation of £8 to £24 is one-third. This is called the Ratio which £8 bears to £24; and there is the same relation or Ratio between 10s. and 30s., because ten is contained as many times in thirty as eight is in twenty-four.

The expression 8 : 24 means the Ratio of 8 to 24, and signifies the same as the fraction $\frac{8}{24}$ (*S. of A.*, 310). Because 10 : 30, or $\frac{10}{30}$, represents the same ratio, the sign (: :) is placed between them, and means that the first ratio is *equal* to the second.

Hence the proportion 8 : 24 : : 10 : 30 may be read—

As eight *is to* twenty-four, *so is* ten *to* thirty; or,

The ratio of 8 to 24 *equals the ratio of* 10 to 30.

There can never be any Ratio except between quantities of the same kind. Therefore the first and second terms must always be of the same name, and the third and fourth also of the same name.

Whenever there are four numbers, of which the first bears the same ratio to the second as the third does to the fourth, they are said to be in Proportion (*S. of A.*, 315).

171. If we look at these four numbers—

8 : 24 : : 10 : 30

we observe that there are two terms in the middle, the 24 and 10. These are called the Mean or Middle Terms. There are also two terms at the ends of the line, the 8 and the 30. These are called the Extreme Terms.

Now if we multiply the mean terms together we shall have the number 240, for $24 \times 10 = 240$. But of the two extreme terms, the 8 is as many times less than 24 as the 30 is more than 10. Therefore 8×30 must equal the same as 24×10, or 240 (*S. of A.*, 126 *and* 319).

For the same reason, *whenever four numbers are in proportion, the product of the two extreme terms is equal to that of the two means.* We thus obtain the rule for finding any one term of a proportion which may be required.

172. Rule.—To find any term of a proportion, when any three terms are given, multiply together either the two means, or the two extremes, and divide by the remaining one.

173. Examples of Working.—I. Find the third term of the proportion 15 : 5 :: ( ) : 7.

Here the number required is one of the mean terms. But since by (180) the product of 15 and 7 must be equal to 5 times the unknown number, we must multiply 15 by 7, and divide by 5. Therefore, $\frac{15 \times 7}{5}$, or 21, is the answer; and 15 : 5 :: 21 : 7.

II. Find the first term in the proportion ( ) : 5 :: 24 : 15.

Here the required number is one of the extreme terms. But because the product of the means, or 5 × 24, equals 15 × the first term; $\frac{5 \times 24}{15}$, or 8, is the first term; and 8 : 5 :: 23 : 15.

Exercise XLII.

(*a*)—*Oral.* (1). What number represents the ratio of 27 to 3?

(2). Express the ratio 10 : 12 in lower terms.

(3). Find two numbers having the same ratio as 7 : 9.

(4). What number has the same ratio to eleven as 6 has to 2?

(5). Express in numbers the ratio of a shilling to a crown; of a florin to a halfcrown; of fourpence to threepence.

(6). What is the ratio which 7s. bears to £1? 10d. to 1s.? 7½d. to 9d.?

(7). What is the ratio of two days to a week? Of 3 bush. to 2 pecks?

(8). How is 11d. related to 2s. 6d.? 2 feet to 5 yards? 1½ miles to 8 furlongs?

(9). Place the required term in the following proportions:—

3 : 5 :: ( ) : 15; ( ) : 7 :: 12 : 21.

(10). 5 : 15 :: 7 : ( ); 18 : 90 :: ( ) : 10.

(11). What sum of money bears to sixpence the ratio of 4 to 12?

(12). What length is to a yard as a penny is to a shilling?

(*b*)—*Written.* Express in the lowest terms the ratios—

(1). 27 : 180; 5784 : 396; 1371 : 1695.

(2). 477 : 1629; 217 : 175; 693 : 543.

(3). 7½d. : 1s. 4d.; 4s. 7d. : 10s. 6d.; 1s. 7½d. : 18s. 7½d.

(4). Find the required term in the following proportions:—

75 : ( ) :: 26 : 39; ( ) : 18 :: 27 : 19.

(5). 297 : 15 :: ( ) : 108; 305 : ( ) :: 408 : 1000.

(6). 5376 : ( ) :: 372 : 287; ( ) : 66 :: 1000 : 264.

(7). 2308 : 57 :: 68 : ( ); 1275 : 800 :: 595 : ( ).

(8). 1723 : ( ) :: 3805 : 627; 3586 : 723 :: ( ) : 519.

(9). Find the fourth proportional to 5871, 92, and 106.

(10). Find the fourth proportional to 3·72, 9·6, and ·08.

(11). Find the ratio of 7 cents to half-a-crown.

(12). Find the ratio of the pound troy to the ounce avoirdupois.

RULE OF THREE.

174. *Example.—If five articles cost* 15*s*. 7½*d*., *what will seventeen such articles cost?*

Explanation.—There must be the same proportion between the *prices* as between the *numbers* of the articles. Suppose we make a proportion, and leave the last or fourth place vacant for the unknown term. The sum 15s. 7½d. may be placed in the third. Now because the price of seventeen articles will be greater than the price of five, the fourth term, or answer, will be greater than the third. But when the fourth is to be greater than the third, the second should be greater than the first. Therefore the proportion is—

As 5 is to 17, so is 15s. 7½d. to the answer; or,

5 : 17 : : 15s. 7½d. : (   ).

This sum cannot be solved until the 15s. 7½d. are reduced to some number which will serve as a multiplier. We therefore reduce it to halfpence. By Reduction (30), the sum 15s. 7½d. is equal to 375 halfpence. Therefore the sum is

5 : 17 : : 375 : (   ); or,

Find a number of halfpence which has the same relation to 375 as 17 has to 5. This number will give the price of 17 articles in halfpence.

By (181) the answer to this question is found by multiplying the mean terms together, and dividing by the extreme,

$$\frac{375 \times 17}{5} = 1275 \text{ halfpence} = £2\ 13s.\ 1\tfrac{1}{2}d.$$

The answer, £2 13s. 1½d., is the fourth term of the proportion, and is therefore the price of 17 articles.

175. This process is sometimes called the Rule of Three, because in it *three* terms are always given, and the remaining term is required to be found.

It is usual, for convenience, to make the answer the *fourth* term of the proportion. Whenever this is done, the *third* term must be of the same kind as the answer. For the same reason, the first and second terms must always be of the same name.

176. Observe that the third term was reduced to halfpence before the sum was worked. Whenever a number of two or more denominations occurs in any of the terms, it must be reduced to the form of a simple number of one denomination, otherwise it cannot be used as a multiplier or divisor. *But the first and second terms, if reduced at all, must be reduced to the same name; and the answer is always a number of the same name as that to which the third term has been reduced.*

177. RULE.—Place in the third term that sum mentioned in the question which is of the same kind as the answer. If the answer will be greater than the third term, let the second term be greater than the first; but if the answer will be less, place the less of the two other terms in the second place.

178. EXAMPLES OF WORKING.—If 4 yards of silk cost £1 11s., how many yards can I buy for £26 10s.?

I. £1 11s. : £26 10s. :: 4 : ( )
31s. : 530s :: 4 : ( )

$$\frac{4 \times 530}{31} = 68\tfrac{12}{31} \text{ yds.}$$

II. 1·55 : 26·5 :: 4 : ( )

$$\frac{4 \times 26{\cdot}5}{1{\cdot}55} = 68{\cdot}38 \text{ yds.}$$

The answer is to be yards.

Place 4 yards in the third term.

But £26 10s. will purchase more than 4 yards. The answer will therefore be greater than the third term.

Put the greater number, £26 10s., in the second place.

Reduce £1 11s. and £26 10s. to the same name.

Multiply the second and third terms together, and divide by the first.

Note.—When no lower sums than sixpence are mentioned in the question, it generally saves trouble to reduce the fractional parts of a pound to decimals by (85), instead of to shillings.

179. Since the second and third terms are always multipliers, and the first term always a divisor, it is often possible to shorten the working, by striking out common factors, or dividing both the first term and one of the others by the same number. For example:—

If 2 tons are carried 7 miles for a certain sum, how far will 3 cwt. 2 qrs. be carried for the same money?

cwt. qrs.
3 2 : 2 :: 7

14 : 160 :: 7 : ( )

$$\frac{160 \times \overset{1}{\cancel{7}}}{\underset{2}{\cancel{14}}} = 80$$

The answer is to be distance.

Set down 7 miles in the third term.

But for the same money 3 cwt. 2 qrs. will be carried a greater distance than 2 tons.

Place the greater term (2 *tons*) *in the second place.*

Reduce 2 tons and 3 cwt. 2 qrs. to qrs.

Multiply the second and third terms together, and divide by the first.

Here we observe that 160 has to be multiplied by 7, and divided by 14; but since 7 is a measure of 7 and 14, we may substitute 2 and 1 for 14 and 7, and this does not affect the answer (*S. of A.*, 133).

This operation is called CANCELLING, and may always be used when a multiplier and divisor in the same sum can be divided by a common measure.

Exercise XLIII.

(*a*)—*Oral*. (1). If five articles cost 6d., what will 15 cost?

(2). How many eggs can I buy for 1s. 8d., at five for 2 pence?

(3). At seven for threepence, how many apples can I buy for 1s. 6d.?

(4). Find the price of six articles at five for 2s. 1d.

(5). What is 7s. 6d. in the pound on £20 10s.

(6). If 6 men can dig 20 feet of earth in an hour, how many will dig 50 feet in the same time?

(7). How many coins, worth 1½d. each, are equal in value to 20 fourpenny pieces?

(8). If 20 workmen can finish a piece of work in 8 days, how many could do it in 5 days?

(9). How many articles can I buy for a florin, if five of them cost 3¾d.?

(10). If a labourer earns £35 in 40 weeks, in what time will he earn £14?

(11). If a train runs 20 miles in 30 minutes, in what time will it run 10½ miles?

(12). How many threepenny pieces are equal in value to 36 fourpenny pieces?

(*b*)—*Written*. (1). Find the price of 17 lbs. 2 oz., if 2 cwt. cost £18 10s.

(2). How much does a person owe who possesses only enough to enable him to pay 6s. 5d. in the £1?

(3). What number of yards 5 qrs. wide will suffice to cover the same floor as 76 yards at 3 qrs. wide?

(4). How many pounds avoirdupois can be purchased for £7 10s. 5d., when 13 oz. cost 12s. 8d.?

(5). How much will 3 nails of cloth cost at 4s. 7d. for 2¾ yds.?

(6). A man owes £7,905, and pays 12s. 5½d. in the pound; how much does he pay altogether?

(7). How many coins, worth 7½d. each, are equal in value to 582 coins worth 10¾d. each?

(8). Find the number which is the fourth proportional to 27, 63, and 51.

(9). Four dozen loaves cost £1 1s.; what is the price of 73 loaves?

(10). If a horse travels over 17 miles in 1 hr. 21 min., in what time would he travel 49 miles?

(11). A and B divide the profits of a business in the proportion of 210 to 195. A's share is £567 15s.; what is B's share?

(12). What is the worth of 3 cwt. 2 qr. 17 lb. at the rate of 1s. 7½d. for 3½ lbs.?

(13). If a gentleman whose income is £640 pays £42 6s. 8d. income tax, what should a person pay whose income is £317 10s.?

(14). What is the price of 753 bags of sugar, each containing 1 cwt. 2 qrs. 15 lbs. at 39s. 6d. per cwt.?

(15). If the price of 3052 lbs. be £217, what is the price per cwt.?

(16). What should be the charge for 71,250 cubic feet of gas, at 6s. 6d. per 1,000 cubic feet?

(17). If tea be imported at £11 13s. 4d. per cwt., and be subject to a duty of 1s. 4d. per lb., at what price must a chest containing 2 qrs. 11 lbs. be sold so as to gain 1½d. per lb.?

(18). The ratio of the side of a square to its diagonal is about 70 : 99; find the diagonal of a square field whose side measures 5 chains 27 links.

(19). What is the length of the side of a square whose diagonal measures 27 yds. 2 ft.?

(20). What sum will be raised by a rate of 3½d. in the pound on a parish whose total rental is £7,963 10s.

(21). How many yards of cloth, worth 17s. 2¼d. per yd., ought to be given in exchange for 550 yards of linen, worth 3s. 9¾d. per yd.?

(22). If ¾ of a pound cost 2⅔ shillings, what will be the price of $11\frac{1}{12}$ cwt.?

(23). If a railway carriage proceeds at the rate of 3·5 miles in 7·8 minutes, how long will it take to reach a distance of 212 miles 2 fur. 3 p.?

(24). If 27 workmen perform 219 yards of work, how much will 11 workmen perform in the same time?

(25). If a train runs 30 miles in 64 minutes, how far will it run in 18 minutes?

(26). If 3 cwt. 2 qrs. 16 lbs. of rice cost £3 5s. 10d., how much may be bought for £5 7s. 6d.?

(27). If the shadow of a steeple, which is 160 ft. 4 in. high, measures 210 ft., what is the actual height of a staff whose shadow is 17 ft. 6 in. long?

(28). On what rental was £71 17s. 6d. paid as poor-rate, at 11½d. in the £1?

(29). If ivory be worth £29 15s. per cwt., what is the worth of a tusk weighing 94 lbs. 6 oz.?

(30). What is the price of 219 quires of paper at 14s. 8d. per ream?

(31). An avoirdupois ounce is to a troy oz. as 175 : 192; express 13 lbs. 7 oz. troy in avoirdupois weight.

(32). If a pound troy of silver be coined into 66 shillings, what is the weight avoirdupois of £47·75 in silver?

(33). If £3 17s. 10½d. be the value of an oz. of standard gold, what is the value of a gold tankard weighing 2 lbs. 5 oz. 12 dwts. 3 gr.?

(34). If 1,000 soldiers' coats have to be made, each requiring 2½ yds. of cloth of 5 qrs. wide, how much lining will be required for them if the material employed is 2 qrs. wide?

(35). The ages of two persons are as 17 to 6, and the younger is 24 years old; what is the age of the elder?

(36). A surveyor, after measuring a road, and finding it 2,738 yds. by his chain, discovers that some links are missing, and that the chain is 15 inches too short, what is the real length of the road?

(37). At £1 7s. 4d. per acre, how much land can be rented for £164 19s. 4d.?

PROPORTIONAL PARTS.

180. *Example.—Three persons enter into a speculation together,* A *contributes* £184 10*s.*; B £96 15*s.*; *and* C £76 5*s.*; *they gain* £238 6*s.* 8*d.*; *what is each person's share of the profit?*

Explanation.—We cannot state the proportion in this case until we know what is the total amount of the money contributed by all the partners. To find this we must add £184 10s., £96 15s., and £76 5s. together. They make £357 10s. We have then three questions to solve:—

I. If A contributes £184 10s. of £357 10s., what should be his share of £230 6s. 8d.?

II. If B contributes £96 15s. of £357 10s., what should be his share of £230 6s. 8d.?

III. If C contributes £76 5s. of £357 10s., what should be his share of £230 6s. 8d.?

In all these three cases, as the answer required is *profit*, the total profit should be placed in the third term; and by (177) the other terms should be thus arranged.

As the *whole investment* is to *each man's contribution*, so is *the whole profit* to *each man's share of the profit.*

I. £357 10s. : £184 10s. :: £230 6s. 8d. : A's share.
II. £357 10s. : £96 15s. :: £230 6s. 8d. : B's share.
III. £357 10s. : £76 5s. :: £230 6s. 8d. : C's share.

Hence it follows that the three answers required will be:—

A's share, $\frac{184{\cdot}5 \times 230\frac{1}{3}}{357{\cdot}5} = £123$; B's, $\frac{96{\cdot}75 \times 230\frac{1}{3}}{357{\cdot}5} = £64\ 10s.$

C's, $\frac{76{\cdot}25 \times 230\frac{1}{3}}{357{\cdot}5} = £50\ 16s.\ 8d.$

181. Rule.—Find the sum of the given terms which are of like kind, and make it the first term of as many proportions as may be required.

Place in the second term that one of the given terms which corresponds to the particular part of the answer required. Place in the third term the number which is the sum of all the answers.

182. Example of Working.—*If copper and tin be mixed in proportions of* 25 *and* 3, *how much copper is contained in a mass of the compound weighing* 1 *ton* 17 *cwt.* 3 *qrs.?*

qrs.
28 : 25 :: 151 : ( )

$\frac{25 \times 151}{28}$ = 33 cwt. 2 qrs. 23 lbs.

The sum of 25 and 3 is 28.
Place 28 *in the first term.*
Place 25 *in the second term.*
Reduce 1 t. 17 cwt. 3 qrs. to qrs., and *place it in the third term.*

Work the question as in the Rule of Three.

EXERCISE XLIV.

(*a*)—*Oral.* (1). Divide a shilling between two persons in the proportion of 7 to 5.

(2). Divide 5s. in the proportion of 6 to 4; of 9 to 3; of 5 to 3.

(3). If a gentleman gives £1 away between three persons, so that for every eightpence given to the first sixpence is given to the second, and twopence to the third, what is the share of each?

(4). Divide 100 marbles between two boys, so that one shall have four times the share of the other.

(5). Divide 7 lbs. avoirdupois into two parcels, of which one shall be three times the other.

(6). A compound is formed of two ingredients, mixed in the proportion of 11 to 4; how much of each is there in a weight of 30 oz.?

(7). Two children, aged 10 and 9, are to divide 3s. 2d. between them in the proportion of their ages; what is the share of the elder?

(8). A street is 20 yards wide, but the road is ten times as wide as either of the footways; what is the width of the road in feet?

(9). Three boys are partners in play; the one has 30 marbles, and the other 21, and the third 15, at first; they gain 22; what is the share of the first?

(10). Divide £5 among 4 men, in the proportions of 4, 3, 2, and 1.

(*b*)—*Written.* (1). Three persons contribute £84 10s., £147 17s. 6d., and £190 2s. 6d. respectively, to a speculation which realizes £100 profit, what are their shares?

(2). If 2 persons rent a meadow between them whose annual rent is £18 7s. 6d., and if one put in 15 sheep, and the other 6, what ought each to pay?

(3). If in a certain compound there are 99 parts of pure metal to 13 of alloy, what quantity of alloy is contained in 1 ton 13 cwt. 3 qrs. of the metal?

(4). Divide 14 guineas in the proportion of $\frac{1}{3}$ to $\frac{1}{4}$.

(5). Eleven parts of standard gold are pure metal, and one is alloy; how much alloy is there in 35 oz. 16 dwts. 4 grs. of standard gold?

(6). Air consists of about 79 parts of nitrogen to 21 of oxygen; how much oxygen is there in 15 cubic feet of air?

(7). Two partners agree to share profits in the proportion of $\frac{4}{7}$ to $\frac{1}{14}$; what is the profit of each out of £1,327 6s.?

(8). Standard silver consists of 37 parts of pure metal, and 3 of alloy; if 33 shillings weigh six troy ounces, how much alloy is there in seventeen shillings and sixpence?

(9). A gun, weighing 5 tons, is composed of 7 parts of copper to 5 of iron; how many hundredweights are there of each metal?

(10). Three kinds of tea are mixed together, half a pound of Hyson, $\frac{3}{4}$ lb. of Congou being put to every pound of Souchong; how much of each kind of tea is there in 2 cwt. of the mixture?

(11). A tax of £13 17s. 4d. is to be paid by 3 tenants, whose rentals are £15, £20, and £30 respectively; what is each person's share?

(12). Divide 780 into parts having the ratio $\frac{1}{2}$, $\frac{3}{8}$, and $\frac{5}{12}$?

COMPOUND PROPORTION.

183. *Example.—If a man can build 7 feet of a wall in a day, what length of wall should be built by 3 men in 5 days?*

Explanation.—The number of feet required depends on two things—the length of time, and the number of labourers. If only the time were considered, the question by (177) would be stated thus:—

I. As 1 day : 5 days :: 7 feet : number required.

And the answer to this question would be 5 times seven feet. But if the number of men only were considered, the statement would be—

II. As 1 man : 3 men :: 7 ft. : number of feet required.

And the answer to this question would be 3 times seven feet. But since statement I. increases seven feet 5 times, and statement II. increases it 3 times, the two together increase it 3 × 5, or 15 times. Both statements are combined thus:—

$$\left.\begin{matrix} 1 \text{ day} : 5 \text{ days} \\ 1 \text{ man} : 3 \text{ men} \end{matrix}\right\} :: 7 \text{ feet} : \text{required answer.}$$

$$1 : 15 :: 7 \text{ feet} : 105 \text{ feet.}$$

184. Whenever there are two ratios affecting an answer in this way, the question is said to be in Compound Proportion, or the Double Rule of Three; because there are two sums in Simple Proportion to be *compounded*, or combined into one. This must always be done by multiplying the two first terms together for a new first term, and the two second terms together for a new second term (*S. of A.*, 358).

185. Rule.—Place in the third term the number of the same kind as the answer. Take two terms of like kind, and consider these with the third as a separate sum in Simple Proportion. State this sum by (177), and take another pair of terms with the third as a second sum in Proportion. Arrange this according to the same rule; multiply the first terms together for a new first term, and the second terms together for a new second term, and proceed as in Simple Proportion.

186. Example of Working.—If 12 horses consume 4 qrs. of corn in 16 days, how much will 20 horses require for a week?

$$\left.\begin{matrix} 12 : 20 \\ 16 : 7 \end{matrix}\right\} :: 4$$

$$192 : 140 :: 4$$

$$\frac{4 \times 140}{192} = 2\tfrac{11}{12}$$

The answer is to be corn: *Set down 4 qrs. in the third term.*

I. If 4 qrs. are eaten by 12 horses, more will be eaten by 20 horses.

Therefore *set down* 20 *in the second place, and* 12 *in the first.*

II. If 4 qrs. are eaten in 16 days, less will be eaten in a week. Therefore *set down* 7 *in the second place, and* 16 *in the first.* Multiply 4 by 7 × 20, and divide by 12 × 16.

Answer, $2\frac{11}{12}$ qrs., or 2 qrs. $7\frac{1}{3}$ bush.

Exercise XLV.

(1). If it costs £19 to keep 4 children for 3 months, how much will it cost to keep 8 children at the same rate for nine months?

(2). If 9 bushels of corn will suffice for 8 horses during 12 days, how many days will 24 bushels last 16 horses?

(3). If the carriage of 8 cwt. for 128 miles cost £2·4, what will be the cost of carrying 4 cwt. for 32 miles at the same rate?

(4). If 136 soldiers consume 351 quarters of wheat in 108 days, how many soldiers will eat 1,404 qrs., at the same rate, in 54 days?

(5). If 48 men mow 54 acres of grass in 24 days, how many acres will 16 men mow in 28 days?

(6). If 1,728 barrels of powder are used in firing 24 pieces of artillery during 22 days, for how many pieces will 48 barrels be required in one day?

(7). If 7 persons in a household drink 2 kilderkins of beer in 12 days, how many gallons will be required for 14 persons in 8 days?

(8). If 14 horses eat 40 bushels of corn in 16 days, how many horses will eat 120 bushels in 24 days?

(9). If £48 suffice for the expenses of 12 persons for 8 weeks, for how many persons will £288 suffice for 2 yrs. 40 weeks?

(10). If a spinning frame, containing 216 spindles, each making 1,000 revolutions per minute, produce 250 lbs. of thread in 12 hours, how many pounds will be produced by another frame, containing 96 spindles, each making 1,600 revolutions per minute?

(11). In a factory 1,500 men are employed in making 80 locomotive engines per month; how long would it take 300 men to make 300 such engines?

(12). If 12 men can mow 30 acres in 20 days of 7 hours each, how many men will mow 22 acres in 14⅔ days of 6 hours each?

(13). If a block of stone 3 yards long, 2 yards wide, and 1⅓ yds. thick, be worth £6 15s., what will be the worth of another block of the same material, measuring 7 feet long, 5 feet broad, and 2 ft. thick?

(14). If £108 gain £6 interest in 12 months, what should be the interest on £75 for 9 months?

(15). If when wheat cost 80s. per qr. a sixpenny loaf weighed 24 oz., what should be the weight of a penny loaf when wheat is worth 3s. 4d. per bushel?

(16). If seventeen men earn £10 10s. 4½d. in 5½ days, how much will 23 men earn in 2 days?

(17). If the quality of one farm be to that of another as 7 to 5, and if the former, containing 59 a. 1 r., pays a rent of £120, what should be the rent of the other, which contains 138 a. 1 r.?

(18). If a capital of £250 gain £23 in four months, what will a capital of £1,200 gain in 3 months?

(19). If a man travels 360 miles in 12 days of nine hours long, how many miles will he travel in 7 days of 12 hours long?

INTEREST.

187. *Example.—What is the Interest on £754 10s. at $3\frac{1}{2}$ per cent.?*

Explanation.—*Per Cent.* means per £100, and Interest means the money paid for the loan of the money. This question, therefore, means, "If £3 10s. are paid for the loan of £100, what should be paid for the loan of £754 10s.?" This is a sum in Proportion, and by (186) it should be stated thus:—

$$£100 : £754{\cdot}5 :: £3{\cdot}5 : (\quad);$$

and the answer is $\dfrac{£754{\cdot}5 \times £3{\cdot}5}{100} = £27{\cdot}4075 = £27$ 8s. $1\frac{3}{4}$d.

188. The money lent out at interest is called the Principal; the money paid as Interest on £100 for one year is called the Rate per Cent.; and the sum made up of both Principal and Interest is called the Amount.

189. Questions in Interest are always to be worked by Proportion. But because all Interest is calculated at so much per cent., *One hundred pounds* is always the first term in such a proportion. The money lent is always in the second place, and the Rate of Interest is in the third place.

190. Rule.—To find the Interest, multiply the Principal by the Rate per Cent., and divide by 100.

191. Observe that as the sums of money mentioned in Interest questions seldom contain lower fractions than sixpence, it will generally be more convenient to express them decimally. Division by 100 is very easy, as by (152) it can be worked by moving the decimal point two places.

192. Examples of Working.—I. What is the interest on £1,258 for 7 years at 6 per cent.?

1258	Multiply £1,258 by 6.
6	*Cut off two figures by a decimal point, to divide by* 100.
75·48 = Int. for 1 yr.	
7	Multiply by 7, or the number of yrs.
528·36 = Int. for 7 yrs.	Reduce £·36 to shillings and pence.

Answer, £528·36, or £528 7s. $2\frac{1}{2}$d.

II. At what rate per cent. will £250 amount to £285 in $3\frac{1}{2}$ yrs.?

£285 − £250 = £35 = Int. for $3\frac{1}{2}$ yrs.	*Find the whole interest for the period, and thence find the interest for* 1 *year.*
£35 ÷ $3\frac{1}{2}$ = £10 = Int. for 1 yr.	
250 : 100 :: 10 : ( )	By (177) If £10 be the interest on £250 for 1 year, what is the interest on £100?
$\dfrac{100 \times 10}{250}$ = £4 = Rate per cent.	Work as in Rule of Three.

EXERCISE XLVI.

(*a*)—*Oral.* (1). Find 4 per cent. interest on £100; on £150.

(2). Find interest on £200 at 6 per cent.; on £550 at 3 per cent.

(3). Find 7 per cent. on £1,200; 8 per cent. on £175.

(4). Find* 5 per cent. on £150; on £30; on £160 10s.

(5). Calculate the interest on £300 at 5 per cent. for 7 months.

(6). Interest on £23 10s. for 5 months at 5 per cent.; £256 for 1 year 6 months; £354 for 2 years 7 months.

(7). At 3 per cent. find interest on £150; on £225; on £675.

(8). At 7 per cent. find interest on £1,250 for 4 yrs.; on £1,500 for $2\frac{1}{2}$ yrs.

(9). What is 20 per cent. on £80; on £50; on £400; on £180?

(10). A tradesman gets 25 per cent. profit on a particular article; what must he sell goods at which he buys for £5? £12? 10s. 6d.?

(11). Add 10 per cent. to £20; to £50; to £1; to 18s.

(12). Add 15 per cent. to £150; 20 per cent. to £18.

(*b*)—*Written.* Find the interest on—

(1). £354 at 5 per cent. for 1 yr.; £1,683 at 4 per cent. for 1 yr.

(2). £562 at 6 per cent. for 1 yr.; £1,983 at $3\frac{1}{2}$ per cent. for 1 yr.

(3). £847 10s. at 4 per cent. for $2\frac{1}{2}$ years; £2,537 at 3 per cent. for 7 years; £1,386 5s. at $2\frac{1}{2}$ per cent. for 4 yrs.

(4). £189 at $1\frac{1}{2}$ per cent. for 6 yrs.; £2,078 at $3\frac{1}{4}$ per cent. for 5 yrs. 3 m.; £3,275 at $7\frac{3}{4}$ per cent. for 2 yrs.

(5). £276 15s. at 6 per cent. for 3 yrs.; £1,837 at $2\frac{1}{4}$ per cent. for 11 years.

(6). What will £783 amount to in 5 years 9 months at 5 per cent.?

(7). What will £1,264 amount to in 15 months at $3\frac{1}{2}$ per cent.?

(8). What will £563 amount to in 4 years 17 weeks at 5 per cent.?

(9). Find interest on £230 10s. for 1 year 183 days at 4 per cent.

(10). Find the interest at £1,000 for 1,000 days at $3\frac{1}{4}$ per cent.

(11). What will £1,200 amount to in 17 months at $2\frac{1}{2}$ per cent.?

(12). In what time will £100 amount to £140 at 5 per cent.?

(13). In what time will £750 become £1,000 at 3 per cent.?

(14). At what rate will £500 amount to £725 in 18 years?

(15). In what time will £1,210 19s. 6d. amount to £1,225 19s. 6d. at $3\frac{1}{4}$ per cent.?

(16). At what rate per cent. must £365 be lent for 95 days to amount to £369 15s.?

(17). A loan of £1,000 is repaid in instalments, as follows: $\frac{1}{4}$ in 6 months; $\frac{1}{3}$ in 12 months, and the rest at the end of two years; what is the total interest which should be paid at 5 per cent.?

(18). A loan of £600 is to be repaid quarterly in equal instalments, in the course of two years; how much interest ought to be paid in all at 5 per cent.?

* Since 5 is one-twentieth part of 100, we may always find five per cent. on any sum of money for a year, by *calling the pounds shillings*. A month's interest may be found by calling the pounds pence. For at £5 per cent. the interest on £1 for a year is 1s., and for a month it is 1d.

DISCOUNT.

193. *Example.—If I am under an engagement to pay £500 a year hence, what sum ought to be deducted from the debt, if I pay it now, interest being at 5 per cent.?*

Explanation.—This is not an ordinary question in Interest. The £500 mentioned in the sum is not Principal; it is the Amount which my present debt will reach if it is left unpaid for a year; and both principal and interest are included in this amount. We have to find how much of the £500 is interest on the present debt, and to deduct it from the whole amount.

To do this we must form a Proportion Sum. If £100, due at this moment, were left unpaid for a year, the debt with its interest at 5 per cent. would amount, in that time, to £105. Therefore, a debt of £105 due a year hence is equal in value to a present debt of £100. The question is,—

If £5 be the deduction which should be made from a debt of £105 due a year hence, what deduction should be made from £500, due at the same time?

By (177) the statement is—

£105 : £500 :: £5 : ( )

$$\frac{500 \times 5}{105} = £23{\cdot}809, \text{ or } £23\ 16s.\ 2\tfrac{1}{4}d.$$

194. This deduction is called Discount. It means the interest which, added to the Present Value, will make up the whole amount of a debt in a given time. The calculation of Discount differs from that of ordinary Interest, because *in Interest sums the principal is given, and in Discount sums the amount is given.* In both cases the interest is required to be found. But in the latter we must first fix on another sum of money, and find what it would amount to at the given rate and time, and then form a proportion. The sum usually fixed on for convenience is £100. The first term is always £100 + its interest for the required time; the second is the given amount; and the third is either £100 or the interest on £100, according as the present value or the discount is demanded.

195. In business, True Discount of this kind is rarely used. Ordinary discount is usually calculated as interest, the debt being considered as principal.

196. Rule.—To find the True Discount, make the following proportion:—

£100 + its interest : Amount : : Interest on £100 : ( ).

197. To find Present Value, make the following proportion:—£100 + its Interest : the Amount : : £100 : ( ).

EXERCISE XLVII.

(*a*)—*Oral.* Deduct ordinary discount in the following cases:—

(1). *Ten per cent. from £100; from £50; from £300; from £250.

(2). Twenty-five per cent. from £100; from £400; from £20.

(3). Five per cent. from £100; from £75; from £320; from £68.

(4). Twenty per cent. from £100; from £60; from £95; from £225.

(5). Take 25 per cent. from £2 10s.; from 18s.; from 15s.

(6). Take 50 per cent. off £79; from £124; from £16 10s.

(7). Deduct 12 per cent. from £100; from £700; from £250.

(8). Take five per cent. from £21 10s.; from £18; from £230.

(9). Take 10 per cent. from £32 5s.; from £17 10s.; from £183.

(*b*)—*Written.* Find the true discount in the following cases:—

(1). On £250 at 5 per cent. for 2 years; on £725 at 4 per cent. for 3 years; on £123 at 2 per cent. for 3½ years.

(2). On £1,000 at 6 per cent. for 4 years.

(3). On £278 at 5 per cent. for 7 years; on £628 at 3 per cent. for 2 years.

(4). Find the true present worth of a bill for £300, payable six months hence, interest being at 5 per cent.

(5). Find the true present value of £1,350, due two years hence, when interest is 3½ per cent.

(6). What sum of money, invested now at 4 per cent., will amount to £1,000 in 3 years?

(7). If £7,510 be the amount which accumulates in 2 years at 4½ per cent., what is the principal?

(8). If at the end of 4 years I draw from a bank the sum of £1,320, including principal and interest, how much of it is interest, supposing £2 10s. to have been the rate per cent.?

Find the ordinary bankers' discount on the following bills:—

(9). A bill for £184, drawn on the 16th of October, and payable on the 16th of January, at 5 per cent.

(10). £2,308, drawn on the 13th of February, and payable on the 27th of September, at 3 per cent.

(11). £5,163 drawn on the 31st of June, and payable on the 8th of August, at 4 per cent.

(12). £6,271, drawn on the 17th of January, and payable on the 3rd of April, at 6½ per cent.

(13). £238, drawn 20th September at four months, and discounted on the 3rd of October, at 3 per cent.

(14). £150, drawn 6th of January at six months, and discounted on the 12th of March, at 8 per cent.

(15). £250, drawn 16th of June at three months, and discounted the 9th of July, at 7 per cent.

(16). £75, drawn 21st of January at five months, and discounted on the 3rd of April, at 4½ per cent.

* Observe that 25 per cent. is one-fourth, or 5s. in the £1; 20 per cent. is one-fifth, or 4s. in the £1; 10 per cent. is one-tenth, or 1 florin in the £1; 5 per cent. is one-twentieth, or 1s. in the £1.

COMPOUND INTEREST.

198. *Example.—What interest will accumulate on £300 in a year and a half at 4 per cent., the interest being payable half-yearly?*

Explanation.—In this case the interest, as it becomes payable, must be added to the principal; and the next half-year's interest must be calculated on the whole amount. There are here, therefore, three separate sums.

I. By (195) Interest on £300 for 6 months at 4 per cent. is £6. Therefore, at the end of the first half-year the principal amounts to £306.

II. By (195) the Interest on £306 for 6 months at 4 per cent. is £6·12, or £6 2s. 5d. Therefore, at the end of a year the principal amounts to £312·12, or £312 2s. 5d.

III. By (195) the Interest on £312 2s. 5d. for 6 months at 4 per cent. is £6·24, or £6 4s. 10¼d. Therefore, at the end of 1½ years the principal amounts to £318·36, or £318 7s. 2½d. The total Interest which has accumulated on the £300 is, therefore, £18 7s. 2½d.

199. This is called Compound Interest. It differs from Simple Interest, because it is calculated on the amount of the Principal and Interest from time to time, and not on the principal alone (*S. of A.*, 382). It is always greater than the Simple Interest on the same sum for the same period; thus, the Simple Interest on £300 at 4 per cent. for 1½ years is only £18.

200. Rule.—Find the Simple Interest for each year or other period at the termination of which the interest is payable; add the results successively to the principal.

201. Example of Working.—What is the compound interest on £1,150 for 2½ years at 3 per cent.?

$\frac{1150 \times 3}{100}$ = £34·5 = £34 10s. = Interest on the first year.

1,150 + £34·5 = £1,184 10s. = Principal at the beginning of the second year.

$\frac{1184{\cdot}5 \times 3}{100}$ = £35·535 = £35 10s. 8½d. = Interest on 2nd yr.

1184·5 + £35·535 = £1,220 0s. 8½d. = Principal at the beginning of third year.

$\frac{1220{\cdot}035 \times 1{\cdot}5}{100}$ = £18·3 = £18 6s. = Interest on last half-year.

1238·335 − £1,150 = £88·335 = £88 6s. 8½d. = Compound Interest for 2½ years.

Exercise XLVIII.

(*a*)—*Oral.* (1). Find the compound interest on £100 at 5 per cent. for 2 years.

(2). To what will £50 amount in 3 years at 5 per cent.?

(3). Find the compound interest on £100 at 10 per cent. for 1½ years, payable half-yearly.

(4). To what sum will £200 amount in 2 years, at 4 per cent.?

(5). What interest will accrue on £250 in 3 years at 1 per cent.?

(6). Find the amount of £1,000 for 3 years at 10 per cent.

(*b*)—*Written.* (1). Find the sum to which £250 will amount in 3 years at 6 per cent.

(2). Calculate the compound int. on £230 for 3 yrs. at 7 per cent.

(3).	„	„	1,750 „	2½	„	3	„
(4).	„	„	300 „	5	„	·2½	„
(5).	„	„	1,850 „	4	„	3¼	„
(6).	„	„	1,250 „	3	„	2½	„
(7).	„	„	840 „	4	„	5	„

(8). To what sum will £730 amount in 3 yrs. at 5 p. c. com. int.?

(9).	„	1,200	„	2½ „	4	„	„
(10).	„	180	„	4 „	6	„	„

(11). What is the compound interest on £670 at 4 per cent. for 2 years, interest being payable half-yearly?

(12). To what sum will £500 amount in a year at 5 per cent. if the interest be paid quarterly?

(13). Find the difference between the simple and the compound interest on £1,000 for 3 years at 5 per cent.

(14). Calculate the difference between the sum to which £540 would amount in 5 years at simple and at compound interest at 4 per cent.

(15). In what time will £25 amount to £30 at 5 per cent. simple interest?

(16). At what rate per cent. will £300 become £350 in 3 years at simple interest?

(17). What sum will amount to £685 in 2 years at 4 per cent. simple interest?

(18). How much interest has accumulated if at the end of 2½ years a person receives £340 as the amount of an investment at 2 per cent. simple interest?

(19). What deduction ought to be made from a bill of £150 due six months hence, when interest is at 6 per cent.?

(20). If I borrow £75 of a friend for 3 months, for how long ought I to lend him £100, to repay the obligation?

(21). Find the difference in annual income between investing £325 at 2½ and at 3¼ per cent.?

(22). When the income tax was levied at sixteenpence in the £1, what was that per cent.?

(23). If at simple interest £256 amounts to £300 16s. in 3½ years, what is the rate per cent.?

STOCKS AND SHARES.

202. *EXAMPLE I.—What must be paid for £712 15s. 6d the 3 per Cents., at 97¾?*

EXPLANATION.—By the 3 per Cents. are meant share the National Debt of England, on which Interest is paid of the public Funds. These shares are the property, ei of persons who originally lent money to the Governmen of their representatives. Since the money which has been lent has been expended by the State, the lender not possess the right to claim a return of their money, only the right to receive £3 per annum from the Governn for every £100 they have lent, until the principal is rep This right can be transferred from one person to anotl and may be at any time purchased in the Stock Excha where Government Securities are regularly bought and s Therefore, £100 *Stock*, as it is called, constitutes the ho a creditor to the nation for the sum of £100, and gives h right to claim 3 per cent. interest on that sum every half-y But this Stock is cheaper at one time that at another. is worth most when the general interest of money is when other investments are scarce, and when, therefore, interest on the Government debt becomes desirabl capitalists. It is worth least when money is most in requ and when, therefore, the general interest of money is (*S. of A.*, 390).

The question refers to a time when £100 Stock is w £97 15s., or 97¾. At such a time, since the actual valu a nominal £100 is only £97 15s., the actual sum for whi nominal £712 15s. 6d. can be purchased is smaller in same proportion. The question is therefore one in the of Three.

"If £100 Stock be purchasable for £97 15s., for sum can £712 15s. 6d. be purchased?"

By (177) this sum may be stated and worked thus:—

$$100 : 712{\cdot}775 :: £97{\cdot}75 : (\quad)$$

$$\frac{712{\cdot}775 \times 97{\cdot}75}{100} = £696{\cdot}737 = £696\ 14s.\ 9d.$$

203. *EXAMPLE II.—What Stock can be purchased £1,240 at 88¼?*

EXPLANATION.—This question, otherwise stated, is:—

"If £88 5s. will purchase a nominal £100, what sum £1,240 buy?"

The statement by (177) is as follows:—

$$£88{\cdot}25 : £1240 :: £100 : (\quad)$$

$$\frac{1240 \times 100}{88{\cdot}25} = £1405{\cdot}098 = £1405\ 1s.\ 0\tfrac{1}{4}d.$$

Exercise XLIX.

(*a*)—*Oral.* (1). For what can I purchase £200 stock at 95?

(2). How much must be given for £300 stock at 87½?

(3). How much stock can be purchased for £270 at 90?

(4). If 4 per Cent. stock could be purchased at 80, what would be the actual interest per cent.?

(5). If the 3 per Cents. can be purchased at 90, what is the real interest per cent.?

(6). When money is worth 6 per cent. at what price should stock be sold realizing 5 per cent.?

(*b*)—*Written.* (1). For what sum can £1,240 be purchased in the 3 per Cents., at 88⅜?

(2). When funds are at 92¼, how much stock can be bought for £1,675?

(3). What sum will be lost by buying £1,250 stock at 91¼, and selling at 90⅞?

(4). If I lay out £4,000 in the purchase of 3 per Cents. at 87⅛, what annual income shall I derive from the investment?

(5). What should be the half-yearly dividend on an investment of £1,000 in the 3½ per Cents. at 96?

(6). What sum would be realized by selling out £3,726 at 87⅜?

(7). If the actual interest of money be 4½ per cent., at what price should the 3½ per Cents. be quoted?

(8). What must be the market value of the 3 per Cents., in order that after deducting the income-tax of 1s. 4d. in the pound, they may yield 4 per cent. interest?

(9). What rate of interest arises from money invested in stock bearing interest at 7 per cent.; at £172 10s.?

(10). What is the difference of income resulting from a transfer of £3,000 in the 3½ per Cents. at 93, to the 3 per Cents. at 85?

(11). In which stock is it more advantageous to invest; in the 3¼ per Cents. at 91⅜, or in the 3½ per Cents. at 93⅝?

(12). What sum do I gain if I invest £625 in the 3 per Cents. at 91⅜ and sell out at 93¼?

(13). When the 3 per Cents. are at 91¾, what amount of stock can I buy for £1,725, and what is the actual interest per cent. which I receive for my investment?

(14). In 1752 the 3 per Cents. were quoted at £106 7s. 6d., and in 1797 at £47 12s. 6d., calculate the difference in the current rate of interest at these periods.

(15). If I transfer £750 stock in the 3 per Cents. at 81⅞ into the 4 per Cents. at 92⅜, how much of the latter stock can I buy?

(16). If I buy 17 railway shares at 47⅛ per £50 share, and 25 shares at 101¼ per £100 share, paying ⅛ per cent. brokerage on the nominal value, how much does the transaction cost me?

(17). When the 3 per Cents. are at 81⅛, and the 3½ at 95¼, for what sum can I purchase £1,725 in each stock.

PER CENTAGE.

204. **BROKERAGE.**—*Example.—A stockbroker charges* $\frac{1}{8}$ *per cent. commission on all the transfers he makes; what will he gain by selling* £750 *stock?*

Explanation.—By $\frac{1}{8}$ per cent. is meant one-eighth of £1, or 2s. 6d. for every £100 sold. The question is therefore one in proportion; "If 2s. 6d. be charged for every £100, what is charged on £750?" The statement is,

£100 : £750 :: 2·5s. : ( )

$$\frac{750 \times 2{\cdot}5}{100} = 18{\cdot}75\text{s.} = 18\text{s. } 9\text{d.}$$

205. **GAIN PER CENT.**—*Example.—A person invests* £2,350, *and finds that in a year it has increased to* £2,455 15s.; *what has he gained per cent.?*

Explanation. — The sum which has been gained is £2,455 15s. – £2,350, or £105 15s.; therefore the question stated as a sum in proportion is:—"If £105 15s. be the interest accruing on £2,350, what is the interest on £100?"

£2350 : £100 :: £105·75 : ( )

$$\frac{100 \times 105{\cdot}75}{2350} = 4{\cdot}5 = £4\ 10\text{s. per cent.}$$

206. **INSURANCE.**—*Example.—If a tradesman insures his goods at* 17s. 9d. *per cent., what annual premium does he pay on* £3,000?

Explanation.—By "premium" is here meant the annual sum paid as security from loss by fire. If this be at the rate of 17s. 9d. per cent., the sum will take this form:—

£100 : £3000 :: 17·75s. : ( )

$$\frac{3000 \times 17{\cdot}75\text{s.}}{100} = 17{\cdot}75\text{s.} \times 30 = £26\ 12\text{s. } 6\text{d.}$$

207. **STATISTICS.**—*Example.—In the year* 1856, *when the population of England was about* 19,500,000, 635,043 *children were born and* 425,703 *deaths were recorded; what was the rate of increase in the population?*

Explanation.—We have here first to find the total increase within the year; this is 635,043 — 425,703, or 209,340.

The question now is, "If 209,340 is the increase on 19,500,000, what is the increase per cent.?" This must be stated thus:— 19500000 : 100 :: 209340 : ( )

$$\frac{209340 \times 100}{19500000} = 1{\cdot}0735 \text{ per cent.}$$

208. Statistical returns, and tables relating to population, employments, education, and many other subjects, are usually calculated at per cent. All questions of this kind can easily be reduced into the form of Proportion sums, and the answer is generally best expressed in decimals.

Exercise L.

(*a*)—*Oral.* (1). In a school of 400 boys, 20 per cent. only can work decimal fractions, how many are unable to work that rule?

(2). An income-tax collector receives 1 per cent. for his trouble, what will he have for collecting £750?

(3). What is the commission, at 5 per cent., on £178? on £235 10s.? on £2 5s.?

(4). If I buy for 4d. and sell for 8d., what do I gain per cent.?

(5). If I buy a thing for a shilling and sell it for 9d., what do I lose per cent.?

(6). A school increases from 80 to 90 scholars in a year, what is the rate of increase per cent.?

(7). At thirty shillings per cent. what will it cost to insure property worth £1,250?

(8). If the population of a town was 12,000 in 1841, and it increased six per cent. in the next ten years, what did it amount to in 1851?

(9). What sum of money is 50 per cent. greater than £95?

(10). How much will a traveller, whose commission is 4 per cent. on his orders, receive for obtaining three orders of £40, £50, and £60?

(11). If a collector, who is paid 5 per cent. commission, receives £17 10s. for his trouble, how much has he collected?

(12). If a merchant lose 20 per cent. on an investment of £1,350, what is the sum he obtains for his outlay?

(*b*)—*Written.* (1). What is the commission, at ½ per cent., on £375?

(2). Find 1¼ per cent. on £753; and 2⅝ per cent. on £374 5s.

(3). A successful speculator, who invests £235, makes a profit of 75 per cent.; what sum does he receive?

(4). If goods cost £12 17s. 6d., at what price must they be sold to gain 12½ per cent.?

(5). Of 1,250 soldiers 26 per cent. are in hospital, 32 per cent. in the trenches, and the rest in camp; how many remain in camp?

(6). If linen cost 2s. 10½d. per yd., at what price must it be sold to gain 15 per cent.?

(7). Add together 65 per cent. on 60, and 78 per cent. on 70.

(8). Suppose £13 6s. 8d. be spent in the purchase of apples at 3s. 4d. per bushel, and one-fourth of them be wholly damaged and wasted, and the rest sold at 50 per cent. profit, what is gained on the whole?

(9). If eggs be sold at 5 for threepence, at what price must they be sold to gain 20 per cent.?

(10). If an article sold at £7 1s. gives the seller a profit of 13 per cent., what did he give for it?

(11). The weekly receipts of a railway company are £4,800 15s. 6d., the working expenses are £15,303 7s. 2d. per calendar month; what dividend per cent. can the company pay?

(12). If 10 per cent. be gained by selling tea at 5s. 6d., what lost or gained by selling it at 4s. 10d.?

MISCELLANEOUS QUESTIONS.—LI.

(*a*)—*Oral*. (1). Nine times the fifth part of twenty?

(2). How many fourths are there in 26? How many thirds in 17

(3). What is the difference between $\frac{5}{7}$ of 21 and $\frac{4}{7}$ of 35?

(4). Out of a crown piece what change shall I have after payin for 3 yds. of ribbon at $7\frac{3}{4}$d., and 2 pairs of gloves at 1s. 6d. each?

(5). By selling an article for a shilling I gain 50 per cent.; wha did I give for it?

(6). Add together the fourth of 48, the fifth of 90, and the sixt of 96?

(7). What is $\frac{1}{2}$ per cent. on £150? Find $\frac{3}{8}$ per cent. of £700.

(8). What is the price of an ounce at 2s. per pound? at 5s.? at 6s.

(9). What are three weeks' wages at 18 shillings per month?

(10). If I buy an article for 6d., and gain 150 per cent. profi for what must I sell it?

(11). Add 5 per cent. profit to £200; 6 per cent. to £150 8 per cent to £725.

(12). At 7s. per day what will be the wages of a workman fc 3 weeks 4 days?

(13). Seven pounds of sugar at $4\frac{1}{2}$d.? nine pounds at $7\frac{3}{4}$d.?

(14). If I take five steps in three seconds, how many steps shall take in an hour and a half?

(15). If a cabinet maker can make 36 workboxes in 5 days, i what time will he make 198?

(16). Add the product of $18\frac{1}{8}$ and 5 to the sum of $2\frac{1}{3}$ and 8.

(17). Find the continued product of 3, 4, 5, and 6, and also thei least common multiple.

(18). What is the greatest common measure of 240, 100, 50, and 95

(19). What must be given for 3 ounces at 8s. per pound?

(20). A school which commenced with 100 boys increased durin two years at the rate of 10 per cent. per annum, what was th number of pupils at the end of the second year?

(21). Take 25 per cent discount off the following sums—17s. 6d £1 5s., £2 9s.

(22). What is the second term in the proportion 8 : ( ) :: 17 : 51

(23). At 5 for 2d., what is the price of 100 oranges? of 250?

(24). Find $\frac{2}{3}$ of $\frac{4}{7}$ of 49? $\frac{1}{8}$ of $\frac{3}{4}$ of 64?

(25). Find the difference between $\frac{3}{4}$ of a florin and $\frac{5}{8}$ of half-a crown.

(26). At what rate per cent. simple interest will a sum of mone double itself in 40 years?

(27). What is the price of half a pint of wine at £1 1s. 4d. pe gallon?

(28). What fraction of 17s. 6d. is 3s. 8d.? What fraction of gallon is $1\frac{1}{2}$ pints?

(29). Express as decimals of £1, the price of 3 articles at 7s. 6d each; of 5 at 19s. each; of $7\frac{1}{2}$ lbs. at 1s. 6d. per lb.; of $\frac{1}{5}$ of 16s. 3d

(30). What are $\frac{15}{7}$ of 21? $2\frac{1}{8}$ of 30? $5\frac{4}{5}$ of 72? $\frac{24}{25}$ of £1.

(31). A weaver can make $\frac{3}{7}$ of a yard of velvet in a day, in how many days can he make 42 yards?

(32). Find a number which is as many times greater than 6 as 19 is greater than 12.

(33). If a collector who is paid 10 per cent. receives £7 10s. for his trouble, what has he collected?

(34). After spending a fifth of the money in my purse, I have £1 8s. left, how much had I at first?

(35). What sum of money is that of which, when $\frac{3}{7}$ are spent, £24 remain?

(36). If a tradesman incurs a debt of £100, and pays $\frac{1}{4}$ of it at once, being allowed 10 per cent. discount; one-half in 6 months, for which he is allowed 5 per cent. discount; and the rest in 12 months, for which no allowance is made; what sum does he pay altogether?

(*b*)—***Written.*** (1). What is the difference between $1+1+\frac{1}{2}+\frac{1}{6}+\frac{1}{24}$ and $\frac{15}{7}+\frac{2}{5}$.

(2). Find the cost of $674\frac{1}{2}$ dozen of hose at the rate of 2s. $9\frac{3}{4}$d. for 5 pairs.

(3). If $14\frac{1}{4}$ cwt. can be carried 100 miles for 36s., how many lbs. may be carried 36 miles for the same money?

(4). If 12 oxen plough 8 a. 2 r. 4 p. in 7 days, in what time will 50 oxen plough 240 acres?

(5). What is the difference between the interest on £654 10s. for 1 year 3 months at 4 per cent., and the true discount on the same sum for the same time?

(6). The weight of a cubic inch of water is 253·17 grains, that of a cubic inch of air ·310,017 grains; what volume of air is equal in weight to a cubic inch of water?

(7). A tradesman purchases 19 lbs. of butter at 1s. 3d. per lb., and 39 lbs. of tea at 4s. 8d. per lb.; he pays £2 10s. in cash, and the rest in cloth at 6s. 9d. per yard; how much cloth is given?

(8). What is the cost of caulking the deck of a vessel containing 1,120 sq. ft., at 5s. $11\frac{1}{2}$d. per sq. yard?

(9). What is the cost of milling 10 pieces of cloth, each 72 yds. long and $\frac{3}{4}$ broad, at 2s. 5d. per length of 10 yards?

(10). How many times is an angle of 57·29578 degrees contained in an angle of 180 degrees?

(11). The mean sidereal year of the earth is 365·2563612 days, and that of Saturn 10759·2198174 days; find the number of years in the year of Saturn.

(12). A grocer mixes 20 lbs. of tea at 6s., 40 lbs. at 5s. 6d., and 19 lbs. at 4s. together, and sells the whole at 6s. per lb.; what does he gain per cent.?

(13). A ship sails with a supply of biscuit for 60 days, at a daily allowance of 1 lb. per man; after being at sea 20 days, 5 men are washed overboard, and damage sustained which will cause a delay of 24 days, and it is then found that each man's share must be reduced to $\frac{5}{7}$ lb.; find the original number of the crew.

(14). Find the greatest common measure of 126, 217, and 175; and also the least common multiple of 162, 108, 81, and 54.

(15). What number, multiplied by $\frac{5}{9}$ of $\frac{3}{7}$ of $3\frac{1}{15}$, will produce $2\frac{1}{4}$?

(16). Find the value of $\frac{(2\frac{1}{4} - \frac{2}{3}) \times 1\frac{5}{6}}{\frac{1}{5} \times (3\frac{1}{3} + \frac{13}{36})}$?

(17). Find the product of $\frac{156933}{19557}$ and $(\frac{314175}{100000} \div \frac{31860}{100100})$ both as a vulgar fraction and as a decimal?

(18). If a room be 26 ft. 4 in. long, 12 ft. 7 in. wide, and 13 ft. 6 in. high, what will be the cost of papering it with paper 4 ft. wide, at 6d. per yd.—allowing 1d. per sq. yd. for labour, and deducting for a door 7 ft. 6 in. by 5 ft., and 2 windows 10 ft. 3 in. by 6 ft. 4 in.?

(19). A father devised $\frac{7}{18}$ of his estate to his elder son, and $\frac{7}{18}$ of the remainder to the younger, and the surplus to the widow; the shares of the two sons differed by £524 6s. 8d., what was the widow's share?

(20). A grocer buys 567 cwt. of sugar at £1 19s. $10\frac{1}{4}$d., per cwt., and mixes it with 1,161 cwt. at £2 2s. $6\frac{1}{2}$d.; at what price should he sell the mixture to realize a profit of 12 per cent.?

(21). What is the difference between the present value of £750, due 9 months hence, at 5 per cent. per annum, and that of £720, due 2 months hence, at 3 per cent. per annum?

(22). A merchant sells goods of the value of £420 for £406 5s. 9d. ready money, how long does he allow credit, the discount for present payment being $2\frac{1}{2}$ per cent.?

(23). A debt of £450 is to be discharged by three payments; £150 immediately, £100 192 days hence, and the remainder 9 months hence; what is the present value of the whole debt at 5 per cent. per annum?

(24). What must be paid for 5 casks of sugar, the gross weight of each being 4 cwt. 19 lbs., the weight of the empty casks being 19·23 lbs. each, the value of the sugar $4\frac{1}{2}$d. per lb., and the charge for carriage being at the rate of £3 17s. 6d. for 8 casks of similar size?

(25). How many times does the clock strike in 4 years?

(26). If $\frac{5}{7}$ of a cwt. cost $\frac{3}{19}$ of £100, what will be the cost of $\frac{2}{3}$ of 1 qr.?

(27). Three farmers hold a farm in common; one pays £97, another £79, and the third £100, as their shares of the rent; a rate of £34 is levied on the farm, what is each man's portion?

(28). It costs a tradesman £5 5s. to insure his goods at 15s. per cent., for what sum is he insured?

(29). Express decimally the difference between 4·692307 and $5\frac{9}{13}$.

(30). In 9 days 25 men can unload a ship; but at the end of 5 days 6 of the men are removed, and replaced by 5 boys. In what time will the work be finished, supposing the work of a boy be computed at $\frac{2}{3}$ of that of a man?

(31). If A can finish a work in 20 days, and B in 30 days, in what time will the work be finished by both together?

(32). Find the present value of a debt of £643 8 fl. 7 c. 5 m., due months hence, at six per cent. per annum.

(33). A young man received £$66\frac{2}{3}$, which was $\frac{3}{5}$ of $\frac{1}{2}$ of his elder brother's share, and $3\frac{1}{2}$ of that portion was $1\frac{1}{4}$ times the father's estate; what was the father's estate?

(34). If at a certain bridge two-horse vehicles are charged 4d., one-horse carriages, 2d., and passengers, $\frac{1}{2}$d.—and if in one day for every 5 two-horse carriages there were 9 with one horse, and ten foot passengers—how many of each passed over, supposing the day's receipts amounted to £94 15s. 10d.?

(35). A ship worth £25,000, and insured for £16,250, is lost; if $\frac{1}{6}$ of the ship belonged to A, $\frac{1}{5}$ to B, and the rest to C, what is C's share of the loss?

(36). Suppose English money were computed in francs or ten-penny pieces, how would the following sums be expressed; £97 10s., £283 13s. 4d., £1 17s. 9d.?

(37). The population of the town of Banbury rose in 7 years from 8,220 to 9,800, what was the rate of increase per cent. per annum?

(38). If $\frac{3}{5}$ of a yard cost £$\frac{7}{12}$, what will $\frac{9}{15}$ of an English ell cost?

(39). How much tea at 6s. 6d. per pound should be given in exchange for 1 cwt. 2 qrs. of coffee, worth 1s. 9d. per lb.?

(40). What will it cost to purchase £723 in the 3 per Cents. at $87\frac{3}{8}$ per cent., commission being $\frac{1}{8}$ per cent.?

(41). If a salesman disposes of woollen goods to the amount of £1,250, cotton goods to the amount of £587 10s., and miscellaneous articles to the value of £1,123 15s., what will be his commission on the whole at $1\frac{3}{8}$ per cent.?

(42). What sum is that which, after being put to interest for 4 years 3 months at $2\frac{1}{2}$ per cent., amounts to £725?

(43). An American dollar weighs 412·5 grains, of which $\frac{1}{10}$ is alloy; suppose pure silver to be worth 5s. 1·375d. per troy ounce, what should be the value of 75 dollars in English money?

(44). A person insures his life for £4,500 at £3 7s. 9d. per cent., what is the annual premium which he pays?

(45). If a ship be worth £11,230, and the premium for insuring her be £9 10s. per cent., for what sum should she be insured so that the policy shall cover both cargo and premium?

(46). If 7 needlewomen can finish a certain quantity of work in $10\frac{5}{8}$ days of $9\frac{3}{5}$ hours each, how long would it take 3 to do twice the same work, reckoning 10 hours to the day?

(47). An English sovereign is worth 25·22 French francs; express £23 2s. 6d. in French money, and 1728·35 francs in English money?

(48). What is the weight of a gallon of water, containing 277·274 cubic inches, when a cubic foot of water weighs 1,000 oz. avoirdupois?

(49). If a boy can do as much in 8 days as a man can in 3 days, how long will a man be doing what a boy can in 2 days?

(50). What is the difference between 4 square feet and 4 feet square?

(51). If three persons own a ship, and the share of the first is $\frac{5}{7}$ of the whole, that of the second $\frac{5}{10}$, and that of the third £$535\frac{5}{7}$, what is the worth of the ship?

(52). Three men start walking round a field $2\frac{1}{4}$ miles in circumference, at the rates of $4\frac{1}{2}$, 5, and 3 miles an hour respectively; in what time will they all arrive together at the starting place?

(53). In a school open 11 times a week, 145 are present 3 times, 152 twice, 150 four times, and 147 twice; what is the average attendance?

(54). Express the ratio between the sum and difference of $\frac{1}{13}$ and $\frac{5}{8}$ in its lowest integral terms.

(55). A carpet manufacturer buys wool at $5\frac{3}{4}$d. per lb.; if $4\frac{3}{4}$ lbs. are required for 1 yard of carpet, and he has to pay for weaving and other materials $10\frac{1}{2}$d. per yard, required the gain or loss by selling 27 pieces, each containing $114\frac{1}{2}$ yds. at 3s. 3d. per yard?

(56). If a leather merchant exchanges 17 English hides, each weighing 19 lbs. 8 oz., at 2s. $1\frac{1}{2}$d. per lb., for 13 foreign hides, each 29 lbs. 4 oz., at 1s. 7d. per lb., will he receive or pay money, and how much?

(57). How many square feet are there in a sheet of paper, $1\frac{1}{2}$ feet and $\frac{1}{8}$ of an inch long, and $\frac{3}{4}$ of a foot and $\frac{3}{8}$ of an inch wide?

(58). If I buy goods for £950, and sell $\frac{1}{3}$ of them so as to gain 8 per cent., for how much must I sell the remainder so as to gain 15 per cent. on the whole?

(59). A man travels 640 miles in 12 days of 16 hours duration, in how many days of 12 hours duration will he travel 720 miles?

(60). A, B, and C advance £7,140 for business in the proportions of 6, 5, and 4 respectively; they gain £436 5s., what is the amount of capital and gain in each case?

(61). If iron paling costs 3s. 7d. per yard, what will be the expense of enclosing a garden 123 yds. 2 ft. long by 123 feet broad?

(62). A bankrupt failed for £8,790; he paid three dividends, of 2 florins 4 cents, of 1 florin 5 cents 6 mils, and of 2 florins 3 cents. 9 mils respectively; how much did his creditors lose in all?

(63). A person invests £4,800 in the 4 per Cents. at 80, and at the end of each half-year invests the dividend which he receives in the same stock, and at the same price; what will he receive as dividend at the end of the third half-year?

(64). What sum put out to interest on the 1st of February at 11 per cent. would amount to £2,000 on the 30th of October in the same year?

(65). The United States dollar is reckoned in exchange as worth 4s. 6d., and is divided into 100 parts called cents; express £174 15s. in American money; and 1,936 dollars 27 cents in English money.

(66). A Prussian thaler is divided into 30 silver groschen, and is worth about 3s. English; express £278 15s. 6d. in thalers and groschen, and 3,396 th. 25 s. g. in English money.

ANSWERS TO EXERCISES.

I. (*b*)—(1) Twenty-seven; fifteen; three hundred and seventy (2) Three thousand one hundred and eighty-five; fifty; six hundred and seventeen. (3) Four thousand and seventy-three; two hundred and nineteen; five hundred and four. (4) One thousand seven hundred and twenty-eight; three hundred and twelve; five thousand one hundred and seventy-two. (5) Ten; thirty-nine; eight hundred and twenty-one. (6) Seventy-one; four hundred and thirteen; five hundred and eighty-six. (7) One hundred and eleven; three thousand and twenty-seven; five hundred and fifteen. (8) Three hundred and twenty; one thousand one hundred; two thousand one hundred and seventy-one. (9) One thousand and seventeen; two thousand one hundred; eleven thousand and one. (10) Six thousand and five; one thousand three hundred and seven; sixteen thousand. (11) Five thousand and twenty-eight; seven hundred and thirteen thousand nine hundrdd and one; thirty-eight thousand seven hundred and five. (12) Five millions seven hunhundred and three; twenty millions nine hundred and thirty-eight thousand four hundred and fifteen. (13) Sixty-three millions two hundred and eight thousand seven hundred and fifty-three; four thousand and ninety-eight millions three hundred and eighty-two thousand and seventy-five. (14) Twenty millions seven hundred and forty thousand and three; five hundred millions sixty-eight thousand three hundred and seventy. (15) Seven millions two hundred and nine thousand eight hundred and sixty-five; four hundred and ten millions three hundred and twenty thousand and seventy-eight.

II. (*b*)—(1) 213; 706; 92. (2) 180; 701; 1,119. (3) 3,400; 906; 508. (4) 7,014; 990; 5800. (5) 6,374; 2,511; 78,324. (6) 4,000,780; 5,000,007; 644,358; 80,000,005. (7) 84,301; 933,000; 47,006,300. (8) 920,608,000; 438,345; 11,011. (9) 24,000,314; 79,201; 60,004. (10) 87,003,020; 24,000,709; 80,006.

III. (*a*)—(1) 21; 34. (2) 275; £28; £45. (3) 45; 31. (4) 38; 30. (5) 33; 51; 83. (6) 45; 65. (7) 66. (8) 71; 152. (9) 34; 31; 54. (10) 51; 48; 64. (11) 7th, 14th, 21st, and 28th.

(*b*)—(1) 2,057. (2) 22,491. (3) 68,364. (4) 90,176. (5) 253,926. (6) 60. (7) 1,639. (8) 51. (9) 117. (10) 449. (11) 658,838. (12) 130,404. (13) 739,524. (14) 84,760. (15) 77,452. (16) 180,912. (17) 1,190,826. (18) 1890,720. (19) 1,861,195. (20) 704,984. (21) 404. (22) 7,206. (23) 385,309. (24) 7,651. (25) 97,208. (26) 9,326. (27) 14,515. (28) 18,421. (29) 24,595. (30) 42,615. (31) 1,296. (32) 90. (33) 654. (34) 955. (35) 2,641. (36) 65,025,813. (37) 958. (38) 325. (39) 902. (40) 179. (41) 1,121. (42) 61,675. (43) 1,237. (44) 155. (45) 1,901. (46) 62,956. (47) 100,590. (48) 6,762,320.

(49) 39,249,605. (50) 1066; 1087; 1100; 1135; 1154; 1189; 1199; 1216; 1272; 1307; 1327; 1377. (51) 3,460,293.

IV. (*a*)—(1) 8; 8. (2) 29; 9. (3) 8; 14. (4) 13; 18. (5) 19. (6) 27. (7) 56; 55. (8) 57. (9) 24. (10) 82. (11) 9; 34; 25. (12) 23; 24; 72. (13) 49; 65; 6. (14) 21; 30. (15) 4382; 3. (16) 3; 16, 7; 2. (17) 19; 63; 28; 86.

(*b*)—(1) 91. (2) 189. (3) 666. (4) 2,872; 2,028. (5) 962,389. (6) 92,636. (7) 12,558. (8) 131,175. (9) 121,690. (10) 36,657. (11) 4,775. (12) 330,848. (13) 279,849. (14) 4,578. (15) 2,032. (16) 5,987; 297,027; 428. (17) 2,539,371; 376,774; 1,379. (18) 2,602,542; 270,164. (19) 484; 33. (20) 2,392; 129. (21) 5,569. (22) 139,012. (23) 14,208. (24) 473. (25) 117. (26) 246,382. (27) 83. (28) 397,592. (29) 843,659. (30) 3,160,702. (31) 4,077. (32) 209,340. (33) 31,957,000; 26,296,900. (34) 66. (35) 586. (36) 4,508. (37) 1603; 1,625. (38) 171. (39) 714. (40) 1080; 486. (41) 136. (42) 11. (43) 501. (44) 11,538,175,158. (45) 61. (46) 5,695. (47) 48,625.

V. (*a*)—(1) 78; 120. (2) 96; 144. (3) 60; 240. (4) 126; 112; 153. (5) 72; 144. (6) 120; 224 (7) 168; 172; 520. (8) 480. (9) 324. (10) 7,416. (11) 3,888. (12) 405; 1,024. (13) 362,880. (14) 182. (15) 384. (16) 115; 183; 231. (17) 102; 264. (18) 174; 369; 4,338. (19) 420; 287; 630. (20) 2,096; 1,386; 3,487.

(*b*)—(1) 1,171. (2) 720. (3) 2,189,538. (4) 22,918,432. (5) 8,651,490. (6) 2383446. (7) 1,250,790. (8) 2,246,909. (9) 1297160. (10) 24,715,881. (11) 406,144. (12) 2,167,396. (13) 4,342,188. (14) 4,561,488. (15) 286,840. (16) 3,956,496. (17) 197,382. (18) 169,440. (19) 410,520. (20) 24,660. (21) 16,236. (22) 27,432. (23) 3,096. (24) 17,100. (25) 25,184 (26) 12,330; 1,652. (27) 882. (28) 424. (29) 608. (30) 439. (31) 35,532. (32) 2,016. (33) £9,264. (34) 543.

VI. (*a*)—(1) 143. (2) 336; 432. (3) 1,200. (4) 325; 1,008. (5) 255; 644. (6) 940; 1,220; 1,780. (7) 840; 3,440. (8) 588. (9) 9.000. (10) 1,750; 408. (11) 30; 252; 672. (12) 816; 24,000; 810.

(*b*)—(1) 53,334. (2) 1,375,974. (3) 2,365,588. (4) 76,123,472. (5) 30,681,698. (6) 15,332,328. (7) 12,842,424. (8) 761,150,070. (9) 25,721,332. (10) 128,797,614. (11) 11,463,764. (12) 69,217,285. (13) 38,277. (14) 564. (15) 851,620; 2,464,484. (16) 172. (17) 1,601,613. (18) 20,655. (19) 504. (20) 7,579. (21) 973,930. (22) 46,584,180. (23) 146,052,688. (24) 169,559,520. (25) 1,703,520. (26) 51,300. *(27) 1,511,100.* (28) 670,032. (29) 4,948,208. (30) 436,414.

(31) 80,042. (32) 144,025,596. (33) 137,922,520. (34) 110,103,616. (35) 5,562,981. (36) 697,618,368. (37) 99,991. (38) 20. (39) 8,160. (40) £387,731. (41) 8,496. (42) 504. (43) 1,227. (44) 92,928. (45) 87,808. (46) 2,686. (47) 2,943. (48) 6,375. (49) 13,870. (50) 668,224. (51) 24,840. (52) 230,480.

VII. (*a*)—(1) 6. (2) 12. (3) $8\frac{4}{13}$. (4) 17. (5) $7\frac{4}{7}$; $6\frac{8}{13}$. (6) 1. (7) 8. (8) 20; 24; 30; 10. (9) 35; 21; 15. (10) 60. (11) 81; 54; $40\frac{1}{2}$. (12) 5; 9; 9. (13) 91; 53; 96. (14) 103; 32; 35. (15) 30; 24; 25. (16) 4.

(*b*)—(1) $142\frac{6}{7}$. (2) £3. (3) 7,988. (4) $4,578\frac{1}{7}$. (5) $26,358\frac{5}{8}$. (6) $2,227\frac{4}{9}$. (7) 5,464. (8) $6,666\frac{2}{3}$. (9) $24,135\frac{1}{4}$. (10) $158,813\frac{3}{4}$. (11) $4,677\frac{4}{7}$. (12) $314,093\frac{4}{7}$. (13) $5,980\frac{5}{9}$. (14) $7219\frac{1}{5}$. (15) $27,106\frac{3}{8}$. (16) 24. (17) 3,056. (18) 113. (19) 168. (20) 3,168. (21) 327. (22) 2,288. (23) $2,766\frac{2}{9}$. (24) £387. (25) $78\frac{13}{30}$. (26) $23\frac{3}{8}$. (27) 1,452. (28) $447\frac{11}{12}$. (29) 338. (30) $142\frac{2}{9}$. (31) 519,481.

VIII. (*a*)—(1) 2; 6. (2) 4. (3) 25. (4) 6. (5) 15; 12; 16; 30; 73. (6) 12. (7) 20. (8) 89,00. (9) 17. (10) $31\frac{3}{8}$. (11) 20; 40. (12) 50; 40. (13) 135; 620. (14) 6. (15) 90. (16) 24; 18; 9; 6. (17) 200,000.

(*b*)—(1) $38\frac{399}{780}$. (2) $16\frac{235}{327}$. (3) $1,739\frac{308}{315}$; $12,212\frac{19}{52}$. (4) $132\frac{23}{74}$. (5) $398\frac{20}{519}$. (6) 28. (7) £358. (8) $21\frac{93}{181}$. (9) 126. (10) $15,138\frac{10}{19}$. (11) $220,365\frac{20}{23}$. (12) $240,536\frac{37}{41}$. (13) $95,967\frac{40}{53}$. (14) $2,136\frac{26}{102}$; $2,084\frac{470}{521}$; $28,662\frac{97}{148}$. (15) $1,221\frac{19}{27}$; $812\frac{183}{503}$. (16) $11,855\frac{9}{816}$; $4,566\frac{40}{219}$. (17) $16,148\frac{143}{318}$; $16,559\frac{15}{429}$. (18) $2,800\frac{708}{782}$; $45,734\frac{10}{136}$. (19) $15\frac{11}{56}$; $29\frac{8}{193}$. (20) $403\frac{18}{25}$; $596\frac{9}{45}$. (21) 768. (22) 272. (23) $169\frac{23}{59}$. (24) 37.

IX. (*a*)—(1) 27. (2) 6; 3. (3) 18; 30; 42. (4) 30; 45; 10; 6; 5. (5) $22\frac{1}{4}$; 45; 72. (6) 12; 35. (7) 12; 54. (8) 36; 27. (9) 6. (10) 28; 36.

(*b*)—(1) $10\frac{10}{11}$. (2) $21,663\frac{5}{6}$; $21,493\frac{1}{2}$. (3) $29,594\frac{2}{3}$; 40,205. (4) $14,350\frac{1}{2}$; $1,126\frac{2}{7}$. (5) $961,171\frac{1}{5}$; $371,608\frac{2}{3}$. (6) 102; 5,560. 777,791. (7) 440 yds. (8) 30,000. (9) 15 days. (10) 226,409,304,186. (11) $11\frac{13}{38}$. (12) $9\frac{17}{42}$; $247\frac{9}{11}$. (13) $2,374\frac{23}{45}$. (14) 286; 9 yrs. $10\frac{136}{143}$ m. (15) 120; 191; $38\frac{1}{8}$. (16) $6\frac{1}{32}$. (17) A, 475; B, 210; C, 315. (18) 763. (19) 240; 140; 100. (20) $85\frac{793}{24272}$. (21) $957,561\frac{1}{2}$; (22) 8,460. (23) $8\frac{13}{14}$.

X. (*a*)—(1) 19; 26; 41. (2) 21; 51; 68; 148; 90. (3) 40. (4) 44; 57. (5) 40; 36; 90. (6) 90; 144. (7) 10,800; 4,500. (8) 960; 480; 80; 60. (9) 200. (10) 11; 82; 120. (11) 135; 252; 202; 308. (12) 164; 66; 175; 206. (13) 130; 173; 37; 151. (14) 14; 44; 88. (15) 24; 52; 192; 70. (16) 120; 330; 1,440; 947.

(*b*)—(1) 16,743; 43,522; 28,495; 102,460. (2) 12,000.

8,000; 2,840. (3) 7,164; 51,267; 11,826. (4) 1,120s., 3,360 fourpences, 14,440d. (5) 13,920; 8,928. (6) 3,390; 6,480. (7) 35,520; 3,000; 2,280. (8) 8,049; 70,634. (9) 1,104,444; 708. (10) 200,640; 7,260. (11) 4,856½; 6,336; 44,220. (12) 11,200; 17,472; 1,698. (13) 129,024; 3,109; 108,416. (14) 109,440; 2,472; 8,286. (15) 862; 12,960; 32,241. (16) 1,613. (17) 27,104; 529. (18) 23,255. (19) 4,000; 65,340; 22. (20) 224; 544; 560. (21) 279; 1,608. (22) 2,880; 5,478; 68,580. (23) 3,648; 1,220.

XI. (*a*)—(1) 2¼d., 3¼d., 5½d. (2) 6¾d., 8¾d., 1s. 3¾d. (3) 4¾d., 6¾d. (4) 1s. 3¾d.; 1s. 10d.; £1 5s. (5) 3s. 4d.; 4s. 5d.; 6s. 4d. (6) 2s. 2d.; 3s. 4d.; 7s. 10d. (7) 4s. 3d.; 3s. 9d. (8) £1 19s. £2 18s.; £10 9s. (9) £2 14s. (10) £3 4s.; £8 8s.; £8 2s. (11) 9s. 7d.; 2s. 5¼d.; £3 10s. (12) 5s. 8d.; 17s. 6d. (13) 25s.; £8 12s. 6d. (14) 6 lbs. 4 oz.; 1 cwt. 0 qr. 20 lbs. (15) 2 hr. 5 min.; 3 wks. 2 days; 2 days, 5 hrs.; 3 yrs. 11 m. (16) 1 yd. 0 ft. 3 in.; 28 yds.; 2 m. 1 fur.; 1 yd. 4 in; 9 yds. 2 ft.

(*b*)—(1) £58 16s.; £87 8s. 2d. (2) 10s. 5d.; £13 10s. 8d. £112 9s. 2½d. (3) £775 19s. 6d.; £254 16s.; £86 1s. 6½d. (4) £150 4s. 6d.; £6 7s.; £426 15s. 9½d. (5) £90 6s. 7d. £413 14s.; £2,708. (6) £1,207 5s. 4d.; £1,030 14s. (7) £2 10s.; £78 2s. 6d.; £259 2s. 5d. (8) 6 + 7s. 2d.; 26 + £3 3s. 9d.; 4 + £1 14s. 1d. (9) £187 5 fl. 6 c. 3 m.; £127 9 fl. 6 c.; £17 5 fl. (10) 72 fl. 8 c. 6 m.; 217 fl. 8 c. (11) 18 m. 2 f. 28 p. 4 yds.; 271 m. 3 f. 32 p. 3 yds. 1 ft. 10 in. (12) 44 f.; 106 f. 28 p. 4 yds.; 281 f. 10 p. 3 yds. (13) 781 a. 1 r.; 18,246 a.; 67 a. 1 r. 36 p. 5 yds. (14) 1 r. 23 p. 23¼ yds. 0 ft. 16 in.; 17 r. 1 p. 25¾ yds. (15) 558 cwt. 0 qr. 4 lb.; 35 cwt. 1 qr. 24 lbs.; 6 cwt. 3 qr. 25 lbs. 4 oz. (16) 517 tons 19 cwt. 1 qr. 10 lbs. 11 oz.; 9 tons 15 cwt. 0 qr. 7 lbs.; 6,250 tons. (17) 19 st. 10 lbs.; 1,427 st. 7 lbs. 8 oz.; 1,790 st. 8 lbs. (18) 1 lb. 11 oz. 9 dwts. 7 grs.; 2 lbs. 1 oz. 18 dwts.; 17 lbs. 3 oz. (19) 109 cub. yds. 24 cub. ft.; 42 cub. ft. 287 cub. in. (20) 99 wks. 1 d. 10 hrs. 40 m.; 13,113 d. 16 hrs. (21) Dec. 10, 1784.

XII. (*a*)—(1) 2s. 6¼d. (2) 16s. 9d. (3) 5s. 8d. (4) 13 wks. 1 d. (5) 6s. 10d.; 1s. 5½d. (6) 3 yds. 1 ft. 5 in. (7) 3s. 7½d. (8) £1 14s. 9d. (9) 6s. 7d. (10) 1s. 8¼d.; 18s. 11d. (11) £2 5s. 10½d.; 2s. 5d.; 19s. 9½d. (12) £5 0s. 2d.; £19 15s. 8d.; £4 10s. 9d.

(*b*)—(1) £37 13s. 8¼d. (2) 175 17s. 5½d. (3) £164 19s. 5½d. (4) £192 14s. 0¾d. (5) £67 5s. 6d. (6) £56 12s. 7d. (7) £2 18s. 3d. (8) £6 16s. 3d. (9) £42 16s. 8½d. (10) £8 4s. 11¼d. (11) £8 10s. 9¾d. (12) £86 1s. 8¾d. (13) £184 8s. 11½d. (14) £3,799 5s. 1¾d (15) £1,370 16s. 10d. (16) £156 3s. 2½d. (17) £168 15s. 1¼d. (18) £9,586 16s. 2d. (19) £19 7 fl. 5 c. 3 m. (20) £37 1 fl. 1 c. 8 m. (21) £7 6 fl. 3 c. 6 m. (22) £20 6 fl. 2 c. 2 m. (23) £16 5 fl. 3 c. 1 m. *(24) £29 6s. 1¼d.* (25) 10 tons 14 cwt. 3 qrs. 20 lbs. (26) *5 tons 14 cwt. 1* qr. 4 lbs. 8 oz. (27) 9 cwt. 0 qr. 20 lbs. 9 oz.

(28) 8 lbs. 5 oz. 9 dwts. 6 grs. (29) 1 lb. 4 oz. 19 dwts. 1 gr.
(30) 9 m. 3 f. 12 p. 4½ yds. 2 ft. (31) 15 l. 3 f. 27 p. 3½ yds.
(32) 94 yds. 2 ft. 8 in. 2 b. c. (33) 35 a. 3 r. 19 p. (34)
46 a. 3 r. 4 p. (35) £83 3s. 8d. (36) 160 yds. 1 ft. 11 ins.
(37) £4 2s. 1d. (38) £20 7s. 2d. (39) 176 sq. yds. 8 sq. ft. 72 sq. in.
(40) 4 yds. 2 qrs. 2 nls. (41) £290 9s. 4½d. (42) £295 12s. 6d.
(43) 215 a. 1 r. 7 p. (44) 128 d. 17 h. 55 m. (45) 2,448 pints.

XIII. (*a*)—(1) 1s. 6d. (2) ¾d. (3) 5s. 1d. (4) 8¼d.,
4½d., 9¾d., 1¼d., 3½d., 2½d., 5½d. (5) 1s 1½d., 7½d., 1s. 4¼d.,
8¾d., 2d., 5¼d. (6) 1s. 10¼d., 9¼d., 4½d., 6¾d., 8½d., 2s. 4¾d.,
1s. 10½d., 1s. 2½d. (7) 8½d., 3s. 8¾d., 2s. 5½d. 4s. 0¾d., 4s. 3½d.,
1s. 4½d., 9¾d. (8) 2s. 8¾d., 1s. 5½d., 7s. 10¼d., 9s. 0½d., 6s. 4¼d.,
8s. 4½d., 5s. 6¼d. (9) 5s. 3d., 12s. 6d., 16s. 4d., 17s. 4¼d., 1s. 2½d.,
16s. 4¼d. (10) 15s. 8½d., 17s. 4¼d., 1s. 5¼d., 3s. 9d., 8s. 5d., 17s. 7½d.
(11) 6 inches. (12) 18 days. (13) 7¼d., 1s. 5¾d.
(14) 1s. 5¾d., 1s. 10¼d.

(*b*)—(1) £1 13s. 2d. (2) £1 18s. 5¼d. (3) £310 5s. 4½d.
(4) £514 7s. 2¾d. (5) £6,191 6s. 8½d. (6) £4,078 5s. 7¾d.
(7) £642 4s. 11d. (8) £3,063 10s. 10d. (9) £183 14s. 9d.;
£235 7s. 10d. (10) £68 10s. 9d.; £2,805 17s. 4d.
(11) £5,523 16s. 7d.; £2,073 7s. 8½d. (12) £1,417 2s. 8d.
(13) £2 6s. (14) £1 12s. 10d. (15) £4 13s. 9d.
(16) £6 1 fl. 4 c. 4 m.; £8 2 fl. 5 c. 4 m. (17) £11 1 fl. 4 c. 5 m.
£13 0 f. 6 c. 5 m. (18) 5 fl. 8 c. 3 m. (19) 10,591 farthings.
(20) £1,008 6s. 8d. (21) 5 lbs. 3 oz. 16 dwts. 6 grs.
(22) 2 lbs. 10 oz. 17 dwts. 6 grs. (23) 9 dwts., 18 grs.;
1 oz. 19 dwts. 12 grs. (24) 3 tons 1 cwt. 2 qrs. 10 lb.; 2 cwt. 0 qr. 1 lb.
(25) 4 cwt. 1 qr. 11 lbs.; 8 cwt. 8 lbs. (26) 9 lbs., 9 oz.;
80 lbs. 14 oz. 8 drs. (27) 4 m. 3 fur. 23 p.; 1 m. 6 fur. 12 p.;
21 m. 6 fur. 34 p. (28) 82 m. 1,477 yds.; 8 m. 5 fur. 34 p. 5 yds.;
9 f. 7 p. 2 yds. (29) 14 cwt. 2 qrs. 11 lb. (30) 1 ton 2 cwt. 2 qrs. 8 lb.
(31) 6 tons 13 cwt. 18 lbs. (32) 83 m. 7 fur. (33) 33 a. 2 r. 8 p.
(34) 6 a. 1 r. 18 p. (35) 129,024 in. (36) 34 qrs. 3 b. 2 pks. 1 gal.
(37) 2 gals. 1 pt.; 2 gals. 3 qts. 1 pt. (38) 6 qrs. 6 b. 1 gal.;
15 qrs. 1 pk. 1 qt.; 5 combs 1 gal. (39) 10½d. (40) 38 d. 7 hrs. 25 m.
(41) 916 lbs. 8 oz.; 937 lbs. 8 oz. (42) 5 m. 1,100 yds.
(43) £1 9s. 11½d.

XIV. (*a*)—(1) 1s. 1½d.; 2s. 7¼d. (2) 9s.; 19s. 3d.; 9s. 2d.;
£1 2s. 6d. (3) 13s. 11d. (4) 8s. 8d. (5) 1s. 4½d.; 2s. 9¼d.;
5s. 7½d.; 4s. (6) £2 2s.; £1 7s. 6d.; £1 9s. 2d.; £2 4s.
(7) 17s. 1d.; 8s. 6½d.; 6s. 3¼d. (8) 6s. 6d.; 12s. 9d.; 16s. 8d.
(9) 4s. 6¾d. (10) 2s.; 4s. 6d.; 7s. 3d.; 6s. 9d. (11) 8s.;
16s.; £1 18s.; £4 7s.; £3 18s.; 3s. 9d. (12) £1 10s.; £3 6s. 8d.;
£7; £2 10s.; £5. (13) 12s. 6d.; 2s. 4d.; 7s. 6d. (14) 3s. 1½d.; 5s. 5d.
(15) 5s. 4d.; 9s. 6d. (16) £1 3s. 9d.; £3 6s. (17) 13s. 3½d.;
13s. 8¼d.

(*b*)—(1) £46 10s. (2) £7 8s. 6d. (3) £139 16s. 8d.
(4) £131 17s. 10d. (5) £1,360 8s. 8¾d. (6) £628 0s. 8½d.

(7) £96 17s. 11d. (8) £1,016 1s. $10\frac{1}{2}$d. (9) £372,210 0s. 11d. (10) £3,945,536 11s. 6d. (11) 8,458 19s. $8\frac{1}{4}$d. (12) £111,940; £18,241 16s. 6d.; £235,061 8s. (13) 92,338 0s. 5d.; £60,376 14s. 2d. (14) £407,325 19s. 6d.; £802,731 7s. $3\frac{3}{4}$d. (15) £285,915; £607,365 2s. 6d.; £171,399 14s. 4d. (16) £1,132,057 4s. 10d.; £74,007 10s. $7\frac{1}{2}$d.; £166 14s. 6d. (17) £159,430 8s. 6d.; £13,991 12s. 6d.; £13,207 2s. 8d. (18) £165 9 fl. 7 c. 1 m.; £1,360 2 fl. 8 c. 2 m. (19) £3,284 6 fl. 5 c. 8 m. £1,653 8 c. 7 m.; £31 9 fl. 2 c. (20) £273 2 fl. 4 m.; £611 8 c. 8 m. (21) £826 3 fl.; £128,060. (22) £67 15s. (23) £11 15s.; £14 3s. 6d. (24) £10 2s. 6d.; £7 14s. 8d. (25) 6s. 8d.; 5s. 9d.; 16s. $2\frac{1}{4}$d. (26) 17s. $10\frac{1}{2}$d. (27) £7 17s. 3d. (28) £2 10s. $5\frac{1}{2}$d. (29) 46 lbs. 5 oz. 15 dwts. 6 grs.; 16 lbs. 11 oz. 3 dwts. (30) 17 lb. 5 oz. 17 dwts. 9 grs.; 576 lbs. 9 oz. 1 dwt. 16 grs. (31) 5 oz. 9 dwts. 16 grs.; 1 lb. 1 oz. 9 dwts. 5 grs. (32) 1 t. 1 cwt. 23 lb.; 2 t. 4 cwt. 1 qr. 23 lbs. (33) 4 tons 17 cwt. 3 qrs. 14 lb.; 186 tons 2 cwt. 1 qr. 18 lbs. (34) 346 lbs. 10 oz.; 46 lbs. 3 oz. 2 drs. (35) 17,867,520,000. (36) 94 m. 2 fur. (37) 4 fur. 24 p. 5 yds. (38) 4,239 m. 6 fur. 14 p. $2\frac{1}{4}$ yds. (39) 132 m. 7 fur. 14 p.; 525 m. 5 fur. 21 p. $\frac{1}{2}$ yd. (40) £145 12s. (41) 634 tons 15 cwt. 2 qrs. 4 lbs. 5 oz. (42) 43 yds. 2 qrs. 3 nls. (43) 4 tons 18 cwt. 15 lbs. 12 oz. (44) 145 qrs. 1 pk.; 1,831 qrs. 6 bush. 1 pk.; 66 qrs. 3 bush. 1 pk. (45) 1,336 m. 2 fur. 36 p. 2 yds.

XV. (*a*)—(1) $1\frac{1}{3}$d.; $1\frac{1}{3}$d.; $\frac{1}{3}$d. (2) $1\frac{1}{4}$d.; $4\frac{1}{4}$d.; $\frac{3}{4}$d. (3) 10d.; 6d.; 5d.; $7\frac{1}{2}$d.; $2\frac{1}{2}$d.; $3\frac{3}{4}$d. (4) 6d.; 4d.; 2d.; 3d.; $1\frac{1}{3}$d. (5) 6d.; 1s. 3d.; 10d.; 3d.; 5d. (6) 5s.; 3s. 4d.; 10d.; 1s. 8d.; 2s. 6d. (7) 6s. 8d.; 5s.; 4s.; 3s. 4d. (8) 2s. 6d.; 2s.; 1s. 8d.; 1s. 4d.; 1s. 3d. (9) 1s.; 10d.; 8d.; $7\frac{1}{2}$d.; 5d. (10) 8d.; 2s. 6d. (11) 9d. (12) 2s. 2d. (13) 8. (13) 48. (15) 8d.; 3s. 6d. (16) 1s. 6d.; $1\frac{1}{2}$d. (17) 4d.; 2s. 3d.; 4s. $7\frac{1}{2}$d. (18) 1s. $6\frac{1}{2}$d.; 10s. 10d.; £1 13s. 4d. (19) $8\frac{1}{7}$d.; 1s.; 7d. + $\frac{6}{7}$; 4s. 6d. (20) 1s. $11\frac{1}{3}$d.; 4s. $3\frac{3}{5}$d.; 2s.

(*b*)—(1) £25. (2) £1 3s. 6d. (3) 7s. 11d.; 15s. $5\frac{5}{7}$d. (4) £55 6s. $7\frac{3}{5}$d.; £14 0s. $10\frac{1}{2}$d. (5) £60 14s. $5\frac{3}{4}$d.; £58 16s. $5\frac{11}{17}$d.; £45 19s. $4\frac{1}{5}$d. (6) £22 4s. $4\frac{23}{35}$d.; £4 6s. $10\frac{11}{17}$d.; £18 1s. $6\frac{66}{83}$d. (7) £37 5s. $2\frac{6}{59}$d.; £6 17s. $10\frac{13}{23}$d. £140 7s. $7\frac{53}{78}$d. (8) £45 17s. $2\frac{21}{71}$d.; £6 14s. $9\frac{59}{117}$d.; £8 10s. $0\frac{60}{147}$d. (9) £12 8s. $2\frac{25}{49}$d.; £350 19s. $2\frac{1}{7}$d.; £6 4s. $9\frac{3}{11}$d. (10) £15 17s. $2\frac{15}{23}$d.; £70 17s. 4d.; £142 3s. $11\frac{3}{7}$d. (11) £4 18s $4\frac{661}{724}$d.; £17 3s. $7\frac{49}{93}$d. (12) £135 7s. $7\frac{65}{88}$d.; £46 2s. $5\frac{1}{4}$d. (13) 251 10s. $4\frac{11}{20}$d.; £2 19s. $0\frac{93}{111}$d.; £3 12s. $2\frac{1}{4}$d.; £83 19s. $2\frac{3}{4}$d. (14) £4 6 fl. 2 c. 6 m.; £3 4 fl. 1 c. 9 m. (15) £1 2 fl. 8 c. $0\frac{8}{27}$ m.; £0 3 fl. 5 c. 0 m. (16) £1 3 fl. 9 c. $6\frac{2}{3}$ m.; £1 3 fl. 8 c. $4\frac{3}{7}$ m.; £1 4 fl. 1 c. $0\frac{4}{9}$ m. (17) £1 1 fl. 6 c. $7\frac{110}{111}$ m.; £1 1 fl. 8 c. 4 m. *(18)* $6\frac{2}{11}$ m.; 5 fl. 6 c. $2\frac{5}{7}$ m.; 25 c. $1\frac{13}{17}$ m. (19) £1 2s. $1\frac{1}{4}$d. *(20)* £2 3s. 7d. (21) 267,517. (22) 12 yrs. (23) $561\frac{1}{7}$.

(24) 540. (25) 2 ft. 0$\frac{4}{7}$ in.; 3 yds. 0 ft. 11$\frac{3}{8}$ in. (26) 15 p. 4 yds. 1 ft. 1$\frac{1}{2}$ in.; 1 m. 4 p. 182 yds. 0 ft. 8 in. (27) 6 fur.; 5 fur. 158 yds. 8$\frac{5}{17}$ in. (28) 2 fur. 3 p.; 8 p.; 3 yds. 5$\frac{1}{7}$ in.; 21 yds. 2 ft. 2$\frac{14}{23}$ in. (29) 23,760. (30) 12,960 steps. (31) 1 ft. 2 in. (32) 3 r. 27$\frac{5}{6}$ p.; 2 a. 5$\frac{6}{7}$ p.; 1 a. 5$\frac{3}{8}$ p. (33) 1 a. 22$\frac{15}{16}$ p.; 3 a. 2 r. 23$\frac{6}{11}$ p.; 1 a. 1 r. 29$\frac{1}{3}$ p. (34) 1 r. 28$\frac{2}{3}$ p. (35) 8 a. 2 r. 34$\frac{4}{5}$ p. (36) 14 a. 1 r. 10$\frac{2}{5}$ p. (37) 1 oz. 15 dwts. 0$\frac{6}{7}$ grs.; 7 dwts. 14$\frac{1}{5}$ grs.; 6 dwts. 8 grs. (38) 7 oz. 13 dwts. 20$\frac{4}{13}$ grs.; 6 oz. 14 dwts. 13$\frac{1}{3}$ grs.; 1 oz. 8 dwts. 15 grs. (39) 15,621$\frac{9}{11}$. (40) 2 oz. 3 dwts. 8 grs. (41) 10 cwt. 3 qrs. 9 lbs. 5$\frac{2}{3}$ grs.; 1 cwt. 3 qrs. 3 lbs. 8 oz.; 14 lb. 1 oz. 9$\frac{3}{5}$ grs. (42) 1 lb. 5 oz. 5$\frac{5}{13}$ dwts.; 3 lbs. 8 oz. 7 drs.; 1 cwt. 15 lb. (43) 46$\frac{20}{31}$. (44) 4 lbs. 8 oz.; 1$\frac{1}{4}$ pts. (45) 3 bush. 2 pks.; 1 qr. 1 cmb. 2 pks. 1$\frac{11}{12}$ gals.; 3 qrs. 3$\frac{3}{7}$ pks. (46) 12 gals. 3 qts. 0$\frac{13}{18}$ pts.; 4 gals. 1$\frac{7}{8}$ pts.; 1 gal. 1 qt. 1$\frac{5}{18}$ pts. (47) ·5787 oz. (48) 3 a. 3 r. 11 p. (49) 8 m. 14 sec. (50) 20$\frac{400}{571}$. (51) 112$\frac{2}{5}$. (52) 237$\frac{464}{525}$.

XVI. (1) £1 14s. 5d. (2) £37 15s. 8d (3) £48 19s. 4d. (4) £62 5s. 0d. (5) £30 9s. 6d. (6) £71 18s. 6d. (7) £2 14s. 10½d. (8) £27 12s. 8¼d. (9) £8 16s 9d. (10) £12 5s. 9d. (11) £90 12s. 8d. (12) £3 13s. 8d. (13) £10 3s. 8d. (14) £262 15s. (15) £26 14s. 10½d.

XVII. (*a*)—(1) 2s. 7½d. (2) 9s. 6d; 5s. (3) 16s. 8d. £1 7s. 1d.; £3 2s. 6d. (4) £1 6s. 0½d.; 18s. 9d.; £1 16s. 5½d. (5) £3 7s. 6d.; £4 8s. 8d.; £4 10s. 7½d. (6) £1 17s. 4d.; £2 16s.; £3 10s.; £2 9s. (7) £1 11s. 6d. £7 0s. 7½d.; £14 12s. 6d. (8) £3 0s. 10d.; £6 16s. 10½d.; £10 12s. 11d. (9) £3 0s. 0d.; £11 18s. 6d.; £5 17s. (10). £1 10s. 4d; 13s. 4d.; £3 9s. 8d. (11) £130 13s. 4d.; £84; £653 6s. 8d. (12) £2 8s.; £3 18s.; £5 17s.; £1 7s.

(*b*)—(1) £60 3s. 9d. (2) £284 8s. 11d.; £3,967 9s. 4d½.; £1,189 14s. 4d. (3) £248 16s. 10½d.; £87 10s. 1½d.; £178 12s. 1½d. (4) £395 18s.; £2,052 9s. 7½d. £1,243 5s. 1d. (5) £35,607 15s. 9d.; £8,170 10s. 6d.; £4,567 10s. 0d. (6) £7,883 7s. 8½d.; £11,196 18s. 0d.; £1,479 18s. 3d. (7) £531 12s. 9¾d.; £14,306 4s. 10d.; £3,614 10s. 0d. (8) £3,790 4s. 2d.; £641 12s. 10½d.; £11,619 7s. 6d. (9) £3,598 13s. 6¼d.; £12,316 19s. 9d.; £47,209 18s. 0d. (10) £4,208 8s. 11d.; £4,393 10s. 6d.; £2,722 10s. 0d. (11) £2,314 10s. 9d.; £7,940 13s. 8d.; £63,466 14s. 0d. (12) £515,220 8s. 9d.; £74,054 4s. 0d. (13) £13,498 8s. 6d.; £10,110 14s. 0d.; £18,014 8s. 0d. (14) £3,148,110 17s. 6d.; £56,863 7s. 0d. (15) £8,522 2 fl. 5 c.; £4,053 7 fl. 8 c. 4 m.; £6,456 6 fl. 3 c. 2 m. (16) £91,672. (17) £133 6 fl. 3 c. 2 m. (18) £275 14s. 9½d. (19) £681,098 18s. 10d. (20) £670,179 10s. 9¼d. (21) £541,931 18s. 6d.

XVIII. (*a*)—(1) 13s. 4d. (2) 5¼d. (3) 11s. 3d.; £1 4s. 6d.; £1 4s. 6d. (4) 5s. 11d.; 2s. 9d. (5) £1 5s. 6d.

(6) £1 5s. 8d.; 6s. 8d. (7) £1 16s. 8d.; £5 17s. 6d. (8) £4 14s. 6d.; £8 8s. 0d. (9) £3 0s. 0d.; £5 1s. 3d. (10) £290. (11) £215; £115. (12) £16 13s. 4d.; £425; £133 6s. 8d.

(*b*)—(1) £60 11s. 0d. (2) £168 11s. 11$\frac{3}{4}$d.; £316 17s. 6d. (3) £94 15s. 6d.; £10 10s. (4) £20 3s. 4d.; £34 2s. 6d. (5) £642 8s. 4$\frac{1}{2}$d.; £529 15s. 10$\frac{1}{2}$d. (6) £194 19s. 8$\frac{1}{4}$d. (7) £213,543 6s. 10d. (8) £34 17s. 11d.; £57 0s. 7$\frac{1}{2}$d. (9) £85 1s. 4$\frac{1}{4}$d. (10) £13 14s. 4$\frac{3}{4}$d. (11) £81 2s. 4$\frac{3}{4}$d. (12) £888 8s. 8$\frac{1}{4}$d. (13) £17 17s. 6d.; £1,328 13s. 7$\frac{1}{2}$d. (14) £161 10s. 0d. (15) £82 9s. 5d.

XIX. (*a*)—(1) 5 fl. 1 c. 6 m. £1 3 fl. 4 c. 1 m.; £2 2 c. 9 m. (2) £7 7 fl. 7 c. 5 m.; £1 9 fl 2 c.; £1 1 fl. 6 c. 5 m. (3) £6 1 fl. 4 m.; £2 4 fl. 8 c. 3 m.; £1 8 fl. 6 c. 2 m. (4) £4 6 fl. 8 c. 7 m.; £1 3 fl. 1 c. 2 m.; £2 2 fl. 8 c. 5 m. (5) £3 1 fl. 8 m.; £5 3 c.; £9 3 fl. 2 c. 5 m. (6) £1 3 fl. 7 c. 5 m.; £3 9 fl. 1 c. 7 m.; £2 3 fl. 5 c. 8 m. (7) £1 4 c. 1 m.; £7 8 c. 7 m.; £8 1 fl. 2 c. (8) £2 1 fl. 6 c. 7 m.; £1 9 fl. 7 c. 8 m.; £2 3 fl. 6 c. 7 m. (9) 1 c. 7 m.; 7 c. 5 m.; 1 fl. 2 c. 5 m.; 5 fl. 2 c. 5 m. (10) £1 6s. 11$\frac{1}{4}$d.; £8 2s. 9d.; £9 4s. 2d. (11) 13s.; £1 4s. 10$\frac{1}{4}$d.; £8 4s. 2$\frac{3}{4}$d. (12) £10 18s. 8$\frac{1}{4}$d.; £6 9s. 0$\frac{3}{4}$d.; £5 6s. 11$\frac{1}{4}$d. (13) £1 17s. 10$\frac{1}{2}$d.; £2 8s. 8$\frac{1}{2}$d.; £7 4s. 9$\frac{3}{4}$d. (14) £61 4s. 2d.; £9 2s. 9$\frac{1}{4}$d.; £12 6s. 11d. (15) £17 6s. 11$\frac{3}{4}$d., £2 8s. 4$\frac{1}{2}$d.; £1 6s. 11$\frac{1}{2}$d. (16) £3; £1 2s. 2$\frac{3}{4}$d.; £5 6s. 10$\frac{1}{4}$d. (17) £1 16s.; 14s. 5d.; 1s. 3$\frac{1}{2}$d.; 5$\frac{3}{4}$d.

(*b*)—(1) £86 8 c. 6 m.; £184 4 fl. 4 c. 7 m.; £3,799 2 fl. 5 c. 7 m. £1,370 8 fl. 4 c. 1 m.; £156 1 fl. 6 c. (2) £6,191 3 fl. 3 c. 5 m. £4,078 2 fl. 8 c. 2 m.; £642 2 fl. 4 c. 5 m.; £3,063 5 fl. 4 c. 1 m.; £183 7 fl. 3 c. 7 m.; £235 3 fl. 9 c. 1 m.; £68 5 fl. 3 c. 7 m.; £2,805 8 fl. 6 c. 6 m.; £5,523 8 fl. 2 c. 9 m.; £2,073 3 fl. 8 c. 5 m.; £1,417 1 fl. 3 c. 3 m. (3) £7 4 fl. 2 c. 5 m.; £111,940; £18,241 8 fl. 2 c. 5 m.; £255,061 4 fl; £11 7 fl. 5 c.; £14 1 fl. 7 c. 5 m. (4) 3 fl. 9 c. 5 m.; 7 fl. 7 c. 3 m.; £55 3 fl. 3 c. 1 m.; £14 4 c. 3 m.; £60 7 fl. 2 c. 3 m.; £58 8 fl. 2 c. 2 m.; £45 9 fl. 6 c. 7 m.; £22 2 fl. 1 c. 8 m.; £4 3 fl. 4 c. 3 m.; £18 7 c. 8 m.; £37 2 fl. 5 c. 8 m.; £6 8 fl. 7 c. 7 m.; £140 3 fl. 8 c. 2 m.; £45 8 fl. 5 c. 9 m.; £6 7 fl. 3 c. 9 m.; £8 5 fl. 1 m.; £12 9 fl. 1 c.; £350 9 fl. 5 c. 8 m.; £6 2 fl. 3 c. 7 m.; £15 8 fl. 6 c.; £70 8 fl. 6 c. 6 m.; £142 1 fl. 9 c. 8 m.; £4 9 fl. 1 c. 9 m.; £17 1 fl. 8 c. 1 m.; £135 3 fl. 8 c. 2 m.; £46 1 fl. 2 c. 1 m. (5) £13 3 fl. 8 c. (6) £80 1 fl. 8 c. 4 m. (7) £590 8 fl. 1 c. 2 m. (8) £13 4 fl. 7 c. 2 m.; £23 8 fl. 1 c. 2 m. (10) 35,256 farthings; 36,725 mils. (11) 237 m. (12) £7·054. (13) 2 c. 6 m. (14) £60,083 3 fl. 3 c. 3 m.; £300,416 6 fl. 3 c. 6 m.

XX. (1) 27 ft. 11 in. 9″. (2) (a) 36 ft. 0 in. 6″; (b) 389 ft. 6 in. 10″ 8‴. (3) (a) 39 ft. 4 in. 10″ 2‴; (b) 206 ft. 8 in. 10″ 6‴. (4) 109 ft. 11 in. 7″ 6‴ 5⁗. (5) 237 ft. 3 in. 7″ 6‴. (6) 48 yds. 4 ft. 5 in. 8″. (7) 3 r. 23 yds. 5$\frac{1}{4}$ ft. (8) 35 [illegible] squares.

(9) 504 ft. 2 in. (10) 475 ft. 3 in. 7″. (11) 44 ft. 8 in. 8″. (12) 23 a. 2 r. 34 p. 17 yds. (13) $261\frac{1}{3}$. (14) (a) 324 ; (b) 8. (15) $25\frac{5}{7}$. (16) $22\frac{3}{7}$. (17) 9 a. 2 r. $31\frac{1}{2}$ p. (18) (a) $2\frac{1}{3}$; (b) $1\frac{1}{4}$. (19) 1,$177\frac{3}{4}$ ft. (20) £12 2s. (21) 10 a. 1 r. 33 p. 12 yds. $5\frac{3}{4}$ ft. (22) 371,200 a. (23) 600 ft. (24) 23 ft. 9 in. (25) 12 ft. 6 in. (26) 1 r. 4 p. 13 yds. 4 ft. (27) 27 ft. (28) 35 yds. 1 ft. 3 in. (29) 54 yds. 1 ft. $9\frac{3}{5}$ in. (30) $5\frac{1}{2}$ ft.

XXI.—MISCELLANEOUS EXERCISES.

(*a*)—(1) 105. (2) 47. (3) 10. (4) 6. (5) 19. (6) 68. (7) 2. (8) 252. (9) $8\frac{1}{3}$. (10) 1s. $7\frac{1}{2}$d. (11) $3\frac{1}{2}$d. (12) 8s. $1\frac{1}{4}$d. (13) 18s. $3\frac{1}{2}$d. (14) 16s. 6d. (15) 80. (16) $133\frac{1}{3}$. (17) 124. (18) 112. (19) 11s. 8d. (20) 225 sq. ft. (21) £3. (22) £22. (23) 240. (24) £1. (25) $11\frac{13}{17}$ weeks. (26) 8 days. (27) 400. (28) 73. (29) £1 2s. $8\frac{1}{2}$d. (30) 272. (31) 490. (32) £2 9s. 5d. (33) £2 5s. 11d.

(*b*)—(1) £12 13s. 7d. (2) £385 5s. (8) Friday. (4) 21 of each. (5) 13 a. 2 ch. (6) £3 8s. 4d. (7) £17 17s. 6d. (8) 68,040. (9) £6,781 13s. 4d. (10) 522. (11) £3 11s. $4\frac{3}{4}$d. (12) 137 2s. gain. (13) 2 w. 2 d. 10 h. 20 m. (14) £14 3s. $6\frac{2}{3}$d. (15) 12s. 10d. (16) 15s. (17) (a) 6 h. 36 m. ; (b) 137,280 ft. (18) 43′ $5\frac{29}{32}$″. (19) 2 a. 0 r. 5 p. 3 y. 6 ft. (20) £2 11s. (21) £165,914 12s. 3d. (22) £1,344,262 10s. (23) $4\frac{1}{2}$d. (24) 5,067 gal. 0 qt. $1\frac{1}{2}$ pt. (25) £55 0s. 4d. ; £27 10s. 2d. ; £13 15s. 1d. (26) 15 yds. (27) 158. (28) 21 a. 3 r. 38 p. $5\frac{1}{2}$ yds. (29) 13,085,292 qr. 4 b. (30) £500 3s. $11\frac{3}{4}$d. (31) $483\frac{187}{256}$ sq. m. (32) £148. (33) £7 10s. $2\frac{1}{2}$d. (34) 5s. $5\frac{5}{8}$d. (35) $420\frac{3}{8}$ tenpenny pieces, $77\frac{8}{9}$ American dols. (36) 7 lbs. 3 oz. 14 d. $9\frac{1}{4}$ grs. (37) £2 10s. (38) £116 15s. (39) £2,675, £1,605, £1,070. (40) 41. (41) 704. (42) £26 4s. 7d. (43) 2,945 yds. 1 qr. 1 nl. (44) £600. (45) £14,630 4s. 6d. (46) 2 cwt. 3 qrs. 12 lbs. (47) £2 10s. $11\frac{81}{44389}$d. (48) £439 10s. (49) £17 4s. 3d. (50) £12 5s. (51) 1 ton 17 cwt. 3 qrs. (52) $327\frac{22113}{23503}$. (53) 7,825. (54) 1s. $9\frac{1}{3}$d. (55) 9,803. (56) £118 12s. $0\frac{3}{4}$d. (57) £194,039 8s. 3d. (58) £176,572 8s. 3d. (59) 144. (60) £377,520. (61) £442 19s. 3d. (62) £5 6 fl. 1 c. 3 m., or £5 12s. $3\frac{1}{4}$d. (63) £1 7 fl. 1 c. $3\frac{3}{5}$ m. (64) $52\frac{1}{2}$ doz. (65) £130 3s. 6d. (66) £2,966 8s. (67) £142 16s. (68) 3,505. (69) 1 h. 35 m. 20″. (70) £275. (71) 40. (72) 4,320. (73) 1,240. (74) 27. (75) 823 A.U.C. (76) £1,185 9s. $6\frac{3}{4}$d. (77) 33 sq. ft. (78) 76,500. (79) (a) $1\frac{139}{363}$; (b) 21. (80) 22,032 ; 14190. (81) 74,385. (82) £9,032 8s. (83) (a) $368\frac{40}{77}$; (b) $181\frac{8}{9}$. (84) 134 a. 0 r. $15\frac{105}{121}$ p. (85) 11 in. 3″. (86) £39 0s. $1\frac{1}{2}$d. (87) 112 nearly. (88) £8 7s. $5\frac{1}{4}$d.

ANSWERS TO EXERCISES

IN "ARITHMETIC FOR BEGINNERS," PART II.

XXII. (*a*)—(1) Prime 29, composite $8 = 2^3$; $15 = 5 \times 3$; $22 = 2 \times 11$. (2) Prime 7, comp. $35 = 5 \times 7$; $63 = 7 \times 3^2$; $100 = 5^2 \times 2^2$. (3) Prime 19, 37, composite $27 = 3^3$, $39 = 3 \times 13$. (4) Prime 11, comp. $36 = 3^2 \times 2^2$; $68 = 2^2 \times 17$; $120 = 5 \times 2^3 \times 3$. (5) Comp. $64 = 2^6$; $34 = 2 \times 17$; $49 - 7^2$; $78 = 2 \times 3 \times 13$. (6) Prime 23, comp. $54 = 3^3 \times 2$; $132 = 11 \times 2^2 \times 3$; $141 = 3 \times 47$.

(*b*)—(1) Prime 587, comp. $340 = 2^2 \times 5 \times 17$; $624 = 2^4 \times 13 \times 3$. (2) Prime 193, comp. $74 = 2 \times 37$; $518 = 2 \times 259$. (3) Comp. $412 = 2^2 \times 103$; $1{,}000 = 5^3 \times 2^3$; $218 = 2 \times 109$; $615 = 5 \times 3 \times 41$. (4) Comp. $723 = 3^2 \times 11 \times 7$; $514 = 2 \times 3^2 \times 7$; $862 = 2 \times 431$; $500 = 5^3 \times 2^2$. (5) P. 167, 347, 281, comp. $219 = 3 \times 73$. (6) Comp. $2174 = 2^2 \times 541$; $3{,}052 = 2^2 \times 7 \times 109$; $4{,}096 = 2^{12}$. (7) Pr. 149, comp. $3{,}261 = 3 \times 1{,}087$; $5{,}782 = 2 \times 7^2 \times 59$; $320 = 2^6 \times 5$. (8) $2{,}172 = 2 \times 23 \times 47$; $3{,}638 = 2 \times 1{,}319$; $1{,}236 = 103 \times 2^2 \times 3$. (9) 2; 3; 5; 7; 11; 13; 17; 19; 23; 29; 31; 37; 41; 43; 47; 53; 59; 61; 67; 71; 73; 79; 83; 89; 97; 101; 103; 107; 109; 113: 119; 131; 137; 139; 149; 151; 157; 161; 167; 173; 179; 181; 183; 191; 193; 199.

XXIII. (*a*)—(1) 5; 3. (2) 2; 7. (3) 5; 14. (4) 10; 18. (5) 3; 40. (6) 3; 4. (7) $1\frac{1}{2}$d.; 4d. (8) 3s. 4d.; 3d.

(*b*)—(1) 30; 2. (2) 9; 17. (3) 17; 11. (4) 57; 86. (5) 86; 9; 31. (6) 42; 9; 813. (7) 217; 1,885. (8) $3\frac{1}{2}$d. (9) 12s. 6d. (10) 1s. $4\frac{1}{2}$d. (11) 1d.

XXIV. (*a*)—(1) 24; 60. (2) 30; 120; 90; (3) 60; 432. (4) 300; 385. (5) 126; 280. (6) 75; 240; 924; 396. (7) 12; 60. (8) 120; 210.

(*b*)—(1) 480. (2) 1,690; 3,927; 46,512. (3) 15,150; 16,632; 1,188. (4) 2,520; 1,608,789; 231,660. (5) 83,700; 651,695; 6,930. (6) 15,960; 30,900; 840. (7) 600; 27,000; 127,680.

XXV. (*a*)—(1) 20; 60. (2) 49; 12; 48. (3) 66; 100; 44. (4) 24; 24; 42. (5) 10; 56; 36. (6) $7\frac{1}{2}$d.; $\frac{3}{4}$d.; 8d. (7) 2s.; 3s. $1\frac{1}{2}$d.; 1s. 9d. (8) 8s.; 5s. 3d.; 13s. 4d. (9) $2\frac{11}{12}$ days; 1 lb. 12 oz.; $14\frac{2}{3}$ f. (10) $\frac{4}{5}$; $\frac{17}{19}$; $\frac{33}{100}$; $\frac{1}{5}$. (11) $\frac{3}{8}$; $\frac{7}{12}$; $\frac{13}{16}$; $\frac{7}{8}$. (12) $\frac{19}{40}$; $\frac{73}{80}$; $\frac{57}{80}$; $\frac{7}{8}$. (13) 35; 40; 45. (14) 112; 19; 104. (15) 3s.; 3s. 6d. (16) 25s.; 2s. 6d.; 1s.; 1s. 8d. (17) $\frac{2}{5}$; $\frac{7}{32}$; $\frac{11}{12}$. (18) $\frac{5}{6}$; $\frac{2}{3}$; $\frac{2}{3}$; $\frac{4}{5}$; $\frac{2}{5}$. (19) $\frac{1}{3}$; $\frac{5}{11}$; $\frac{1}{3}$; $\frac{1}{4}$; $\frac{11}{12}$. (20) $\frac{13}{28}$; $\frac{16}{66}$; $\frac{33}{40}$; $\frac{29}{36}$.

(*b*)—(1) £4 13s. 9d.; £2 16s. $7\frac{1}{2}$d. (2) 28 lbs.; 11 h. 12 m. *(3) 620 yds.*; 102 lbs. (4) $\frac{19}{450}$; $\frac{151}{400}$. (5) $\frac{59}{3630}$; $\frac{139}{672}$.

(6) $\frac{19}{40}$; $\frac{149}{882}$; $\frac{1}{32}$. (7) $1\frac{10}{81}$; $\frac{107}{117}$; $\frac{13}{21}$. (8) 6s 3d.; 309 lbs.
(9) $24\frac{8}{9}$ days; $9{,}978\frac{2}{11}$ lb. (10) $\frac{11}{80}$; $\frac{47}{2240}$; $\frac{63}{3520}$.
(11) $\frac{3}{352}$; $\frac{147}{320}$; $\frac{63}{3520}$. (12) $\frac{3}{11}$; $\frac{7}{15}$; $\frac{1}{9}$. (13) $\frac{5}{8}$; $\frac{27}{101}$; $\frac{11}{80}$.
(14) $\frac{220}{527}$; $\frac{27}{1624}$. (15) $\frac{5}{7}$; $\frac{2499}{3941}$; $\frac{17}{21}$. (16) $\frac{213}{715}$; $\frac{117}{190}$.
(17) $\frac{19}{61}$; $\frac{151}{219}$. (18) £35 12s. 6d.; 4,479 ft. 6 in.
(19) 38 lbs. $4\frac{1}{2}$ oz. (20) $\frac{13}{18}$; $\frac{5}{12}$; $\frac{8}{9}$; $\frac{4}{5}$; $\frac{2}{3}$.

XXVI. (*a*)—(1) 3s. 4d.; £2 5s.; 1 lb. 12 oz. (2) $2\frac{5}{10}$; 1s. 3d.; 2s. 1d.; $5\frac{3}{4}$d. (3) 4s.; 6s. 9d.; £3 12s.
(4) 58; 45; 29. (5) 32; 140; 270. (6) $9\frac{1}{2}$; $1\frac{1}{14}$; $5\frac{1}{9}$.
(7) $2\frac{1}{11}$; $15\frac{2}{3}$; $7\frac{5}{9}$. (8) $12\frac{2}{9}$; $10\frac{5}{6}$; $24\frac{1}{2}$. (9) $\frac{37}{9}$; $\frac{43}{8}$; $\frac{39}{5}$.
(10) $\frac{23}{12}$; $\frac{71}{13}$; $\frac{37}{9}$. (11) $\frac{26}{4}$; $\frac{33}{4}$; $\frac{36}{7}$.
(*b*)—(1) $50\frac{7}{10}$; $51\frac{7}{11}$. (2) $265\frac{3}{5}$; $284\frac{14}{15}$; $44\frac{2}{9}$.
(3) $111\frac{10}{21}$; $93\frac{11}{18}$; $94\frac{12}{23}$. (4) $\frac{408}{24}$; $\frac{132}{11}$; $\frac{219}{15}$.
(5) $\frac{190}{11}$; $\frac{473}{18}$; $\frac{107}{25}$; $\frac{161}{13}$. (6) $\frac{397}{14}$; $\frac{83}{15}$; $\frac{311}{34}$.
(7) $\frac{226}{125}$; $\frac{292}{19}$; $\frac{7346}{275}$. (8) $\frac{192}{35}$; $\frac{3632}{960}$; $\frac{427}{98}$.
(9) $\frac{757}{108}$; $\frac{3300}{928}$; $\frac{10991}{1007}$.

XXVII. (*a*)—(1) $\frac{4}{12}$; $\frac{3}{12}$. (2) $\frac{3}{4}$; $\frac{6}{7}$. (3) $\frac{7}{28}$ and $\frac{4}{28}$; $\frac{1}{10}$ and $\frac{6}{10}$; $\frac{3}{10}$ and $\frac{9}{10}$. (4) $\frac{7}{21}$; $\frac{15}{21}$; $\frac{12}{30}$; $\frac{25}{30}$; $\frac{3}{8}$; $\frac{2}{8}$.
(*b*)—(1) $\frac{72}{90}$, $\frac{70}{90}$, $\frac{27}{90}$; $\frac{1}{12}$ and $\frac{6}{12}$; $\frac{275}{495}$, $\frac{180}{495}$, $\frac{198}{495}$.
(2) $\frac{50}{60}$, $\frac{28}{60}$, $\frac{55}{60}$, $\frac{42}{60}$; $\frac{140}{168}$, $\frac{84}{168}$, $\frac{27}{168}$; $\frac{350}{550}$, $\frac{770}{550}$, $\frac{418}{550}$, $\frac{495}{550}$.
(3) $\frac{45}{48}$, $\frac{32}{48}$, $\frac{16}{48}$; $\frac{1848}{1320}$, $\frac{720}{1320}$, $\frac{165}{1320}$, $\frac{110}{1320}$; $\frac{288}{1008}$, $\frac{184}{1008}$, $\frac{224}{1008}$, $\frac{504}{1008}$.
(4) $\frac{54}{900}$, $\frac{36}{900}$, $\frac{765}{900}$, $\frac{50}{900}$; $\frac{10}{60}$, $\frac{35}{60}$, $\frac{28}{60}$, $\frac{9}{60}$; $\frac{50}{170}$, $\frac{34}{170}$, $\frac{140}{170}$.

XXVIII. (*a*)—(1) $\frac{5}{6}$. (2) $\frac{5}{6}$; $\frac{17}{18}$. (3) $\frac{17}{20}$; $\frac{3}{4}$. (4) $\frac{1}{42}$; $\frac{7}{20}$.
(5) $\frac{3}{10}$. (6) $7\frac{5}{6}$; $10\frac{9}{20}$. (7) $5\frac{7}{8}$; $8\frac{11}{15}$. (8) $3\frac{4}{7}$; $\frac{5}{8}$.
(9) $7\frac{2}{7}$; $7\frac{1}{4}$. (10) 13s. $8\frac{1}{2}$d.; 7s. $2\frac{3}{4}$d. (11) $\frac{1}{6}$; $\frac{19}{40}$.
(12) $\frac{13}{70}$. (13) $\frac{4}{7}$; $7\frac{4}{5}$. (14) $7\frac{3}{4}$; $24\frac{11}{18}$.
(*b*)—(1) $1\frac{121}{168}$; $\frac{79}{288}$. (2) $1\frac{25}{132}$; $3\frac{9}{155}$. (3) $36\frac{11}{12}$; $12\frac{83}{171}$.
(4) $22\frac{5}{7}$. (5) $4\frac{9}{35}$; $2\frac{38}{45}$. (6) $1\frac{310}{693}$. (7) $2\frac{219}{280}$.
(8) $5\frac{1}{15}$; $12\frac{362}{697}$. (9) $159\frac{7}{30}$; $7\frac{1423}{1710}$. (10) $4\frac{11}{68}$. (11) $\frac{13}{150}$.
(12) 11s. $6\frac{1}{4}$d. + $\frac{1}{84}$d. (13) $5\frac{229}{720}$. (14) $10\frac{359}{420}$. (15) £$3\frac{3}{5}$.
(16) $28\frac{2}{7}$. (17) 54. (18) $1\frac{3}{7}$ h. (19) £$2\frac{7}{8}$. (20) 240.
(21) $\frac{13}{40}$. (22) £$6\frac{2}{3}$. (23) $49\frac{1}{11}$. (24) $19\frac{1}{5}$ m. (25) 15 h.
(26) $77\frac{11}{40}$ lbs. (27) $17\frac{89}{252}$. (28) $\frac{13}{60}$. (29) $4\frac{19}{24}$ yds. (30) $6\frac{4}{11}$.

XXIX. (*a*)—(1) $2\frac{4}{7}$; $2\frac{1}{3}$; $1\frac{2}{3}$. (2) $5\frac{5}{7}$; $1\frac{1}{3}$. (3) $1\frac{12}{25}$; $2\frac{1}{4}$d.
(4) $1\frac{3}{4}$; $\frac{3}{10}$. (5) $2\frac{1}{3}$; $1\frac{26}{29}$. (6) $1\frac{2}{3}$; $9\frac{15}{17}$. (7) $1\frac{1}{5}$; $\frac{7}{13}$.
(8) 13; $31\frac{3}{7}$. (9) $7\frac{1}{2}$; $10\frac{1}{4}$. (10) 64; 18. (11) $33\frac{2}{11}$; 46.
(12) $\frac{1}{7}$; $\frac{7}{24}$; $\frac{1}{5}$. (13) $\frac{5}{39}$; $\frac{4}{77}$. (14) $\frac{2}{63}$; $\frac{5}{54}$. (15) $\frac{7}{60}$; $\frac{19}{60}$.
(16) $\frac{5}{114}$; $\frac{4}{41}$. (17) $\frac{3}{7}$; $\frac{3}{5}$. (18) $1\frac{2}{15}$; $\frac{2}{17}$. (19) £1 4s. (20) $\frac{5}{56}$.
(*b*)—(1) $\frac{33}{56}$; $12\frac{5}{11}$. (2) 88; $167\frac{5}{8}$. (3) 27; $25\frac{3}{5}$.
(4) £12 16s. $1\frac{7}{12}$d.; £22 8s. $3\frac{11}{16}$d.; £251 0s. $6\frac{3}{8}$d. (5) 69 yds. 2 ft. 6 in. (6) 56; $11\frac{43}{115}$. (7) $13\frac{1}{2}$; $\frac{1}{2}$. (8) £$321\frac{7}{8}$; £$931\frac{13}{16}$, (9) £128; £$948\frac{4}{5}$. (10) $681\frac{5}{8}$; $309\frac{3}{5}$.
(11) $\frac{2}{17}$; $\frac{4}{21}$; $\frac{2}{9}$. (12) $\frac{57}{1744}$; $\frac{2}{453}$. (13) $\frac{35}{1139}$; $\frac{1}{14}$.
(14) £$\frac{23}{36}$; $1\frac{75}{128}$. (15) $8\frac{7}{8}$; $4\frac{193}{200}$. (16) 3s. $9\frac{3}{8}$d.; £1 0s. $4\frac{16}{21}$.
(17) 2s. $2\frac{5}{8}$d; 4s. $1\frac{5}{12}$d. (18) $\frac{13}{132}$; $\frac{5}{648}$; $\frac{243}{476}$. (19) £$6{,}609\frac{3}{5}$.
(20) $20\frac{1}{8}$ pints. (21) $231\frac{1}{5}$ lbs. (22) 31. (23) $1\frac{81}{}$ =
(24) £410. (25) 59 yds. $9\frac{1}{3}$ in. (26) $697\frac{357}{924}$.

XXX. (*a*)—(1) $\frac{1}{6}$; $\frac{8}{15}$; $\frac{1}{10}$. (2) $\frac{1}{6}$. (3) 10d. (4) $\frac{1}{6}$. (5) $\frac{5}{6}$; $\frac{3}{4}$. (6) $9\frac{9}{10}$; 4; $22\frac{23}{99}$.

(*b*)—(1) $\frac{7}{12}$; $\frac{12}{35}$; $14\frac{1}{2}$. (2) $4\frac{37}{63}$; $14\frac{7}{8}$. (3) $\frac{189}{200}$; $3\frac{29}{77}$. (4) $11\frac{1}{4}$; $\frac{1}{2}$. (5) $52\frac{8}{9}$; $\frac{63}{4250}$. (6) $\frac{5}{168}$. (7) $\frac{146}{165}$; $1\frac{3}{8}$; $59\frac{10}{33}$. (8) $\frac{19}{2025}$. (9) £36 18s. $2\frac{1}{4}$d; £2 12s. $3\frac{9}{28}$d.; £4 8s. $10\frac{117}{128}$d. (10) $945\frac{3}{4}$ yds. (11) $\frac{3}{10}$. (12) $541\frac{215}{672}$ sq. yds. (13) $1\frac{2159}{2520}$; $\frac{11}{24}$.

XXXI. (*a*)—(1) $\frac{8}{9}$; $1\frac{11}{24}$; $1\frac{4}{5}$. (2) 14; 18. (3) 10; 35; 22. (4) 60. (5) 8; 40. (6) £5,000.

(*b*)—(1) $\frac{39}{77}$; $\frac{14}{27}$; $9\frac{11}{13}$. (2) $2\frac{43}{45}$; $3\frac{1}{8}$. (3) $\frac{12}{23}$; $7\frac{31}{60}$. (4) $12\frac{12}{17}$; $1\frac{121}{159}$; $\frac{77}{320}$. (5) $3\frac{3}{73}$; $1\frac{133}{171}$; $2\frac{121}{198}$. (6) $1\frac{1}{27}$; $\frac{176}{861}$; $1\frac{38}{77}$. (7) $4\frac{47}{392}$; $2\frac{212}{825}$. (8) £5 15s. 6d.; £1 7s. $11\frac{1}{2}$d.; £17 4s. $4\frac{14}{45}$d. (9) $20\frac{4}{55}$ times. (10) $19\frac{17}{52}$ times. (11) $1\frac{359}{2667}$; $\frac{245}{837}$; $2\frac{93}{362}$.

XXXII. (*a*)—(1) $\frac{4}{5}$. (2) $\frac{7}{40}$. (3) $\frac{1}{50}$; 16. (4) $\frac{3}{28}$; $\frac{5}{49}$. (5) $\frac{3}{80}$; $\frac{1}{768}$. (6) $\frac{1}{70}$; $\frac{1}{192}$; $\frac{3}{280}$. (7) $\frac{11}{144}$; $\frac{29}{36}$. (8) $\frac{8}{7}$; $\frac{48}{9}$. (9) $\frac{19}{132}$; $\frac{169}{240}$.

(*b*)—(1) $\frac{3}{140}$. (2) $\frac{25}{12}$; $\frac{48}{17}$. (3) $\frac{40}{189}$; $\frac{11}{288}$. (4) 55; $\frac{69}{140}$. (5) $\frac{37}{20}$; $\frac{1}{320}$. (6) $\frac{1}{11}$; $\frac{280}{3}$. (7) $\frac{13}{8960}$; $\frac{700}{3}$. (8) 420; $\frac{1}{10368}$. (9) $\frac{7200}{17}$, $\frac{120}{17}$; $\frac{5}{119}$. (10) $\frac{19}{41216}$; $\frac{19}{368}$; $\frac{304}{23}$; $\frac{153000}{368}$. (11) $\frac{127}{160}$; $\frac{127}{102400}$. (12) $\frac{315}{10648}$. (13) $\frac{36}{19}$; $\frac{3}{38}$; $\frac{3}{380}$; $\frac{3}{1900}$. (14) $\frac{184}{17}$; 540. (15) $\frac{23}{400}$. (16) $\frac{3067}{4480}$. (17) $\frac{7}{352}$. (18) $\frac{66}{25}$. (19) $\frac{67}{504}$. (20) 201; $\frac{67}{21620}$. (21) 243,210. (22) $\frac{269}{33520}$. (23) 2 fur. 26 p. $4\frac{1}{5}$ yds. (24) 237 cwt. 3 qrs. 14 lbs.

XXXIII. (*a*)—(1) 81. (2) $16\frac{1}{3}$. (3) 30. (4) 2,025 (5) $\frac{17}{120}$. (6) $2\frac{2}{3}$. (7) £4 3s. 4d. (8) 6. (9) $\frac{2}{3}$; $\frac{5}{6}$. (10) $10\frac{2}{3}$d. (11) $\frac{1}{6}$; 10d. (12) 40. (13) $\frac{13}{42}$. (14) $5\frac{5}{11}$. (15) $\frac{1}{3}$; $\frac{151}{188}$. (16) $10\frac{1}{2}$. (17) $1\frac{4}{5}$. (18) 11 sh.

(*b*)—(1) $\frac{11}{420}$. (2) $\frac{403}{945}$. (3) $13{,}714\frac{2}{7}$ poles. (4) $\frac{8}{15}$, $\frac{2}{15}$, $\frac{1}{15}$. (5) $\frac{8711}{900}$. (6) $\frac{143}{240}$; $\frac{497}{1728}$; $25\frac{9253}{14400}$. (7) 5s. $9\frac{2}{15}$d.; 18s. $9\frac{7}{12}$d. (8) £11 2s. $10\frac{1}{2}$d.; £10 8s. $4\frac{1}{32}$d.; 14s. $4\frac{7}{16}$d. (9) 12 cwt. 1 qr. $23\frac{3}{7}$ lbs.; $181\frac{7}{8}$ lbs.; 541 weeks $4\frac{17}{18}$ days. (10) $\frac{27}{5}$. (11) £3,478 10s.; £10,900 17s. 6d.; £2,577 5s. (12) £195. (13) 6 a. 2 r. 39 p. (14) $\frac{807}{4649920}$. (15) $\frac{115}{146}$. (16) 60 days. (17) $\frac{2}{19}$. (18) $\frac{514}{3465}$. (19) Sulphur 28 lbs., charcoal 42 lbs., nitre 210 lbs. (20) $\frac{21}{40}$. (21) $\frac{15}{56}$. (22) 30. (23) $\frac{1}{275}$. (24) £760. (25) $\frac{2421}{2451}$. (26) 15s. $0\frac{1}{2}$d. (27) $\frac{15}{16}$. (28) $6\frac{3}{7}$ m. (29) $3\frac{1}{3}$d. (30) $\frac{69}{94}$; $1\frac{789}{3682}$; $\frac{3555}{24822}$. (31) $8\frac{38}{315}$; $7\frac{1}{2}$. (32) 33. (33) £1 3s. 10d. (34) £5,000. (35) $\frac{71}{168}$.

XXXIV. (1) ·3; ·51; ·085. (2) 1·1; ·007; ·000193. (3) ·7; ·14; ·065. (4) 1·08; 3·6; 12·03. (5) 7·006; 2·38. (6) ·003; ·0101; 5·0007. (7) 9·108; 12·7; 20·4. (8) 30·24; 50·9; 2·18. (9) ·6; 3·14; 2·8. (10) $4\frac{1}{10}$; $7\frac{86}{1000}$; $13\frac{47}{100}$. (11) $12\frac{938}{1000}$; $\frac{17}{1000}$; $7\frac{103}{1000}$. (12) $1\frac{7}{10000}$; $13\frac{4705}{10000}$. (13) $6\frac{18753}{1000000}$; $1\frac{29}{10000}$; $2\frac{9706}{10000}$. (14) $25\frac{36}{100}$; $1\frac{7803}{100000000}$. (15) $79\frac{680352}{10000000}$; $4\frac{1073285}{10000000}$. (16) $21\frac{96}{1000}$; $\frac{3507}{100000}$. (17) $210\frac{971}{1000}$; $\frac{5638271}{10000000}$. (18) 723·5; 410·69; 270. (19) ·7; *·738; 4096.* (20) ·3287; ·05069; ·00013728. (21) ·30790; *·071684; 796·3.* (22) ·18; 17538; ·070638. (23) 703·86;

1590·85 ; 7·263 ; ·862 ; 57638·94. (24) ·0069 ; ·58321 ; 179·6 ; ·3057 ; 2·786 ; ·09072. (25) 123 ; 7·96 ; 5830 ; 15070 ; 3278·6 ; 509·78. (26) ·01796 ; ·002083 ; ·000059 ; ·723 ; ·215 ; ·01729 ; ·34625.

XXXV. (*a*)—(1) ·1. (2) ·25 ; ·5 ; ·75. (3) ·5. (4) ·2 ; ·9 ; ·55. (5) 2s. ; 4s. ; 14s. ; £6 10s. (6) 5s. ; 6s. 10½d. ; £1 12s. ; £183 8s. ; £20 9s. 5d. (7) £2 18s. ; £4 3s. ; £1 1s. 5d. ; £627 16s. £1,224 6s. 5d. (8) 5 ; 2. (9) 25 ; 10. (10) ·6 ; ·625. (11) ·75 ; ·2 ; ·375. (12) ·04 ; ·05 ; ·5.

(*b*)—(1) ·71428 ; ·2 ; ·8. (2) ·3 ; ·625 ; ·88235. (3) ·75 ; ·53. (4) ·493 ; ·29 ; ·155. (5) ·4259 ; ·4375 ; ·38756. (6) 8·5 ; 5·25. (7) 2·875 ; 21·21052. (8) ·0925 ; ·57142. (9) 12·1 ; ·04210. (10) 3·6136 ; 1·71428. (11) 1·375 ; ·57960. (12) ·42475 ; ·76122. (13) ·52197 ; ·68493. (14) 5·4 ; 1·53214. (15) 8·18 ; 3·92156. (16) ·05144.

XXXVI. (1) 101·209. (2) 15·935. (3) 10·867. (4) 114·1377. (5) 959·0483. (6) 40·52753. (7) 15156·66886. (8) 200·0211. (9) 25·749445. (10) 227·5024. (11) ·357. (12) 1·381. (13) ·403015. (14) 5·8311004. (15) 502·21 ; 26 grains.

XXXVII. (1) 10·645 ; 12·2676. (2) 43·54 ; 3·1268 ; 2·051. (3) 27·6248 ; 11·8372 ; ·0522. (4) ·3352 ; ·4693 ; 47·106. (5) 1·2035 ; 5·083. (6) 4·2515 ; 33·5. (7) 101·45463. (8) 644·414 ; ·017 ; 53·9946. (9) ·85. (10) ·2318. (11) 36·002. (12) ·099. (13) ·146. (14) 1·660714. (15) ·796.

XXXVIII. (1). 4036·45 ; 747·804 ; 144·781. (2) 929·91852 ; 426·07056. (3) 2267·16 ; 5767·6032. (4) 10323·459696 ; 1072·614532. (5) 16550·248 ; 1110·41304. (6) ·00595. (7) ·19431. (8) 89·952225. (9) ·00000053946. (10) 202·62928 ; 400·5805. (11) 32·642244 ; 1·811667. (12) 170·837226. (13) 134·58034. (14) ·07619. (15) 13·8375 ; 1·58535 ; 234·375. (16) 380·571. (17) 334141·402. (18) 44363·840. (19) 9·875. (20) 333·80692. (21) 117·04936022. (22) 728·9271. (23) 1387·5625 p. (24) 8431·425. (25) 110·53572. (26) 2150·05031. (27) ·185905. (28) ·43. (29) 18995·3955 grs. (30) 595·23494.

XXXIX. (1) 2·6434 ; 1·58604 ; 1·1328857142. (2) ·083538461 ; (3) 18·8728 ; 254·616375 ; ·296. (4) ·1430575 ; 100 ; 1700. (5) 20 ; 164·28571 ; 576·20612. (6) 6033·3 ; 254·36 ; 28·652. (7) 151·761904 ; 173·10212 ; 242·8235294117. (8) 65·40074 ; ·03096212 ; 25·047317. (9) 2·91809 ; 6·2322974. (10) 17·329 in. (11) ·12625 links. (12) 30·8185 grs. (13) 22·916. (14) 4·11764705835. (15) 5000. (16) 1678·5714. (17) 3·9286. (18) 84·857142. (19) 106·875 ; 14·28125. (20) 18·472. (21) ·16290384615. (22) ·015471 ; 1·36590869 ; 2·94

(23) 1·53852. (24) 1074·679. (25) ·75 ft. (26) 44·137931 p. (27) 28·25 nearly. (28) ·31798 ft. nearly.

XL. (*a*)—(1) £2 18s. 9¼d.; £5 1s. 2½d.; £1 15s. 10¼d. (2) £1 17s. 1½d.; 4s. 7¼d.; £1 9s. 6¾d. (3) 6s. 6¼d.; 14s. 5d.; £1 0s. 2d. (4) 16s. 2¼d.; £1 6s. 0½d.; 11s. 7¼d.; £172 16s. (5) 3s. 5¼d.; 3s. 8¾d.; 12s. 6½d.; £7,326 10s. 9¼d. (6) £1·483; £12·079; £185·318. (7) £·133; £·264; £·525; £124·688. (8) £22·562; £4·093; £1·35. (9) £·816; £·414; £·995; £208·325. (10) £·018; £·032; £·005; £1·028. (11) £·028; £·56; £·04; £·739.

(*b*)—(1) £1·88641; £28·84478; £12·38958; £47·65937. (2) 27·375s.; 49·3125s.; ·9583s.; ·39583s. (3) ·925d.; 283·25d.; 2964d. (4) ·15833; ·39367. (5) ·52976; ·010208. (6) ·3468$\dot{7}$; 1·375. (7) ·985; 634·68. (8) ·02241; ·17928; 39·45$\dot{6}$. (9) 3·45 g.; 883·2 qts.; 1766·4 pts. (10) ·01924 w.; ·13471 d.; 194 m. (11) ·005078 cwt.; ·0002539 tons. (12) 6969·6 ft.; 51·3 ft. (13) £1 17s. 6d.; 11s. 10½d.; 2d. (14) 1531·2 ft. 13·104 lbs.; 7 cwt. 3 qrs. 5 lbs. 9 oz. (15) 179 gal. 1 qt. 3 gills; 218 lbs. 8 oz. 8 dwts.; 11 lbs. 5 oz. 6 dr. (16) 21 a. 1 r. 23 p. 21 sq. yds. 7 ft. 2 in.; 31 a. 3 r. 16 p.; 103 a. 10 p. 24 yds. 1 ft. 115 in. (17) Julian year greater by 11·14004 min. (18) 5·4924 m. (19) ·015584 m. (20) 4·3496 m. (21) 3280·916 ft. (22) 2·6812 tr. lbs. (23) 31 a. 3 r. 20 p.

XLI. (1) ·8825. (2) ·62; ·32. (3) $\frac{108}{35}$. (4) 383 a. 3 r. 1 p. (5) ·77307. (6) £4·24772. (7) £2 10s. 4¾d. (8) 5 m. 3 f. 39 p. 1 yd. 1 ft. 9 in. (9) 4 ft. 11·0273345 in. (10) 720. (11) ·15. (12) £971 14s. 3d. (13) 142·272 in. (14) ·101$\dot{3}$ yds. (15) 24855·429 m. (16) 6464·92. (17) 157·635 c. f. (18) £1,450 13s. 4d. (19) £5·67; ·625 of £5. (20) 820. (21) ·84042 g. (22) 20·0$\dot{3}$. (23) £258 7s. 7¾d. + $\frac{23}{25}$. (24) 20. (25) 883345·17; 2,192 inches. (26) ·05. (27) 7·215. (28) £4,250. (29) £290·6139. (30) £26,400. (31) 17s. 6d. (32) ·14285; ·125. (33) £40·516. (34) 1·484. (35) £·3463491$\dot{6}$. (36) 125·6228592. (37) ·096. (38) 205·584 inches. (39) £70·824. (40) $\frac{319}{420}$; ·7595237. (41) £4·73$\dot{6}$. (42) 6·0134 lbs. (43) 90·796. (44) 33·88$\dot{6}$. (45) 1236·399. (46) £2·23125; £4·029; £·0889. (47) £262·5. (48) £232·352736. (49) 5050·31835 inches. (50) 57·72 lbs. (51) 10s. 10½d. (52) 660.

XLII. (*a*)—(1) 9. (2) 5 : 6. (3) 14 : 18. (4) 33. (5) 1 : 5; 4 : 5; 4 : 3. (6) 7 : 20; 10 : 12; 15 : 18. (7) 2 : 7; 6 : 1. (8) 11 : 30; 2 : 15; 4 : 1. (9) 3 : 5 :: 9 : 15; 4 : 7 :: 12 : 21. (10) 5 : 15 :: 7 : 21; 18 : 90 :: 2 : 10. (11) 2d. (12) 3 inches.

(*b*)—(1) 3 : 20 : 482 : 33; 457 : 565. (2) 53 : 181; 31 : 25; *231 : 181.* (3) 15 : 32; 55 : 126; 77 : 89. (4) 112½; $25\frac{1}{10}$. *(5) 2138*$\frac{2}{5}$; $747\frac{31}{102}$. (6) $4147\frac{19}{31}$; 250. (7) $1\frac{322}{577}$; $378\frac{1}{3}$.

(8) $283\frac{1253}{1903}$; $2574\frac{133}{733}$. (9) $1\frac{3881}{5871}$. (10) ·031. (11) 14 : 25. (12) 2304 : 175.

XLIII. (*a*)—(1) 1s. 6d. (2) 50. (3) 42. (4) £2 6s. (5) £7 13s. 9d. (6) 15. (7) 64. (8) 32. (9) 32. (10) 16. (11) 15·75. (12) 48.

(*b*)—(1) £1 8s. $4\frac{3}{4}$d. + $\frac{1}{8}$. (2) 3·1169 times. (3) $45\frac{3}{5}$. (4) 16 lbs. $10\frac{3}{5}$ oz. (5) $3\frac{3}{4}$d. (6) £4,924 1s. $10\frac{1}{2}$d. (7) $834\frac{1}{5}$. (8) 119. (9) £1 11s. $11\frac{1}{4}$d. (10) 3 h. 53 m. + $\frac{8}{57}$. (11) £527 3s. $11\frac{1}{7}$d. (12) £9 9s. $10\frac{5}{7}$d. (13) £21 0s. $0\frac{5}{16}$d. (14) £2,382 6s. 9d.; £2,429 18s. $9\frac{3}{56}$d. (15) £7 19s. $3\frac{21}{100}$d. (16) £23 3s. $1\frac{1}{2}$d. (17) £11 17s. $3\frac{1}{2}$d. (18) 7 ch. 45·3285 l. (19) 19 yds. 1 ft. 8·242 in. (20) £116 2s. 8d$\frac{1}{4}$. (21) 122 yds. (22) £224 17s. $5\frac{1}{15}$d. (23) 473·034 m. (24) $89\frac{3}{5}$ yds. (25) $8\frac{7}{16}$ m. (26) 5 cwt. 3 qrs. $14\frac{59}{79}$ lbs. (27) $13\frac{13}{38}$ ft. (28) £1,500. (29) £25 1s. 3d. (30) £8 0s. $7\frac{3}{5}$d. (31) 9 lbs. $4\frac{1}{2}$ oz. avoirdupois. (32) 9 lbs. $14\frac{1}{2}$ oz. avoir. (33) £115 4s. $11\frac{1}{2}$d. (34) 6,250 yds. (35) 68 yrs. (36) 2,696 yds. 8 in. (37) $120\frac{29}{41}$ acr.

XLIV. (*a*)—(1) 7d.; 5d. (2) 3s. and 2s.; 3s. 9d. and 1s. 3d.; 3s. $1\frac{1}{2}$d. and 1s. $10\frac{1}{2}$d. (3) 10s.; 7s. 6d.; 2s. 6d. (4) 80 and 20. (5) 1 lb. 12 oz. and 5 lbs. 4 oz. (6) 22 oz. and 8 oz. (7) 1s. 8d. and 1s. 6d. (8) 50 ft. (9) 10. (10) £2; £1 10s.; £1 and 10s.

(*b*)—(1) £20; £35; £45. (2) £13 2s. 6d.; £5 5s. (3) 3 cwt. 3 qrs. $10\frac{3}{4}$ lbs. (4) £8 8s. and £6 6s. (5) 2 oz. 19 d. $16\frac{1}{3}$ g. (6) 3·15 cub. ft. (7) £1,225 4s. and £102 2s. (8) 4 d. $18\frac{6}{11}$ g. (9) 2 tons $18\frac{1}{3}$ cwt. of copper, and 2 tons $1\frac{2}{3}$ cwt. of iron. (10) Hyson $49\frac{7}{9}$ lbs., Congou $74\frac{1}{3}$ lbs., Souchong $99\frac{5}{9}$ lbs. (11) £3 4s.; £4 5s. 4d.; £6 8s. (12) 360, 240, and 180.

XLV. (1) £14. (2) 16 days. (3) 6s. (4) 1088. (5) 21. (6) $14\cdot\dot{6}$. (7) 48. (8) 28. (9) 4. (10) $177\cdot\dot{7}$. (11) $18\frac{3}{4}$ m. (12) 14. (13) $38\frac{3}{5}$s. (14) 3·27669. (15) 12 oz. (16) £5 3s. 6d. (17) £200. (18) £82 16s. (19) £280.

XLVI. (*a*)—(1) £4; £6. (2) £12; £16 10s. (3) £84; £14. (4) £7 10s.; £4; £8 0s. 6d. (5) £8 15s. (6) 9s. $9\frac{1}{2}$d.; £19 4s.; £45 14s. 6d. (7) £4 10s.; £6 15s.; £20 5s. (8) £350; £262 10s. (9) £16; £10; £80; £36. (10) £6 5s.; £15; 13s. $1\frac{1}{2}$d. (11) £22; £55; £1 2s.; 19s. $9\frac{1}{2}$d. (12) £172 10s.; £21 12s.

(*b*)—(1) £17 14s.; £67 6s. $4\frac{3}{4}$d. (2) £33 14s. $4\frac{3}{4}$d.; £69 8s. 1d. (3) £84 15s. $5\frac{3}{4}$d.; £532 15s. $3\frac{3}{4}$d.; £138 12s. 6d. (4) £17 0s. $1\frac{1}{2}$d. £354 11s. $1\frac{1}{4}$d.; £517 12s. 6d. (5) £49 16s. 3d.; £454 13s. $1\frac{1}{4}$d. (6) £1,008 2s. 3d. (7) £1,319 6s. 0d. (8) £684 16s. $0\frac{1}{2}$d. (9) £13 16s. 10d. (10) £89 0s. $9\frac{3}{4}$d. (11) £1,242 10s. 0d. (12) 8 yrs. (13) $11\frac{1}{9}$ yrs. (14) $2\frac{1}{2}$ per cent. (15) 4 m. 2 w. 2 d. (16) 5 per cent. (17) £72 18s. 4d. (18) £135.

XLVII. (*a*)—(1) £90; £45; £270; £225. (2) £75; £300; £15. (3) £95; £71 5s.; £304; £64 12s. (4) £80; £48

£76; £180. (5) £1 17s. 6d.; 13s. 6d.; 11s. 3d. (6) £39 10s.; £62; 85s. (7) £88; £616; £220. (8) £20 8s. 6d.; £17 2s.; £218 10s. (9) £29 0s. 6d.; 15 15s.; £164 14s.

(*b*)—(1) £22 14s. $6\frac{1}{2}$d.; £77 13s. $6\frac{3}{4}$d.; £8 0s. $11\frac{3}{4}$d. (2) £193 10s $11\frac{1}{2}$d. (3) £72 1s. $5\frac{3}{4}$d.; £35 10s. $11\frac{1}{4}$d. (4) £292 13s. 8d. (5) £1,261 13s. $7\frac{3}{4}$d. (6) £892 17s. $1\frac{1}{2}$d. (7) £6,889 18s. $1\frac{3}{4}$d. (8) £120. (9) £2 6s. $4\frac{1}{2}$d. (10) £42 17s. 5d. (11) £22 1s. $3\frac{3}{4}$d. (12) £6,186 3s. $11\frac{1}{2}$d. (13) £2 2s. $7\frac{1}{2}$d. (14) £3 16s. $3\frac{1}{4}$d. (15) £3 6s. $1\frac{3}{4}$d. (16) 8s. $10\frac{1}{2}$d.

XLVIII. (*a*)—(1) £10 5s. (2) £57 17s. $7\frac{1}{2}$d. (3) £15 15s. 3d. (4) £216 6s. $4\frac{3}{4}$d. (5) £16 0s. 6d. (6) £1,331 0s. 0d.

(*b*)—(1) £297 15s. 1d. (2) £51 15s. $2\frac{1}{2}$d. (3) £134 8s. $5\frac{1}{2}$d. (4) £39 8s. $4\frac{1}{4}$d. (5) £252 9s. $7\frac{3}{4}$d. (6) £96 2s. 3d. (7) £181 0s. $0\frac{1}{2}$d. (8) £845 1s. 4d. (9) £1,323 17s. 7d. (10) £227 4s. 11d. (11) £55 4s. 7d. (12) £525 9s. $5\frac{1}{2}$d. (13) £7 12s. 6d. (14) £8 19s. 10d. (15) 4 yrs. (16) $5\frac{5}{9}$. (17) £634 5s. 2d. (18) £16 3s. $9\frac{1}{2}$d. (19) £4 10s. (20) $2\frac{1}{4}$ months. (21) £2 8s. 9d. (22) $6\frac{2}{3}$. (23) 5.

XLIX. (*a*)—(1) £190. (2) £262 10s. (3) £243. (4) 5 per cent. (5) $3\frac{1}{3}$ per cent. (6) $83\frac{1}{3}$ per cent.

(*b*)—(1) £1,098 12s. $9\frac{3}{4}$d. (2) £1,815 14s. $4\frac{1}{2}$d. (3) £10 18s. 9d. (4) £137 2s. $10\frac{1}{2}$d. (5) £33 17s. 1d. (6) £3,255 11s. $10\frac{1}{4}$d. (7) £72 4s. $5\frac{1}{4}$d. (8) £70. (9) £12 1s. 6d. (10) £7 0s. 5d. (11) The latter. (12) £12 16s. $9\frac{1}{2}$d. (13) £1,880 2s. 2d. and 3·216 per cent. (14) £3 9s. $4\frac{3}{4}$d. (15) £663 14s. 8d. (16) £3,336 11s. 3d. (17) £1,405 17s. 6d. and £1,643 1s. 3d.

L. (*a*)—(1) 320. (2) £7 10s. (3) £8 18s. and £11 15s. 6d. and 2s. 3d. (4) 100 per cent. (5) 25 per cent. (6) $12\frac{1}{2}$ per cent. (7) £18 15s. (8) 12,720. (9) £142 10s. (10) £6. (11) £350. (12) £1,080.

(*b*)—(1) £1 17s. 6d. (2) £9 8s. 3d.; £10 15s. $2\frac{1}{10}$d. (3) £411 5s. (4) £14 9s. $8\frac{1}{4}$d. (5) 525. (6) 3s. $3\frac{3}{4}$d. (7) £93 6s. (8) £1 13s. 4d. (9) 25 for 1s. 6d. (10) £6 4s. $9\frac{1}{4}$d. (11) 25; 48. (12) $3\frac{1}{3}$ loss.

CPSIA information can be obtained
at www.ICGtesting.com
Printed in the USA
LVHW031311210223
739960LV00008B/813

9 783375 143602